UNSPEAKABLE THINGS

AN ORPHIC ASSASSIN NOVEL

SAM LUNA

CAPSAICIN PRESS

For The Glorious Dead

Unspeakable Things
An Orphic Assassin Novel

Sam Luna

The more you hurt, the better the song is.

—Loretta Lynn

PROLOGUE

Los Angeles, California; Present Day

The mountain lion's sandpaper tongue ran up Damien's cheek. The wet nose followed, sniffing.

"I'm up," Damien said, reaching over and scratching the cat beneath her California Department of Fish and Wildlife-issued radio collar. *C-33* was written across the collar's fabric in bold black marker.

C-33 jumped off the mattress, her giant paws leaving indentations in the sheets. Damien sat up and checked the time on his clock radio next to the bed. He had managed to get three hours of sleep.

After he showered, shaved, and dressed, he checked the ammo in his 9mm pistol and dropped it into his overnight bag, which was still packed from his trip to New York City days earlier. He stepped outside, the light breaking through the marine layer in an ethereal haze.

Damien's red Mustang convertible was covered in a fine layer of ash from a recent nearby brush fire. He got inside, lowered the top, and set his bag on the passenger seat.

When he put the car in reverse, the mountain lion reappeared, leaping into the backseat. Her claws tore at the upholstery as she found her footing.

Damien killed the engine and glanced at her in the rearview mirror. *What do you think you're doing?*

I'm going with you.

Why?

Why not?

Damien considered this for a moment. *What if I get pulled over? What will you do then?*

I'll feed.

On a cop? For a speeding ticket?

Frustrated, C-33 sighed and shook a fly off her head. *You won't get pulled over.*

I speed.

Don't speed.

Damien couldn't argue with the logic. *Fine. Keep your head down.* He backed out of the driveway.

———

They arrived in Denver moments after midnight. Damien drove through the city and into a suburb, finding a spot in the parking lot of a church to camp.

C-33 yawned. *Now what?*

We wait.

For what?

For dawn.

And then?

And then I'll go to work.

Who?

Who what?

Is it?

Damien cracked his neck. *An ophthalmologist.*

A what?

An eye doctor.

What did she do?

It's a he.

What did he do?

He killed a rhino.

A what?

An animal.

I kill animals.

You kill animals to eat. He killed this animal for sport. A trophy.

I see.

Rhinos are endangered.

Where?

Africa.

Where?

A place far from here.

How did he get there?

Damien's eyes grew heavy. He closed them and lay back against the headrest. *He flew in a plane, I assume. Wake me with the sun, please.*

The cat's sandpaper tongue woke him up seven hours later.

Thanks.

They arrived for his eye appointment fifteen minutes early. Sign-carrying protesters paraded in front of the medical building, police car lights flashing.

Damien kept driving then pulled over to the curb a block away.

I shouldn't be here, C-33 said.

It's fine, Damien assured her.

What will we do?

Get in the trunk.

What?

Get in the trunk.

Damien squeezed the fob on his keychain, and the Mustang's trunk popped open. He pressed a button, and the rear window rolled down, the lion slipping through it like a snake. The car jostled as the mountain lion's weight shifted from the backseat into the trunk.

Damien got out of the car, scanning for any casual passersby who might have witnessed the 150-pound cat slinking around.

He shut the trunk and the cat growled.

Relax.

Damien got back into the driver's seat and U-turned toward the medical center. He steered the convertible through a sea of protestors and local news cameras. Security guards on either side simultaneously waved him through and pushed back the mob.

A police officer held up a hand as he approached the building. Damien pressed the brakes and rolled down the window.

"'Morning," he said.

"'Morning," said the officer. "You got an appointment or do you work here?"

"I have an appointment," Damien replied.

"With who?"

"Dr. Rumbold."

The officer waved over another uniform.

"What's going on?" Damien said.

"We need to search your vehicle, sir," the officer said.

"What?" Damien asked. "Why?"

"We have a security situation," the officer replied, gesturing to the protestors, "as you can see."

Damien twisted around in his seat as if noticing them for the first time. Signs bearing slogans such as ANIMAL PRINTS, NOT ANIMAL SKINS and TROPHY HUNTERS KILL FOR KICKS bobbed over the heads of the mob.

"Geez," Damien said. "What's this all about?"

"Your doc shot himself a giraffe or something couple weekends ago," the officer said.

"A rhino," said his partner.

"Right, rhino. Open your trunk, sir."

"Excuse me?" Damien replied.

"Your trunk," the officer repeated. "Please open it."

Damien put the car in reverse.

"Screw this."

"Whoa, whoa, whoa," the officer said.

"No, forget it."

"Sir..."

"This is absurd," Damien said, braking. "I'm not going to submit to a damned *pat down* to get a prescription for contacts. Tell Rich I'll reschedule."

The cops exchanged a look.

"You're a regular of his?" the officer asked.

"A *regular*?" Damien sniffed. "Yeah, I'm a regular. *And* his golf coach. *And* his amateur therapist when he and Maureen... Look, guys, it's all good. I gotta go."

Damien again put the car in reverse. The officer knocked on the car's hood.

"Okay, guy. Go on through."

Damien sighed. "Sorry I lost my temper," he said. "You guys are just doing your job."

"Drive on through, sir."

Damien offered the officers a smile and parked his convertible in a space near the entrance. The sledgehammer he had purchased to pulverize Richard Rumbold's skull lay stashed in the trunk, along with the mountain lion. Both would wait there, for now.

This is foolish, the mountain lion said from the confines of the trunk.

Relax, Damien replied.

He passed through another row of police officers and into the lobby, the protestors' cries fading as the automatic doors shut behind him. Damien consulted the directory and rode the elevator to the third floor and office of the Vision Specialists of Greater Denver.

A weary medical assistant glanced up from her computer screen as a lean, handsome man with neatly coiffed black hair and striking green eyes entered the empty waiting room.

"Be right with you," she said.

Damien waited patiently as she finished her typing and smiled when her eyes met his. "Hi," he said.

"Hi," she said, shoulders dropping.

"Busy morning, huh?" Damien said.

The medical assistant shook her head as if to say, *You have no idea.*

"Name?" she asked.

"Stone," Damien said. "Jack."

"I need to see your drivers license and insurance card, please."

Damien handed them over. She set them on the counter and entered them into her system, then handed them back, along with a clipboard.

"This is our new-patient form," she said. "Please take a seat and fill it out."

Damien sank into a pastel-colored chair, underneath a framed photograph of the African savanna. He checked random boxes and scribbled out an address that didn't exist. The receptionist called out his fake name a few minutes later.

Dr. Richard Rumbold looked tan, fit, and tired. He extended a handshake as he entered the examination room.

"Jack," he said. "Welcome."

Damien pumped his hand. "What in the world is going on out there?" he asked.

"Don't get me started," Richard said. "And thanks for pretending you don't already know."

"I don't," Damien said, with all the sincerity in the world.

Richard plopped onto a stool and rubbed his eyes. "Long story. Look up at that chart for me." He wheeled the stool across the carpet and pulled the phoropter across Damien's face. "And peek through that bad boy if you would please, Jack."

Damien leaned forward and peered through the lenses.

"Read line ten for me," Richard said.

"L, E, F, O, D, P, C, T," Damien read.

"Perfect," Richard said. "And eleven."

"F, D, P, L, T, C, E O," Damien read.

"Great," Richard said, twisting a knob on the projector. "See if you can do that bottom line right there for me."

"P...E...Z..." Damien said. "I think that's an 'O'... That's an 'L'...or maybe a 'P.'"

"Giving you trouble?" Richard said.

"Yeah," Damien said. "Blurry."

"Yup," Richard said, and rolled on his stool to a low lying

desk, picking up a ballpoint pen and scratching something out on Damien's chart.

"Never worn glasses or contacts?" he asked.

"Not as of yet," Damien replied.

"Well, I think you're gonna start. Lean forward."

Richard rolled back to the instrument and presented Damien with a variety of magnifications. Damien pretended to choose between them, his vision already perfect.

"Okay," Richard said, standing from the stool. "Lean back in that chair and look at the ceiling. Let's do some drops."

Richard stood over him, a dropper in one hand, tissue in the other. He squeezed a drop of solution in each of Damien's eyes and handed him the tissue. Damien dabbed the fluid running down his cheeks, his vision blurring.

"Sit forward for me," Richard said, pulling a new machine around. Damien rested his chin onto the slit lamp, squinting at the bright light boring into his dilated right eye.

"Good," Richard said. "Nice and wide."

Only a few days had passed since Damien tossed corrupt Wall Street executive Andrew Griggs out of an office high rise window in Manhattan, but it felt like months. When Damien was working, he was happy. When he wasn't, he fell into anxiety and depression. The time he was willing to wait between kills was growing shorter and shorter. All he could think about was the satisfying cracking sound Richard's head would make when it connected with the sledgehammer, the one still in its hardware store bag in the trunk outside, next to C-33.

"Whoa," Richard said, jerking backward from his side of the lenses. "You okay?"

Damien rubbed his eyes. "It kinda burns."

"Look back through there for me," Richard said.

"One sec," Damien replied.

He knew his eyes had gone black. He knew Richard had seen it happen and, like most people encountering the phenomenon, wanted a second look to be sure.

Damien thought of otters floating on their backs, holding hands. He thought of Mr. Rogers putting on his sweater. He thought of Jesus Christ in the desert, turning clay into birds.

Only then did he look back through the machine.

Richard stared into Damien's corneas for a long time. He had never encountered the same quality of green in a patient's eyes, not once in the thousands he'd examined during his twenty-year career.

"Can I blink?" Damien asked.

"Yeah," Richard said, sitting back. "Sure."

Damien pocketed the eyeglass prescription he would never use and exited to the parking lot. A local news reporter rushed toward him, microphone extended, and Damien slipped on a pair of sunglasses.

"Sir? Sir?"

Rather than ignore her and continue to the car he stopped, offering a smile. "Yes?"

The cameraman hovering behind the reporter switched on a light connected to his camera, even though the sky was cloudless, the sun harsh.

"Are you a patient of Dr. Rumbold's?"

"I am."

The reporter pushed the microphone closer to Damien's face. "Can I ask you a few questions?"

"Sure," he replied, knowing better but saying it anyway.

"Does what Dr. Rumbold did bother you at all?"

"What did he do?" Damien asked.

"He killed an endangered animal," the reporter said, brushing her hair out of her face in the morning breeze.

"My understanding is he had a permit to do so," Damien said.

"So it doesn't bother you?" the reporter asked. "You'll continue to patronize his practice?"

"Of course I will," Damien said. "He's done nothing wrong."

The reporter opened her mouth to ask another question, but Damien held up his hand. "Look," he continued, "the only problem here is you, meaning the press. This man hunted an animal legally. And now you in the media want to stir your base up with some crazy story and destroy his reputation. I'm sorry, but I just won't have it."

The reporter started to ask another question, but Damien again held up his hand. "That's all I got to say."

Damien walked toward his convertible. The mountain lion grumbled as he approached the vehicle. He pressed the keychain and opened the door locks, headlights flashing. As he guided the Mustang out of the parking lot, he saw the number of protestors had doubled.

What now? C-33 asked.

Damien waved to the group of cops as he passed, and they waved back.

We wait.

For what?

For him to leave.

When will that be?

A while.

What will we do until then?

Like I said, we'll wait.

When can I get out of the trunk?

Damien checked the rearview mirror, the protestors and police growing smaller.

Soon.

———

C-33 spent most of the day in the backseat, napping. Damien passed the time strategically moving the car up and down the boulevard. The protestors eventually thinned down to a few people in lawn chairs, only one of whom held up a sign, which read, MURDER IS NOT A SPORT.

Richard emerged from the office building three hours after sunset. The last police car parked in front of the medical center didn't follow the ophthalmologist as he exited the lot in his BMW. Damien made a U-turn off the curb and followed him at a distance through the suburban streets.

———

Floodlights washed over the empty driving range's manicured green. Richard set his ball on the tee and straightened, exhaling with relief. He would drive a bucket of balls then go home and drink a Scotch, or three.

His first drive hooked right, landing just short of the fifty-yard marker. He plucked another one out of the bucket and set it, breathing in a lungful of warm summer air. He addressed the ball, peering down the range.

The mountain lion's eyes flashed like headlights, and Richard dropped his club.

"What the fuck?" he muttered.

A man stepped into the slot next to him, setting his golf bag on the ground.

"'Evening," the man said, bending over to place a ball, his back to the doctor.

He lowered his rented driver off his shoulder and whacked it, sending it 300 yards down range in a perfect arc.

"Holy shit," Richard said, shading his eyes under the range's lights. "Nice shot, dude."

"Gerta," the man replied, still facing away.

"Sorry?" Richard said.

"Gerta," the man said again. "That's what they named her. The Oxford scientists. She was fourteen years old. Before you shot her, that is."

The mountain lion roared. Richard's head whipped toward the sound.

"How'd it make you feel, Richard? Shooting her, I mean," the man said.

The mountain lion roared again.

"Powerful?"

The mountain lion roared again.

"Important?"

The mountain lion roared again.

"Is that..."

"A mountain lion?" Damien said, turning around. "Yes. It is. Just showed up on my doorstep one day. Follows me wherever I go. She's a real sweetheart."

Richard now clearly recognized him as Jack Stone, but Damien didn't give Richard the opportunity to address this.

"You'd better run," Damien said, trading his driver for the sledgehammer tucked inside his rented golf bag.

"I... What?" Richard said.

"I said, you'd better run."

The mountain lion sprinted down the green,

muscles rippling under her butterscotch fur. Richard turned back to Damien in time to see the sledgehammer swing in a circle toward his head. It connected with his jaw, breaking it. Richard crumpled to the ground.

C-33 sailed through the air where Richard's body had stood moments earlier. The cat landed on all fours, nails skittering on the concrete.

Why?

To give him a fighting chance.

Why?

It's no fun otherwise.

Fun for you. I'm hungry.

Yeah. Well.

Richard sprang to his feet, clutching his jaw. He saw the mountain lion regain its footing and ran for it.

Damien held up a hand, stopping C-33 in her tracks. She growled.

Just wait.

When Richard crossed the fifty-yard marker, he dared a glance over his shoulder, eyes wide with panic. Damien lowered his hand, and the mountain lion bolted.

"You know something, Richard?" Damien shouted. "Trophy hunting *is* a sport!"

Richard ran. The mountain lion easily overtook his stride, leaping onto his back and sinking her claws into his trapezius. She tore his scalp off with a single bite.

Richard screamed, crumpling into the grass. C-33 spat his hair out of her mouth, bit into his neck, and paralyzed him.

The lion rolled Richard onto his back. She placed her mouth over his nose until his heart stopped beating under her paw.

Once he was dead, she feasted. Damien hit golf balls as she did, impressed by his swing.

Finished?

Almost.

Finish up, please.

Okay, fine.

A groundskeeper found Richard Rumbold's remains at five o'clock the following morning. Damien and C-33 were halfway back to Los Angeles by this point, the warm desert wind rippling through their hair as they cruised down the highway.

Back at his home in the Hollywood Hills, Damien collapsed onto his bed for an afternoon nap. Seventeen hours later, his phone's alarm woke him up, the buzzing in his pocket a reminder of his appointment that morning at the Past-Life Hypnotherapy Partners of Los Angeles on Wilshire Boulevard.

Angela hugged Damien as he entered her office, a first.

"Hi," he said, taken aback.

"Hey," she said. "How's life?"

"Good," Damien said. "You?"

"Oh, just dandy. Thanks."

Angela was letting her gray roots grow in, her hippie ensemble of choice for the session a long orange dress made from hemp. She swung her arms as they walked down the hallway, the copious bracelets covering her wrists chiming musically.

Damien sat in the overstuffed chair across from her. Angela reached out and switched on the light on the coffee table. It pulsed under the plastic casing, blue then green then red then yellow.

"Relax," she said. "Let's do some breathing."

They breathed together. When Damien rested his head against the chair, Angela tapped a button on her phone.

"Recording," she said. "Damien, keep breathing."

Damien did so.

"I think we're past the cowboy," Angela said. "The outlaw. Yeah? Breathe."

Damien listened to the sounds of traffic. He recalled Richard Rumbold's screams, his scalp sliding off his skull like a shower cap.

"The woman," she continued. "You speak of her frequently. Take me there. A woman. Germany, I think. Georgia, sometimes? Look at the light. Breathe. No rush."

Damien inhaled and exhaled.

"Good," the hypnotherapist said. "No rush. The light. Look at it."

Damien did.

"The woman. Georgia, yeah? Is that where she is? She's in a couple of places. Germany too. Yes? Look at the light. Good. Breathe. *The woman*. Let's relax. Take our time."

Damien remembered the crunching sound Richard's bones made as the mountain lion consumed his dead body.

"Good," Angela said. "Good, Damien."

The light pulsed. Damien's blinking slowed as if he were drugged.

"Love that," she continued. "You're relaxing. Breathe. We have nothing but time. All the time in the world. The woman. Georgia. Tell me about her. Breathe. Good. You're safe. Germany. Watch the light. Breathe in on a count of four. Go into the light, Damien. Hold for a count of seven. A woman.

And release on a count of eight, slowly. Georgia. Germany. Can you take me there? And release on a count of eight, slowly. Breathe in on a count of four. Hold for a count of seven. Georgia. Germany? Tell me about her. Go into the light, Damien. And release on a count of eight, slowly. Breathe in on a count of four. Go into the light, Damien. Hold for a count of seven. And release on a count of eight, slowly. The woman."

Damien went into the light.

PART I

GOLEM

1

Hades, Banks of Acheron

Before Georgia there was Hades, and a thousand-mile trek across its chalky-white ground. There is no silence there, or sound, and no darkness, or light. To remember it is to recall a single day, as no two are different, and every one is the same. Hell is the absence of everything.

Giant stone markers red as blood—the only color there —bordered the path. Snickering demons hid behind these rocks, taunting the Orphic staggering blindly on bare feet through the scorched sand. The demons waggled their reptilian tongues and rolled their milky unblinking eyes, dragging their claws against the stones and whispering discouragement. *If only you would lie down*, they hissed. *And sleep. Lie down and it will all be over. You* need *a rest. You* deserve *one.*

Damien walked this void for a hundred years, and then one day he fell to his knees and crawled. Insanity arrived late in his journey, a welcome friend that allowed a retreat into fantasy. Lies were a relief here. They were all he had left.

Then there was *the demon*: translucent and beautiful and horrifying, laughing atop her great white rock. His broken mind couldn't comprehend her existence. The tactile reality of the golden cylinder on the chain around his neck was all that remained.

He tugged at the chain until it broke and fumbled the tiny container open. Inside the cylinder he found a parchment, given to him the morning of his death at the Orphic Temple.

"I am but mortal flesh, a child of the gods," he read aloud. "Take pity on me, and allow me to drink from the sacred water."

The demon cackled.

"Yes, yes, yes! Drink, Chindi. Drink!"

Chindi. The word meant something. A name. He'd been a human being once, something other than the wretched creature now shivering in the ashes, blistered and bloodless.

"Why do you call me that?" he whimpered.

Her breath washed over him, blanketing his naked skin with the stench of death. His eyes met hers, radiant suns eclipsed by black moons, set within a long equine skull, skin as clear as water. She grinned, baring a thousand fangs.

"Because it amuses me," she said. "Now *drink*."

The Pool of Memory sat beneath a Cyprus tree. Damien pulled himself to it, hand over hand, digging what remained of his fingers into the alabaster sand and willing his emaciated body toward its waters. When he arrived, he dared a glance at his reflection, confirming that he was no longer a man but a carcass, a rotten puppet dancing on the ends of the demon's strings.

Damien drank the water and immediately reincarnated as a baby girl in early twentieth-century America, a child with no memory of the trials already endured in lifetimes previous, nor any notion of the peril soon to come.

And thus the Orphic Assassin was reborn.

2
_____

Mama found the Nazi dolls while cleaning Dee's room. She sat on the bed with them for a long while, unsure what to think. It wasn't just the appearance of the toys that bothered her. It was more that the person who constructed them had recently celebrated her twentieth birthday.

She could hear Dee downstairs in the kitchen eating a third helping of Hoppin' John, a New Year's Day recipe made to bless the inhabitants of the house with luck in the year ahead. When she walked up the staircase, Mama took a deep breath.

Her petite daughter stood in the doorway, dark hair dangling into her green eyes, frozen at the sight of her mother holding the Nazis in her white apron. Smoothing back her unkempt bob, Dee swallowed hard and opened her mouth to speak. When no words came forth, Mama spoke first.

"What in God's name are these?"

Dee's silent tongue still tasted the excellent Carolina peas, cooked without bacon fat. Her mother couldn't understand why her only child preferred them that way any more than she could comprehend why pictures of Adolf Hitler, Hermann Goring, and Heinrich Himmler had been stitched onto the bodies of cotton-stuffed dolls, then hidden behind the cedar hope chest beneath her window.

"Dee? Answer me."

Her behavior had confused and even frightened her Mama for as long as she could remember. She was getting bone tired of concocting lies to comfort her.

"They're dolls, Mama," she said.

"I can see that," Mama replied. "Why are these men's faces on 'em?"

Dee's mind raced for an excuse. Finding none, she offered the simple truth.

"Because I put them there, Mama."

Her mother let the dolls tumble out of her hands, wiping one palm against the other as if they were covered in filth.

"And *why* did you do that is my meaning. Don't sass me, girl."

Dee looked up at the ceiling.

"Don't you roll those eyes at me."

"Mama."

"Don't *Mama* me."

Dee leveled her gaze at her mother.

The truth was that they were the tenth set of Nazi dolls she'd made. The previous nine were similarly crafted, the pictures trimmed from *Life* magazine. Then she had taken them into the woods, hours after dark while her parents snored across the hall from her room.

Once there she pulled out a box of blue-tipped matches from her purse, an item procured from the same corner drugstore that had sold her the magazines. Next she lit a match, allowing the sulfur smell to sting her nostrils for a moment. She touched the flame to a doll's foot. She always started with the foot and always the *right* foot. She didn't know why; it was just how she liked to play her game.

The flame flared as it fed on dry cotton. The doll would be consumed in an instant—the Nazi's picture charring black, edges curling.

The changes to Dee's body that took place when this occurred fascinated and embarrassed her. The sensation started in the center of her body, washing warmly and deliciously down her legs. It then spread up her stomach, over her chest and, moving against gravity, trickled up to her throat. It was the best feeling in the world.

If she'd had a mirror, she would see that her eyes then went over black, the bright green eclipsed by a void. Dee never brought a mirror on these outings, of course, so she had no idea the phenomenon took place.

The doll would burn and she'd move to the next, her chest rising and falling with each quickening breath. When she finished burning them, she lay on the forest floor, spent, her wide black eyes fixed on the stars above.

Dee figured her mother didn't need to know any of that.

"I was just foolin' about, Mama," she said. "That's all."

Her mother peered down at the dolls, Hitler's black-and-white face stern and openmouthed, ranting and raving at a crowd of German soldiers halfway across the world from Marietta.

"Well, the dishes need doing anyway," she said, kicking the dolls across the hardwood with a house slipper. She brushed past her daughter and down the staircase without another word.

Dee picked up her dolls and lay with them across the mattress. Soft winter sunlight washed over her creations, illuminating Goring's and Himmler's faces. She placed Hitler on his feet.

"*Fur das Varterland,*" she whispered, pulling the doll's right arm into the Nazi salute she had only seen in newsreels. "*Sieg heil, sieg heil, sieg heil.*"

Her German was improving, the pronunciation feeling effortless after two months of practice. Her French was also coming along nicely, her Russian less so. She had work to do.

The cedar hope chest contained six books: *Les Miserables* by Victor Hugo, *War and Peace* by Leo Tolstoy, and *The Metamorphosis* by Franz Kafka, all in their original French, Russian, and German, respectively. Their English-translated companions accompanied each tome. While not exact, they were giving Dee a general command of the three languages. The next step was to find French, Russian, and German people to practice with.

The kitchen sink tap opened up downstairs, and Dee rolled onto her back. She would go down in a moment, yank a kitchen towel off the front of their wood-burning stove, and dry the dishes with her mother. Their hips would sway to the radio broadcast of Duke Ellington or Ella Fitzgerald or Bing Crosby. Later they would eat supper, most likely leftover Hoppin' John.

Then they'd sit by the radio, stitching on a quilt and listening to *Fibber McGee and Molly* or Jack Benny or whatever music caught her mother's fancy. Then to bed at nine, Mama's and Daddy's snores filling her childhood home, Dee slipping out the window with her dolls and her matches, heart pounding.

She set Hitler on the mattress and went downstairs.

Dee noticed the posting on the way to the grocer's the next morning, her usual Tuesday errand for coffee and laundry soap and Mama's cigarettes, printed on card stock and tacked to the telephone pole a half block down from the Attica residence on Juniper Street. It read:

Attention, Residents
UNITED KLANS OF AMERICA, INC.
Will Present a Program
THIS SATURDAY at 8:00 P.M.
PARADE ON JUNIPER STREET
NO PARKED AUTOS ALLOWED
COME HEAR THE TRUTH!
THE WHITE PUBLIC ONLY!
THE GRAND DRAGON OF GEORGIA
& OTHER GOOD SPEAKERS

Dee read it twice before continuing on her way. The flyer hung from every other telephone pole, as well as the corkboard in front of Tully's Grocery. She bought the coffee, soap, and cigarettes and went back home. Dee observed several other white people stop and read the flyer with the same curiosity she had. When she got home, she didn't mention them to her mother.

The week passed as most did, boring and uneventful. When Saturday night arrived, Dee made sure to be on their front porch, bowl of beans in hand, ready for the show.

3

Juniper Street, Marietta, Georgia; January 1945

Dee liked her beans Southern style: ham, garlic and onion, minus the ham. She simmered them for three hours, then ate them piping hot, huffing and puffing her cheeks until they were cool enough to swallow. This annoyed her Mama to no end, but Dee didn't care. She liked her beans a certain way, and beans were pretty much all that she ate; Mama just needed to deal with it.

Juniper Street was clear of parked cars, long ropes hung with red flags strung between the telephone poles. A few hundred people had converged for the evening's presentation, all white per the flyer's admonition. Dee sat on her porch swing, chewing her hot beans as the crowd noise swelled along with *Amos 'n' Andy* on the radio inside the house.

The Klan appeared all at once, dressed in white robes and tall pointy hats. Their polished black leather loafers clipped and clopped along Juniper Street, their faces obscured by white sheets, dark eyeholes cut in the featureless masks.

Every man carried a torch in one hand, a Bible in the other. A red-robed Klansman at the head of the parade—the Grand Dragon—called out a command, and the procession halted.

"Dee? Where you at, honey?" Mama called from inside the house.

"On the porch, Mama," Dee replied.

The radio audience laughed as Amos or Andy got up to one of their typical high jinks.

"Come inside, Dee."

"I'm fine out here, Mama."

"*Damienne Attica.*"

Dee rolled her eyes, pinching the skin on the bridge of her nose.

"Just be a minute."

A man in a tan fedora clapped on the sidewalk below.

"White people!" he shouted. "Blessed are these eyes to see *white people* living on this street!"

Dee shook her head.

"*White* men and *white* women," the man in the fedora roared. "Praise God!"

When the Grand Dragon hoisted his torch in the air, everyone along the sidewalk whooped and hollered. Dee picked up her bowl of beans, wide eyed, as if the events before her flickered on a movie screen.

The Grand Dragon raised his Bible and the crowd of Klansmen parted, a boy of no more than twelve running up the aisle, a wooden cross hoisted over a shoulder. The crowd cheered as the boy placed it in a Christmas tree stand. The red-robed man dipped his torch to the cross, igniting it in flames.

"We shall ever be devoted to the sublime principals of pure Americanism, and valiant in the defense of its ideals and institutions!" the Grand Dragon bellowed. "It is our earnest desire to promote real patriotism toward our civil government, honorable peace among men and nations, and protection for and happiness in the homes of our people!"

Dee burst into laughter.

One of the Klansmen lining the sidewalk turned around to the sound. The man, a portly sort whose robe barely concealed the girth underneath, stepped away from the rally.

He ambled up onto the Attica's lawn, toward the skinny young woman slapping her knee, chuckling.

"What'cha laughing at?" the fat Klansman asked her.

Dee flipped the bangs out of her face, and pointed at him. "Why you, of course."

"That so?" the Klansman replied.

Dee set her beans down and leaned forward on the swing, no longer laughing. "Do you have any idea just how ridiculous you all sound? Not to mention *look*?" she asked him. "I'll say one thing for the Nazis. They dress better."

The Klansman glared at Dee through his hood's eyeholes. She grinned back wickedly.

"Halloween was months ago, Mister," Dee continued. "Why don't you go ahead and lift that mask of yours so I can see your face."

The man partially lifted his hood, revealing a thick red beard. He then hocked up a mouthful of phlegm and spat it onto the mailbox, tobacco-stained saliva running over the neat white lettering that spelled out ATTICA. Then he shuffled back into the crowd.

The grin didn't leave Dee's face, green eyes sparkling in the low light. The front door hinges squeaked open and closed, and Mama was at her side.

"Get inside, girl!"

Mama gripped Dee's earlobe, a technique not employed since her childhood.

"Get in, now," her mother huffed. "Come on."

Once they were inside, her mama slammed the front door so hard the walls shook.

"What the hell you doin' sitting out there?," Mama said. "Huh?"

"Just find it interesting," she shrugged. "Is all."

"*Interesting?*" her mother asked. "Daddy will be home tomorrow. Want me to tell him his only daughter was sitting out on the porch, talking foolishness with some strange man for all the neighbors to see?"

"We weren't talking, Mama," Dee said.

Her mother went to the radio and turned up *Amos 'n' Andy* until it drowned out the rally outside.

"You want your tea?" Dee asked.

Mama nodded. Dee went to the kitchen to prepare a blend of chamomile and lavender picked from their garden. She filled the kettle with water from the tap and peered through the curtains.

Short. Potbelly. Red beard.

The Grand Dragon gesticulated wildly as white-skinned hands stuck out of the robed throngs before him, raised high in testimony. She recalled a similar fervor depicted in the newsreels at the Strand movie theater downtown, mobs of Germans transfixed by *der Fürher*. The kettle whistled, and she pulled it off the flame, the radio crackling with static. Mama twisted the knobs, searching for her evening program: a preacher who read from the Bible each night in a deep sonorous voice.

Short. Potbelly. Red beard. Dee couldn't get his face out of her head.

She handed Mama a cup wrapped in a kitchen towel.

"Thank you," she said, tone curt. Mama rocked back and forth in her chair, listening to the preacher read from Leviticus.

"I'm going upstairs, Mama. You okay?"

"Just fine." Her mother sighed. Dee took the stairs two at a time.

"Your Daddy's gonna be home tomorrow," Mama called over her shoulder.

Dee stopped one step before the top, gripping the handrail. "Yes he is, Mama. You come up to bed soon now."

"Surely will," her mother replied.

Dee collapsed into her pillow, which was cool and inviting. Her windows were wide open and the smell of torch fuel burned her nose. The humidity mercifully had broken, but now Klansmen's chants, not the stifling heat, would keep her up into the wee hours.

"America first!"

Dee flipped over, trying to find the spot in her mattress that allowed her to drift to sleep.

"They will not replace us!"

She gripped the first Nazi doll she found in the darkness. Himmler and his jowly mustached face.

"America first!"

"They will not replace us!"

"America first!"

Dee jumped up from the mattress, shutting her window with such force that the glass spider-webbed.

Daddy arrived at noon the next day, tall and handsome in his suit and tie.

"There's my girl."

Dee hugged her father's neck, breathing in his after-shave. "We missed you, Daddy."

"And I missed you, girl of mine," he replied, kissing her forehead.

Mama appeared at the top of the staircase.

"George," she said.

"May," he replied. "Get on over here." Her parents embraced.

That evening, they ate supper around the table as a family: celebratory steak and potatoes for Daddy and Mama, leftover beans for their vegetarian daughter.

Dee and her mother listened to Daddy's tales of life on the road as a traveling insurance salesman.

"And Mr. Samuelson said, 'Mr. Attica, you are one silver-tongued devil, sir, that's what you are...'"

Dee and Mama laughed at his stories. After dinner, Mama and Daddy listened to *Amos 'n' Andy* wrapped up in each other's arms, smiling at the jokes, midlife's wrinkles unfolding around their tired eyes. The sight did Dee's heart good.

She excused herself and went upstairs to bed. The Nazi dolls awaited her, tucked beneath the mattress. She held them up in the waning moonlight.

Short. Potbelly. Red beard.

Tap, tap, tap.

Dee awoke to sunlight pouring through the curtains.

Tap, tap, tap.

A tiny shadow was on the other side. Dee sat up. Hitler, Himmler, and Goring glared at her from the floor with their monochrome eyes.

Tap, tap, tap.

Dee slid the curtains open. A brown sparrow sat, its little head bobbing.

Dee crouched, meeting it at eye level.

Hi, she said.

Hello, the bird replied.

Dee waited for more. When nothing else was said, she made the bed, pulling the sheets taut. She had enjoyed many conversations with many, many birds in her lifetime, and they all went much like this one: "Hello" and "hi." That was usually it.

Short. Potbelly. Red beard, the bird said.

Dee whipped her head around. *What did you say?* she asked.

Short. Potbelly. Red beard, the bird repeated.

Dee's green eyes widened.

"What happened to your window?" another voice asked from behind.

She let out a shout and the sparrow flew away.

"Daddy, you scared me to death," she said.

"I can see that."

Her father walked across her bedroom to the cracked glass, mug of steaming coffee in hand.

"It was like that when I went to sleep last night," Dee said.

George traced a finger down the fissure in the window and clucked his tongue. "Won't get to this until Saturday," he murmured.

"You leaving again?" Dee asked. "So soon?"

"Have to," her Daddy said, straightening. "Not that folks are buying anything right after Christmastime."

Dee was thrilled at the news of her father's upcoming trip and deeply ashamed for being so. His absence made her nightly forays into the woods much easier to pull off, Mama being a deep sleeper and Daddy the exact opposite.

"How's she doing?" he asked her, sipping on his coffee.

"Mama's okay," Dee said, acutely aware of the Nazi dolls on the floor between them, an issue she was sure her mother hadn't imparted to her husband, at least not yet. "You know."

"She seems tired to me," her father said. "You two been gettin' on okay?"

The sparrow returned to the windowsill.

Are you coming or aren't you? it asked.

Cold sweat broke out across Dee's skin. The bird spoke so loud and clear she couldn't believe her father didn't hear it.

Well?

"Will you look at that?" Daddy said. "That there bird's lookin' at you like you're its mother." He tapped the glass with a knuckle. "Hey, *chee-pee chee-pee chee-pee,*" he said. The bird didn't move. "Think it's sick or something?"

"Seems okay to me," Dee said, kicking her Nazis under the bed. "Daddy, I should get ready."

Her father's expression indicated a sudden awareness that he was in his grown daughter's bedroom, and she was in a sheer nightgown.

"Yes, right," he said, and shuffled back from the window, coffee cresting over the top of his porcelain mug and landing on the hardwood floor with a plop. Dee clenched her teeth with relief when he regarded the spill apologetically, the dolls safely tucked out of view.

"Mama's got your beans on," he said, and left the room.

Well? the bird said.

Dee nodded. The bird expanded its wings, fluttering

down into the garden and landing in what would be a rutabaga patch come spring.

The bird gazed up at her. *Well?*

I'm coming, Dee said, picking her robe off the hook by the dresser. She ate breakfast downstairs with her parents, as fast as she possibly could.

4

Woods, Marietta, Georgia; January 1945

The bird flew over her head, Dee alternating her attention from the flapping of its wings to the forest floor beneath her feet.

This way, the bird told her.

Rotten leaves covered the ground, brown and baked by the pale winter sun. It wasn't freezing yet, but it was cold enough. Dee wiped her runny nose with the pink mittens she always wore, products of her mother's ceaseless knitting hobby.

As they walked through the woods, Dee stumbled over the occasional hole in the ground, doorways to warrens of skunks, foxes, and rabbits. She heard the little animals chattering underground, hundreds of tiny voices whispering like the wind.

How much farther? she asked the sparrow.

Farther, it replied.

Dee never had spoken this much to a bird before. She was lightheaded, outside of her own body.

The bird took the long way round to Owensmouth Road,

skirting Marietta's thoroughfares in favor of a secret forest route. After an hour's journey, they arrived.

The Harrell Farm sat in the distance, the cabbage fields surrounding it bare and frostbitten. The Harrells were a prominent family, one of the oldest in Marietta. Deacon Harrell, the patriarch, had retired as its deputy mayor. His daughter Callie owned the sewing shop on Main Street. Dee's mother bought yarn there. She wasn't sure why the bird, now perched on her shoulder, had guided her to their farm.

Short. Potbelly. Red beard.

"Here?" she asked aloud. The bird flew off, disappearing into the slate-gray sky.

A Ford pickup rolled down Owensmouth Road, weaving from one side to the other. A man with a red beard sat in the driver's seat, ball cap perched back on his head, a Pall Mall dangling from his lips. As he steered onto the road that led to the farm, Dee slowed her gait, observing the truck pull into the property. When the taillights flickered, she situated herself behind a telephone pole and peered around it.

The truck door opened, and the gut emerged before the beard. It was the same man from the rally, the same one who had lifted his white hood and spat tobacco juice over her family's mailbox.

Dee sucked in her breath. Only when the man walked inside the farmhouse, screen door clattering shut behind him, did she emerge from behind the wooden pole and run across Owensmouth Road.

Dee hid in the hay barn, rubbing her mittens together for warmth. The sun's path poured through the slats in the wooden roof high above her head; she used that to mark the time.

The bird had guided her here and she had followed, pretending all the while that there was some greater plan. There wasn't. Now she was in a strange man's barn, cold and defenseless and quite possibly mad.

The sound of the farmhouse screen door opening sent her low to the ground. Dee held her breath as boots scuffled down steps, stalking through the dirt. Then a woman's shrill twang rang out from the farmhouse in the chilly afternoon air.

"Bocephus McInnes, what in the Lord's name do you think you're doing?"

The hay barn doors slid open and Bocephus McInnes, the short man with the red beard and potbelly, staggered inside, prompting Dee to shrink back farther into the shadows. He was clearly intoxicated, milk bottle half full of moonshine gripped in his chubby fingers.

"Mind your own fuckin' business, Callie!" he hollered back.

The screen door slapped open and closed, and new footsteps marched toward the barn. Callie Harrell entered, charging up behind Bocephus and snatching the bottle from his hand. "Get back inside," she commanded.

"Don't boss me, woman!"

"Matter of fact, I am your boss, Bo!" Callie screeched. "You drive here drunker than a hoot owl and now you're going where exactly?"

"Huntin'," Bo slurred. He weaved his way across the barn to a large leg-hold animal trap that hung from a chain on a wall, its steel jaws brown and rusted.

"Huntin'," Callie repeated, incredulous. "Skunked as you are."

"Aw, shut up now!" Bo bellowed. He gripped the trap on either side and yanked it off the barn wall.

"You're a child growing older," Callie said. "That's what you are. Not a handy*man*. More like handy*boy*."

The weight of the trap sent Bo backward into the hay, onto his rear. His teeth clicked together, and he burped loudly.

Callie burst into laughter. "You got what you *deserved*, Mr. McInnes!"

Bo rolled over onto his belly. Dee held her breath as they spat more insults at each other. Eventually they finished their squabble, and Callie left the barn, tossing a few more barbed words over her shoulder as she did. The barn doors slid closed. Now it was just Dee and Bo, the former crouched behind a hay bale, the latter flat on his back, incapacitated. When Bo started snoring, Dee made her escape.

She sprinted across Owensmouth Road, chancing glances back toward the barn. No one witnessed her disappear into the treeline, navigating her way home through the dark woods.

⸻

Dinner had gone cold, and Dee knew she'd never hear the end of it. Her mother interrogated her as to her whereabouts as she cleared plates, her father out on the porch smoking a cigarillo in the cold, preferable to listening to yet another battle play out between his wife and daughter. Dee silently endured her Mama's rant then excused herself to her room, bringing her Nazis from underneath the bed and huddling with them under the covers.

She lay awake, trying to strategize a plan. She felt certain about what she wanted to do but hadn't a clue how to go about doing it. This along with the bright, full moon outside her window made sleep all but impossible. After four hours of insomnia she gave in, whipping the covers off and sitting on the edge of her bed, sweating with anxiety.

The blue-tipped matches were deep in the hope chest across from her bed, the gasoline can hidden in the woods a mile north, in the clearing where she played her game.

Tap, tap, tap.

I hear you.

Tap, tap, tap.

I said I hear you. Please go away.

Tap, tap, tap.

Dee lay back on her mattress, waiting for dawn.

Dawn came and went with her father, Mama fussing over his sack lunch and thermos of coffee, imploring him to return home safely. He offered his usual assurances and left.

Dee listened to Daddy's coupe cough and sputter as the engine turned over. When it faded down the block, she ventured downstairs, hoping her Mama had forgotten the previous evening's transgressions. As it happened, she was too preoccupied by her husband's departure to pay her daughter any mind. Relieved, Dee ate her breakfast of cold beans and bread.

The usual morning chores kept the women a safe distance apart. When her mother left on an errand, Dee brought the matches out of the hope chest and ventured into the woods for her can of gasoline.

5

Harrell Farm, Marietta, Georgia; January 1945

Bocephus McInnes kept to a routine from which he never wavered. In the mornings, he left the Harrells' farm and drove his pickup three miles to the Savercool Gin Company, a factory that produced and serviced gin mills for much of the rural south. Bo was a mechanic and an inebriate, and after his eight-hour shift he repaired to a bar not far from the factory. He drank until he staggered out or was dragged out, truck weaving down the country roads back to the Harrell farm.

That was Bo's daily routine. Dee had spent the past week following him, sometimes guided by the sparrow, sometimes not. Now it was Sunday, and she was again hidden in the hayloft; so far the day had gone much like the previous six.

Deacon Harrell spread chicken feed and called the pigs around a bucket of corncobs and potato skins. Callie Harrell stepped out with coffee, and they drank it on the porch, watching the sun rise. Then they went inside for breakfast:

pancakes and bacon, which Dee smelled from the hay barn. Another hour passed and they emerged in their Sunday fineries, sliding into the front seat of Mr. Harrell's ruby-red Studebaker. Deacon guided the car down the thin strip of dirt road that led to the highway.

Bo appeared an hour later, bed headed and unshaven. This morning he wore overalls without a shirt, his gut hairy and fish belly white in the hazy sunlight. Dee followed his weaving path to the barn from her vantage point in the loft.

Bo now entered, .22 rifle in one hand, bottle of whiskey in the other. He leaned the rifle against the wall and slugged off the bottle, grimacing.

"Sho 'nuff," he muttered, and took another drink. He set the bottle down and wiped the sleep out of his eyes. As he squinted at the blank wall where his animal trap usually hung, Dee pulled off a mitten, biting her knuckle.

Bo walked toward the space where the trap was supposed to be, just as she hoped. His left foot found it first, a few inches below the hay, right where Dee had buried it.

The trigger squeaked, and the steel jaws slammed shut around his tibia, snapping it like a twig. Bo crumpled to the ground, screaming. Dee slid her other mitten off and descended the ladder.

"Well hey there, Bo," she said. "Remember me?"

Bo gripped his knee above the compound fracture, the bone tenting the pant leg grotesquely. When Dee appeared, Bo shouted at her, his face contorted in agony and confusion.

"Hey! You! Fetch a doctor or sumthin'!"

Bo eyeballed the young woman as she rushed to a corner of the barn, her left hand holding her sweater closed against the frosty morning air. She reached under the hay and produced a can of gasoline, then twisted off the cap and poured it into a milk pail.

"Where's your little costume?" she asked. "Not playing dress-up today?" Bo lay back, groaning.

Dee reached into her sweater pocket and brought out a cardboard canister of TreeSweet frozen orange juice concentrate, pulling the string and unspooling the contents into the milk pail.

"Recipe I've been working on," she explained.

"The fuck *you* doin', girlie?" Bo exclaimed. "Go get me some fuckin' help!"

The orange juice fell into the bucket of gas with a plop, steam swirling up and out of the pail.

"Makes the gas *stick* in just such a way," she said.

Dee used a hand shovel to mix it up while Bo went white with shock. She wanted him fully conscious for the next part, so she hurried it along, pouring the contents of the bucket over his head and body. Bo coughed and sputtered as the gasoline and orange juice ran into his eyes.

"The...*hell*...you doin'?"

Dee reached into her other coat pocket and brought out a box of blue-tipped matches. Her hands shook as she removed one and struck it along the grain, potassium chlorate giving birth to a flame.

Then her green eyes turned black, and she dropped the match onto Bo's foot, the one not caught in the trap. Dee always started with the foot and always the *right* foot. She didn't know why; it was just how she liked to play her game.

The flame caught the gasoline fumes first, wrapping the fat man in an ethereal blue shroud. Then the oxygen sucked out of the air and his skin burst into flames. Dee stumbled backward, eyes wide and black, mouth open in awe.

Bo howled and writhed, his clothes, skin, and the straw

beneath him exploding with fire. Putrid black smoke rose in a straight line above his flailing body. Dee stamped out the burning hay, unable to avert her gaze from the immolated man convulsing at her feet.

His cheeks melted away, exposing ruined, yellow teeth. His hair turned to ash; his hands curled into fists, fingers roasted. Dee wiped the sweat out of her eyes as a familiar warmth spread up her body from her toes. It was nothing at all like when she had burned her Nazi dolls. It was a thousand times better, maybe even ten thousand times.

Short. Potbelly. Red beard.

Dee spotted a bird in the rafters. It was the sparrow, peering down at her with eyes as black as hers.

Yes, Dee replied.

Short. Potbelly. Red beard.

Yes. Thank you.

Hitler, the bird said.

Dee's breath caught in her throat.

What did you say?

Bo's eyeballs popped in his skull with a hiss, his facial features unrecognizable as human, everything burned away save his yellowed teeth.

Hitler.

Another sparrow joined her bird, then another and another. They each said the same name.

Hitler. Hitler. Hitler. Hitler.

I hear you, Dee said.

Hitler.

I said I heard you.

Dee slipped out of the barn, pumped with adrenaline. Somehow she managed to make it across the road, Bo's death stink in her nostrils all the way home.

Christmas in Connecticut was still playing at the Strand movie theater. Dee arrived a half hour early, seating herself in the third row from the back, directly in front of the WHITES ONLY sign strung across the aisle. She chose a seat dead center, picking her popcorn out a kernel at a time. By the time the lights went down, the theater had filled to just under half. The screen crackled, and the projector's light washed over it, trumpets announcing the latest newsreel.

A parade of Allied soldiers marched across the screen in black and white. *"Stopping Von Runstedt's unceasing march into Belgium, the Americans defend against German counterattacks!"*

Seats jostled around Dee as the rows filled up around her.

"Destroyed American hardware on the road ahead is a testament to the Nazis' attempt to stop the Allied's offensive toward Cologne!"

Soldiers trudged across a bridge somewhere in Europe, rifles slung over their shoulders, exhausted eyes acknowledging the camera filming them.

"The Ardennes is awash with Allied soldiers of every stripe. To stop Nazi infiltration, mines are placed every few yards along the roads."

Dee shifted in her seat, palms sweating. The weapons and hardware in the newsreel beckoned to her, calling across an ocean to a girl munching popcorn in a small Southern town.

"Roadblocks are set up. A tank is hidden beneath a mountain of straw. The Nazis have tried everything, even dressing up in the clothes of fallen American heroes in an attempt to cross our lines!"

She wanted to be a part of it. If she could have walked

through the screen and into the world of warfare on the other side right then and there, she would have.

"New supplies of ammunition are dropped from the skies, picked up by our brave boys and put to use immediately."

The first bird flew in unnoticed, alighting on the chair back directly in front of Dee. The second caught the attention of a white man in the second row. He waved at it with his hat.

"Get on now," he said. "Get!"

The third passed the second, and the others found their way onto empty seat backs. Then the rest of the flock followed, singing:

Hitler.

Hitler. Hitler.

Hitler. Hitler. Hitler. Hitler. Hitler.

Hitler.

Dee covered her face, the murmuring of the crowd drowning out the newsreel. She begged her pardons and made her way down the row and out to the aisle. She hurried through the lobby, employees waving the birds toward the doors.

Hitler. Hitler. Hitler. Hitler. Hitler. Hitler. Hitler. Hitler. Hitler. Hitler. Hitler.

Dee ran through the parking lot. There were birds everywhere, in the dark winter sky and in the leafless trees, weighing down the branches.

Hitler. Hitler. Hitler. Hitler. Hitler. Hitler. Hitler. Hitler. Hitler. Hitler. Hitler.

Dee ran all the way home.

Mama was waiting up for her when she got there, seething with anger at her daughter's lateness but not speaking about it. Dee went to bed without a word.

In the morning, she would rise, dress, and enlist in the Woman's Army Corps at the recruiting center on Wilton Street. With any luck, she'd be on the next boat to Europe.

But first she dreamed.

6

Cape Sounion, Attica Peninsula; The Month of Pyanepsion 434 BC

When Dee dreamed it was of her first life, the one lived centuries earlier on the Grecian peninsula that had given her a name. Here she was a boy called Damien of Attica, murderer of a wealthy merchant named Nicomedes, the man who had killed his father for not throwing a wrestling match in the Olympian games for profit. Here she had been exiled for her crimes, banished into the Athenian wilderness and rescued by a mysterious man named Scylax, who claimed to be an Orphic monk.

While the other students learned their scriptures and played their lyres, Damien slept. As his classmates said their evening prayers to the Gods he awoke, readying for his night's lessons with Scylax, now his master. The boy who had plunged a dagger into Nicomedes's heart was not meant to sing songs and recite poetry to the animals like the other children, not anymore. Now he was a creature of the night, the only pupil of a man with eyes the color of the setting sun.

They sat in the Great Round Room, on a stone wheel laid flat. It was here where Orphic monks' throats were ceremoniously cut, sending the devoted into the first of ten reincarnations: voyagers on the Grievous Cycle.

"What frightens you above all else?" Master Scylax asked, his yellow eyes shimmering in the near total darkness.

Damien sat before him, legs crossed, mirroring his master.

A black scorpion, its exoskeleton shining in the torchlight, crawled over Scylax's shoulder and lifted its dagger-tipped tail high.

"What scares you more than anything?" Scylax asked again, his voice a whisper.

Damien contemplated the question for a while before answering, a lesson hard won over the past year as his master's pupil. "Many things scare me," he said.

"That is the truth," Scylax said, his bloodless lips twisting into something like a smile. "But what scares you *most of all*?"

Damien silently wished for a cup of wine. Something about the drink unleashed the truth within him, making it so much easier to tell Scylax all the things he wanted to know. He hadn't taken so much as a sip since they had begun their lessons a year prior, though not a day went by that he didn't crave another taste of it.

"Tell me," Scylax whispered.

"I'm afraid of the dark," Damien said. "I'm afraid of small spaces that I can't get out of. I'm afraid my heart will stop beating. I'm afraid that my next breath will be my last."

"You are afraid of death then," Scylax said.

"Yes," Damien replied.

"That is the truth," Scylax replied, and bowed his head. "But that is not what scares you most of all."

Scylax closed his eyes. Damien remained still as his master sat like this for a long while, as he often did.

"Why are you here?" he finally asked Damien.

"Because I killed people, Master," Damien answered. "I killed the man who murdered my father, and I was banished. And now this is where I live."

"And how did killing this man make you *feel*?" Scylax asked.

"Good, Master."

"You killed others besides."

"Yes, Master."

"Who?"

"Two sodomites. They attacked me."

"And how did killing *them* make you feel?"

"Good, Master."

Scylax dragged one of his long fingernails over the surface of the stone wheel, scraping a thin line into the granite. "Everything you want, and have ever wanted, is on the other side of Fear," he said. "For fear is a liar. It is a monster inside your head. It whispers untruths, and you listen to it. *Believe* it. *Honor* it. It is your true master."

"No," Damien replied. "You are."

"You lie to me now, as it lies to you," Scylax said, his sallow skin darkening. "In the Temple of Orpheus, there is a price to pay for dishonesty."

"I swear to the Gods I am telling the truth," Damien said, thinly veiled panic in his voice.

Scylax struck him so fast and hard he didn't know what hit him. He smelled blood in his nostrils, and Scylax slapped him again, across the other cheek this time. Damien clutched his stinging face.

"You have talent," Scylax said. "A certain kind of skill. But it is merely clay. Unshaped and useless in the world beyond these walls. The *truth* is that there is nothing special about you. Your struggle is that of every living thing on earth: the search for love, and safety and warmth. When that is threatened, you all too willingly sell your courage to *fear* in exchange for the slightest of hopes that you will be spared discomfort. Tell me that you know I am right."

"You are right, Master," Damien said, wiping blood from his chin.

Scylax struck Damien again. "*Pain* is an illusion. *Fear* is an illusion. *Safety* is an illusion," he intoned.

"Yes, Master," Damien said, blood dripping off his lips.

A sudden shift in wind, a quick flash of his Master's cloak, and then nothing save the torchlight. An invisible breath blew it out, leaving Damien alone in the darkness.

He assumed the tugging sensation at his tunic was Master Scylax. When he turned around, however, nothing was there, only darkness. With a sickening realization, he understood something was crawling up his back.

A scorpion pulled itself up his tunic with its claws, the weight of its body nauseatingly heavy. Damien endured its agonizing progress across his shoulders, up his neck, and to the top of his skull. The scorpion finally rested there, clinging to his scalp.

Damien sat on the stone wheel like this, waiting for dawn.

7

W.A.C. Recruiting Center, Marietta, Georgia; January 1945

Dee woke with a gasp. She sat up in bed and swatted at her hair, relieved when a scorpion didn't tumble out of it and onto the mattress.

She collapsed back onto her pillow, listening to her mother run coffee beans through the grinder in the kitchen downstairs.

"'Morning, Mama."

May sipped her coffee, cold morning light casting a blue glow across the counter. Her daughter stood in the doorway fully dressed, winter coat and all.

"Going somewhere?" May asked.

"Yes, Mama," Dee said, and poured a cup from the steaming pot on the stove.

The women drank their coffee in silence. Dee finished hers first and rinsed the mug under the tap. She was halfway out the door when her mother spoke again.

"Better wear your mittens," she said. "It's freezing out there today."

Dee clenched her jaw and didn't answer; she just pivoted on her foot and marched back up to her room.

Her mother was right, of course. The day was unusually frigid, and Dee had only forgotten the mittens in nervous anticipation of her morning at the Army recruiting station. Back in her room she went straight to the place where she always kept them: on top of the radiator next to her closet, the place where they went from cold and soggy to warm and crispy, a delicious feeling that lasted most of the way to her morning bus.

They weren't there.

Dee jammed her hands inside every pocket of her coat and every drawer in her bureau. She checked under the bed; only her Nazi dolls were there, staring back at her, and a cold realization washed down her body.

She had left her mittens in the Harrells' barn.

When Bo had stepped into the animal trap, Dee had pulled them off, setting them on the floor of the hayloft and descending to the man and his shattered leg. She stopped thinking at that point, propelled only by her unstoppable desire to burn the Klansman alive.

And they were still there.

Dee covered her mouth to keep herself from screaming in the quiet morning gloom. She couldn't risk another sojourn to the Harrells' farm. The mittens would be found, if they hadn't already, and conclusions would be drawn one way or the other. Nothing could be done about it now.

Dee scurried down the stairs, hands shoved in her coat pockets so her mother wouldn't notice they lacked the pink mittens crafted especially for her daughter the previous winter.

"Where you goin' anyway?" her Mama snapped, patience at an end.

Dee mumbled something and strode out across the short lawn, shoes crunching over the snowfall. Bocephus McInnes's brown tobacco sputum still clung frozen over the name ATTICA on the mailbox by the sidewalk. Remembering his shrieks as his face melted off his skull, Dee smiled beneath her scarf.

A beautiful pin-up wearing a uniform in front of a waving American flag asked the question in large, blue font:

ARE YOU A GIRL WITH A STAR-SPANGLED HEART?

Dee did a little jump of excitement as she read the rest of the poster hanging inside the window of the Army recruiting center:

JOIN THE WAC NOW! THOUSANDS OF ARMY JOBS NEED TO BE
FILLED!
WOMEN'S ARMY CORP
UNITED STATES ARMY

As she placed her shoe on the first step into the station, her vision went fuzzy. She loosened her scarf, sucking in a lungful of cold air and willing herself to calm down. Only when she was composed enough that she might speak whole sentences did she go inside.

The clacking of typewriters echoed off the walls. A radio somewhere broadcast the news of the day: the Japanese had launched a counterattack against the British at the Irrawaddy River in Burma.

Sergeant Haft, a pristinely groomed man in uniform, glanced up from a pile of paperwork. The ceiling lights glinted off the short black hair slicked flat against his scalp. Dee smelled his aftershave from ten feet away.

"Help you with something?" he asked, tucking his pencil behind an ear. Dee noticed his clean fingernails, trimmed to the quick.

"Yes, sir," she said, immediately disliking the way her voice sounded. She cleared her throat and drew up her spine. "Yes, sir," she repeated, more confidently. "Where may I sign up, sir?"

Haft sat back in his chair. "Sign up for what?"

Dee reread the sign on the door to confirm that she had in fact walked into an army recruiting station and not the post office.

"The army, sir," she answered.

The sergeant's eyebrows shot up. "I see. Did you bring your letter?"

"Letter?"

"Your recruitment letter," he said.

Dee gripped her coat pocket as if one could be in there.

"I don't... No," she said.

"Did you leave it at home?" he asked, sighing with impatience.

"No, I... What letter, sir?"

Haft held up a finger that indicated Dee should wait there, then walked into a back office.

She studied the posters lining the walls while he did, one in particular catching her eye. Another classic beauty marched arm in arm with a gray-haired man wearing a top hat covered in stars and stripes. MAKE A DATE WITH UNCLE SAM! it read.

A throat cleared. The young soldier had returned with a much older one, wearing the same tan uniform but adorned with pins and medals across the breast pocket.

"Hello," he said. "I'm Colonel Hall. What's your name, miss?"

"Attica, sir. Dee."

"Miss Attica, it's nice to meet you," he said, and whispered something to the sergeant.

"Yes sir," he replied.

"This way, please," Colonel Hall said, indicating Dee should follow him around the counter. She did, to an office at the end of the hallway.

The colonel gestured to a seat in front of his desk and Dee sat. A ship in a glass bottle was positioned next to a brass nameplate that read, COLONEL WILLIAM HALL.

"I understand you'd like to sign up for the Army, Miss Attica," he said, smiling under his trimmed gray mustache.

"Yes, sir," Dee replied. "Very much so."

"The Women's Corps were partly my idea, you know," he said. "It's my opinion that if men can serve active duty, so can women."

He tilted his head in such a way Dee understood she needed to respond to this.

"Couldn't agree more, sir," she replied.

"Now Miss Attica... Sorry, remind me of your first name?"

"Damienne. But folks call me Dee."

"Dee," he repeated. "Damienne Attica. Damienne, Dee Attica. See now, I've never heard of you. And I'm on the committee that puts together the list of gals we'd like to see enter our corps. Only the best and brightest. Once you're picked, you get a letter. Sergeant Haft out there tells me you don't have one, is that so?"

"That's right, sir," Dee said.

"And there's our problem," Colonel Hall continued. "What school would I have missed you at when I visited?"

"School, sir?" Dee asked.

"We mainly recruit from college campuses."

There wasn't enough time in the day to inform the colonel of her disastrous foray through the Georgia Public School system. Her refusal to put her hand down in class when she knew the answer, her disgust at the subpar textbooks she was taught from. She instead graduated from high school and read every book she could get her hands on at the Marietta Public Library. Her discipline record didn't lend itself to a college career, however.

"I don't attend, sir," she said.

"And that's just fine," the Colonel said with a shrug that made the pins on his uniform shirt rattle. "Just fine. This man's army—or should I say, *woman's* army—doesn't require it. It was a starting place for us is all."

A knock came at the door, and a woman in uniform entered, one Dee guessed to be around her mother's age.

"Sir, Sergeant Haft said you asked to see me?" she said, appearing surprised to find Dee in his guest chair.

Dee rose, smoothing down the front of her dress. She

held her shoulders back and straight, like the female officer did.

"Yes, Corporal. Sit, please," Colonel Hall said, and both women sat.

Dee adjusted herself so the woman needn't turn too far to look at her.

"Miss Attica, this is Corporal Adams. She works with us in our recruiting efforts for the WAC."

"Miss Attica," Adams said with a nod.

"Ma'am," Dee replied. Her mouth was dry, and she wished for a glass of water, though wouldn't dare ask for one.

"I was just about to ask Miss Attica *why* she wants to join the army, Corporal."

"Yes, sir," Adams said, and both officers stared at Dee.

Dee crossed her legs, trying to formulate an answer they might want to hear.

"Well, sir...ma'am, I suppose I want to join for the same reason anybody else does," she said. When she spoke no further Hall nodded at Adams, who asked the follow up question.

"And why is that?"

Dee winced at the condescension in the corporal's tone.

She answered that way because there could be no other reason to voluntarily leave her home for war-torn Europe. She didn't know she would really be expected to spell it out for them.

"Why to kill Adolph Hitler, Corporal," she said, making sure her tone held a similar quality as Adams's.

Colonel Hall slapped his hand on his knee. "Ha!" he said, and smoothed his mustache with a finger. "Can't think of a better reason myself. But you of course know, Miss Attica, that the Women's Army Corps isn't a combat unit.

And without a college education you would likely be assigned as...*support* of other WAC's, in more specialized assignments."

Dee's heart sank.

"Do you understand what the colonel means, Miss Attica?" Corporal Adams said.

"Yes ma'am," Dee replied. "And yes sir. I would do whatever is asked of me."

The officers glanced at each other.

"Say for example, you were asked to cook dinner for a *thousand* troops," Colonel Hall said, as if there could be no greater mission in the war. "Think you could do it?"

Dee made beans and that was about it. Those beans were excellent, however.

"Sir, I think I can do anything I put my mind to."

"Fine," Colonel Hall said, standing. The two women did the same. "Fine. Miss Attica, Corporal Adams here will have you fill out an address card at the front desk. I'll happily take you under consideration, along with our recruiting committee. If it's decided that you're a qualified candidate for potential enlistment, you'll receive a letter in the mail. How does that sound?"

The colonel beamed. Dee returned the best smile she could muster.

"I think that's just wonderful, sir," she said. "I do hope to hear from you."

8

Attica Residence, Marietta, Georgia; January 1945

Dee spent the next three days pretending to read books on the sofa under the living room window, one with a clear view of the mailbox at the end of the drive. She and her mother danced around each other when doing chores, speaking only when necessary. Dee was finishing *The Sun Is My Undoing* by Marguerite Steen for the fifth time when Mama entered the living room and sat on the opposite end of the couch.

Dee turned a page, not acknowledging her presence.

"Girl, put that book down."

Dee did so.

"Something wrong, Mama?"

"What's his name?"

Dee picked her bookmark off the floor. "*Him*, Mama? *Him* who?"

"Him whoever you were with all day and night last week."

"I wasn't with anyone, Mama."

"Where were you, then?"

"Walking. Reading."

"Walking? In the freezing cold? You trying to catch your death?"

"I was at the library, Mama."

This struck her mother as plausible.

"Dee. You're either gonna have to find a rich man, get a job, or go to school," Mama said. "You know I prefer school and job, in that order."

The sound of a car engine snapped Dee's attention out the living room window.

"You waiting for someone?" Mama asked, following her gaze to the curb.

The family coupe cruised up in front of the house. Dee and her mother jumped off the couch.

"Oh, my word!" Mama cried.

George stepped out of the front seat, a bouquet of flowers in his hand. Mama ran for the front door and swung it open.

"George! What in the world?"

May slid down the icy walkway, waving her arms in excitement. The couple embraced, and when she caught her father's eye, Dee waved from the window.

"Dee! Come and hug your daddy now!" May called to her.

"We can hug inside, honey," George said. "Cold as a well digger's shovel out here."

"Dee! Get!"

Another engine sound, the one Dee had been waiting for. The mail truck pulled up behind the coupe.

Dee ran outside.

"Daddy!"

George held her tight. Dee's eyes traveled over to the mailman in the red cap who was sliding letters into the box.

"Wait," Mama said, her smile fading. "Why are you back so soon? Something happen? You get fired?"

Laughing, George released Dee. She couldn't take her eyes off the mailbox as the postman shut the small door, lowered the flag, and walked to the next house.

"Nothing of the sort happened," George said, throwing his arms over his wife's and daughter's shoulders. "I made my quota early is all. And came straight back to my best girls lickety-split."

Dee slipped out from under her father's arm. "I'll get the mail, Daddy."

"I'll get it," George said. "Gotta get my things out of the trunk anyway."

"I'll get your things, Daddy," Dee said.

"Take your father inside and pour him his drink," Mama said. "I'll bring everything inside." With that, she snatched her husband's keys out of his hand and headed for the coupe.

"No use arguing with your mama," George said, and they walked toward the house, Dee casting glances back at her mother.

George settled into his overstuffed chair by the radio and kicked his shoes off.

"Oh, Lord, yes." He sighed. "Good to be home. Yes, sir."

Dee dropped an ice cube in a tumbler and splashed Old Underoof rye over it. She walked it past the living room window; the sight of her mother reading a letter in the middle of the frozen driveway without a coat nearly made her drop it.

It had come.

She passed the drink to her father, who accepted it with a warm smile.

"These eyes sure are glad to see you, sweet girl," he said.

"Drink up, Daddy," Dee replied.

"Pardon me?" George said.

"Your whiskey," Dee continued. "Drink it."

The front door creaked open, and Mama entered, stopping first to hold herself upright in the doorway. She finished reading and dangled the paper from her hand.

"May?" George said, rising from his chair and setting the rye on the coffee table. "What is it?"

"I think that's for me, Mama," Dee said, stepping in front of him. May nodded.

"Then why did you open it?" Dee asked, and plucked the letter from between her mother's fingers. It read:

Miss Attica,

On behalf of the Army Service Forces, I hereby invite you to enlist in the Women's Army Corps. Should you choose to do so you are required to report to this station on Monday, February 12th. You will then be assigned a furlough of one month to put your civilian affairs in order. You also may instead report on Monday, January 22nd, prepared to depart immediately for Fort Oglethorpe.

If you do not wish to enlist into the Army Service Forces, please disregard this invitation and do not report.

Colonel William Hall

Dee gripped the edges of the letter, wrinkling the paper. Her father gently took an edge, and she released it.

George's face fell as he read. "What's this all about?" he said, voice barely above a whisper.

"It's the army, Daddy. They want me to join."

"That can't be," May said.

"Why?" Dee asked.

"Because you're just a girl."

"I'm a woman, Mama. And women can join the Army," Dee said, careful to watch her tone in a room thick with tension.

"You are *not joining the army*, Dee!" Mama shouted.

"May, let me see this again." George reread the letter then handed it to his daughter. "What are you going to do?"

"She's not doing *anything*!" Mama exclaimed.

"May," George said again, his voice rising. "Dee. What are you thinking, honey?"

"I'm thinking..." Dee said, excitement flooding her chest. "I'm thinking I want to go."

May marched across the room and snatched the letter out of Dee's hands.

"I'mma *tear this up!*"

"Mama! No!"

Dee chased her mother around the room, George asking both for calm. When May made a motion to tear the letter in half, Dee grabbed her arm to stop her.

"That's enough!" George never had raised his voice to either of them. Both women appeared taken aback.

"May, give that back to Dee."

May shook her head ruefully, dropped the letter on the floor, and stalked up the staircase, slamming their bedroom door behind her.

Dee reached down and picked it up, rereading "I hereby invite you to enlist" once again.

"Dee, honey." George sat in his chair, rye whiskey in

hand. "The Army? What about school? Not sure where this is all coming from."

Dee folded the invitation letter back into thirds. "Army Service Forces" was stamped in black ink in the upper-left-hand corner. It was addressed to "Miss Damienne Attica," the first letter she had ever received.

"Daddy, I want to show you something."

The wooden floorboards creaked as they walked past the bathroom, May sniffling within. Dee led George into her bedroom, shut the door, and twisted the lock.

"Sit down, Daddy."

George sat on the bed, the hand stitched baby dolls of Dee's youth arranged in front of the headboard. Dee got on her knees and reached under it, bringing up two handfuls of an altogether different kind of doll. She held them out and George took them.

"Your mama told me about these," he said, looking them over.

"What did she tell you?" Dee asked.

"She told me...she told me you made them," he said, dropping them onto the mattress. "Didn't know what for."

"I burn them, Daddy."

George's eyes widened.

"I burn them."

George looked away, out the window.

"I have these thoughts, Daddy, and I can't make them stop. You remember Miss Adeline's cat? The way we used to sit with each other on the porch all day? Talking? How upset Mama got? Said that cat was the *Devil*..."

George shook his head, wincing at the memory.

"Thing is, I don't want to worry you or Mama about anything like that ever again. Not ever. But this? This is something I *have* to do, even if it worries you. Even if it scares you. Look around you, Daddy. I'm a twenty-year-old woman, still playing with dolls in a little girl's bedroom. Thing is, I don't want to play games anymore. I don't want to pretend. And I don't want to be a little girl. I want to grow up. It's time. *Past* time. And to do that I have to go, Daddy. You hear me? I have to *go*."

Dee rose from the mattress.

"Now. You want to tell her that or should I?"

Dee packed her only suitcase with clothes, George and May arguing downstairs. Daddy repeated the phrase "her adult decision," while Mama wore out "no child of mine." After placing the last folded blouse in her luggage, she picked the Heinrich Himmler doll from the bed and turned in a circle with him, taking in her childhood room one last time.

She tossed the doll back into the pile with the others. They lay in a heap, pieces of cotton and stitching and magazine paper.

Just enough space remained in her suitcase for the books Dee figured she needed on her journey: *Les Miserables*, *War and Peace*, and *The Metamorphosis*. She set the original French, Russian, and German editions in first, and stacked the English translations on top.

Dee had a feeling she would meet some French, Russian and German people to put her linguistic skills to the test soon.

When her parents stopped fighting, she went back downstairs. They ate supper in silence: chicken and mash for George and May, beans as always for Dee. Halfway through *Amos 'n' Andy*, May excused herself and went to her room. George listened to the evening news as Dee cleared plates and did the dishes, careful to run the sink tap low so her father kept the radio volume down. Then she went to bed.

9

W.A.C. Recruiting Center, Marietta, Georgia; January 1945

Like a child waiting on Christmas dawn, Dee didn't sleep at all that night, listening for the creak of her parents' door so she could run down the stairs and open her presents under the tree. When their bedroom door finally opened, she allowed them a few moments in the kitchen to start the coffee.

George and May waited for her downstairs, on the couch. Only there were no presents like so many of those Christmas mornings and no sparkling tree. There was only their sadness and fear.

Dee stood fully dressed, suitcase in hand. Her parents stared out the dark living room window at nothing.

"You wanting breakfast?" her Mama asked.

"No thank you, Mama," Dee said. "Not hungry."

George pointed to the suitcase. "What in the world are you packed up for?"

Mama gasped. "What on *earth*?"

"The letter said you report February twelfth," George

said, standing. May followed. "That's damn near a month from now."

"War might be over in a month," Dee said. "We stopped the Germans before the Meuse."

"The *what now*?" Mama said.

"The Meuse River," Dee continued. "The German offensive could be finished. Hard to say right now. The Nazis already retreated out from the Ardennes forest. Mr. Churchill's saying it was the greatest battle of the war. And the *Luftwaffe* aren't flying anymore. Can you imagine? The whole German air force, not dropping any more bombs, or troops. By the time February comes, there might not be an army to join. I'll have missed the whole darn thing. And that is *not* going to happen. Mama, Daddy, I love you. And I'm going. Now."

Dee set her suitcase down and hugged her parents. They hugged her back, searching for words to keep her from leaving. They found none. Dee turned around and walked out the front door.

"Dee! *Dee!*"

It was her father, following her down Juniper Street in the coupe.

"Let me drive you, honey."

"I can walk, Daddy," she called over her shoulder.

"Please."

Dee stopped. The coupe glided up next to her. She opened the back door first and placed her suitcase inside. Then she got in next to her father. Radiator heat blasted through the vents, and she shivered. George rubbed her shoulder in an effort to warm her.

The rising sun shone on downtown Marietta, ice crystals already melting off car windows and roof eaves lining the thoroughfare. When they pulled up to the recruiting station, it was dark inside.

"Looks closed," George said.

"Seems to be," Dee said.

"Guess we'll wait," George said. He twisted the coupe's radio dial.

Jazz, Ella Fitzgerald, Gene Autry and then the news crackled through the speakers. George cranked up the volume. "Catch myself up on some of what you already seem to know," he said.

An announcer read the morning's news.

"*...and our weakened Seventh Army. General Eisenhower pushed on to the bitter end, our boys fighting valiantly to rid the Ardennes of the Nazi scourge. Greatly outnumbered, they fought in the bitter cold to ensure an Allied victory.*"

"Just like you were saying," George said.

"They repeat the same thing, Daddy," Dee replied.

They listened a while longer, Dee trying to picture life in the Ardennes forest. Sleeping under snow-covered trees, waking to the sounds of Wehrmacht shelling, what night and the total darkness that followed might bring. She imagined Nazis screaming as the Americans retaliated, toppling ancient oaks and willows in a storm of fire.

"Dee." George pointed to a young man in a crisp uniform keying into the recruiting station. It was Sergeant Haft, his Brylcreem-groomed hair shining brightly under the lamp above the door.

"That's the sergeant, Daddy," Dee said, and took her father's hand.

"I'll write. First chance I get."

"Call, honey," George said, pained. "You *call*, first phone you come to. And every one after. Here."

George reached for the glove box and twisted the knob; it fell open, receipts and maps and business cards tumbling forward. He fished under the detritus and produced a handful of nickels and dimes.

"Here."

Dee cupped a palm, accepting the change. Tears rolled down her father's cheeks.

She slid over in the coupe's front seat and hugged him tightly. "Don't cry, Daddy. Please." George wept. Dee gripped him closely. "I'm going to be *fine*, Daddy. Just fine. They'll send me to some mess hall to cook and clean with the other girls and I'll come home knowing how to make all your favorite dishes. Mama's too."

This lie pleased her enough that she elaborated on it. "The sergeant himself said I wouldn't be going anywhere dangerous. Might not even make it overseas."

George pulled back, wiping his face. "That so?"

"Mm-hmm," Dee said. "Only thing to worry about is me getting fat on all that army cooking."

George laughed despite himself.

"There you go," Dee said. "Now Daddy, you listen to me, and you listen good. You listening?" George nodded. "When I send letters home, you read them to Mama. I don't think I'll have anything too exciting to write home about, but you read 'em to her anyway."

"I will," George said.

"Promise?"

"I promise, honey."

"Good," Dee said, opening the coupe's door. "Now no more blubbering. You tell Mama the same. I love you. And you'll hear from me soon. War will probably be over before I get halfway in that door."

Dee got out of the car, retrieved her suitcase from the back seat, and ascended the steps to the recruiting station.

George waited until she disappeared behind the door before pulling away from the curb.

Sergeant Haft appeared startled to have such an early arrival in the office, brow furrowing with confusion when Dee set her suitcase on the floor. She produced the recruitment letter and laid it flat on the counter between them.

"'Morning, sir," she said.

"Uh. 'Morning," the sergeant replied. "What's this now?"

The sergeant read it over. When he finished, he jerked a thumb to the calendar on the wall behind his chair.

"You know how to read one of those, gal?"

"Yes, sir."

"Then why are you here?"

"Wanted to get a head start on things, sir."

"A head start?"

"Yes, sir."

"Well, allow me to teach you US Army rule number one," the sergeant said. "And that is what you *want*..."

The front door opened. Sergeant Haft stood at attention.

"Good morning Colonel Hall, sir."

"Good morning," Colonel Hall replied. He didn't look at the sergeant when he said it, only at Dee, also standing at attention, shoulders back, feet together, chin high.

"And to you, Miss Attica," he continued. "You look right and ready this morning, eh?"

"Yes, sir," Dee said. "I surely am, sir."

"At ease, please," the colonel said, removing his coat. Sergeant Haft retook his seat.

"Seems to me the recruitment letter I sent you specified a certain date to report for duty, Miss Attica," he continued. "I highly doubt that date was *today*."

"Sir, that's exactly what I was telling her," Sergeant Haft interjected. "I said to her, I said..."

Colonel Hall held up a hand, stopping his speech. "Miss Attica? Did the letter not specify a certain date?"

"It did sir," Dee said. "And I don't mean to disobey an order. Thing of it is, sir, the Allied counteroffensive in the Ardennes speaks to progress. Great progress that might spell the end of the German advance. If that's the case, the war in the European Theater might be over sooner than later."

"You seem to know a great deal about our operations, Miss Attica," the colonel said. "I'm impressed."

"Thank you, sir."

"There are a great many fronts in this conflict, of course. What if you were to be deployed somewhere else? In the Pacific, say?"

"I'm not going to the Pacific, sir."

Sergeant Haft spat out a laugh and shook his head. "Got us a live one, all right," he mumbled.

"Is that so, Miss Attica?" Colonel Hall said, amused.

"Yes, sir. I'm going to Europe."

"And why there specifically?"

"As I told you and the corporal the other day, sir," Dee continued, "that's where Adolph Hitler is."

The colonel's smile dropped. He took a step toward Dee, hesitating before taking another.

"Sir?" asked Sergeant Haft. Something about the colonel's expression alarmed him.

"Quiet, Sergeant," the colonel said.

Dee remained at attention as Colonel Hall approached her. He towered over her diminutive frame, much too close to be polite, manners and custom the farthest things from his mind.

When Dee had said the name "Adolph Hitler," something very strange occurred. The colonel felt certain he'd seen it, but it happened so fast he couldn't be sure.

Her green eyes had turned black. If asked, he'd have sworn on the Bible that it was true. Colonel Hall stared into those eyes now, losing himself in their emerald hues. His feet felt nailed to the floor by them. After half a minute of this, he stepped back, unsteady on his feet. He gripped the counter's edge and cleared his throat.

"Sergeant..."

Sergeant Haft had followed the entire exchange, open-mouthed.

"Sir."

"What time's the next bus to Oglethorpe?"

Sergeant Haft scrambled through some papers on his desk. He found a bus schedule and flipped it right side up, then traced his finger down the lists of departures and arrivals.

"Next bus headed out Oglethorpe way is oh nine hundred, sir."

"Miss Attica will be on it," Colonel Hall said.

"Yes, sir."

"Miss Attica?"

"Yes, sir."

"Welcome to the United States Army."

Dee couldn't suppress a wide grin. "Yes, sir. Thank you sir."

The colonel brushed past her, walking down the hallway to his office.

Dee faced the sergeant. He jabbed a finger toward the seat against the opposite wall.

"Sit. Down."

Dee picked up her suitcase. "Yes, sir."

She walked the six blocks to the Marietta Bus Depot.

Dee had filled out a few pages of paperwork before being handed a bus voucher. Sergeant Haft had rushed through the intake process, seeming to want nothing to do with her. Dee guessed he had never encountered a woman like her before.

The terminal line lurched forward. Dee tapped a shoulder in front of her. "You have the time?"

The lady in the purple pillbox hat confirmed it was nearly a quarter to the hour. Dee squinted at the long line ahead and marched to the front of it.

"Excuse me," said the man at the counter glaring at Dee as she approached. "You just wait your turn."

"Sir, I..." Dee began.

"Wait your turn."

"Sir, I'm..."

"Wait. Your. Turn."

Dee dropped her bag.

"Sir, I'm fixing to join the United States Army today!" she shouted. All chatter in the terminal ceased. Dee continued. "I have a voucher here for Fort Oglethorpe, which departs in fifteen minutes. I cannot be late. Now either take my ticket and show me to my bus, or you can explain my lateness to

Colonel William Hall at the US Army recruiting station on Wilton Street. Now what's it going to be, hmm?"

The counter agent sat in stunned silence, along with every other person in the vicinity. Then a porter appeared at Dee's side, hand extended.

"Let me see that, miss."

Dee handed it to the elderly gentleman in the red cap and tie.

"Bus for Oglethorpe leaves out of door six. Right over there."

Dee followed his finger to a group of soldiers in uniform on the far side of the terminal, smoking cigarettes and chatting amiably.

"Thank you very much," she said, and picked her suitcase off the floor.

10

Bus Depot, Marietta, Georgia; January 1945

The bus was packed by the time Dee stepped onto it, cigarette smoke clouding the air as she dragged her suitcase down the aisle to the back row of seats. Only a handful of her fellow passengers weren't in uniform. The only other person who wasn't a man besides her was the bus driver. She settled into a single seat next to a window.

"Under the bus," a voice said.

Dee's head whipped toward a blond soldier with a pencil mustache across the aisle.

"Excuse me?" she said.

"*Under* the bus," he repeated. "Your suitcase is what I meant," he said, reaching out a hand. "Here."

The man took the handle of her suitcase and walked it back down the aisle and off the bus. He placed it in the luggage compartment beneath and returned, a smile on his thin face.

"It'll be the first one off now," he said, resuming his seat. "Lucky you."

"Thank you," Dee said. "Most kind."

"Iggy," the man said, extending a hand. Dee shook it.

"Dee," she said. "Thanks again, Iggy."

"My pleasure, Dee," he said. The soldier next to Iggy slapped his arm and asked for a cigarette. As he fished one from his pocket, Dee observed her feet were planted on a crumpled newspaper on the floor.

It was the *Marietta Daily Journal*. After smoothing it across her lap, she read the headline: *BURNING DEATH OF LOCAL FARMHAND DECLARED A HOMICIDE.*

She checked the date. It was Wednesday's paper, just three days prior. Dee eyeballed her fellow passengers warily, as if being seen reading the article might implicate her in the murder.

Authorities investigating the burning death of Marietta resident Bocephus McInnes, 29, have concluded that his death on the Harrell farm property this Sunday last was an intentional act and thus a homicide. An investigation has been opened.

"We have every reason to believe Mr. McInnes was murdered in cold blood," Detective Jasper Kimmet said at a press conference. "We're asking the public for any and all information that might lead to the arrest of the person or persons responsible."

Miss Callie Harrell, daughter of former Marietta Deputy Mayor Deacon Harrell, discovered Mr. McInness burned to death in the family barn Sunday morning after church.

"I smelled smoke and went outside," she told the Journal. *"When I got there, the fire was already out and to be honest with you, I didn't even see him at first. Everything was incinerated. And then I saw him lying there. He was burned so badly he didn't even look like a person anymore."*

Police are questioning employees of the Savercool Gin

Company, the factory where Mr. McInnes had been employed since...

"Smoke?"

Dee jumped in her seat, the newspaper crumpling in her fists.

"Didn't mean to startle you," Iggy said, pack of cigarettes in his hand, the tip of a Pall Mall poking out of the foil.

"Don't smoke, but thank you kindly," Dee said.

"Surely," Iggy said. He stuck the Pall Mall in his mouth.

The bus doors closed.

"This bus is headin' to Fort Oglethorpe. Ain't no stops in between!" the driver called back. "Fort Oglethorpe! No stops!"

Excitement overtook the tension in Dee's chest. She gazed out the window as the bus backed away from the terminal and eased itself onto the road that led to the highway out of Marietta.

She wasn't at all sure she would ever see it again.

Dee stepped off the bus a few hours later. She retrieved her suitcase and followed the throng of soldiers hoisting duffel bags over their shoulders into Fort Oglethorpe. She had no idea where to go.

"Lost?"

Iggy sidled up next to her, baring a sizable pair of buck-teeth in his amiable smile and tipping the green army-issued cap on his blond head.

"Think I might be," Dee said.

"Where you hoping to get to?" he asked.

Dee set the suitcase down and retrieved a folded stack of paperwork given to her at the recruiting center.

"Let me see," Iggy said, taking it from her. "Well. Says here you're in the Women's Army Corp." He shaded his eyes in the late-afternoon sun, pointing to an entrance across a lawn yellowed by winter. "Intake canteen. Building forty-five. You'll start over there, same as everyone."

"Thanks for all the help today, Iggy," Dee said. "Much appreciated."

"Good luck to you, Dee."

"Same to you."

Dee had made it halfway across the campus when Iggy called out her name. He jogged up to her, out of breath under the weight of his duffel.

"I *know* you from somewhere," he said. "Where have we met before?"

"Don't think we have," Dee replied.

"Ever been to Sandwich, Illinois?" Iggy asked.

"Never been anywhere except Marietta," Dee said. "And now here."

Iggy shook his head. "Gosh darn it. I *know you*."

"Maybe I look like someone else," Dee offered.

"Maybe," Iggy said. "What's your last name?"

"Attica."

Iggy wagged his finger at her.

"See, I know that name! And dang it if I don't know from where."

He had kind eyes that appeared older than the young face they were set in. Dee shrugged. "Don't know," she said.

"Maybe I'll see you around," he finally said, "and remember."

"Maybe," Dee said.

Iggy laughed. "You take good care, Dee."

"You do the same, Iggy."

"Short for 'Ignatius,'" he said. "If that rings any bells."

Dee shrugged again. Iggy shook his head.

"I know I know you!"

Dee continued into Fort Oglethorpe.

Female recruits packed the intake canteen. Dee searched the sea of faces for an empty seat and, finding none, settled for a spot along the wall.

Two hours passed, Dee mopping her brow under the heating vent blasting above her head. A barrel-chested officer with stripes on his sleeve strode into the room, clipboard in hand. The chatter echoing around the canteen died down to a whisper.

"Listen up," the lieutenant barked. "When your name is called, line up in fives, starting at the yellow line."

They were called up by their last names, preceded by "Miss."

"Now," the lieutenant said, again addressing them, "how many of you have done your medicals?"

A few hands went up. They were pulled from the group and told to follow a red line painted on the floor, down a hallway.

"Rest of you will have your physical, in alphabetical order." The lieutenant consulted his clipboard. "Attica, Damienne."

Dee sat on a cold table in a cold room, an even colder stethoscope traveling up and down her back.

"Lie down," the doctor said, tightening her hair bun with a rubber band. She appeared overworked and in a rush, her uniform hanging loosely off her lanky frame. She pressed her fingers into Dee's abdomen under the thin paper gown she had been made to change into.

"Pregnancies?" the doctor asked.

"Sorry?" Dee asked.

"Have you ever been pregnant?"

"No, ma'am."

The doctor ran a rubber mallet along Dee's elbow and knee joints, then told her to dress. She was then directed down the hallway toward a wooden bench.

Over the next hour and a half, the bench cleared as women went in and out of the army psychiatrist's office, but Dee never sat on it, preferring to stand.

"Attica."

A small, bald, bespectacled man in uniform sat at his desk, smoking a pipe. What little hair he had splayed out in brown wisps above his ears.

"Miss Attica," the man said, "I'm Dr. Wroe. Sit, sit."

Dee took a seat across from Dr. Wroe's desk.

"And how are we today, Miss Attica?"

"Well, sir. Yourself?"

"Fine, fine," he said. "Miss Attica, I'm here to evaluate your mental fitness to serve in the United States Army. Much like your physical fitness was evaluated moments ago. Do you understand?"

"Yes, sir."

"*Why* do you want to join the Army, Miss Attica?"

Dee considered the real answer before giving the safer version.

"To serve my country, sir."

"Married?"

"No, sir."

"But you'd like to be one day, yes? Have a family?"

Dee had never given the matter a moment's thought and said so. The doctor was clearly perturbed by that answer.

"Miss Attica, you do like *boys*, eh? Men? Want to snag yourself a handsome fella some day? Hm?"

Now Dee understood what he was asking. Of the many things that separated her from the other schoolgirls growing up, this was chief among them: she had not a bit of interest in the opposite sex. This caused more than a few to taunt her as a bulldicker or butch broad, but she didn't have any interest in women either, at least not sexually. Other things consumed Dee's imagination, none of which she deemed wise to share with Dr. Wroe.

"Yes, sir," she said. "Of course I do."

Now satisfied, he scratched a sentence down in her file and closed it flat.

"Welcome to the army, Miss Attica."

"Thank you, sir."

11

Barracks 22, Fort Oglethorpe: January 1945

Dee was issued a khaki shirt, skirt, and jacket. She changed into them with the other women in Barracks 22, their assigned housing unit. The taciturn barracks corporal bellowed her instructions, the recruits scrambling to fold and stuff their footlockers with the civilian clothes they had arrived in. The first lesson of the day was how to stand at attention facing out from their respective bunk, feet together, arms at their sides.

"Repeat after me," shouted the corporal. "I. Your name."

"I, Damienne Attica..." Dee said, swelling with excitement, and repeated the oath along with her fellow recruits.

"...do solemnly swear I will support and defend the Constitution of the United States against all enemies, foreign and domestic; that I will bear true faith and allegiance to the same; and that I will obey the orders of the president of the United States and the officers appointed over me, according to regulations and the Uniform Code of Military Justice. So help me God."

Dee exhaled. She was in the army, at last.

Over the next week, she learned the army way: how to make a bed, how to shine her shoes, how to clean a toilet. She had done all these things in Marietta, but she was now instructed those civilian methods were sorely lacking. Her childhood bed didn't have hospital corners, for example, the bedspread so squared and tight a nickel bounced off it. Dee savored the newness of it all, the regimentation of her daily activities. When they were told boot camp commenced that Monday morning at oh five hundred, she barely slept in anticipation of its rigors.

They learned to march and drilled until each and every woman was in lockstep with the other. Dee was never once out of rhythm, landing every footfall perfectly. Her drill instructors noted this and put her at the front. "Like Attica does it," they commanded the others.

They ran, and ran some more, Dee always at the head of the line, arms pumping. She couldn't recall running anywhere a day in her life, but never once did she stop to catch her breath like most did, or fall to her knees and vomit into the grass with the rest. "Outstanding, Attica" was a familiar refrain from the officers.

At chow she shunned the meat for the vegetables, drawing strange looks from the other women when she sat down with a tray of steamed carrots, the fruit cup, and nothing else. She didn't socialize with anyone in particular, only stared out the window, her green eyes a million miles away from the chatter surrounding her.

On the Friday of the first week of boot camp, the regiment learned an obstacle course. They wore gas masks for the drill, a detail Dee loved. She took to the exercise like a duck to water, and as she emerged from a crawl through thirty yards of wooden sawhorses, a whistle blew.

"Private Attica! Front and center!"

Dee jumped to her feet and sprinted for the formidably sized drill instructor. She stopped a few feet short of him and stood at attention, barely out of breath as she pulled off her mask.

"Private Attica reporting as instructed, Drill Sergeant!"

"Lieutenant Burrows wants to see you in his office, Attica!" he roared. "ASAP! Move it out!"

"Yes, sir!" Dee dropped her mask and bolted across the lawn.

She waited on a bench, same as her first day, only this time blissfully alone. A man's voice calling into the hallway pierced the silence.

"Enter."

Lieutenant Burrows, still trim in his fifties, returned her salute and offered her a seat. "Your instructors tell me you're doing a fine job, Attica. Best in your class."

"Wonderful to hear, sir," she replied.

"They say you run a five-minute mile."

"Apparently so, sir."

"You run track in school?"

"No, sir."

Burrows appeared flummoxed by this. "Play sports?"

"No, sir."

"I understand you and your platoon went on a map-reading exercise out in the forest. And you led your squadron back in record time. *Without* a compass."

"I have a good sense of direction, sir."

Burrows smiled. "What do you want to do in the army, Attica?"

"Go to Germany, sir. Since you asked."

"Go to Germany."

"Yes sir."

"And do what, exactly?"

Dee chased the true answer out of her head before speaking. "Help win the war, sir."

Burrows sat forward in his chair. He didn't blink, and so neither did she. "Well. I don't think we'll be sending you quite that far, Private," he finally said. "But I am recommending you to the officer candidate class we offer female recruits at Oglethorpe. How does that strike you, Attica?"

"Will I go to Europe, sir?" Dee asked.

"I think you just might," Burrows replied.

"Then sign me up, sir. And thank you."

Burrows sat back in his chair. "Do you know what *chutzpah* is, Private Attica?"

"*Chutzpah*?" Dee repeated. "Don't think I do, sir."

"Well, you have it," Burrows said. "In spades."

———

Dee fairly skipped back out to the grounds, rejoining the platoon and running the perimeter of Fort Oglethorpe twice before being released to chow. The women staggered into the mess hall, glistening with sweat on a twenty-degree evening. Plastic trays were grabbed, and they made their way through the line, meat loaf and mashed potatoes slopped into the appropriate indentations in the plastic receptacles. Dee waved it all away, anticipating the green beans at the end of the row.

"You got something against my meat loaf?" the cook said, loud enough for the others to hear.

"Certainly not," Dee said. "Don't eat meat is all."

She secured her ladle of green beans and went to a seat by the window, sun dipping into the gray horizon as she ate.

"Hey," a voice said. "Attica."

A group of recruits stared at her, disheveled after a day of drilling.

"Where you from?" a woman asked.

"Marietta," Dee answered.

"Marietta," the woman repeated. "And what? They don't eat meat out there?"

"And does everybody run as fast as they can from one place to the other?" another asked.

"Without a compass?" a third chimed in.

The table broke into laughter. Dee smirked and went back to her green beans.

January–February 1945

She was up at five o'clock each morning for "Reveille," tearing off the bedsheets and remaking the bunk to army standards. Next was chow, the easiest meal for her to procure: a bowl of steaming beans, followed by a two-mile run. Officer training classes followed, her favorite part of the day.

She learned how to use a gas mask, how to do a handspring, how to drive a stick shift. There were map-reading classes, first-aid classes, health and hygiene classes. She joined and eventually led her company's color guard. It was about this time the national press took notice of the WAC, and Dee's mother and father awoke one late-winter morning to discover their daughter on page A3 of the *Marietta Daily Journal*, front and center in a four-by-six photograph carrying her company's flag across the field, two rows of women behind her, smiles beaming.

"*Marietta resident Damienne 'Dee' Attica leads her WAC platoon across the grassy fields of Fort Oglethorpe,*" the caption read.

"Well, I'll be," George said, clipping out the article with a pair of scissors.

Dee elevated marching to the level of art, rightly suggesting to the instructors that marching columns should be arranged with short women like her in the front and the tall women in the back, a complete reversal of protocol. She explained that the band music they marched to required twenty paces a minute with thirty-inch steps, and shorter women trying to keep up with the taller made for less-than-perfect turns. Her superiors agreed, reversed the order, and the next time the WAC color guard marched for Oglethorpe brass, the base commander paid Lieutenant Burrows a personal compliment.

"They march beautifully, John. I'll give you that," the commander said.

Burrows called Dee into his office later that afternoon.

"Reporting as instructed, sir," Dee said, saluting smartly.

"At ease, soldier," Burrows said, and indicated she should sit. "Outstanding presentation today, Attica. There were a lot of important eyes on you and your unit. You did yourself and the WAC proud."

"Thank you, sir."

"Graduation is in two weeks. Excited?"

"Very much so, sir."

"We need to discuss your classification upon graduation," Burrows said. "Your *job*."

"Yes, sir."

"Thing of it is, Attica, is that you're young, and you're a woman. And young women, officers or not, don't lead people in the United States Army."

Dee shifted in her seat, making sure to keep the pleasant smile on her face.

"Sir, I put in a request to be a truck driver," she said. Driving a truck put Dee behind the wheel, a useful tool in her overall plan. That, and truck driving wasn't cooking, the job classification she expected to be placed in.

Lieutenant Burrows dismissed this with the wave of a hand. "Public relations is where you belong. I see you as the face of the Women's Army Corps."

"Public relations, sir?"

"Recruitment," Burrows said. "Getting other girls riled up to join the service. What a tremendous thing it is, et cetera. Send you around to college campuses. What do you think?"

Dee studied her lap, searching for an answer. College campuses weren't a boat over to Europe. If she went along with the idea, the war might be over by the time she secured an assignment that took her overseas.

Tap, tap, tap.

Lieutenant Burrows made a face and wheeled around in his chair. A tiny shadow was outlined behind the curtained window.

Tap, tap, tap.

"What the Devil?" he said, and rolled his chair to the window.

He pulled the curtain back to reveal a sparrow, sitting on the ledge. When it caught Dee's eye, it spoke.

Hitler, it said.

I know, Dee replied.

Hitler, the sparrow said again.

"Will you look at that?" Burrows said. "Cheeky little fella." He tapped the windowpane. The bird didn't move. "Huh," he said, and closed the curtain. "Now," he continued, "tell me, Attica. What do you think?"

Tap, tap, tap.

The lieutenant rose from his chair and opened the curtains. He pulled the window up in an effort to shoo the bird away, but it flew inside instead.

"Damn it all," Burrows said, the sparrow alighting on top of the bookcase behind Dee's chair.

Hitler. Hitler.

To Dee's ears, the bird was shouting.

"Allow me, sir," she said, standing. Dee locked eyes with the bird. She put out her hand; it fluttered through the air and landed in her palm.

"Well, don't that beat all," Burrows said.

I hear you, Dee told the bird. *Enough now.*

She walked to the window and released it outside. The sparrow flew away.

Dee shut the window and drew the curtains.

"Sir. I appreciate your thinking I'm worthy to represent the WAC in such a way. I truly do," she said. "But whatever classification the army sees fit to put me in, I hope it's one that will take me to Europe and our fighting boys. I want to help them, sir, if I can."

Burrows nodded. He pictured the bird, perching itself into her hand without a moment's hesitation. There was a silence, the senior officer staring at Dee as if she were an optical illusion or a puzzle to solve.

"Will that be all, sir?" she finally asked.

"Yes," Burrows said. "I'll take our discussion under advisement. Dismissed."

Dee saluted and left.

Graduation day found George and May in the wooden
stands surrounding the Oglethorpe training field. The day
was cloudless and chilly, May shading her eyes from the
brilliant sunshine with the graduation day program, which
outlined the morning's ceremonies.

"Can you see her, George?" May asked her husband,
scanning the uniforms lined up at the field's edge.

"I'm looking," George replied.

A hundred yards away, Dee also was searching, trying to
make out faces in the stands and finding it impossible. She
checked the position of her hands around the pole of the
American flag in her grip, noting the slight breeze ruffling
the star-spangled fabric.

Lieutenant Burrows walked the line, the WAC soldiers
squaring their shoulders as he passed, and stopped in front
of Dee.

"Attica."

"Sir."

"How are we this morning?"

"Ready, sir."

"Outstanding," Burrows said, and backed up so all the
women lined up behind Dee heard him.

"'Morning," he called out.

"'Morning sir," the WAC platoon answered as one.

"This presentation is the culmination of your training.
You ladies left your hometowns to be here. Left Mobile and
Phoenix. Sacramento and Boston and Jacksonville. Seattle
and Marietta."

This last town he said directly to Dee.

"A lot of people don't think women can serve in the United States Army as soldiers. I happen to strongly disagree with that sentiment. I look to you—to each and every one of you—to help me prove them wrong. Now who's with me?"

"Sir, we are, sir!" the platoon answered.

Burrows planted his feet. "Atten-*tion!*"

The thunderclap of 250 women coming to order quieted the stands across the field. The steady beat of a drum began, and the women marched in place.

"Left, right, left, right, left," Burrows called out, and Dee stepped forward, leading her class across the field.

They kept in time with the drum, parading through the grass toward the spectators. The women to Dee's left and right kept perfect rhythm as they had for hundreds of drills before, the State of Georgia and Fort Oglethorpe's flags slightly dipped in deference to the one Dee held ramrod straight. A nearly imperceptible movement above her eyeline caused her to glance up its pole, only for a second.

It was the sparrow, perched atop the head of the brass eagle just above the stars and stripes, twittering.

Dee suppressed a smile and called out a command. "Company...*halt.*"

Every woman's last foot fell onto the grass in seamless unison.

The names were called in alphabetical order, which George and May figured meant they wouldn't wait too long before their daughter was called onto the platform erected above the grass.

"Attica, Damienne."

Her parents craned their necks as Dee ascended the steps, press camera bulbs flashing. A small congregation on the stage waited to receive her, including Congresswoman

Edith Nourse Rogers, dressed in white. She was one of the first women to serve in Congress, and when her eyes met Dee's she beamed.

Major General Frederick Uhl presented her a diploma and a small silver bar. Dee held her chin high as he pinned it to her lapel. She was now a third officer in the Women's Army Corp, equivalent to a second lieutenant.

"Congratulations, Officer Attica."

Never had Dee heard her name sound so sweet.

"Yes, sir," she said, saluting. "Thank you, sir."

———

After the ceremonies, the graduates were free to do what they wished with the rest of the day. Most spent it with their families, Dee included. The Atticas shuffled through the crowd to her father's coupe in the parking lot, waxed within an inch of its life for the special occasion. They drove into town, Dee directing them to Dellah's Diner on the corner of Peachtree and Fifth, a joint willing to cook her Southern-style beans minus the ham, just the way she liked them.

"On the right," she said.

"Looks to be a line," May said.

Dellah's was packed, a beleaguered waitress taking down names at the door. A hand-lettered banner was strung above the entrance: WELCOME, OGLETHORPE GRADS!

"Officers and their families first, please!" the waitress hollered.

"That's us," Dee said, taking her parents hands.

"What's us?" May asked.

"I'm an officer now, Mama," Dee said. "Follow me."

Dee pulled her parents toward the front of the line. When they arrived the waitress was gesturing to a silver bar on the uniform of a young Black woman, flanked by her beaming parents. Dee recognized her as a member of the 6888th Central Postal Directory Battalion, the segregated unit that trained in another part of Fort Oglethorpe. Her uniform name badge read *Scott*.

"Congrats, girl," the waitress said to the Lieutenant with a wink. "Let me get you folks seated. Won't be two shakes of a lambs' tail."

The waitress went in search of a table and waved the trio to a booth by the window. The Scott family was about to follow when a white, hairy arm barred their path.

A burly man in overalls glowered at them, his family lined up behind him.

"We'll take that table, thank you," he said.

"They were here first," Dee said. May poked her daughter in the back.

Overall's turned to her, eyes narrowed. "What you say?"

"I said they were here first," Dee repeated calmly. "And she's an officer."

"*Dee*," May hissed under her breath. The Scott family just watched the exchange, wide-eyed.

Overalls snorted. "Uniform or not, no niggers sit before me and mine, not around here."

Dee guessed that, say, biting the man's nose off his face and spitting it onto the diner's linoleum floor would probably result in her arrest and expulsion from the army. Such a scenario didn't serve her purposes, not at all. She could have done that, and in other circumstances gladly would have, expect for the diner full of patrons now warily eyeing the exchange.

Another white man appeared, this one in uniform. He gripped Overall's wrist, yanking it out of the doorway and flattening him against the wall with a forearm across the throat. A small gasp went up among the patrons.

It was Iggy.

"Like Lieutenant Attica said, officers first," Iggy spat, going red, and pointed to Lieutenant Scott. "See that bar on *her* uniform? That means she's an officer, too. You raise this arm of yours to her one more time and I'll break it for you. Get me?"

When Overalls nodded his understanding, Iggy released him.

The waitress led the Scotts to their booth. Iggy now turned his attention to the Attica family, Dee grinning up at him.

"Sorry about that, ma'am," Iggy told Dee. "And these must be your parents."

Iggy offered his hand to George and May and shook them in the now-total silence of the restaurant.

"Mr. Attica, Mrs. Attica. Good to meet you both," he said.

"Thank you, Iggy," Dee said. "Thank you very much."

Iggy snapped a smart salute. "Yes, ma'am," he said, and went out the front door to take his place in the back of the line.

"Right this way," the waitress said, returning with menus in hand.

The clatter of silverware resumed. George and May ordered soup and sandwiches, Dee her usual bowl of beans.

She told them about her classes, the marches, and the endless drills. They listened, taking a bite of their sandwiches here and there as their daughter illustrated the world of discipline and order from which she had just emerged.

She was well aware what her father would ask when she stopped to take a breath and eat a spoonful of beans. His question arrived right on cue.

"So what's next?" he asked. "Where are they sending you?"

Dee swallowed and dabbed her mouth with a napkin. She set it back in her lap before giving the answer she'd rehearsed in the mirror the night before.

"Nowhere," she lied. "Gonna stay right here in Georgia and recruit other women into the WAC."

"You *are*?" May said, brightening.

"Yep," Dee said. "I'll visit colleges, give speeches, you know..."

"Here," her father said, smiling. "In Georgia."

"Yes, Daddy," Dee said.

"Well all right then." He took his wife's hand across the table and squeezed it.

The truth was that Lieutenant Burrows had again summoned Dee to his office the previous afternoon. Army brass was ordering a number of WACs overseas to join the 3341st Signal Service Battalion. It would take hundreds of women to fill critical positions such as switchboard operators, teletype operators, and couriers.

Dee accepted this assignment gratefully, on the spot. They would leave for Chattanooga the next morning and then a flight bound for Washington, DC. From there they would board a C-54 cargo plane for Prestwick, Scotland, and eventually travel to the Signal Center in France.

Had her parents known this, lunch would be ruined. So Dee kept the lie, and the smiles on their faces, and they ate a meal as a happy family, perhaps for the last time.

12

C-54 Skymaster Transport Plane, Somewhere Over the Atlantic Ocean; February 1945

Dee sat strapped into her bucket seat, thirty thousand feet over the Atlantic Ocean. A single light above her head illuminated the letter she had written on her hardback copy of *Les Miserables*.

She signed her name and flipped it back over.

Dear Mama and Daddy,

I'm writing you from a place I truly never thought I'd ever be. I'm in an airplane, on my way to Scotland. Can you imagine? The plane is called a C-54. It has four propellers, and it's the biggest plane I've ever seen. It's usually used as a flying hospital, bringing injured soldiers back to the US (Mama, that won't be me!).

There are a bunch of women from my unit at Oglethorpe, all of us officers. We're going to be in charge of a very important mission: overseeing the switchboard centers in Paris!

You're probably very unhappy with me now that you know I

won't be staying in Georgia, like I said I would. But I knew if I told you the truth, you'd get upset, and worry needlessly. I'm very safe and will continue to be so. Being a switchboard operator isn't a dangerous mission! Paris has been liberated for over a year, and there's really no chance to be put in harm's way there. My only concern is that someone in France will be able to cook a decent pot of beans!

Please keep good thoughts for me and the other ladies in my platoon. We've worked so hard to prove ourselves worthy to call ourselves officers in the United States Army. We get funny looks wherever we go, but we hold our heads high. Times will change, and something tells me we're a part of that. Be proud of me is what I think I'm trying to say.

I've been looking out the window all day, but now it's dark and I should get some rest. I'll mail this first thing when I get to Scotland, so the envelope will have some funny stamps and things. Please keep it for me so I can see what it looks like when I return.

I'll write if I can, but please understand I'll be very busy with my mission. Don't worry—instead think of all the things I'll be seeing and the people I'll meet and know I've never been happier. I'm serving my country and doing my part to bring this terrible war to a swift end. I really do think it'll be over in a matter of weeks or months, and I'll be back home before you know it.

Take care. And again, DON'T WORRY, please!

Love,

Dee

Dee read the letter a couple more times before folding it and tucking it into the book. She then unbuckled her lap belt and peered around the back of her seat. The other passengers were asleep.

She reached under her seat and pulled out her rucksack, "Attica" written across the canvas in black marker. She undid the outer buckle and retrieved a thick map from within a pocket, unfolding it across her lap. It was Europe; at least the version before the Wehrmacht had begun its mechanized march across it. Dee traced her finger from Scotland to Britain, Britain to France, France to the German border. The blue emptiness of the ocean was filled with her scribbling, distances between major ports and cities written in both miles and kilometers.

Dee had no intention of using her time in Europe to run a switchboard. How she got to where she needed to go was yet to be determined, but like everything else she figured she'd make it up as she went along.

The map went back in the rucksack, and she twisted around in the hard seat, trying to find a comfortable position. The drone of the C-54's engines eventually lulled her into sleep and dreams.

13

Cape Sounion, Attica Peninsula; The Month of Pyanepsion 434 BC

Damien spied from his hiding place in the cypress bushes as the other students ran inside from the meadow, summoned by the clanging of the dinner bell, leaving their musical instruments behind in the grass. Ignatia lingered, tuning the strings on her lyre. She played a few chords before stopping, sensing his presence. Waving, Damien emerged from the bushes.

Ignatia opened her arms. Damien ran to her, and she pulled him into a hug.

"There you are," she said, and kissed the top of his head. "I've missed you, Damien."

"I've missed you too," he said, burying his nose in the curls of her hair, breathing in their sweetness. She held him like this for a while; Damien would have fallen into a peaceful sleep there if she allowed him.

"Who did this to you, Damien?" she asked, gently touching the swollen cut on his cheekbone. "Tell me."

If Damien told her, she'd go to one of the headmasters,

and Scylax would beat him harder for it. Ignatia didn't know what he was learning in the temple each night, didn't know it was a world apart from his former days of games and songs and talking to birds.

"I fell out of bed," he said, for lack of a better lie. "I had a bad dream."

Tears stung Damien's eyes at her tenderness. He missed her presence in his life more than he could say.

"Damien, you weren't placed in Master Scylax's class as a punishment," she said. "You were put there because that's where you belong."

"I miss *your* classes. And Master Praxis's too," Damien said, struggling to hold back his tears. "I miss making music and talking to the birds."

"I know. And I miss you. *We* miss you. But Damien, you know how to make music. You know how to talk to birds. We have nothing left to teach you. Master Scylax does."

Damien wiped his eyes. She averted her gaze to the sea as he collected himself.

"He scares me," Damien said.

Ignatia laughed, to his surprise. "He scares me too!" she said brightly. "And Master Praxis."

"Really?" Damien asked.

"Of course, really!" she said. "With those great big yellow eyes of his and that face. He looks like a wolf! He scares everyone, Damien."

Relieved to hear he wasn't alone, Damien sighed.

"Master Scylax is a child of the Gods, Damien, as you are, as I am, as we all are," Ignatia continued. "He was chosen to teach here by Orpheus, may he be blessed. It is no accident that he found you in the wilderness. There is *purpose* to your being his pupil and he your master. You just have to give it time. All the answers you seek will be illuminated by the Gods' graces. That's all any of us can hope for. Do you understand?"

He nodded. She tousled his hair.

"There. That's better. Now get back to your room and prepare for your night's lessons. I'll see you again, and soon. Okay?"

Revitalized, Damien raced to his room. Ignatia was more than a teacher to him; she was his best friend.

The sun fell and the torches in the temple windows bloomed to life. Damien summoned his courage and walked across the meadow to his class.

Master Scylax sat upon the stone wheel, legs crossed, hands resting in his lap. Damien entered the Great Round Room and sat before him, crossing his own legs and folding his hands as if he were Scylax's mirror. After a while, the master raised his head, his yellow eyes glinting within the hood of his cloak.

"The woman who plays the lyre. What is she to you?" he asked, his voice flat.

"Ignatia? She is—*was*—my teacher," Damien explained nervously.

"That is the truth but not the answer to my question," Scylax replied. "My question was 'Who is she to *you*?' The woman teaches a great many of the other children music. But they do not seek her out in the meadow. Nor are they held in her arms like an infant. Nor are they...*soothed* by her." He reached out a hand and lifted Damien's chin, bringing his eyes back to his. "I ask again. Who is she, to *you*?"

"She is my friend," Damien replied.

"Your *friend*," Scylax said. "I see. Do you count all of your instructors in the Orphic Temple as friends? Is Master Praxis your friend? Am *I* your friend?"

Damien shifted in his seat, his mind racing for an answer that would appease Scylax.

"Well?"

"Master, s-she took a special interest in m-me," Damien stammered. "She helped me remember how I came here. Remember *you*, Master, finding me in the wilderness."

Master Scylax's eyes bored through Damien. Yet his expression gave no indication of his feelings about his pupil's response.

"She is your *friend*," he said. "That is the *truth*."

The torches went out, and Damien was enveloped in darkness. Scylax's next words came an inch from his right ear, the cold breath sending shivers down his spine.

"Now I know what scares you most of all," Master Scylax whispered.

And then he was gone.

14

Port Glasgow, Scotland; February 1945

The *Ile de France* sounded its mighty horn as it docked. Thousands of troops eager to end an eleven-day journey fraught with seasickness and the specter of roaming German U-boats lined up against the deck railing. Dee spotted her contingent among them and waved.

Gawkers stole glances at her face, her uniform, at the silver bar signifying her rank. Salutes were slow to come here, bewildered male soldiers with no prior concept of a WAC officer acknowledging a woman for the first time in their life as a superior.

The last of the 3341st Battalion stepped down the gangplank. A Red Cross unit greeted them on the dock to provide medicine and fresh supplies, along with coffee and doughnuts. Dee listened to the women tell tales of fifty-foot swells that bobbed the ship like a cork, as well as the terrible food. A man stepping off the ship caught her eye.

"Iggy!" Dee called out.

Dee excused herself from the group and ran after him.

"Iggy!"

His face lit up as Dee approached.

"Lieutenant Attica," he said, dropping his rucksack and saluting smartly. Dee returned it.

"What brings you to Glasgow?" she asked, tapping the stripe on his sleeve. "*Sergeant.* Congratulations. What are your orders?"

Iggy produced a sealed envelope from a pocket in his uniform. "General Orders—Top-Secret—Eyes Only" was stamped across it.

"You haven't opened it?"

"No, ma'am," Iggy said. "Figured I'd wait until I landed."

"Well," Dee continued. "Here you are."

Iggy carefully tore an end of the envelope, drew out the letter, and handed it to her.

"You read it, ma'am."

"Those are *your* orders, Sergeant," Dee said. "Eyes only."

"Please," Iggy asked sheepishly. "I'm kinda nervous, truth be told."

Dee unfolded the paper and scanned its contents. "I have good news and bad news," she said.

"Yes, ma'am."

"The good news is you've been assigned mechanic detail with the 3341st Battalion. The bad news is we..."

Dee swept a hand to the throng of women chatting over coffee and doughnuts on the dock.

"... we are the 3341st Battalion. You're going to be fixing courier trucks, Sergeant."

A wide grin broke across Iggy's face. "That sounds just fine to me, ma'am."

"Then fall out, Sergeant," Dee replied.

"Yes, ma'am," Iggy saluted, and picked up his rucksack.

15

Signal Center, Paris, France; February 1945

The 3341st worked three eight-hour shifts around the clock running their switchboards. Dee was present for every hour those first few days, prompting more than one enlisted woman to ask her if she ever slept or ate. As it happened, Dee did neither, her body thinning under her uniform. She tightened the belt around her khaki skirt to the last hole and kept working. She believed it her duty to make sure the operation was well in hand before she deserted her post.

She chose a Sunday night to do it. Curfew was ten o'clock on Sundays, and Mondays were so busy at the Signal Center that the number of soldiers spared to look for her would be minimal. She hoped to be far outside of Paris by the time her absence was discovered.

She sat on the edge of her hotel bed, grateful that her rank afforded her a private room. Most of the others had roommates, which would have made these preparations extremely difficult, if not impossible. She checked the contents of her rucksack in the glow of a street lamp outside the window. Map, compass, first aid, extra clothes, a magnesium fire starter, a canteen, waterproof matches, a signaling mirror, snare wire, and a candle. All of it was Army issued, and all of it perhaps useful, but there was one item she hadn't procured, one that was not even a consideration for the soldiers of the WAC.

"A gun," Dee whispered, as if doing so might make one appear on her pillow. "You need a gun, girl."

It was a bridge to be crossed later. For now, she needed to get out of the hotel without being detected.

One last inspection of the room for any clues regarding her disappearance, and she was in the hallway, her footsteps quiet and deliberate. Shadows moving beneath the glowing door cracks that lined the corridor indicated not every soldier was asleep. When she got to the staircase she winced, the first step squeaking so loud she was certain it had awoken half the battalion.

Dee had rehearsed the escape the previous four nights. A guard kept watch at the hotel reception desk in six-hour shifts, but a wall separated that area from a service entrance near the back. Dee pulled off her boots on the last step, hugging that wall as she shuffled across the marble tile in her stocking feet. She slipped out the back door and into the alley, which stunk of fish heads and rotting vegetable trimmings tossed out by the hotel's kitchen staff. She replaced her boots and started down the alleyway for the quiet boulevard one block away.

A lantern shone from beneath one of the courier trucks parked against the alley wall; as she got closer, she spotted a pair of legs sticking out from underneath it. For a moment she considered turning around and attempting the opposite route, but she'd have to pass in front of the hotel lobby's expansive front windows to do so. It was a greater risk than the one she now faced. She tucked her head down into her scarf and kept moving.

She was almost out of the alley when a man's voice stopped her in her tracks.

"Going somewhere, ma'am?"

Iggy rolled out from under the truck on a mechanic's creeper. He sat up, wiping his greasy hands on a rag.

"Midnight stroll?" he asked. When Dee didn't return his smile he jumped up, brushing off his clothes. "Didn't mean to pry, ma'am."

Dee went through her options. She could simply turn around and continue without a word, an action that would arouse much suspicion when it was relayed to Iggy's superiors.

She could make a weak excuse, all of which would be thrown into doubt by the heavy rucksack on her back and the very unladylike boots on her feet. Those she had procured from the men's canteen, explaining to the clerk that they were for a male colonel overseeing her unit. He hadn't questioned this lie, thankfully, and now she had footwear appropriate for a long march.

She chose a third option.

"Well, Iggy," she said, in disbelief that she was saying the words as she said them. "Since you asked, I'm...leaving."

The sergeant mechanic rubbed his chin, leaving a smudge of black oil on it.

"Ma'am?"

"And you'll need to report it in the morning, I suppose," Dee continued, sweating under her heavy uniform coat. "When the general wakes up."

"Report what, ma'am?" Iggy asked.

"That I have gone absent without leave, of course," Dee replied.

"Why would I do that?"

"Because I'm deserting my post and it's your duty to report criminal activity."

Iggy shook his head. "Don't think I will."

A loud voice bursting into song made both of them jump. A disheveled Frenchman wove down the alley, a bottle of cheap port dangling from his hand.

"Ah!" the Frenchman exclaimed, spotting them. "Americans! *Tres bien!*"

He dropped the bottle, the shattering glass echoing down the alleyway. The Frenchman staggered up to Iggy, grabbing his cheeks and planting a kiss on his lips.

"*Mes heroes!*" the man cried.

"What's that mean?" Iggy asked, wiping his mouth.

"He says you're his hero," Dee said.

The Frenchman resumed his stumble down the alley, singing "The Star-Spangled Banner" in broken English.

Iggy turned to her. "Ma'am. Can I tell you something?"

"Go ahead," Dee said.

"I dream about you sometimes," Iggy said.

"Sergeant," Dee replied. "Are you sure you want to pursue this line of thinking with a superior officer?"

"No, ma'am. Now listen," Iggy continued. "I don't mean dream about you like I dream about Veronica Lake. I mean I dream about you and me as friends. *Old* friends. I'm not making any sense, am I?"

"Afraid not, Sergeant," Dee replied.

"What I mean is...in this dream, we're in a desert, see? Cactuses and mountains and coyotes, the whole shebang. I've never been to no desert in real life, never seen a cactus *or* a coyote. You get me, ma'am? But I'm there. And it's as real as me standing right here in Paris, let me tell you. And you're there, and I'm there, together. Thing is I'm not *me* me, though, I'm...well, ma'am. I'm an Indian."

"An Indian," Dee said.

"Yes, ma'am," Iggy continued. "And you're a cowboy. With a hat, and a couple of six shooters on your belt. You look a lot like Gary Cooper, come to think of it."

"Sergeant, you're telling me that in your dream I'm a man?"

"Yes, ma'am."

"Then how can it be me?"

"The eyes," Iggy said without hesitation. "You've got those same big green eyes of yours. And you and me are brothers, see. *Blood* brothers. Riding across the Old West on our horses, just like Tex Ritter and Dave O'Brien in *Gangsters of the Frontier*. You ever see that movie?"

"No."

"Ma'am, you're looking at me like I've got two heads, but I'm telling you the God's truth. And I'll tell you another thing. I knew what those orders were in my pocket that day at the Scotland docks because I requested this assignment. Ever since I saw you get on that bus in Marietta, something inside me said, 'Go where she goes and look out for her.' Get your back, like. And I *also* knew I wasn't gonna be just fixin' trucks over here. I didn't know what we would be doing, but it wasn't gonna be that. So, ma'am, at the risk of being impertinent to an officer, I'll ask you again: where are you going?"

There was nothing insincere about Iggy, no trickery or deception. He was speaking from his heart.

"All right, Iggy, I'll tell you," Dee said. "I'm going to get myself to Berlin somehow. And when I get there, I'm going to find Adolph Hitler. And execute him." She waited for

Iggy's laughter or at the very least his incredulity. "I'm serious," she said.

"Yes ma'am," Iggy said. "I know you are." He gestured to the truck behind him. "We'll get there a lot faster in this than we will walking," he said.

"*We?*" Dee asked.

Iggy got inside the truck and revved the engine. He leaned out the window as he switched on the headlights.

"Yes, ma'am," he said from the front seat. "Hop in. Best make as much time as we can before sun up."

Dee had absolutely no reason to, but she trusted the skinny man with the pencil mustache sitting behind the wheel unequivocally. She too sensed they had known each other for a lot longer than a few weeks. There had been no dreams of a desert on her part, only of an ancient temple on a peninsula by the clear blue sea. Those dreams were as real as Iggy had described his, and she found herself placing the rucksack in the back of the truck as if that had been the plan all along.

Dee got into the front seat. She and Iggy glanced at each other, the truck engine idling.

"Where'd you learn to speak French?" he asked.

"Books, of course," Dee replied. "Better buckle up, Sergeant."

"Yes, ma'am," Iggy said, and pulled his seat belt across his lap before clicking it into place. He put the truck in gear and drove into the Paris night.

16

Roadside, Troissy, France; February 1945

They drove past rubble and craters, evidence of four years of bombing to rid the country of the Nazi scourge. They drove past checkpoints, showing their papers; Dee catching looks here and there but always waved through to the next road, the next town, the next village; Dee leaning out the window, frigid winter air numbing her face but not caring, taking in pastoral farmhouses and landscapes she had only read about in books checked out from the Marietta Public Library. They drove until a thin pink band of light illuminated the horizon.

They drove until the truck ran out of gas.

"Dang," Iggy said.

Dee stepped out of the truck and onto the roadside, grateful for her thick-soled boots. She wore every layer of clothing the army had seen fit to issue her, pulling her winter coat tightly around her shoulders, happy to find it sufficiently warm.

Iggy let down the truck's tailgate and fished around,

producing a can of gasoline. "Back in business," he said, unscrewing the cap.

"Don't," Dee said.

"Ma'am?"

"How far will a gallon of gas take us?" she asked.

Iggy did math in his head. "Not very far, ma'am."

"That's right," Dee said. "This truck has taken us as far as it can."

Iggy tightened the cap and set the can back in the truck. "What now, then, ma'am?" he asked, worry on his young face.

"Iggy," she said, "if you're having second thoughts, I understand. That last checkpoint we passed was only a couple clicks back. You walk there and hitch a ride back to Paris and use the trip to come up with a plausible excuse. Pretend you never saw me and you'll be fine."

Iggy's expression darkened as he took a step toward Dee. "I will do no such thing," he said. "I was simply asking what we were doing next. Awaiting my orders is all, ma'am."

Dee reached out and snapped the top two buttons on Iggy's coat closed.

"Hungry, sergeant?"

"If there was food I would eat it, yes, ma'am."

"Well, there is," Dee said, opening the back door of the truck to retrieve her rucksack.

She faced Iggy, her hands hidden behind her back. "Right or left?" she asked.

"Left," Iggy said. Dee brought it around, revealing a can of beans.

"What was in the right hand?" he asked. Dee showed it to him, revealing another can of beans.

"Beans it is, I guess," Iggy said.

They sat on a wooden fence bordering a sloping field of frozen grass, eating cold beans out of Army-issued tins. Iggy got to the bottom of his and scraped his spoon around. A light snow fell.

"Pretty good, huh?" Dee asked. She ate slowly, luxuriating in the taste. She had only room for six cans in her rucksack and wanted to savor them while she still could.

"I dunno about *good*," Iggy replied. "But food is food."

The morning sun angled overhead, spilling light through the fir trees and snow in a celestial fog. There was the sound of movement in the treeline as a herd of horses entered the clearing, thin from winter and months of wartime neglect.

"Look," Iggy said.

"I see them," Dee said, and stepped down off the fence.

She inched toward them, mindful of the sound the frost made crunching underneath her boots. The horses glanced up from their foraging, whinnying nervously.

"They spook pretty easily, ma'am," Iggy said. "Don't think they'll let you get too close."

The animals scrutinized her warily as she approached. Then a magnificent black stallion trotted toward her.

"Guess they're friendly," Iggy called out from the fence.

The horse abruptly stopped at the sound of his voice. Dee raised her open palm to the animal.

"Quiet, please, Sergeant."

"Yes, ma'am," Iggy replied. "Sorry."

Dee motioned for the horse to continue toward her. It did, its black coat shimmering in the low winter sun.

"Will ya look at that?" Iggy whispered.

The stallion placed the bridge of its nose against Dee's open palm, nuzzling it.

Hello, it said.

Hello, Dee replied.

She ran her hand down its thin mane, its backbones jutting up from the skin.

We're so very hungry, the stallion told her.

I see that, Dee replied.

It's been terrible here.

I know it has.

We're frightened here.

I know you are.

Will you save us?

Dee had never felt as helpless in her life. She rejected all the comforting lies she could tell the horse and instead settled on the simple truth.

I don't know if I can yet.

Dee called back to Iggy. "Sergeant!"

"Yes, ma'am!"

"We walk from here!"

"Yes, ma'am!"

"Bring my rucksack. And the gas can."

"The gas can, ma'am?"

"They come in handy, I've found," she said. "From time to time."

17

Troissy, France; February 1945

Dee and Iggy trudged through the forest, rucksacks strapped to their backs. Fresh snowpack sparkled ahead like diamonds, perfect and unspoiled. Without proper snowshoes, however, it was nearly impossible to navigate.

"Maybe we should have ridden the horses," Iggy said.

"They're too weak, Sergeant," Dee replied. "Besides, you ever ridden a horse?"

"No, ma'am. You?"

"No."

A low-hanging branch heavy with snow gave way and dumped its frozen white contents over Iggy's head. He shook it out of his blond hair and off the back of his neck.

"Beats walking, though," he said.

Noonday sun broke through the clouds. Dee spotted a fallen tree trunk and let the rucksack slip off her shoulders.

"Let's rest a minute," she said.

They sat on the ancient log, one of hundreds in the forest felled by bombing or artillery shells. Iggy brought out a flattened pack of Pall Malls from within his coat, half empty.

"I don't know if I should have one or save them for later," he said.

"Later might not come," Dee replied. "Smoke 'em while you got 'em."

Iggy shook out a cigarette and passed it to Dee.

"Don't smoke," Dee said.

"That's right," Iggy replied. "So you said."

"When?"

"On the bus." Iggy lit his Pall Mall.

"Seems like a long time ago already," Dee said.

"Yes, ma'am. Sure does."

Iggy smoked as the horses slogged across the forest floor, heads sagging. The black stallion whispered to Dee as they passed.

Hurry, it said.

———

The cold end of machine guns on the back of Dee's and Iggy's necks signaled they weren't alone in this forest.

"Aw, hell," Iggy said, raising trembling hands.

The stallion broke eye contact, loping behind the herd. If there had been a threat to her safety, it would have warned her, so Dee relaxed.

"*Les mains en l'air,*" a woman's voice said.

Dee grinned. They were Allies. "We're Americans," she replied in French. "There's no need for that."

The cold muzzle left her skin, and a thin blond woman with cornflower-blue eyes and an aquiline nose walked around to her. "What are you doing out here?" the woman asked in French. "You get lost or something?"

Others emerged from the trees, dressed in winter coats and hats, weapons and bandoliers slung across their chests, eyes ringed with fatigue.

"What's she saying?" Iggy asked.

"Wondering if we're lost," Dee replied. She explained in French that they were not lost.

"How do you speak French so well?" the Frenchwoman demanded, wiping the strawberry-blond hair out of her eyes.

As Dee went for her rucksack, the sound of a dozen machine guns being cocked echoed through the forest.

"Easy," the Frenchwoman admonished her. "Move slowly."

Dee pulled her arm back. "What is your name?" she asked.

The woman took a step back, lowering her gun. "Clementine."

"Nice to meet you, Clementine. I'm Dee. This is Iggy. He doesn't speak French. Now may I answer your question? It's in here."

Clementine ordered the others to lower their weapons.

Dee opened her rucksack and pulled out her copies of *Les Miserables*: one in French, one in English.

"I learned from these," she said, handing them over.

Clementine brightened at the sight of the books. She let her machine gun dangle off its strap and opened the hard-back. The checkout card from the Marietta Public Library was glued to it.

"*Mare...ee...etta*," Clementine sounded out, "Georgia."

"That's where I'm from," Dee said. "Marietta, Georgia."

"Your accent is excellent," Clementine said, handing them back. "So...the Americans are letting girls into their army now?"

"Yes," Dee said. "After a fashion."

Iggy raised a hand above his head. "Mind telling me what you two are going on about, ma'am?"

"Clementine and I are getting acquainted is all," Dee said.

"And what does he do?" Clementine asked. "Besides sit there with a stupid look on his face?"

"Well, so far Iggy here has been my driver."

"Where from?"

"Paris."

"And where are you going?"

"Berlin."

Clementine burst into incredulous laughter. "They are going to Berlin!" she announced to the assembled. Most laughed in return, many responding that they too would like to go.

"We're going to Colmar," Clementine said. "You know where that is?"

Dee unclasped the outer pocket of her rucksack, removed her map, and unfolded it over the tree trunk. "No," she said. "Please show me."

Clementine pored over Dee's meticulous straight lines, which zigzagged between Scotland, England, France, and Germany.

"Here," she said, placing a nicotine-stained finger on the French-German border before tracing it back across the map. "And we're here. Four hundred kilometers away."

"Is that where some Germans are?" Dee asked.

"Oh, yes," Clementine replied. "Fucking bastards won't leave."

"Well, we would very much like to join you," Dee said. "If we may."

Clementine spotted the gas can next to Dee's rucksack. "She has fuel!" she called out.

"Does she have *coq au vin*?" a soldier responded.

"Or *boeuf bourguignon*?" said another.

"Will you idiots shut the fuck up?" Clementine snapped. "Xavier, come over here. Bring the Bitch."

The man called Xavier emerged, a heavy pack swaddled in a green tarp hanging off his shoulders. He set it down and picked up the gas can.

"Hey now," Iggy said, standing. "That ain't yours."

"The fuck is your problem?" Xavier said.

"I don't know what the hell you just said," Iggy replied, "but I sure don't like the tone you said it in."

"Iggy, it's fine," Dee said. "Let him."

"Yes ma'am," Iggy said, and took a step back. Xavier got to a knee, unscrewed the gas cap, and brought it to his nose. He sniffed and winced.

"We need gas for the Bitch," Clementine said to Dee. "May we?"

"And what is that?" Dee asked. "The...Bitch?"

"Xavier, show them."

Xavier slid the tarp off the pack, revealing a flamethrower.

"Oh, my," Dee said, stepping toward it. "Oh, goodness me."

"*Flammenwerfer,*" Clementine said. "Got it off a German pig Jacques over there shot between the eyes. Works great. We fucking love it. Xavier calls it the Bitch, so now we all do. But, it's out of gas."

"May I?" Dee asked, holding out her arms. Xavier handed it to her.

Dee cradled the flamethrower as if it were a newborn child. "Oh, goodness," she said to it. "Look at *you*."

18

Countryside, France; February 1945

The platoon marched through the forest, Clementine and Dee bringing up the rear.

"Your army doesn't know you're out here, do they?" Clementine asked, smoothing her hair back across her scalp.

"How did you know?" Dee asked.

"You have no weapons," Clementine said. "You aren't dressed right. You are a woman. Nothing about you adds up." She clapped her hand on Dee's back. "Just like me."

"And you?" Dee asked. "What's your story?"

Clementine plucked a cigarette from behind her ear and lit it from a Zippo engraved with a swastika. "I am French," she said with a shrug. "Everybody fights. Well, not *everybody*. Some people are content to be shit on and kiss fascist ass. When the war is over, we will find them and deal with them."

They marched on with the platoon of bedraggled Frenchmen. Some were in uniform, others in the last clothes they had grabbed before the Wehrmacht had taken occupation of their village or town years earlier. Iggy waved as if to say "Is everything all right?" Dee nodded.

"Is he in love with you or something?" Clementine asked. "That it?"

"Iggy? No," Dee said. "He's just looking out for me is all."

"And do you need that?" Clementine asked. "Looking after?"

"No."

"I didn't think so. So he's in love with you."

Dee took a deep breath of the cold countryside air. "It's beautiful here."

"Yes," Clementine said. "It is."

The French soldiers walked on, fingers on triggers, scanning the trees warily. After three more hours of marching, Xavier held up a fist, and they stopped, finding seats on the ground. Cigarettes were passed around.

"Don't smoke?" Clementine asked Dee. She shook her head.

"You must be hungry all the time," Clementine replied. "Smoking kills the appetite, no?"

"Don't give it much thought." Dee reached into her rucksack and pulled out Kafka's *The Metamorphosis.*

"What's that?" Clementine asked. Dee showed her the cover. "You read German?"

"Just had a feeling I'm going to be speaking to some German people soon," Dee said. "Just like I had a feeling I'd be speaking French."

"So you *speak* German?"

"Yes."

"As well as you speak French?"

"I don't know," Dee said, "but I'll soon find out."

Cigarette smoke rushed out of Clementine's nostrils.

"You're a very interesting person. Are all people in George like you?"

"George-*uh*," Dee corrected. "And no. I don't think so."

"I don't think so either," Clementine said.

Xavier and another man with a dark beard appeared on either side of Clementine, lying worn, weather beaten maps over the snow-covered leaves.

"This is the last place they crossed," Xavier said, tracing along a river. "The Americans are here, watching the bridge. I say we go *here*, then *here*, then *here*."

Clementine drew her finger down the route as Dee flipped open a page in *The Metamorphosis*: Gregor, now an insect, hid under his couch while his sister cleaned up after a dinner of rotten food, the only cuisine he now enjoyed. The absurdity of this sequence always made Dee laugh, and she did so now.

Clementine strapped her machine gun over a shoulder. "All right then. We meet the Americans in Chátenois. And you two," she said, gesturing to Dee and Iggy, "you two stick with me."

Dee marched behind Xavier, who wore the *flammenwerfer* on his back, gas sloshing in the tank hypnotically.

Iggy sidled up next to her. "Ask you something, ma'am?"

"You don't have to ask permission every time you want to ask a question, Iggy."

"You ever shoot a gun before, ma'am?"

Dee allowed her eyes to slip from the flamethrower to Iggy. "No. You?"

"In Basic, yeah, but not since," he said, then lowered his

voice to a whisper. "You sure we should be following these people?"

"You know a better way to get to Berlin?"

"Well, ma'am, that's the thing. They're *not* going to Berlin. They're going to Shat...*shat...*"

"Châtenois," Dee finished for him. "It's a town outside of Colmar. That's where some Germans are. From there it's about twenty clicks to the German border. To get to Berlin you first have to get to the border. Understand, Sergeant?"

"Yes, ma'am."

"Do you want to turn around and walk back to Paris? That option is always available to you."

"No, ma'am."

"Good. Then onward we go."

A snow owl glided above them, landing on branches here and there to rest its wings. The platoon took no notice of it as they marched through the forest, but it soon made its presence known.

Dee's head whipped around at the sound of its screeching. The command she issued was loud and firm enough that the entire platoon obeyed it.

"*Halt!*"

Three dozen French soldiers came to a sudden stop, Clementine among them. The owl alighted on a branch above Dee's head; she listened to it intently.

Clementine followed Dee's gaze up to the bird. "We stopped so you could look at an owl?"

"No. This forest ends at a road ahead," Dee said in French. "There's an ambush there. Twenty Wehrmacht. MG-42s. We're headed straight into them."

"How the hell do you know that?" Xavier asked.

"Yes," Clementine said. "How?"

"I just know," Dee said. "We should go left here. Flank them north of their position."

A stocky man with an ugly scar across his forehead emerged from the crowd, giving Dee a once-over.

"Who is this?" he asked his fellow soldiers. "And why should we listen to her?"

Many murmured in agreement. "And him," he continued, thrusting his chin toward Iggy. "Why aren't they with the other Americans? We don't know these people."

"I agree," someone called out.

"Me too," said another.

"Do we think they are who they say they are?" the stocky soldier went on. "And now we maneuver on her orders? The fuck I will."

The platoon voiced their solidarity. Iggy leaned in to Dee. "What are they saying?"

"They don't believe me," she replied.

"Well, how *do* you know? I mean really?"

"Sergeant, you're here because you had a dream I was a cowboy, and suddenly the veracity of *my* thinking is in question?"

Iggy faced the French alongside her. "Good point."

Dee raised her hand, and the soldiers quieted down. "If you don't believe me, send a scout," she said. "Prove me wrong."

The owl screeched again, peering down at the French soldiers with giant eyes.

"Xavier, take Victor and Louis," Clementine said. "Go check it out."

The three men peeled off from the group, jogging from the platoon until they disappeared into the treeline.

The rest just paced, staring at Dee and the owl. Iggy seemed unsure where to look or what to say.

The owl's head bobbed around on its neck. *It is good you are here,* it told Dee. *Orphic.*

Dee had heard the word once before, in childhood. She didn't know what it meant then and still didn't, and told the owl so.

It is what you are, the owl said. *Orphic.*

Repeating it doesn't help me understand.

There is no other word for it.

Is it a name?

No. It is a way.

Help me understand.

It is a path.

A path to where? Am I on it?

Yes.

The sound of crunching leaves and snow signaled the return of the scouting party. Xavier doubled over, catching his breath.

"It is just as she said. Machine-gun nest. Fifteen that we could see, probably more. MG-42s."

"Tank?" Clementine asked.

"Not that we saw," Louis said.

"Count our grenades," Clementine replied. "We attack them from the north. Give them everything we've got. Once this scum is tits up, we'll take the 42s and anything else we want."

The platoon counted up their guns and grenades, bandoliers exchanged so every soldier was evenly armed.

"Why don't I get a gun?" Iggy asked.

"What did he say?" Clementine asked. Dee translated. "Pierre, give him your pistol."

"Why?" Pierre groused.

"Just fucking give it to him. He's no use without one."

Pierre pulled a revolver out of his waistband and tossed it to Iggy, who caught it.

"What about her?" Pierre asked.

"Dee's with me," Clementine said. The platoon continued onward, making a sharp left through the trees and angling north of the Wehrmacht's position on the road ahead.

Clementine put her arm over her new friend's shoulder, and they marched into the woods.

19

Country Road, France; February 1945

Dee's first look at real-life Nazis proved unremarkable: bored soldiers not much older than teenagers in olive-colored helmets and jackets, languidly manning their MG-42s and guarding an all but deserted road in French farm country.

Clementine observed them through a pair of binoculars. "We should use the RPG," she whispered, lowering them.

"It's our last one," Xavier replied from the back.

"They'll turn those 42s around on us before we get halfway across the road," she countered. "There isn't a choice."

A thin man in a beret emerged from the group, carrying an oblong object wrapped in a Nazi flag. He unwrapped it, and the platoon passed the rocket-propelled grenade launcher up to Clementine. She rested it on her shoulder and peered through the sight, aiming for the Nazi machine-gun nest.

Breathless, the soldiers waited for her to pull the trigger.

Clementine dropped it to her side. "Fuck," she said. "I think I might miss."

A rustling in the spruce trees above their heads brought everyone's attention skyward. Snow showered down; when it cleared, the soldiers stood amazed at what this revealed.

More snow owls, dozens of them, perched among the branches.

"They're called a Parliament," Dee said, strolling among the platoon. "I think they're here to help us."

"Help us?" Clementine asked. "How?"

"I'm not entirely sure," Dee replied. "But perhaps they'll be the distraction we need."

Dee locked eyes with the largest of the snow owls.

Ask us, and we will, the owl said.

Ask us, another said, and the others joined in. *Ask us. Ask us. Ask us.*

Dee raised her hand to them.

"What are you doing?" Xavier asked.

"I'm not sure," Dee said. "It's like I told Iggy. I'm making this up as I go along."

When Dee dropped her arm, the owls exploded off the branches, their enormous wingspans generating enough down draft to whip the soldiers' hair around their heads. The Parliament glided across the country road, straight for the Germans on the other side.

A young Wehrmacht soldier finishing a cigarette jumped to his feet, gripping the arm of the machine gunner closest to him. "Klaus. *Klaus.*"

"What?" Klaus said, and spun around.

"Holy *shit*," he said, and the owls were upon them.

Klaus lost his helmet when he fell to the ground, an owl with talons the size of his fingers burying them into his pink scalp. Many in the Wehrmacht squad fired indiscriminately into the air, white wings and black claws swirling around bewildered faces.

"Now," Clementine commanded. "*Go!*"

The French platoon let out a battle cry and charged.

The owls pinwheeled skyward as the rocket-propelled grenade popped out of Clementine's launcher and hissed across the road. It found its target, a pair of bloodied Germans scrambling for the triggers of their MG-42s, terrified at the sight of the Free French Army charging toward them. The grenade detonated, shrapnel tearing through the soldiers and sending severed limbs arcing through the air.

Dee made a move to join the assaulting French, but Iggy held her back.

"You don't have a weapon, ma'am!" he shouted, arm braced against her chest. "I won't let you get yourself killed!"

Machine guns crackled and grenades exploded, voices in French and German comingling in the chaos of battle. Then the percussive thunder of an MG-42 kicked off.

A German soldier managed to commandeer the nest back, covering the road in a withering blanket of machine-gun fire. The owls flocked above the battle, screeching.

Xavier lay on the cobblestone, holding his leg. Blood squirted out of the bullet hole, and he cried out in pain, begging any of his comrades in earshot for help.

"Stay here," Dee told Iggy.

Pierre fired his way to the machine gunner, putting the German down with a rifle shot through the head. No sooner did Pierre capture the MG-42 than he too was struck down, falling next to the German he had killed seconds earlier, dead.

Dee ran across the road, dropping to the ground beside Xavier. Blood poured from either side of his leg. She remembered her first-aid classes in officer training and pulled up his shirt.

"It *hurts*," Xavier told her through gritted teeth. "Christ."

Dee removed the leather belt from his trousers. She looped it around his thigh and yanked it as tightly as possible without tearing the strap in half.

Xavier groaned. "That means it's tight enough," Dee said, and the Frenchman regarded his leg. The tourniquet had slowed the bleeding to a trickle.

"Bullet went all the way through," Dee told him. "You'll make it. Now sit up for me."

She took both his arms and pulled him up to sitting, then guided them out of the straps holding the *flammenwerfer* to his back.

Dee hoisted the flamethrower over her shoulders. She gripped the nozzle and beheld the bloodshed before her, as well as the owls circling in the sky.

When she looked back down at Xavier, her eyes were black. "*Viva la France,*" she said, and ran into battle.

———

Clementine found cover behind a hay wagon, bullets splintering the wood and piercing the straw inches above her head. She pulled the bandolier around her neck and reloaded her weapon.

She held her rifle across her chest, stamping down adrenaline and summoning the courage to cover the others with a salvo of gunfire. She got as far as standing when an ear-splitting noise brought her back to her knees.

She wasn't the only one. Soldiers, French and German alike, dropped their weapons and covered their ears, an unearthly howl filling the air and paralyzing their senses.

Clementine fell to her side, trying to cry out, her voice catching in her throat.

Dee charged toward the German position, the parliament of owls swirling around her. Her black eyes shimmered, light radiating from the orbs, her face contorted in a scream. The howling came from her yet *not* from her: it came from *everywhere*, Dee and the birds and the trees and the ground beneath their feet. She planted her boots in the snow and pulled the *flammenwerfer*'s trigger.

Fire ejected from the nozzle, bathing the Germans in flames. The howling stopped, mercifully, and the French scrambled for their weapons, Dee's unholy shrieking now replaced by the agonized wails of Wehrmacht soldiers being devoured by fire.

Dee squeezed off another volley of flaming gasoline, the liquid landing on the Germans with a sickening slap as it fused to their skin. The French platoon gaped in horror as the Germans thrashed about, many calling out for their mothers, others for God's mercy. Many of the Frenchmen couldn't take the sight or the sound of it anymore, and began firing into the fallen enemy soldiers, putting them out of their misery.

"No!" Dee bellowed. "*Let them scream!*"

The owls flapped their great white wings and landed on the bodies, tearing at ears and lips and cheeks with their beaks, feasting on the dead and the not-yet dead. Dee relished all of it, her eyes fading from black to green. When the last of the dying Germans fell silent, she came back to herself and found her compatriots staring at her.

Even Xavier, lying in the road with his badly injured leg.

Even Iggy, now emerged from the forest, pistol in hand.

After an interminable silence, one of the Frenchmen removed his cap and took a cautious step toward Dee.

"Golem," he said.

Another soldier also removed his cap and sank to his knees on the frozen road. "Golem," he said.

Iggy arrived at Dee's side. "What's that word mean?" he asked.

"I'm not sure," Dee said.

Clementine parted the crowd, lighting a cigarette. She contemplated Dee anew, trying to reconcile that the young woman from Marietta, Georgia, and the soldier who had immolated an entire squad of Germans were the same person.

"I don't know what she is," Clementine said, "but she's not a golem or any other fucking superstitious thing."

"She is a *golem*," the man on his knees insisted, then raised his arms and prayed aloud in Hebrew.

"No," Dee said. "She's right. I'm a soldier like any of you. Just doing my part."

"Just doing your part?" Clementine said, spitting tobacco. "You fucking massacred those assholes. You and these birds. These birds, that do whatever you say."

"I don't talk to birds," Dee said, embarrassed.

"Oh, I think you do," Clementine said. "We all saw what you did. Dee, the American from Georgia." She flicked her cigarette into the pile of roasted Wehrmacht and squared herself with Dee. Clementine peered into her bright-green eyes, trying but failing to convince herself that what she had seen was real. "Maybe you are what you say you are," she finally said. "Just a soldier. Maybe war has made us all crazy."

"I'm not crazy," Xavier said, hobbling next to her on the shoulder of a fellow partisan. "I saw it too."

"It doesn't matter," Dee said. "What matters is that I get to Berlin. Who will help me do that?"

"And what will you do there?" Clementine asked. "Assuming you make it there alive? I don't think even these owls will save you from the million Nazi pigs waiting for you in the city streets."

"What I do when I get there is my affair," Dee said. "Will you help me or won't you?"

Clementine scanned the platoon. Pierre's body was being carried between two soldiers, the men placing him on the cold grass. Miraculously, he was the only KIA in a battle that might have easily halved their numbers.

"Okay, Dee from Georgia," Clementine said. "I will help you."

Dee started to take the *flammenwerfer* off her back.

"No, no," Clementine said. "That is yours."

"It's Xavier's," Dee said. "I only took it from him because he was injured."

"Dee, it is *yours*," Clementine said with finality. "You and that bitch are made for each other."

20

Church, Chalons-En Champagnes; February 1945

The platoon buried Pierre in a French flag behind a church with its roof still intact and made camp inside for the night. Dee chose a pew near the back, away from the others. Rations were passed around: salted venison and crusty bread and hard, moldy cheese. Dee settled for a can of beans from her rucksack.

She chewed her dinner, staring at a large carving of Jesus Christ crucified on a wall. He hung there, eyes closed, red paint indicating blood dripping from puncture wounds in his hands, feet, and side. Dee always found it a remarkable depiction, one ubiquitous in the churches of Marietta but never adequately contemplated. Crucifixion was to her the most gruesome form of execution ever devised, a diabolical contraption that ensured an agonizingly slow death for its victim. What kind of mind had come up with it? Her thoughts wandered back to the Harrells' barn and Bo, his leg caught in the jaws of his own animal trap. There was plenty of wood about the property, and a cross would have been fairly simple to construct. Perhaps with a little more planning and preparation...

Iggy stepped over the pew and plunked down onto the hard wooden bench next to her. "Ma'am," he said, chewing half a bread roll. Dee held out the can of beans and spoon to him. "All yours, ma'am," he said. "Thanks anyway."

They ate together. Some of the French cast wary glances in Dee's direction, but she pretended not to notice.

"A lot of these fellas are Jewish," Iggy whispered. "One of 'em has enough English that we could sort of make out what the other was saying. Found out what a 'golem' is."

"Do tell," Dee said, spooning up another mouthful of beans.

"A golem is a mythical creature," Iggy continued. "Made from the earth. Mud, and such. Clay."

Dee nodded and glanced back up to the crucifix.

"You religious, ma'am?" Iggy asked. "Been saved?"

"No, Sergeant," she said. "Don't think I'm a candidate for the saving graces of Jesus Christ."

"Don't say that," Iggy replied. "Jesus said 'Repent, for the kingdom of heaven is at hand.'"

"He did," Dee said, setting her empty can down. "He also said, 'That which you do to the least of my people, that you do unto me.' If that's the case, a lot of good Christians in Marietta have quite a bit to answer for when they reach the pearly gates."

"So you know the Bible," Iggy said.

"I've read it," Dee said. "There are some interesting stories."

"Well, ma'am, I wouldn't call them *stories* so much as—"

"Sergeant," Dee said, cutting him off, "I'm very tired. As you must be."

Iggy crumbled the weeks-old roll in his fist, crumbs scattering to the floor. "Darn it," he said. "I feel like I've been no help at all to you, and that wasn't my intention. Not in the slightest."

"That's not true," Dee replied.

"Sure it is. I've been as useless to you as a submarine with screen doors."

Dee laughed. "See? You made me laugh. That's not nothin', you know." She placed a gentle hand on his shoulder. "You've been a friend to me ever since I got on that bus, Iggy. We deserted the army together, for pity's sake. We can write to each other from prison after our court martials."

Now Iggy was laughing.

"See there?" Dee said. "Don't sell yourself short. A true friend is hard to find these days. Someone you can depend your *life* on."

"You can depend your life on me," Iggy said.

"And you me," Dee said. "Now. Let's get some shut-eye, hmm? Only Jesus knows what tomorrow might bring."

"Hey, now," Iggy said. "You got religion."

"I got something," Dee said. "But right now I'm tired. More tired than I've ever been in my life."

"Yes, ma'am."

Iggy headed to his own pew a row over from Dee's. She bunched the rucksack into a pillow and lay there, listening to the French soldiers softly singing songs from their childhoods. In this time and place, the lullabies sounded beautiful and sorrowful all at once, and they carried Dee into her dreams.

21

Cape Sounion, Attica Peninsula; The Month of Pyanepsion 434 BC

The stone wheel was unoccupied when Damien arrived for his nightly lesson, a small piece of parchment placed where Master Scylax usually sat waiting for him. A single word was written upon it: "*SEA.*"

Did the master mean for him to go to the water? Was this a test? Should he instead wait for the master to appear? Either choice was wrong somehow.

He descended the temple's steps to the meadow. When he arrived at the cliff's edge, he peered down to the beach. There, surrounded by torches, was Master Scylax, waiting for him in the tide.

Damien rushed down the path to the oceanfront. When he got to the bottom, he pulled off his sandals and ran through the sand toward the ring of torches.

The Master sat in a fisherman's canoe, meditating. Damien stepped inside the vessel and sat across from him.

Scylax opened his eyes, the reflection of the torches in their black pupils.

"The fear of death is shared by every living thing," he said. "There is no avoiding it. We live and die and travel around the wheel of reincarnation on our Grievous Cycle. So teaches the great, wise Orpheus, may he be blessed."

"May he be blessed," Damien repeated.

Master Scylax brought the hood of his cloak down from his bald, ashen head. "Give us a push, hm?"

Damien jumped out of the canoe and walked around to the bow. He pushed the small boat with all his might, his feet sinking deeply into the sand. The boat slid into the shallow tide, water rushing around his knees. Damien crawled inside, and the canoe bobbed with the waves.

Master Scylax rowed them toward the sea. The torches on the beach grew smaller and smaller; it wasn't long before they appeared only as tiny red sparks, barely visible through the mist.

Scylax dragged the oars through the water for several hours, his eyes closed, Damien silent and still. There were a few small islands in the area, but try as he might he couldn't see them, the fog over the water impenetrable. As the moon fell and the first hazy band of light appeared on the horizon, panic rose in Damien's throat. There was no food in the boat, no bladder of water. Experience had taught him asking a stupid question resulted in a beating, but as his anxiety reached a crescendo, he was unable to stop himself.

"Master, where are we going?"

Scylax stopped rowing and opened his eyes. "How long did you deliberate before you asked this question?"

"Some time, Master. Forgive me."

"We have traveled throughout the night, far from shore. Dawn approaches. You see there is no food, no water. You *fear* your master will cause you hunger and thirst. *Discom-*

fort. You fear he might even put your very life in jeopardy. Is that so?"

Damien knew better than to lie. "Yes, Master."

"That is the *truth*," the master said. "And as it happens, those fears are well founded. It is likely you won't survive what is about to befall you. Should you live to this journey's end, you will discover *that which you fear most*. What a thing it will be to see what you do when you arrive there."

"Where am I going, Master?" Damien asked, his skin going cold. "What journey?"

"Why, young Damien of Attica, we are in a boat in the middle of the sea," Scylax replied. "Where in heaven's name do you *think* you're going?"

And with that Scylax snatched Damien by his neck, pulled him across the canoe, and tossed him into the water.

Damien surfaced with a gasp, swallowing mouthfuls of water as he flailed in the ocean. Saltwater stung his eyes.

"Master!" he cried. "Master!"

The canoe receded into the fog, oars turning over in the waves.

"Master! Don't leave me here! Please!"

Master Scylax wasn't returning—of that he was certain. He was on his own, in the middle of the sea.

I'm going to die here.

He recalled the image of his slain father, impossibly lifeless in the back of a wagon cart, murdered for refusing to appease the villain Nicomedes and disgrace himself before the Gods and the roaring crowd in Olympic stadium. He remembered his grief-stricken mother, wasting away in bed, frozen snow covering the withered crops outside. Now he would join them in a sea that would swallow him whole without mercy.

Damien cried.

He imagined what it felt like to drown, how terrible it probably was before death's merciful release. Fear and sadness pulsed through his veins, and his limbs grew weak. He floated on his back, waiting for the water to overtake him and send him into the unfathomable depths below.

The sun rose eventually, and the fog cleared. Thin, white clouds formed streaks in the sky, and he took some small comfort in the light of day. He was surprised that a bit of strength had returned to him, and his panic was subsiding. He pulled himself upright and bobbed in the water, taking in his surroundings.

Land was nowhere in sight. The cry of gulls sent his gaze skyward as they circled high above his head.

Gulls.

Damien remembered Master Praxis and the little finch he had entrusted into his care. He was to live with it, feed it, make sure it stayed safe.

The *finch.*

It had repeated one phrase to him, over and over: "*The ocean is forever, and you are a child of the Gods.*"

Damien squinted up at the gulls and closed his eyes. He stilled himself, giving in to the current.

Please help me. I don't know how, but speak to me, as I speak to you. Hear me. I am scared. I am alone. I need your friendship. The ocean is forever, and I am a child of the Gods. The ocean is forever, and I am a child of the Gods. The ocean is forever, and I am a child of the Gods.

Splashes opened Damien's eyes.

A flock of gulls bobbed around him, forming a circle. They cocked their heads, curious. One of the larger gulls paddled its webbed feet, stopping half a foot from Damien's head. It inquired how he had come to be in his current predicament.

Damien described being thrown overboard from the canoe. The gulls laughed, squawking ringing in his ears. He asked how close he was to land.

The gulls just stared, not understanding. Damien asked them again, forming a picture of the seacoast in his mind.

The gulls took to the skies, shrieking.

"No, don't go! Please!" Damien called after them. "Please! Please come back! I'm begging you! Please! *Please don't leave me here!*"

The gulls grew smaller and smaller, soon disappearing altogether.

Damien floated on his back, his skin hot and dry. Thirst crept around his tongue. If he drank the seawater, he'd be dead. His father had taught him that.

He floated on his belly. It was more agreeable than his back, and he bobbed along like this, lifting his head every few seconds for a breath. Now the skin on his neck baked. He prayed to the Gods for another flock of gulls or any living creature to give him aide.

The ocean is forever, and I am a child of the Gods. The ocean is forever, and I am a child of the Gods. The ocean is forever, and I am a child of the Gods.

The sun had slipped across its apex when the gulls returned. He lifted his head and cried out to them.

"Here! I'm over here!"

The gulls had brought others, cormorants and terns and a pelican. The latter took the lead, extending its feet and landing close by with a splash.

Damien lifted an arm and waved. The flock surrounded him. A pelican opened its beak. Dozens of silver fish splashed within its pouch, an offering of food.

"I am not permitted," he said, remembering the temple's

teachings that animal flesh wasn't Orphic food. "I can't. But I thank you, friends. Thank you very much."

The birds asked if he required anything else. Damien replied that he needed a way to get to land. The birds checked among themselves, asking each other if any of them understood what he meant. Damien repeated himself, explaining that he couldn't stay here, that he wasn't a creature of the sea. He would die here and soon.

A small, red-bellied cormorant flapped its wings, assuring Damien that it could retrieve exactly what he needed. The birds then leapt from the water, filling the sky with their calls. They disappeared into the horizon. He thanked them again for their company, even though they were too far away to hear him.

22

Church, Chalons-En Champagne; February 1945

Dee awoke from the dream shivering, a cold emptiness in the center of her chest. She was scared and alone and wanted to be in her bed in Marietta, smelling her parents' morning coffee more than anything in the world.

The church was dark, moonlight streaming through what remained of the stained glass. Most of the platoon was asleep, their snores echoing off the walls. She sat up to find Iggy on his back one pew over, puffs of steam escaping his lips in the frigid night air.

"Ádaa áhólyą́. Haa nízah? Hazhó'ó naniná," he said, talking in his sleep.

Iggy thrashed on the pew and muttered in a language Dee didn't recognize. She reached across and gripped his shoulder.

"Iggy," she whispered. "*Iggy.*"

Iggy sat up, sucking in air. "Holy Moses," he said.

"You're all right," Dee said. "Bad dream."

Shaken, Iggy wiped the sweat off his face. "Had the same one again. You and me. The desert."

"Was I still a cowboy?"

"Yes, ma'am. And I was an Indian. Like always. We..." He squeezed his eyes shut, perspiration soaking his hair as if he'd just run a mile and not woken up in a freezing church.

"You don't have to talk about it, Iggy."

"No ma'am, I *want* to...to *remember*," he said, gripping his head. "We were on horseback. Purple mountains and blue skies. Beautiful. We rode and rode and...we just kept riding."

"Sounds okay to me," Dee said.

"We get to this little town. Folks everywhere. Get off our horses and tie them up to a hitching post, just like in the movies. Go inside this saloon. And these men are in there, drinking. And when they see me they suddenly stand up and pull out their pistols..."

"Goodness," Dee said.

"... and *bam bam bam bam bam*...you pulled yours out first, see? And you shoot 'em all down, one after the other. And they fall like dominoes. Except this one man. The one we've come for. I don't know how I knew that, but in the dream I just *knew*. He's this ugly son of a gun, with a big black beard and rotten teeth. And you—"

"*You* meaning *me*, the cowboy," Dee interrupted.

"Yes, ma'am. You reach across the counter and yank him over it. Pistol whip him 'til his face is just..." Iggy grimaced. "...and you drag him out of there like a sack of potatoes. Tie him up and throw him over the back of your horse. And then we're riding again, riding and riding, and come upon this big ol' rock. And there are *bees* everywhere. You get off your horse and walk right up to them and start talkin' to them! 'Hello friends, good to see you,' and this, that, and the other. And you reach your hand in the crack of this rock and pull out a giant...*honeycomb*. Lick your fingers, thank the bees again in plain English, and then we're riding again."

"Honey is good on beans," Dee said. "Most people don't eat them that way, though."

"Way out in front of us is this big cactus, the kind with, you know, arms?" Iggy continued. "You point it out to me, and we ride up to it. Get off our horses. You pull the bearded guy down off yours and rub the honeycomb into his hair. Tell him 'his days of preying on little Mexican girls is over.'"

The smile left Dee's face.

"And then we tie him to the cactus. And you...you get low to the ground and put your hand on the dirt. Close your eyes. And suddenly...*ants* come out of these holes in the ground. The biggest, reddest ants I've ever seen. Thousands...no, *millions* of them. And just like an army they march up to the bearded guy and up his legs and arms and when they get to his *face*..." Iggy pressed the heels of his hands against his eyes. "...they crawl into his mouth and his ears, and he...he starts making these *sounds* like..."

Iggy abruptly jumped up from the pew.

"God almighty that was the worst dream I ever had, ma'am," he said. "I need to take a walk."

"Go ahead, Sergeant," Dee said. "Get yourself some air."

"Yes ma'am," he replied, and walked down the aisle for the exit.

Clementine woke with the sun. Everything ached. She gripped the back of her pew and pulled herself up to sitting, wincing at what the hard wood had done to her back.

Most of the soldiers were still asleep. Dee sat in the rear of the church, soft morning light falling over her face, her elfin features lined with fatigue. Clementine wondered if she was praying and, if so, to whom.

"'Morning," Dee said in English as the only other woman in the platoon approached.

"Is it just *morning*?" Clementine replied in French. "I thought it was *good morning*."

"It is," Dee said, switching to her language. "But you can just say *morning*."

"English is hard," Clementine replied. "Too hard for me."

"French was no picnic, that's for sure," Dee said. "Harder than Russian."

Clementine sat in the pew in front of Dee's, draping a long, thin arm over it. "You speak Russian?" she asked.

"I think I do," Dee said.

"Say something in Russian."

"*Eto krasivaya tserkov*," Dee said.

"What does that mean?"

"'This is a pretty church'...I think."

Clementine pulled out a pack of cigarettes. "Who are you?" she asked, lighting one. "Really."

"I'm me. Dee."

"Are you a spy?"

"A spy?"

"*Oui.*"

"No."

"Why do you want to go to Berlin?"

Dee shifted in the pew, considering how to answer. She settled for the truth. "So I can find Adolph Hitler and execute him."

Clementine didn't blink; she just tapped an ash off her cigarette and took another drag. "I knew you were going to say that."

"You did?"

"What else is in Berlin but Hitler?"

Dee reached under her pew, brought the *flammenwerfer* into her lap, gasoline and tar sloshing inside.

"You should name it," Clementine said. "It's good luck."

"Maybe I will."

Clementine stubbed out her cigarette and placed the remainder behind an ear.

"Okay, Dee from Georgia," she said. "There is someone you should meet."

23

US 6th Army Group Outpost, Metz, France; March 1945

Doing his best Ty Cobb stance, Sergeant Mike Etheridge tapped his baseball bat on the potato sack that was home base. His red hair had gone shaggy since D-Day, bangs nearly but not yet completely covering his blue eyes. That, along with a prominent under bite and thick stubble spread over a lantern jaw, gave him an appearance not unlike a sheep dog.

The pitcher, a big-eared kid from Nebraska, stared him down.

"Just throw the ball, why don'tcha?" Etheridge taunted.

The private spun around and threw to second, missing by a mile. The baseman chased it down while his runner stole third.

"Goddamn it, Private!" the corporal on third bellowed. "Dizzy Trout you ain't!"

They waited for the ball to be retrieved and thrown to first, then back to Big Ears. Mike swung the bat a couple of times, indicating he was ready for the pitch.

He whiffed it. Three strikes, and out.

"Hey! Mike!"

Mike tossed the bat. It was the platoon's sergeant major calling for him, a wide grin on his face.

"Sir?" Mike called back to him.

The major mimed a cigarette between his fingers and picked an imaginary skirt off his legs, curtsying.

"Meez Clementine iz 'ere to zee oo," he said in a mocking French accent.

Mike gave a salute and jogged off the field, the other men hollering after him.

"All right, lover boy!"

"How'd a jerk like you *ever* manage a dame like that?"

"She got a sister, Mikey?"

"Lucky son of a bitch!"

Mike passed through the opera house that served as the company mess hall, red velvet seats ripped out of the floor and stacked in piles to make way for cots and supplies. Clementine was waiting outside on its stone steps, rifle slung over her shoulder, cigarette dangling off her lips. She appeared beautiful to him, as she always did.

"Mon amour," he said.

"Come here and kiss me," she replied.

He ran down the steps and did as he was asked.

Clementine pulled away and took Mike by the hand, leading him away from the opera house so they could speak in private.

———

They chose a bridge overlooking the Moselle River. She plucked the pack of Chesterfields from his shirt pocket, waving them in the air and taunting him in French as he tried to grab them.

"Sometimes I think you only like me for my cigarettes," he said, taking a seat on the bridge and dangling his feet over the water. She joined him, scooting along the stone until their bodies meshed together.

"I *like* you," she said in her halting English. "But I love Chesterfields!"

Mike's expression made Clementine cackle with glee.

"I say it right, eh?" she said. "You get me!"

"Oh, I get you, *mon lapin*," Mike said.

"*Mon lapin*. Your *rabbit*," Clementine said. "It is sweet how you call me this."

He lit his own Chesterfield, and they allowed themselves a moment's serenity in a country ravaged by war. Twenty feet below, the Moselle trickled along, its flow impeded by patches of gray ice.

"I need...you...do me something," Clementine said, searching her English.

"What's that, *ma cherie*?" Mike asked.

"I need you...go up in your plane."

Mike tapped ash into the Moselle.

"Ain't *my* plane," he said. "It's the army's. What do you need a plane for, baby?"

Clementine shook her head, not understanding.

"Plane," Mike said, and shrugged. "Why?"

"Top of the secret," Clementine said.

Mike laughed. "Top secret, huh?"

"Yes, yes, like that," Clementine said. "Top secret."

She kicked her khaki-clad legs above the frozen water, dusty shirt opened three buttons down from the collar, exposing milky white skin made golden brown by months of living outdoors. The sun also had brought out the freckles on her face, sprinkled across the bridge of her nose and underneath cobalt-blue eyes Mike could have stared into for the rest of his life, if she let him. He couldn't think of a thing she might ask that he would refuse.

"All right," Mike said. "Where and when?"

———

Two nights later, he was at the rendezvous point, Tiger Moth fueled and at the ready. He had come up with some grade-A bullshit to secure the biplane for the evening, impressive even by his standards. Something about rumors of roaming German squadrons sighted east of their position; he noted the suspicion in the major's eyes as he saluted his thanks for permission to perform a reconnaissance mission. He had done what Clementine had asked of him: he had secured wings.

Only now in a cold field did he ask himself *what* she wanted the plane for. The aircraft wasn't armed for a dogfight. It was only good for map making or flight instruction or the type of reconnaissance he had lied to his CO about.

Boy, you're a sucker for a beautiful dame, he thought, stamping his feet on the frosty ground.

It was hours before dawn, but he used binoculars anyway, sweeping the grassy field for any sign of Clementine. He heard her voice first, the French accent high and lyrical.

"Michael!"

"Here!" he called out in the darkness.

Her strawberry-blond hair emerged from the shrubbery, haloed in moonlight. They ran to each other and embraced. Her kiss tasted of the stale pack of Chesterfields she had stolen from him.

"*Mon amour,*" Mike said.

His hat fell off his head and tumbled to the ground as he lifted her off her feet. There were others with her, sticks and leaves crunching underneath their boots.

It was a man, thin and bearded, and a petite white woman. When she spoke American English, his mouth fell open.

"This him?" the woman asked.

"Yes," Clementine said.

The woman walked up to him and gave him a once-over. She wore a tan military-issued jacket and what he immediately recognized as a parachute pack, a swastika stamped on the fabric.

"Where'd you get the chute?" Mike asked Clementine.

"Dead German. Never opened," she replied. "*Sploosh.*"

Mike's eyes met the woman's, bright and green and glinting in the low light of the moon.

"You know how to fly that thing?" she asked.

Mike turned around to the Tiger Moth, the dark-blue paint making it nearly invisible.

"Well, yeah," he said. "Of course I do."

"Good," she said, and addressed the bearded man.

"Iggy. Where's Benny?"

The man pulled what appeared to be a rucksack off his shoulders. The woman took it, cradling it in her arms. Mike now saw it wasn't a rucksack.

It was a flamethrower.

"All right, then, Benny," the woman whispered to the weapon, as if addressing a pet. "You ready?"

"Benny?" Clementine asked the woman.

"You said naming it was good luck," she replied.

"*Oui,*" Clementine said. "Nice name."

Iggy appeared worried.

"I'm gonna be fine, Iggy," the woman told him. "Don't fret."

"Are you *sure* you don't want me to go with you?" he said.

"I'm sure."

"You take good care. Hear me? *I will see you later*, ma'am."

Mike sniffed. *Ma'am?*

Clementine gripped Mike's elbow and pulled him around to her.

"Get her as far in as you can," she said.

"Get her *where*?" Mike asked.

"Germany," Clementine said, as if it were the most obvious answer in the world.

A thunderhead rumbled in the distance. Mike pulled Clementine back to him, kissed her, and they all ran for the plane.

Mike hopped into the bucket, the plane's body sagging with the weight of the second passenger.

The woman clapped a hand on his shoulder. "Let's go."

Clementine gripped the propeller and spun it. "Contact!" she yelled, the plane's engine sputtering. "*Bonne chance!*"

Mike steered the biplane right, away from the group and into the dark borders of the grassy field. He reached under his seat and brought up two pairs of aviator goggles. He strapped one around his scalp and held the other pair over his shoulder. The woman snatched them out of his hand.

"High as you can go," she said over the propeller's hum. Mike gave a thumbs-up.

He climbed out of the field into the stars above. When they leveled out, his passenger exhaled loudly.

"Everything all right there, gal?" he asked.

"Everything is grand," the woman said. "I'm right where I need to be."

A flock of godwits appeared to their right and left, climbing to altitude with the plane. They squawked, tucking their long stick-like legs up into their wings.

"Looks like we got some visitors," Mike said.

"Yeah," the woman replied from the back. "Guess we do."

He pulled back on the controls, bringing the plane up to five then ten then twenty thousand feet. The birds kept pace, stretching their wings and cruising alongside.

"Let me know when we get there," the woman said.

Mike turned around in his seat as she pulled the goggles down over her green eyes and closed them behind the glass.

Mike steered the biplane, keeping a wary eye for roving German Luftwaffe. The godwits chirped among themselves, and after a while, the woman snored.

Mike shook his head. Now he had seen everything.

The German border soon loomed below, dimly lit by farmhouse campfires. Mike flew for almost an hour, until the hair rose on the back of his neck. He had flown into Nazi territory far enough.

"Hey," he said. "Girlie."

The woman sat forward, rubbing her eyes under the goggles.

"That's *Lieutenant* to you, Sergeant," the woman said. "Not 'gal.' Not 'girlie.'"

"Say what, now?" Mike said.

The woman draped her arm over his shoulder, the silver bar on the sleeve signifying her rank brushing his cheek.

"*Lieutenant*," the woman repeated.

"Lieutenant," Mike said, eyeballing it. "Yes ma'am."

"Better," the woman said. "I'll get out here."

The gasoline sloshed in the flamethrower's tank as the woman climbed out of her seat. The godwits twittered and drifted within feet of the plane's wings, bobbing along in the propeller's downdraft.

"Ask you something, ma'am?" Mike said.

"Go ahead," she said.

"Who *are* you?"

The woman lifted a boot out and dangled it over the ground thousands of feet below.

"Lieutenant, like I said," the woman shouted over the roar of the wind, "Attica."

Mike glanced back over his shoulder. She was perched on the edge of the biplane, like a bird about to take flight. "But you can call me 'Dee,' Sergeant," she continued. "Everybody does."

Dee winked, clutched the flamethrower to her chest, and dove head first out of the airplane. The godwits slapped their wings against their flanks and dove alongside her. Dee rocketed down into Germany, the blue pilot light within the flamethrower flickering in the night sky until it disappeared along with her and the flock. Eventually her parachute bloomed open, white and round, like the moon above.

"I'll be damned," Mike said, and guided the plane back toward France.

24

Somewhere Over Germany; March 1945

Dee didn't expect the sudden jolt that accompanied the parachute opening. When the canopy filled with air, it yanked her back up into the sky so forcefully that she dropped Benny, barely catching the flamethrower by its strap. The godwits sailed around her as she struggled to pull the weapon back up into her arms.

"There, there, Benny," she said. "Easy does it."

Iggy had asked about the nickname when they had set out for the airfield. Dee had told him it was her uncle's name, a white lie he had accepted without further discussion.

The truth was too had been having the cowboy dreams, only hers were much different. She wasn't a man, as she was in Iggy's version, and there was no Navajo companion. Instead she looked like herself and the companion was a homesteader, old and cranky, dressed in a green apron and standing behind the dry goods counter of a trading post. Cowboy Dee sat and listened while the gray-haired man drank whiskey and told her things. She never could remember what he had said, but she always awoke warm and safe after these dreams, much unlike those in which she was a boy on a peninsula by the sea.

The man's name was Bennett. That much she did remember. She shortened the name and gave it to the weapon now gripped tightly to her chest. She wished Bennett were here now, talking to her in his gravelly voice and making her feel like everything would work out just fine.

We are here. We are with you.

It was the godwits, their tiny voices drifting around her in the winds carrying the parachute over the German countryside below.

Thank you, she said, and a sudden gust sent the parachute careening to the left.

Dee flailed about, the wind snatching her out of the sky and sending her pinwheeling to the ground below. She tried to twist her body in such a way that the silk might catch a chute full of air and slow her descent, but the ground careened up toward her anyway.

A spruce tree grove loomed below, rapidly approaching. Dee reached out for one of the lines hanging from the half-collapsed canopy, pushing it out and away and allowing the flap to catch an updraft and inflate. Her plunge became a glide, and now she was squarely above the trees, lowering into them.

The branches enveloped her, scratching her face and arms, the canopy snagging the treetops. She dangled two stories above the ground, a fly in a web.

The godwits alighted themselves among the branches, assessing her predicament.

"Well...*shoot*," Dee said.

She couldn't undo her harness and hold on to the *flam-*

menwerfer at the same time, so she let Benny go, noting the thud it made when it hit the ground. She would break her legs if she too dropped from this height.

Dee was halfway through a plan to climb out of the harness and reach a nearby branch when male voices cut through the nighttime silence.

She held her breath, and listened as they approached.

"Over here, in the trees," a voice said in German.

"Where?" said another.

"*There*," the first man said. "It was a parachute, no question. Watched it come all the way down."

She heard footsteps now, growing closer and closer to her position. Two Nazi Waffen-SS men emerged into the tree grove, armed with machine guns.

"Show me where or I'm going back," the larger one said.

"I'm telling you," the smaller said. "It fell right here."

Dee swallowed dryly as the footsteps broke into a run. She looked down as one of the Nazis arrived directly below her feet, picking Benny off the ground.

"Kurt!" he exclaimed. "Look!"

Kurt lumbered up to his companion. Dee let out a long sigh as they surveyed the area where the *flammenwerfer* had been found before gazing straight up at her, in the trees.

"Holy shit, Karl," Kurt said. "That's a lady."

"Get the others," Karl replied.

German soldiers no older than teenagers climbed up the trees, detangling the parachute's canopy from the branches. The godwits harassed them mercilessly as they did, trying to peck at their eyes. The boys swatted them back like flies, cursing all the while.

They lowered her to the ground, Dee landing in the middle of what she counted to be around three dozen soldiers. A towering Nazi officer in a leather trench coat emerged from among the men. A soldier grabbed Dee by the armpits and pulled her to standing.

"Oh, I like her," the *divisionskommandeur* said, his putrid breath washing over Dee's face. The other Waffen-SS whooped and hollered.

"What's your name?" he asked Dee.

Dee answered in the way she was trained to at Oglethorpe in the highly unlikely event that she, an officer in charge of a communications center in suburban Paris, were to be taken as a prisoner of war in Nazi Germany.

"Attica, Dee. Lieutenant, United States Army," she replied in English. "Serial number A611313."

The Germans exchanged astonished looks.

"She's American," the *divisionskommandeur* said. "And an officer. Her I *have* to fuck!"

With that he shoved his hand into Dee's crotch and gripped her tightly.

Dee lunged forward, sank her teeth into the *divisionskommandeur's* nose, and tore it off his face with a single bite.

The officer staggered backward, blood spurting out of the hole left behind. Dee spat the Nazi's nose onto the ground, and the others rushed in, rifle butts connecting with her skull. Dee crumpled, the sound of godwits crying the word *Orphic* the last thing she heard before the darkness.

PART II

THE HYENA

25

Somewhere in Germany, March 1945

When she next opened her eyes Dee was looking into the face of a young girl, perhaps twelve years old, brown hair in braids. Like Dee, she lay on her side, eyes wide and open. Flies buzzed around her head.

"Hello," Dee croaked, her voice thin and weak. "Name's Dee."

The girl just stared.

"Where are we?" Dee asked.

A fly landed on the girl's left eyeball. She didn't blink.

Dee planted her hand on the wooden floor and pushed herself onto her back. When the back of her skull made contact with the wood, she cried out in agony. She gripped a slat in a wall and pulled herself to sitting, an act that took every bit of strength she could muster. Vertigo overtook her, and she fell back onto an elbow, dry heaving. The world swam around the edges of her vision. The ground vibrated beneath her, and when she again managed to sit up, she realized where she was.

A train.

Barbed wire stretched across the boarded-up windows, ice-cold winter air pouring inside the compartment through the cracks. Dee rubbed her eyes, something like mud caking the skin on her face. She wiped it off and brought her fingers into the light that spilled between the wooden slats in the train car's walls.

Blood.

Dee gently probed her scalp, wincing as she found indentations in the flesh. The wounds had frozen over but were still tacky to the touch. Remembering the Germans in the forest, she took in her surroundings.

Dozens of women lay on the floor, all of them dead—some clothed, others naked. Some had exit wounds in their throats, having been shot in the back of the neck. The weather had preserved the bodies, but the stink of excrement hung heavily in the air. Flies coated a bucket in the corner of the room, the source of the smell.

She reached over to the young girl next to her, closing her lifeless eyes. She then rolled onto her stomach and pushed herself to her knees. Dee's vision swam, and she again vomited nothing, her empty stomach clenching. She pulled herself along the wall until she got to the barb-wired windowsill and gripped its edge.

The train rattled along the tracks, the dead women frozen to the floor.

Dee staggered to the door that separated one car from the other. She was barefoot, her new pair of army boots nowhere to be found. Her toes were numb, gripped by frostbite.

An old dead woman lay on her back not far from Dee, dull brown eyes staring into a void, legs swollen and black with decay. At the end of them were a pair of wool socks, wrapped around bloated feet.

Dee lurched forward, collapsing into the pile of bodies. She peeled the socks off the corpse, a good bit of skin sloughing off with them, exposing the bones in the deceased woman's ankles.

Dee pulled them on, groaning as the rough wool scratched her frostbitten skin like broken glass. Then she fell backward, spent.

After some time she wobbled back to the door. The train car's previously deceased occupants had managed to make a hole in the wood so that communication might be made with their neighbors. Dee peered through it.

She estimated a hundred women in the next car over, all very much alive. They huddled together for warmth, steam streaming out of their mouths and nostrils. The youngest and oldest sat in the center, arms protectively wrapped around them by the others. Their wide, terrified eyes stared at the floor, their mouths moving in silent prayer.

"Where am I?" Dee whispered to herself.

She moved about the train car, gingerly removing sweaters and shawls and scarves from the dead. She spoke to them as she did, apologizing for the intrusion on their person, an absurd gesture under the circumstances but one she felt compelled to make. After a few minutes' work, she collapsed to the floor wrapped in the clothing of women whose names she would never learn.

"Thank you," Dee told them, her voice muffled by the clatter of the train over the tracks. "Much obliged."

She drifted in and out of consciousness. Day became night and then day again, and one afternoon the train rattled to a stop.

Male voices pierced the still, frozen air. The walls vibrated as train compartment doors slid open. Dee lay on her side, peering through the slats in the wall and listening to the soldiers bark commands in German.

"Get your ass up, you ugly old cow," an *obersoldat* commanded, and one by one Dee's neighbors fell out of their cars and onto the ground, surrounded by a vast field of snow. A Nazi private walked down the line of women, tossing shovels onto the ground from a wheelbarrow.

"Dig, you stupid bitches," he said in German. "Dig, dig, dig."

Dee saw that the tracks were buried in snow, so deep that it had impeded the train's ceaseless progress toward its unknown destination. The women outside were desperately confused and clearly unable to understand the German being hollered at them; others were too terrified to move a muscle.

"*Schnell! Schnell! Schnell!*" the *obersoldat* roared, spittle flying off his lips. "Move your fucking ugly old asses or I'll kick the shit out of you!"

A few of the women understood, picking up the shovels and chipping away at the frozen bank of snow underneath the train. The rest followed, those without tools falling to their knees and clawing at it with their bare hands.

"*Good*, cows, *good*," the private sneered. "Maybe you're worth something after all."

A woman around Dee's Mama's age dropped her shovel, clutching her stomach in pain. She doubled over, moaning.

The *obersoldat* whipped his head toward the sound. "You," he said, pointing at her with a deerskin-gloved hand. "Get to it."

The woman sank to her knees.

"I said *get to it*, bitch," the soldier barked.

The woman crumpled into the snow.

"She has dysentery," an old woman wearing a headscarf said in French. "Let her be."

The *obersoldat* didn't understand the French, nor did he care a whit about what might ail the woman on the ground. He stalked over to her, his boots leaving deep prints in the powder.

"Stand up," he commanded.

The rest of the women kept shoveling, casting wary glances at the soldier and their fellow passenger in the fetal position at his feet.

"I said *stand up*, bitch," he said. When she didn't, he kicked her in the stomach with the steel-toed tip of his boot. The woman let out a guttural shout, the wind knocked out of her. "Stand the *fuck* up!" he screamed.

The old woman in the scarf approached him, placing a hand on his shoulder. "Sir, please..."

The *Obersoldat* recoiled at her touch, yanking a pistol from the holster on his belt and aiming it at the woman's face. "Back!" he yelled. "Back, I said!"

"Show her mercy," she said. "Please, sir."

The *obersoldat* pulled the trigger. Arterial blood spurted out of the hole his bullet made in the old Frenchwoman's neck. She tipped over into the snow bank, dead.

The concussive sound of the Nazi's weapon going off stopped the shoveling. The young *obersoldat* gaped at the old woman's corpse then broke into surprised laughter.

Dee's vision again blurred, a dull ache overtaking the wounds on her battered skull. She took a step forward, and her legs buckled, sending her back into the pile of dead women covered in frost.

Consciousness came and went. After some time, her

compartment's door opened, a pair of soldiers counting off in German.

"One ...two...three!"

They heaved the old woman's body inside, which landed squarely on top of Dee. The doors slid closed, and after a while the train again rumbled forward.

Dee emerged from beneath the newly arrived cadaver. She cradled the old woman in her arms, the body already stiffening with rigor mortis.

"*Bonne nuit,*" Dee said, and closed the woman's eyes.

Dee sat against a wall, inspecting her head injuries as the train picked up speed. "You're in it now, girl," she told herself, the light through the train car slats fading with the setting sun. "Yes, you are."

26

Ravensbruck Concentration Camp; March 1945

The train traveled one more night and one more day. When darkness again fell, it stopped. Whispered voices in half a dozen languages drifted from inside the cars, high and panicked. Then there was the sound of barking dogs.

Two dozen uniformed women, all tall, all blond, and all running behind leashed German shepherds descended onto the train, black capes fluttering off their backs. A woman in the next car over from Dee's screamed, and the others joined her.

"Out, out, out!" a guard screeched, and the compartment doors slid open. The screaming intensified as the dogs lunged into the cars, jaws snapping.

"Get your stinking asses out! *Now!* Get down here, you filthy cunts! Move!"

Dee understood the German but guessed few of the others did. The sound of compartment doors crashing open and the subsequent screams progressed until Dee's car was up next.

The door trundled open. A statuesque Aryan guard with

a high forehead and blue eyes gasped. "*Mein Gott*," she said, and called back for help. Another guard who could have been her twin, nearly six feet in height with a head of bouncing blond curls, joined her. Their dogs jumped on their leashes, barking ferociously, trying to see inside.

"Frank!" one screeched. "Frank, get down here!"

The soldier who had shot the old French woman appeared, as astonished as the blondes upon seeing Dee standing there amid the corpses. He brought up a flashlight, the beam landing directly in her eyes.

"She's supposed to be dead," Frank said. "I mean, she was dead when we got her."

The trio stared while Dee observed hundreds of women stagger across a snow-covered field toward a stone tower, its twirling spotlight washing over a forest of trees.

One of the blondes snapped to, raising a clenched fist holding a riding crop.

"Come down from there! *Schnell!*"

Dee didn't move.

"I said get down here, you ugly bitch! Move it!"

The German platoon she had encountered in the forest had stripped her winter coat and boots, but she still wore her army-issued uniform shirt. She angled her arm in such a way that the flashlight beam now illuminated the insignia.

"I am an officer in the United States Army," Dee said in crisp, clear German. "If you want me, you'll have to come in here and get me."

The trio exchanged expressions of disbelief. Frank climbed up into the train car and grabbed Dee's arm. She slammed her forehead into his teeth, and he stumbled backward, tripping over a dead body and falling out of the train.

Another blonde blew a whistle and released the German shepherds. The beasts leapt into the train car ahead of their masters, one sinking its teeth into Dee's left arm, the other her right shin.

Dee tried to wrestle them off, but the blondes were soon on top of her, kicking her with the tips of their jackboots and whipping her face with the riding crop. Then Frank was back, fresh blood dribbling off his lips. He punched Dee across the jaw, and she spat in his face.

"Stop fighting!" he screamed.

Dee was pleased to hear worry in his voice. She writhed in their grip, the dogs' jaws locked on to her arm and leg. The Nazis dragged her outside.

Then there were more guards, out of breath from their run across the field. They asked what happened, who this woman was, and why it required so many soldiers to remove her from a train car.

"She's a spy," a familiar voice said. It was Kurt, the Nazi who had spotted her dangling from the tree by her parachute. "She needs to be seen by the *hauptsturmführer*."

"Herr *hauptsturmführer* is asleep," said a blonde. "I'm not waking him up for her."

"I didn't say wake him up," Kurt replied. "I said he needs to know that she's still alive."

"She'll see him all right," the blonde said. "First thing in the morning."

They caught up with the rest of the prisoners from the train, now a teeming mass of starving, injured women falling over each other into the snow. There they were kicked, dragged, or set upon by dogs.

Dee tried to catch a German shepherd's eye. When one finally glowered at her, all she found was rage.

Why are you doing this? Dee asked it.

It didn't answer her; it only barked back ferociously.

The women passed through open gates between two-story-high stone walls. Pitched roofs glowed under spotlights ringing the perimeter of the camp. They passed rows of what appeared to be barracks of some sort, their window-panes coated in black paint.

Dee limped along with the rest, blood dribbling from the dog bites in her arm and leg. Her eye was swelling up where the riding crop had struck, and she felt a tooth coming loose where Frank had punched her jaw. She reached in her mouth, feeling along the bottom teeth, and found it. The molar detached from the gum with little effort, and she dropped it, blood speckling the snow.

The blondes in black capes ran up and down the line, their dogs snarling as they screamed orders at the terrified women.

"Eyes front, cows! Eyes front! Hands at your sides! Don't look at me, bitch! Look ahead!"

They rounded the corner of a gray building with a hand-painted sign above the door, the word REVIER in block letters over a small red cross. *Hospital*, Dee translated. Before them was a field, measuring a hundred yards by fifty. Thousands of footprints were scattered about the dirty brown slush.

"Line up! Five across! Move, move, move!"

The women chattered among themselves, eyes wide with panic. Dee overheard two women around her age whispering their confusion in French and approached them.

"They're saying line up in fives," Dee said in French. "Tell the others."

The French women nodded gratefully. Soon the German demands were being met, women hastily arranging themselves in lines five across, wincing as the dogs lunged at them, barely held back by their flaxen-haired masters.

"Eyes front!" the tall guard who had discovered Dee repeated. "Hands at your sides! Don't move until we tell you!"

A skinny Russian woman wearing a torn green dress and one broken-heeled shoe collapsed two rows ahead of Dee. The black-caped blonde who had struck Dee with the riding crop stalked forward, her leashed dog snarling. The other guards seemed to defer to her, backing away to give her and the dog ample room.

"*Achtung!* Stand up! *Achtung!*"

The fallen woman didn't move.

The guard kicked her in the spine. A small gasp went through the assembled prisoners.

"*Achtung!*"

One of the Russian women broke ranks, going to the woman on the ground and pulling at her arm. The guard whipped her riding crop across the Russian's face.

"Get back in formation, cow!"

The Russian clutched her cheek and resumed her place in line. The guard thrust a finger toward the collapsed woman.

"Greif," she said, and her dog wagged its tail, yelping in anticipation. "*Anbeißen!*" she commanded it.

Greif lunged, encasing the Russian's thin upper arm in its jaws. The woman shrieked and scrambled back to her feet, her green dress now soaked as well as torn.

Chuckling with satisfaction, the guard strolled back to the front of the assembly.

A door opened and closed elsewhere on the field, and another line of women appeared, all dressed in blue-and-white striped dresses, over which they wore thin, ragged coats. Each had a triangle and a number sewn to their clothing. No two triangles were the same color.

They formed an orderly row, hands at their sides and eyes front, like well-trained soldiers. As the blond guard spoke, the women translated in Polish, Russian, French, and Romany. It was difficult to hear them over the loud, nasal German.

"My name is *Frau Oberaufseherin* Ursula Botz," the guard announced. "I'm the head guard here at Ravensbruck Camp. You filthy creatures are now the Reich's prisoners. Tonight you will wash and be placed in quarantine. Should you survive, you will then be put to work in service of *Der Führer*. Now get your ugly faces out of my sight."

The other female guards screeched orders, and the prisoners broke into a run, driven like cattle across the field by cracking whips and dogs snapping at their heels.

"Schnell! Schnell! Schnell!"

They were herded into a large, dimly lit building, bare but for piles of clothing stacked floor to ceiling. Bone-thin women dressed in prison uniforms were waiting for them, colored triangles stitched to their dresses, each holding a pair of hair clippers tethered by fraying cords to electrical outlets in the walls.

"Undress," they said in various languages. Dee was aghast at how sallow their skin appeared under the dangling light bulbs, cheeks and eyes sinking into the hollows of their skulls.

The women in Dee's group protested with indignation at being stripping naked in subzero temperatures. The women in the striped uniforms just shook their heads, again ordering them to remove their clothing.

Haltingly they complied, and when the first woman stood completely naked, a young Romani prisoner motioned her over and started shaving her head. The woman recoiled, objecting in Polish, and yet another bloodless blond guard stepped out from the shadows, an ox-hide whip in her hand, poised to strike.

"Shut your ugly mouth and do as you're told," the guard said.

The Polish woman shrank back from the whip, and the prisoner finished her scalp then dropped to her knees. The Polish woman looked on in shocked silence as the Romani shaved off her pubic hair.

Other women stepped forward, many bursting into exhausted tears as their hair was unceremoniously shorn from their heads. Dee waited her turn, observing the blond guard with the whip. She appeared to be enjoying herself tremendously, chewing her thumbnail and giggling like a schoolgirl.

The door opened, and two male guards entered, one carrying a bottle of Schnapps, half full. He swigged, and the duo laughed at the spectacle.

One of the nude women shrieked at the sight of them, covering her nakedness with her hands. The blonde charged forward and struck her across the buttocks with her whip.

"Schnell!"

The woman cried out, a large red welt blooming across her skin where the whip had struck.

"Don't be shy, darling," one of the male guards slurred. "Nothing we haven't seen before."

The Romani girl on her knees kept about her work, eyes dark and vacant, moving the clippers up and down the woman's lower torso with grim efficiency.

"Next," she said, standing.

Hours later Dee emerged from the building with the others, head and body shaved. Like everyone else, she had given up her clothes, the US Army uniform indifferently tossed in a pile with all the rest. In exchange she now wore a blue-and-white striped cotton dress, a threadbare wool jacket, and a pair of wooden clogs that were already starting to cut into her feet. A red triangle was stitched onto her dress pocket at a guard's instruction, its meaning unclear.

She also had been issued a tan headscarf, now repurposed as a bandage on her left arm, the deeper of the two dog bites. The young Romani prisoner had appeared sickened as Dee's dark hair fell away with the clippers, revealing the wounds on her scalp.

The quarantine barracks were designed to hold half as many women as those now struggling to stuff themselves inside it. Thin, filthy mattresses scattered on the floor were quickly claimed; Dee settled for the corner, against a bare white wall. It was colder there, but at least she was sitting up, giving her skull a chance to heal.

Women streamed in, searching for a place to sit. Many cast furtive glances at Dee, quickly looking away when her eyes met theirs. Poles stuck with Poles, French with French, Russian with Russian. The Romani claimed a corner and sat in a circle, their backs to the others.

A few other women were like Dee: alone, without a tribe to join on the cold wooden floor. Some were German themselves, others suffering from a physical deformity or mental illness. These women huddled in the dark shadows beneath the blacked-out windows, knees protectively drawn up against their chests.

Oberaufseherin Botz appeared in the doorway, her blue

eyes scanning the room under thin, neatly plucked eyebrows. When they found Dee, she pointed with her riding crop.

"You," she said. "Come with me."

The room fell silent as Dee got to standing, her clogs shuffling across the floor.

"You won't need those," Botz said. "Take them off."

Dee slipped her feet out of the shoes.

A woman on the floor sighed with pity at the sight of Dee's frostbitten toes.

"*Schnell,*" Botz said.

Dee followed Botz across the camp. Now that the women from the train were in quarantine, the other guards were nowhere to be seen, nor were their dogs. Light snow falling across the searchlights gave the place an eerie, peaceful calm.

Botz turned around and walked backward, the riding crop held in deerskin-gloved hands tucked behind her back.

"Without your hair you're an ugly little *fotze*, you know that?" Botz said.

"*Fotze*?" Dee asked, unfamiliar with the German word.

Botz giggled. Her ruddy apple cheeks and the tiny white teeth exposed between them when she laughed made her look like a schoolgirl.

"*Cunt*," she translated in English. "Ugly, ugly little cunt," she repeated, switching back to German.

Dee nodded and kept silent, eyes front.

When they arrived at a stone building on the edge of the field, Botz held up a gloved hand and Dee stopped walking.

"In the morning you will be seen by the *hauptsturm-führer*," she said. "He will be in at eight, maybe nine. Who knows? You will stand right here and wait for him. Understood?"

Dee didn't answer.

Botz shivered theatrically and pulled her fur-lined leather coat tightly across her chest. The snow crunched under her jackboots as she approached Dee, stopping inches from her face. Botz eyeballed Dee's swollen feet and clucked her tongue.

"Frostbite," she said. "You might lose those, if Herr *Hauptsturmführer* decides to have a second cup of coffee in the morning."

Botz lifted a jackboot and slammed the heel into Dee's left toes. The white forehead beneath her blond bangs went red with effort as she ground into them.

Dee didn't react; she merely stared ahead at the stone building before her.

Botz grinned and lifted her boot. "See you tomorrow, my ugly little *fotze*."

27

Hauptsturmführer Glockner's Office, Ravensbruck Concentration Camp; March 1945

Dee stood in the snow, everything below her knees frozen and numb. The rest of her shivered uncontrollably, her breath coming in fits, puffs of steam illuminated by the searchlight that beamed down on her from the stone building's roof. She needed to think about something other than how cold she was, so she turned her thoughts elsewhere.

It was the middle of the night here, a place she assumed to be somewhere in Germany. Fraulein Botz had called the place Ravensbruck, although it was impossible for her to know if that was a town or just the name of the camp. Figuring out where exactly this camp was located would be her first order of business.

Germany was six hours ahead of Georgia, and Dee imagined what her parents might be doing. Listening to the radio, no doubt, and Mama having a cup of tea, her Daddy a glass of rye perhaps. They would be listening for news of the war constantly, huddled by the living-room radio, her father offering reassurances that Dee was okay, that she was safe in France, sitting at a switchboard. At this her Mama would feel relief.

Dee smiled at the possibility. Her swollen eye throbbed as she did.

No one on earth had any idea where she was. Mike's plane had flown for some time into Germany, a journey covering hundreds of miles. It was a reckless act on his part, one only a man senseless with love would perform. Dee imagined Clementine and the rest of the Free French Army somewhere warm, gathered around a bottle of Chianti and recounting stories of the strange American who briefly had been in their company.

She thought of Iggy. Her loyal companion across France faced a certain court martial for his desertion, and Dee wasn't sure it had all been worth it. They had bonded over bad dreams, an absurd justification for his blind loyalty, especially given the result. Now she would probably die of hypothermia, and he'd spend years in a prison cell. She shook her head at the senselessness of it all.

After a few more hours passed, Dee abruptly stopped shivering and collapsed into the snow.

———

A siren woke her up. The first light of day streaked across the cloudless sky, stars she knew to be planets fat and twinkling by the fading moon. When she pulled herself up to sitting, a searing pain crept across her scalp. She observed the indentation in the snow where her head had lain, thick with dark frozen blood.

A siren blared from speakers atop the telephone poles ringing the camp. Then it stopped, and a high-pitched whine pierced the brief silence. The sound of a throat clearing echoed off the walls, and a female voice commanded in German, "*Appell! Appell! Appell!*"

Dee cast a quick glance down at her feet. The toes on her right foot were swollen to twice their normal size, the nails black. The nails on the left were scattered in the snow.

"*Appell! Appell! Appell!*"

The sound of doors flying open on their hinges crackled in the air. Women, thousands of them, streamed out onto the frosted field like ants.

They were all dressed in their blue-and-white striped dresses, arranged in groups by the color of the triangle on their uniforms: red, blue, green, black, and, a few, yellow.

The women were gaunt. Most heads were shaved, though some had tufts of hair, sticking up off their heads every which way. They lined up in perfect rows of five, a ritual obviously perfected over months if not years of practice. Dee was reminded of her color guard at Fort Oglethorpe, a place that now felt a million miles away.

Black-caped women appeared, leashed attack dogs trotting at their sides.

"*Appell! Appell! Appell!*"

The prisoners stood stiffly, eyes forward as the guards inspected their ranks.

"Ah," said a voice behind Dee. "You're still alive."

Botz strode toward her through the snow, a steaming mug of coffee in hand. She appeared fresh and well rested, wearing red lipstick and blue eye shadow.

"Come along," she said, motioning for Dee to follow her inside.

A blast of warmth greeted Dee as she hobbled into the building. The feeling in her body started to return within moments of the doors shutting behind her.

Inside the stone building it was clean, immaculately so.

Desks were placed in orderly rows, each topped with an inkwell, a stack of white paper, and a typewriter. Botz drained her coffee cup and set it on a desk; she removed her gloves and motioned toward the stairs.

A large painting of Hitler hung on the wall at the bottom of the steps. Botz abruptly came to a halt, slammed her boots together, and gave it a sharp Nazi salute.

"*Heil Hitler!*" she cried.

Dee stared at the painting: *Der Führer* rendered four times life size.

"*Schnell*," Botz commanded.

Dee was made to stand in a hallway outside a thick wooden door, HAUPTSTURMFÜHRER OTTO GLOCKNER was etched into the brass placard. It was even warmer here on the second floor; Dee let it sink into her pores, sensation returning to her extremities. This included her feet, which throbbed with an excruciating ache.

The sunlight streaming through the windows grew brighter, and more people arrived, all in uniform: some Nazis, some prisoners.

Botz appeared soon after, head high, walking two steps behind a stocky man with a pinched face and round wire-rim glasses perched at the end of a long nose. His thinning brown hair was slicked wetly across his forehead. When he saw Dee for the first time his nostrils flared.

"She is waiting for you, *Hauptsturmführer*, as promised," Botz said, her chest swelling beneath her uniform. She handed him a thin manila folder.

"*Ja, ja, gut*," he said, and Botz opened the door for him. Glockner gave Dee a once-over as he passed.

"Where are her shoes, *Oberaufseherin*?" he asked.

Botz gawked at Dee's feet as if only noticing them for the first time. "Where are your shoes, stupid?" she asked Dee, hands on her hips. "Look at those toes! How careless!" She sighed and made a show of rolling her eyes. "I will have one of the girls fetch her some shoes, *Hauptsturmführer*," she said, and snapped a salute. "Heil Hitler!"

Glockner returned the salute. Botz spun on a heel and marched down the hallway, her jackboots hammering against the tile.

The *hauptsturmführer* opened the file Botz had given him and waggled a finger over his shoulder. "Come in," he said in English.

Glockner's office was filled with furniture, well-appointed treasures pillaged from the homes and offices of Europe's conquered cities. A bronze relief of a German shepherd sat prominently displayed among the various sculptures on a bureau by the bar, a half globe stocked with Scotch and schnapps. The wall behind his desk was decorated with framed insect specimens—a few large beetles but mostly butterflies, their colorful wings spread out across white cardboard. A giant monarch was pinned dead center, just above Glockner's head.

"Sit," he said, also in English.

Dee eased into the leather chair across from his desk, wincing at the stiffness in her frozen muscles.

Glockner licked his index finger and flipped a page in the file. "You bit off a German officer's nose," he read, switching back to his native tongue.

A stuffed bird stood on his desk next to the inkwell, a Steller's jay mounted on a round stand carved from oak.

"You bit off a German officer's nose?" he asked, now a question.

Dee glanced from the jay to the *hauptsturmführer's* beady eyes and shrugged.

Grimacing, Glockner returned to her file. "You were captured a few hundred miles south of here," he continued. "How were you able to get so far into Germany?"

"Where is *here*?" Dee asked, and Glockner's eyes widened behind his wire frames.

"Ravensbruck," he said.

"Where is Ravensbruck?" Dee asked. "What part of Germany is this?"

Glockner's lips turned up in a tight smile. "I will ask the questions. How were you able to get so far into Germany?"

Dee said nothing, only stared. There was knock at the door.

"Enter," Glockner said.

A gray-haired prisoner entered, tray in hand. She appeared relatively healthy and wore a comfortable pair of shoes.

"Your breakfast, Herr *Hauptsturmführer*," the woman said.

"*Ja, ja, gut,*" Glockner replied.

The gray-haired woman set down the tray, a cup of coffee placed next to a thick piece of toast slathered with butter and jam, and a rasher of bacon. The woman hurried out the door without acknowledging Dee and shut it behind her.

Glockner picked up the toast and took a big bite. Jam dribbled down his chin.

He picked up the triangle-folded napkin from the edge of the tray and dabbed his lips.

"The extraordinary circumstances of this meeting are not lost on me," he continued, blowing steam off his coffee. "An American female soldier who speaks perfect German. In my office. When I heard you were here, alive, I couldn't believe it until I saw it with my own eyes. And now you sit casually before me, as if those ruined feet and gruesome dog bites don't cause you agony. You aren't at all what I expected is what I'm trying to say."

"I get that a lot," Dee said.

"Why are you in Germany, and how did you get here?" Glockner asked, daintily licking jam off his fingers.

"Attica, Damienne. Lieutenant, United States Army," she replied. "Serial number A611313."

"Yes, it says that here in your file. That wasn't my question."

"But it's my answer," Dee said. "I'm a prisoner of the German army, am I not?"

Glockner shrugged as if to say, *obviously*.

"Name, rank, and serial number," she said. "That's all you're getting from me."

"Such insolence," Glockner said, slurping coffee.

Another knock came at the door.

"Enter," he said, irritation in his voice.

A girl of no more than fifteen years slid through a crack in the door, arms and legs so thin beneath her prison uniform that the bones were visible beneath her gray skin. She set a pair of wooden clogs on the floor, scurried out, and shut the door behind her.

Glockner peered over the edge of the desk.

"Go ahead. Put them on."

Dee dragged them closer to her feet and gingerly wedged them inside, her toes lighting up with fresh pain.

"*Gut*," Glockner said. "Now then, Lieutenant Damienne Attica, serial number A611313. We have just spent my valuable time having what I call a *discussion*. It's obvious to me that you have no intention of answering my questions. So now we must have what I call an *interrogation*. You see, *discussions* happen here, in my nice office, surrounded by all these beautiful things. *Interrogations* happen elsewhere in the camp, for interrogations are very, very messy, and *wet*. So the room they take place in doesn't have any of these beautiful things. Just bare walls and a floor and a drain." Glockner closed the file on his desk. "And now you may go. We will meet again. At your interrogation."

28

Quarantine Bunker, Ravensbruck Camp; March 1945

Dee walked along the edge of the field in her clogs, their rough wood a welcome respite from the frozen ground. The rows of women who had lined up for whatever *Appell* was were now dispersed to places unknown. Dee had inexplicably been allowed to leave the building without a guard, left on her own to find her way back to the quarantine bunker. This strange development elicited thoughts of how she might escape.

The stone wall that surrounded the camp was two stories high and ringed with barbed wire. Hand-painted signs hung along the interior every twenty feet or so, their message unreadable at a distance. Dee shifted her eyes to the right, making sure no one was watching her, and approached them.

The signs displayed skulls and crossbones and a message in thick black lettering:

VORSICHT! ELEKTROZAUN!

The wire was electrified. Dee studied something amid the barbed coils: fingers.

Dismembered fingers were fused into the wire, black-ened with decay. Dozens of them, left on display.

Dee buttoned up her coat and made her way to the quarantine bunker.

———

It was slightly warmer there, the two hundred women stuffed inside keeping one another alive with what remained of their body heat. When Dee opened the door, a room full of whispering immediately ceased. She searched for a spot on the floor, no one eager to make space.

"Hey. You."

All heads swiveled to a German-speaking woman who sat near the back. She was tall and heavyset, a weary grin on her face. Black roots erupted from a fading dye job, dishwa-ter-blond hair hanging into her smiling eyes. She motioned for Dee to sit next to her.

"Here, darling," she said.

The whispering resumed.

"Excuse me," Dee said in English, making her way through the crowd. "Thank you."

Dee sat down and the woman offered her hand.

"Elsa," she said.

"Dee," she replied, shaking it.

"You are American."

"I am. You're German?"

"Don't hold it against me," Elsa said. "And a whore, to boot. Maybe now you want to sit somewhere else?"

Dee shook her head. "Suits me just fine."

"Your eyes are very beautiful," Elsa said. "Such a marvelous green."

"Thanks. Can I ask you something, Elsa?"

"Of course."

"Where are we? I mean where *exactly*. In what part of Germany is Ravensbruck?"

"Ravensbruck is a hundred kilometers north of Berlin," Elsa replied.

Dee gasped. "A hundred kilometers? That's all?"

"Yes."

Dee crossed her legs and slid the wooden shoes off her feet. Elsa cursed at the sight of them. "These fucking animals," she said.

"Not a card-carrying member of the Reich, I take it?" Dee asked, gripping the edge of a toenail. It came off easily, like a flower petal.

"Christ, no," Elsa said. "Which is why I'm in this place, I suppose. Well, that, and one of my girls gave a soldier the clap. Now I'm an enemy of the state."

Dee set the toenail aside and removed the headscarf from the dog bite on her arm. The bloody holes had frozen over. She moved it to the bite on her leg, which had started to bleed again during her walk across the camp.

"What about you?" Elsa asked.

"Well," Dee said, wrapping the wound. "I took a plane ride over from France. Jumped out of the plane. Landed in a tree, not too sure where. Had a little scuffle with some soldiers. More of them than there were of me, and next thing I know I woke up on a train, which stopped here."

"And now you're an enemy of the state," Elsa said. "Like me."

"I am that, Elsa. Yes indeed."

Giddy, Elsa leaned in close to Dee's ear. "Are you a *spy*?" she whispered.

"No," Dee said.

"Then why did you jump out of plane?" Elsa said, still whispering.

"Can you keep a secret?" Dee asked. Elsa nodded, giggling. "I'm going to find Adolph Hitler," Dee said. "And execute him."

Elsa howled with laughter, once again turning the room full of heads.

"Sorry, sorry," Elsa said, covering her mouth. "I just think that's *wonderful*."

The doors to the quarantine room creaked open, and all chatter ceased. The same group of girls who had shaved their heads and stitched the triangles on their uniforms now entered. One carried a large pot, the others bowls and spoons. The smell of food wafted through the air, and the women started shouting.

The girls distributed the bowls and spoons among frantic, outstretched hands. Dee smiled gratefully to the young prisoner wearing pigtails as she received hers; she was a girl of maybe twelve years old. The girl smiled back, cheeks dimpling in the malnourished hollows of her face.

"What's your name?" Dee asked her in English. She patted her chest. "Dee. *Dee*."

"Hanna," the girl whispered, smiling at being acknowledged.

"Hello, Hanna," Dee said.

"*Witaj*, Dee," Hanna replied in Polish, and continued handing out bowls down the line.

They each received one ladle's worth of soup, which Dee guessed was nothing more than boiled cabbage and potato skins. Still it was warm, and the first food she had eaten since her night in the church with Clementine and Iggy.

"Garbage," Elsa said, dropping the bowl in her lap. "In the city jail they at least gave us sausage."

"Eat it," Dee said. "You'll need your strength."

Elsa sighed and retrieved the bowl, slurping up a spoonful and making a face. "You want mine?" she said.

Dee took the bowl. She consumed both quickly, missing her Mama's Southern-style beans, minus the ham.

She had just set her second bowl down when Botz appeared in the doorway, flanked by two male guards. Her icy-blue eyes scanned the room. When they landed on Dee, they lit up like torches.

"Her," she said, pointing with her riding crop.

The guards charged across the room, bowls of soup clattering to the floor as the women made way. When they got to Dee they stopped, towering over her.

"Stand up," said one of the guards. Dee just stared up at him. "I said *stand up*, bitch," he repeated.

Eyes wide and frightened, Elsa placed a hand on Dee's arm. "Do as they say, Dee."

"What the fat whore said," the other guard barked. "*Now.*"

Dee glanced from Elsa to the guards, her expression blank. The first guard took a step back and kicked her in the face. Several women screamed. Dee didn't make a sound, however. She felt along her jaw, reached into her mouth, and removed another tooth.

"Now they match," she said, holding the bloody molar up to the guards. Then, to the astonishment of all in the room, she smiled. "*Danke schoen.*"

The guards picked her up under the shoulders and dragged her across the floor. Elsa sat there, stricken.

Dee turned and winked.

They pulled her along the narrow paths, Dee using it as an opportunity to take in more of the camp.

Most of the grounds were populated by row after row of barracks, windows shuttered against the cold. Women of all ages and nationalities hurried from one place to the other, eyes cast downward, making obvious pains not to look at Botz or Dee or the two guards manhandling her.

A steeple somewhere outside the camp rose above the western wall, perhaps a village church. A tall brick chimney stood similarly outside the wall to the east, thick black smoke pouring out of its flue.

They passed a building bustling with activity and smelling of cabbage soup, then one with several women outside, scrubbing striped uniforms in pails of ice-cold water. *WASCHEREL,* a sign above them read.

The guards quickened their step as they came upon a building in the farthest corner of the camp, one without windows and surrounded by a barbed-wire fence. Botz moved ahead, opening the padlocked gate with a key and motioning the guards inside, grinning all the while.

It was dark inside, as Dee predicted it would be, lacking windows. The overpowering stench of sweat and urine and feces hung in the air. A switch flipped, and a single light bulb illuminated the room.

It contained what appeared to be dog cages, minus the dogs. There also were a few wooden crates, not much larger than coffins. In the center of the room, under the light bulb, was a gynecologist's exam table, complete with stirrups. It had been outfitted with handcuffs dangling from each corner.

Smiling, Botz observed Dee taking in the view of the room for a moment. Then she stood in front of her, eclipsing it. Dee stared up at her, impassive. Botz nodded to the male guards, and they tightened their grip on her arms.

"How was your lunch, *fotze*?" she asked.

Dee said nothing.

"What was on offer today? Hm?"

Dee studied the floor. Dark stains covered the concrete, in the center of which was a drain.

"Don't want to tell me?" Botz said. "Well, maybe I'll just see for myself."

Botz gripped Dee's shoulders and slammed a knee into her stomach. Dee vomited. Botz crouched to the ground, sifting through the mess with the end of her riding crop. "Let's see. Cabbage. Potatoes. Yummy." She rose and strolled toward the gynecologist table.

"I was thinking today how perfect your German is. You speak it better than some Germans even. The dialect. The pronunciation. *Fantastic*."

Botz ran a gloved hand along the table's metal edge.

"But you can't know *every* German word," she said. "That's not possible. Not unless you were born here. Which you clearly were not."

The *oberaufseherin* hopped up onto the table and swung her legs gleefully.

"Repeat after me," she said. "*Pru...gel...strafe.*"

Dee just stared.

"*Pru...gel...strafe,*" Botz sounded out again. "*Prugelstrafe.* Do you know this word?"

Dee didn't respond.

"No? Well. You will soon learn. I'll give you a hint."

She slid off the table and gripped one of the stirrups.

"This...*this* is *prugelstrafe*. Only our esteemed *Reichs-führer* Himmler himself can approve its administration."

Dee's eyes widened. "Himmler?" she said. "Heinrich Himmler?"

Botz burst into laughter.

"You know of our *reichsführer*? she cried. "Yes! Yes, indeed. He's making a special trip all the way from Berlin to meet you. Isn't that wonderful?"

Botz sauntered back up to her, using the hem of Dee's prison dress to wipe the vomit off the end of the riding crop.

"But first you must rest, eh? It's been a long day."

The guards dragged Dee to one of the coffin-size crates on the floor, dropped her inside, and slammed the lid.

Dee lay in the darkness, listening as an iron latch slid closed; then she heard a padlock click shut. A small hole in the box lid was the only source of air. As soon as Dee discovered this, Botz's blue eye peered through it.

"Sleep, my ugly little *fotze*," she whispered. "*Sleep.* And pleasant dreams."

There was the sound of footsteps and then a door slamming, leaving Dee in the pitch-darkness.

She managed to roll over onto the arm without the dog bite. Her head still throbbed, as did her jaw and eye. Her feet were still numb, a small mercy.

Himmler.

Dee remembered her Himmler doll, crafted from wool and cotton and a black-and-white photo trimmed from *Life* magazine. If what Botz said was true, she would soon meet the man in person. She closed her eyes, enjoying the silence. Botz's wish for pleasant dreams was in no way sincere, of course, but Dee hoped they might be anyway.

29

Isle of Kasos, Greece; The Month of Pyanepsion 434 BC

It took every ounce of sanity Damien could muster not to dip his head into the ocean and take a drink. His tongue had swollen to nearly twice its usual size, which made closing his mouth difficult. The skin on his arms and shoulders had cracked open into blisters. Damien scratched until the blood flowed. The pain he could take, but the itching was unbearable.

The sun passed over his head three times before he stopped doubting he'd really die in the middle of the sea, alone. As the fourth day dawned, an image formed in his mind that he couldn't shake: if he only swam deep enough, far enough, he'd reach Hades and the river Lethe, and drink from its waters, and sleep on its banks.

He had learned of Lethe in his classes at the Orphic Temple. It was there that those who passed forgot everything of life on Earth, provided they dropped to their knees and swallowed its cool water. Damien's tongue burned as he contemplated it, how wonderful his first drink would taste. He just needed to keep swimming, down into the depths.

A sea bird splashed onto the water a few feet from his head, a squirming silver fish in its beak, its scales glimmering under the hot midday sun. The bird slapped it against the water's surface, killing it, then floated to Damien and offered it to him as a meal.

"Thank you, friend," Damien said, his voice coming in a croak. *But I have no need. I am going to Lethe, you see.*

Puzzled, the bird cocked its head. It asked Damien where Lethe was and how he intended to get there.

Below, Damien replied. *Down.*

The bird explained that he would surely drown if a journey into the ocean depths were attempted.

I'll just have to swim fast, Damien said, laughing.

The bird took the skies, shrieking; hundreds of others flocked to join it. There were so many voices that Damien only heard bits and pieces of what they screamed at one another.

Boy. Dead. Drown. Dead. Boy. Drown. Dead.

Damien thanked them for their help, took a deep breath, and dunked his head under the waves. The sun pierced the ocean's depths, all the way to Hades. At the limits of Damien's vision, the water was a deep dark blue, and that's where he would find the liquid that would slake his thirst. He swam, fat air bubbles erupting from his nostrils and trailing up to the glittering surface.

Not long into his journey, the bubbles stopped, and he ran out of air.

He figured if he only swam a little faster, a little farther, he might make it. He kicked harder, but the dark pool below wasn't getting any closer. He peered up to the surface, dismayed at the distance traveled.

Orphic.

Damien stopped swimming at the sound of the word. He

hadn't heard it as much as he *felt* it, rising from the chasms of the Earth below his dangling feet.

Orphic.

They emerged from the darkness, fading into view like stars after sunset. Calm and serene, two and then six, then a dozen.

Damien remembered the old fishermen in Attica telling stories of the monsters they had encountered on their journeys at sea, fearsome creatures just like these. Fins jutted from their sides, cutting through the water like knives.

They sang:

> *The ocean is forever*
> *and we are children of the Gods.*
> *In the south the wind goes warm*
> *and we are children of the Gods.*
> *At night we swim by the stars,*
> *and we are children of the Gods.*
> *We saw further than we ever had today*
> *and we are children of the Gods.*
> *The waters are warm in spring*
> *and we are children of the Gods.*
> *There is perfect quiet in the ocean's solitude*
> *and we are children of the Gods.*
> *The waves are mountains we must climb*
> *and we are children of the Gods.*

A dorsal fin half Damien's height sailed by, and he grabbed it. The leviathan it was attached to rocketed toward the surface with such force that Damien almost lost his grip.

When it broke the surface, he gasped, sucking in a lungful of air.

The birds above were still circling, relief exploding through their flocks at his reappearance. They dipped their wings in salutation, heading back toward land, and left Damien amid the school of great white sharks.

———

They never stopped swimming. Damien clung to his shark's fin as it dashed through the water, the other dozen keeping pace. He glanced back and was amazed to find the creature's tail jutting above the surface twenty feet behind them. He'd never encountered a beast so large; it filled him with both fear and awe.

Thank you, Damien said. *Thank you all.*

As evening approached, a band of color appeared on the horizon. A great shadow hovered above it, and he now understood what it was. The band of color was rocks, the shadow a cliff.

"There!" he yelled. *An island.*

The sharks responded with one voice, the sound striking his body from every angle: *As you like.*

They arrived as night fell, the sky thick with stars. The sharks took him into the shallows, the frigid water turning warm as they neared the island. Damien slid off the shark's back, his toes sinking into sand. His knees trembled as he found his legs again.

We cannot linger.

The sharks swam away and Damien raised his hand. A single voice floated back toward him, carried by the current. It was the voice of the monster that had ferried him these many miles upon its back. The words wrapped around his legs and flowed up his body like blood pumping through his veins.

The ocean is forever.

Soon their fins and the dark water became one, until he could no longer see them.

He collapsed into the sand, sleeping through the night and into much of the next day. He awoke with his tongue so thick with thirst it nearly choked him. Water. Even though he was back on dry land, he still needed to find fresh water.

The island's surface was mostly rock bleached white by the sun. Yellow scrub brush dotted the landscape, no shade in sight. Tiny blackbirds hopped among this vegetation and, along with some lizards, were the main inhabitants of this patch of land in the middle of nowhere.

"Water," Damien said around his ballooned up tongue. "Water."

A white duck with black markings on its neck and eyes waddled alongside him. The smew eyed Damien, its crown of feathers bobbing in the wind. It asked him where he was from and what he was searching for.

"Water," Damien replied.

The smew then said something Damien didn't understand. He asked it to repeat itself.

The smew addressed a gray cormorant on a nearby rock, a wriggling fish clenched in its beak. It apologized for interrupting its meal and asked if it wouldn't mind explaining to the young Orphic where water was found on the island, as it apparently wasn't making that clear. The cormorant threw its head back, swallowed the fish whole, then hopped over. It told Damien that freshwater was where the Rotting were, the Blackness; it was with They who were Black with Rot. It said if Damien kept going the way he was headed, he would find the place they were talking about.

Damien struggled up a steep hill made of stone, slipping in a patch of gravel and skinning his knee. He crested the hill and caught his breath. Smoke rose from the valley below. Where there was smoke there was fire, and fire meant other people. Damien winced as he hopped down the hillside, the sun-baked rocks scorching the bottoms of his feet, his skin soft and mushy after being submerged for four days in salt water.

He reached the bottom and ran toward the smoke. It was a small village, huts made of stone dotting the landscape. They were probably fishermen, which meant there was a boat that could take him back to the Orphic Temple.

As he staggered closer, he realized they weren't fishermen at all. They were children.

A girl Damien's age held a seashell and tossed it into the air. It landed painted side up, and the others squealed in delight, chasing her. Damien loved this game.

"Hello," he said with a rasp. "Excuse me."

One of the little girls whipped her head around to him, and the wind left Damien's lungs.

The girl's face was as featureless as the rocks. Where there should have been eyes there were only indentations in the skin; where the nose was supposed to be, a hole. Her lips were gone, exposing her teeth, and when she waved at him, she did so with stubs, not fingers.

The other children stopped their game. They all had similar deformities, noses or ears or fingers missing—like black, burnt sticks pulled from a fire.

Some waved. Others stared.

The ground rushed up to Damien as he passed out.

30

Strafeblock, Ravensbruck Concentration Camp; March 1945

Dee came out of the dream gradually, dimly aware that she was drowning. Then she bolted upright, spitting up a lungful of water. Laughter rang in her ears as she choked and wheezed. She was still in the crate, the lid now removed. A male guard had filled the box with water while she slept, the hose still running over the floor and into the drain.

"She's up."

Dee rubbed the water out of her eyes, the trio of Nazis fading into view under the light of the single light bulb. Now that she had regained her breath, she was freezing again, sitting in a box of water in single-digit temperatures. Botz and her companions appeared perfectly warm in their gray woolen great coats. The swastika pins on their lapels glinted in the low light.

"Get her out of there," Botz commanded.

A male guard gripped Dee's arm, making sure to choose the one with the dog bite. He dragged her to the gynecologist's table, dripping wet. The other guard joined him, forcing her legs into the stirrups and locking the handcuffs around her wrists.

"*Prugelstrafe,*" Botz said, closing the handcuffs around Dee's ankles tight enough that the circulation to her feet was cut off. "Any idea what it means?"

"Punishment by beating. Something like that," Dee said, staring up to the light bulb.

"Not *something* like," Botz said, smiling. "*Exactly* like. Good, *fotze*. Whoever taught you our language did a marvelous job. Perhaps we'll find out who that was today."

"Franz Kafka," Dee said.

The Nazis exchanged a look.

"Who?" Botz asked.

"He's a writer," Dee said. "Which is why you've never heard of him. See, some of us *read* books, and some of us *burn* them. When the war is over, I suggest trying the former. Assuming you live to see its end."

Botz's porcelain skin flushed red. She reached into her coat and yanked out the riding crop. Dee was bracing for a strike when the doors to the *strafeblock* creaked open. A tall man dressed in a black SS uniform slipped inside. Botz put the crop back into her coat and saluted sharply.

"*Heil Hitler,*" she said.

"*Heil Hitler,*" the man replied, and stepped into the light.

He had a long, pale face with deep-set eyes. His chin sank into his neck as he peered down at Dee, the skull-and-crossbones insignia on his cap glowing under the light bulb. *Life* magazine had taught her this meant he was a member of the *Totenkopf* Division, or Death's Head. When he spoke he sounded tired, bored even.

"May I examine her?" he asked, placing a thumb on Dee's right cheek and pulling her eyelid down.

"You may do whatever you like, Doctor Voss," Botz said.

"But do keep in mind *Reichsführer* Himmler will be joining us very soon."

"Yes," Voss said. "I saw his car coming through the gates on my walk over from the *revier*."

Botz stiffened at this news, adjusting the curly blond bangs across her forehead.

"If you will excuse me, Doctor, I wish to greet the *reichs-führer* personally."

Botz left after instructing the male guards to follow. Now Dee was alone with the Nazi doctor, whose dull brown eyes traveled over her body head to toe.

"I understand you speak German, so I will speak German. Though I do know a little English," he said. Voss ran his fingers along her rib cage. "You are relatively well nourished," he said flatly. "No typhus, I assume?"

Dee said nothing; Voss inspected her feet.

"You will probably lose a few of these to frostbite," he said, pressing gently on her toes. "Can you feel that?"

Dee still said nothing. Voss walked to the head of the table and took one of her handcuffed wrists in his right hand. He shucked the left sleeve of his black uniform and marked the second hand ticking around his Rolex. Dee smelled tobacco on his breath as he exhaled over her face. After a minute, he released her wrist.

"Your pulse is acceptable, under the circumstances," he said. "You will likely survive your interrogation. I would suggest doing what you can to shorten its duration. Only my opinion, of course."

With that he retreated to a corner of the room and sat on a wooden stool. He leaned his head against the wall and folded his arms across his chest. Within seconds he was snoring.

Dee pulled against the handcuffs and stirrups, yanking

her feet up toward her body. She didn't really think she could break free of the restraints, but she had to try.

She lay back, focusing on the light bulb above her head. When Voss had checked her pulse, she caught a glimpse of his watch. It was half past nine in the evening. That meant it was half past three in Marietta. Mama usually started dinner around then, so she and Daddy could eat at five thirty sharp. Five thirty was a little early for Dee, but she would be happy to be there now, breaking green beans or boiling corn or whatever chore her mama had set her to.

After what Dee guessed was a half hour, the doors opened. Voss sat forward on his stool, yawning. Botz entered first, gesturing with a gloved hand that the doctor should stand up. He did, raising a Nazi salute.

A pudgy, bespectacled man walked in, one Dee immediately recognized. Before now she had only seen him in pictures and newsreels, but he now loomed over her, in the flesh. His thin hair was slicked back, closely shaved at the sides. He wore round, clear glasses, and his mustache was trimmed not unlike Hitler's. His gabardine uniform was meticulously adorned with *Waffen*-SS General shoulder boards and *reichsführer* collar tabs, the insignias of his rank. Despite the uniform's splendor, he appeared more like a bank teller than a Nazi general. Heinrich Himmler took a deep breath at the sight of Dee, removing a handkerchief from his pants pocket and dabbing his nostrils.

"Well, well," he said, and refolded the handkerchief. The room was silent as he took pains to make sure it formed a perfect triangle before putting it back in his pocket.

"I am *Reichsführer* Himmler," he said, peering over his glasses. "And what is your name?"

"Attica," Dee said. "Damienne. Lieutenant."

"Aha," Himmler said. "It is my understanding that you

refused to answer *Hauptsturmführer* Glockner's questions. Is this so?"

"It is," Dee said.

"And why is that?" Himmler asked.

"US Military Code of Conduct, Article Four," Dee answered. "When questioned, should I become a prisoner of war, I am required to give my name, rank, service number, and date of birth. I will evade answering further questions to the utmost of my ability. I will make no oral or written statements disloyal to my country and its allies or harmful to their cause."

Himmler blinked rapidly behind his glasses.

"With that in mind," Dee continued, lifting her head from the table, "my name again is Damienne Attica. Lieutenant, 3341st Battalion. Serial number A611313. Date of birth is November first, 1924. What do you say, Heinrich? If I'm still here next fall, will you bake me a birthday cake?"

Botz let out a shout and stomped across the room to the table. "Insolent *bitch*," she hissed. "The *reichsführer* has demeaned himself to speak to you today, and you respond with disrespect? How dare you? You will answer his questions fully. Do you understand me, you filthy piece of shit?"

"Now, now, *Oberaufseherin*," Himmler said. "Please." Himmler craned his neck to look Botz in the eyes, half a foot difference between them. Botz lowered her gaze to the floor. "You are well aware I have deemed that sort of language unacceptable," Himmler said. "It demeans you as a woman of Aryan blood. It is beneath you."

"*Ja, Reichsführer*," Botz replied, her eyes welling with tears.

"No need for that," Himmler said. "And do know I understand what a great deal of stress you are under. Your task is not easy, or enviable. But you must conduct yourself as a lady at all times. You and others like you are the mothers of our Great Reich. It is critical that you behave as such. And that includes language."

"Ja, Reichsführer," Botz repeated.

"Now then," Himmler said, turning back to Dee, "you have made your position perfectly clear to me. And now I will do the same to you."

With that Himmler abruptly left the room.

Botz glared at Dee, the air fragrant with Himmler's aftershave. A few seconds later, the door again opened, and Glockner entered.

He carried a cotton T-shirt in one hand and a fireplace poker in the other. The young male guard accompanying him carried the end of a hose.

Botz grinned as the water ejected from the hose's nozzle. Glockner removed his coat and handed it to Dr. Voss, who folded it over his arm.

Then Glockner took the T-shirt and wrapped it around Dee's face.

A blast of water rushed down her throat. She struggled to spit it up, Glockner holding her tightly against the table with the T-shirt. Dee writhed and coughed. The shirt was abruptly removed.

Dee gasped for breath as Glockner brought the fireplace poker down hard against her ribcage. Dee clenched her fists and tightened her abdomen, absorbing the blows. She blinked water out of her eyes and bit her tongue, determined not to make a sound. They may torture her to death, but never enjoy the satisfaction of her screams as they did. Of that Dee was sure.

Glockner beat her until he was out of breath, the metal rod falling to the concrete floor with a clang. Botz went to pick it up, but Glockner held up a hand, stopping her. He motioned for Voss, who set the *hauptstrumführer*'s jacket on a stool and walked over to Dee.

He again took her wrist with his right hand and checked his watch. Glockner leaned against a wall, wheezing. Botz just stared with her wide blue eyes, the muscles in her jaw clenching and unclenching.

"Steady as a rock," Voss said, releasing Dee's wrist. "Extraordinary. She's in excellent physical condition. You, however, Herr *Hauptsturmführer*, I'm not so sure about."

Botz stifled a laugh, and Glockner let out a roar as he snatched the hose out of the young soldier's hands. He grabbed Dee by the throat, squeezing it and running the hose over her face. Soon all she breathed was water and turned what she assumed were her last thoughts on earth to her mama and home.

31

Attica Residence, Marietta, Georgia; July 1931

Dee remembered a sunny summer's day in Marietta while she drowned, handcuffed to a metal table four thousand miles away from home. In this memory she was six years old, dressed in her favorite green jumper, her hair in pigtails. She sat on the porch with their neighbor Miss Adeline's cat, a tabby named Sassy.

Mama was allergic to dogs and cats, so Sassy became her surrogate pet, provided she stayed outdoors. The animal hopped the fences along Juniper Street until she found Dee, meowing her greeting. Dee patted a spot on the top step, and Sassy sat with her, licking a paw and cleaning her whiskers.

Not long after Dee and Sassy became friends, Mama started crying. She cried while cooking breakfast, was crying when Dee got home from school, cried on Sunday mornings before church. Naturally this alarmed Dee, so she asked her daddy what was wrong.

"She's just sad, is all," Daddy said.

Dee asked why.

"Mommies get sad sometimes," he answered, but Dee suspected something else was going on.

One Sunday, the Sunday Dee reflected on as her body convulsed for oxygen in the *strafeblock*, she approached her mama, who sat on the porch swing with a glass of lemonade. Her mother rocked in it languidly, staring into space, eyes red and swollen from another afternoon in tears.

"Can I sit with you, Mama?" Dee asked.

May nodded, wiping her eyes. "Yes, honey. Of course you can."

Dee climbed up in the swing. It was a hot, sticky day, and she watched the condensation on her mother's glass of lemonade trickle a while before she spoke.

"I'm sorry a baby died inside you, Mama."

May didn't seem to hear her at first. Dee was about to repeat it when her mother's red eyes widened.

"What did you just say?"

"I said I'm sorry a baby died inside you," Dee said. "And that you're so sad."

May dropped her glass. It didn't shatter; it just rolled along the porch, lemonade spilling out into an icy puddle.

"Who told you that?" she asked. "Daddy?"

Dee shook her head.

"Then who?"

"Sassy."

May's face fell into an expression Dee had never seen before. It made her nervous.

"Sassy," Mama said. Dee nodded. "Miss Adeline's cat." Dee nodded again.

May stared at the puddle of lemonade. Dee wanted to help clean it up, but her mother's expression made her feel as if she were glued to the porch swing.

"Why would you say something like that to me?" Mama asked. Her voice was shaking. "Why would you lie?"

"I'm not lying," Dee said.

The vein in her mother's forehead that only appeared when she was very upset was now visible.

"Dee, don't you lie to me."

"I'm not lying, Mama."

"Dee, who told you that?"

Dee opened her mouth to speak, and her mother held up a finger. It was a warning.

"Think very carefully before you answer this time."

Dee sighed and stared down at her bare feet dangling off the porch swing.

"Look at me, little girl."

Dee did as told.

"I asked you a question."

"You'll get mad if I say it again, Mama."

"I'm already mad," May replied. "Tell me the truth and I won't be. Lie to me again and I will be very, very mad. Now who told you that? Was it Daddy?"

"No, Mama."

"Then who?"

Dee braced herself for a slap. "Sassy."

Her mother didn't raise her hand; she only stared at her for a while.

"Go to your room," she finally said. "No supper for you."

Dee ran inside, the screen door slapping shut behind her. She didn't stop running until she was in her room.

She heard her parents talking in the living room downstairs, but couldn't make out what they were saying. At one point their voices rose, and Dee shuffled to the door in her socks, pressing her ear against it.

"...she needs to learn about these things, May..."

"...too young..."

"...let me talk to her. Okay?"

Her father's heavy footsteps up the staircase sent Dee scurrying to her bed. She jumped onto the mattress, picking her stuffed rabbit off a pillow and pretending to play.

A knock and her father stuck his head in. "Dee. Talk with you a second?"

Dee shrugged. Her father walked to the bed and sat down. He smelled like pipe tobacco and shoe polish. It always made her feel safe.

"What's her name again?" George said, pinching one of the long ears on the stuffed rabbit.

"Miss Potter," Dee said.

"That's right. Miss Potter," he said. "And how's she doing today?"

"Okay, I guess."

"Dee, I want you to tell me how you found out about what happened with your Mama. Did you overhear us talking?"

Dee shook her head.

"So how did you know?"

"I don't want to tell you," Dee said.

"Why not?" George asked.

"Because you'll get mad."

"I won't get mad. I promise."

Dee set Miss Potter down. "Sassy told me."

George pressed his lips together. Dee took it as her cue to continue. "She said Mama had a baby in her tummy, but then it died."

"Sassy said that," George said. "That cat from down the street you play with sometimes."

"Yes, Daddy."

"I see."

Formulating his words, George rubbed his palms together. "What happened to Mama is called a *miscarriage*," he finally said. "See, there was a time when you were inside your Mama, when you were a tiny baby about this big." George held his fingers up a few inches apart, the length of a green bean. "And you grew and you grew, and then one day you came out of your Mama and now here you are, pretty as a peach."

Dee liked when her Daddy said she was pretty as a peach.

"A few weeks ago, we found out there was another baby growing inside your Mama, just like you had. And that baby was going to be your little sister or brother."

George's voice caught in his throat. He put his hand over his eyes, taking a deep, shaky breath. When he again faced his daughter, he had tears in his eyes. Dee had never seen this before, and it alarmed her.

"But the good Lord saw fit to take that baby up to Heaven before we could meet it. That was His will, His plan. And even though we know Jesus loves us, losing that baby made your Mama very sad. Made me sad too. You understand?"

"Yes, Daddy."

"And if you overheard Mama and me talking about it, that's okay. That's just fine. We're not mad about that. And you can tell us things, and we can talk about things as a family and you don't have to tell stories or lie, which you know is a bad thing to do. Don't you?"

"Yes, Daddy."

"Well, good then. Now I warmed up some of those beans you like so much. They're in the oven. You want to go downstairs and eat some supper?"

George opened his arms, and Dee jumped into them. He carried her down the stairs and sat with her as she ate her food, Mama listening to the radio in the living room by herself.

A few months passed, and one crisp autumn day May started singing. Dee couldn't recall her Mama ever having sung a note in their house, only in church. That day Mama sang while she cleaned, while she did the dishes, while she cooked.

Dee listened from the porch. Then Sassy trotted down the sidewalk, and they sat together for a while, watching the leaves fall from the trees.

"Honey, come help me, please," Mama called out to her. Dee excused herself and went inside as instructed.

She appeared in the kitchen doorway. A bundle of carrots sat on the kitchen table.

"Peel those for me," May said. "Watch your fingers."

Dee retrieved the peeler from a drawer and went to work. May sang "Jesus Loves Me So" while stirring onions in a pan.

When she stopped singing, Dee set the peeler down.

"Are you singing because you have a new baby inside you, Mama?"

May swung around from the stove, oil flying off the end of her spatula. "What?"

"Is it a baby brother or a baby sister? Do you know?"

May clutched her lower abdomen. The oil started to

smoke, and she moved the pan off the burner, grabbed an oven mitt, and waved it out the window.

"Dee?" she said. "Honey? How do you know that?"

Dee pressed the back of her hand to her mouth, knowing her mother would be furious if she told her.

"I...I just got that news *this morning*, Dee," Mama continued. "At Dr. Creel's office. Nobody knows but him and me. Even your Daddy doesn't know yet."

Dee poked at the carrot peelings, not sure where else to look.

"Dee?" Her mother sounded frightened. "How did you know about that?"

"Sassy told me, Mama. Please don't be mad."

May glanced out the window to the porch, and Dee followed her gaze. Sassy was where Dee had left her, sitting on the top step. She stared back with her big yellow cat eyes and meowed.

Mama was suddenly ill. She rushed to a corner, picking up a broom and storming out to the porch.

"Get!" she shrieked, and Sassy bolted for the street.

May dropped the broom and charged back inside. Her hands shook as she flipped through the telephone directory pinned above the kitchen phone. May picked the receiver off the candlestick base and dialed.

"Yes, Adeline? It's May. Well, I'm not doing so well; that's why I'm calling. No, she's fine. No, George too. Listen, Adeline, you need to keep that cat off my property. Yes. Well she's...no, she's... I... Fine."

May slammed the receiver in its hook and went back to the stove. Dee picked up a carrot peel and nibbled on an orange end.

A few minutes later, Miss Adeline appeared at their gate, marching up the walkway in her housecoat.

"May? Come out here and talk to me face-to-face, now."

Mama slapped her spatula onto the counter and went to the back door, opening it but not the screen.

"What's this all about?" Miss Adeline asked.

"What this is about is you making sure that animal doesn't come around here anymore," May snapped.

"Sassy?" Miss Adeline asked.

"Yes, Sassy," May replied. "What other cat is there?"

"What'd she do to you?"

"I'm allergic, which I've told you a thousand times over."

"But I thought Dee liked to play with her."

"Yeah, well, she scratched her."

Dee gasped at the lie; Sassy hadn't done anything of the sort.

"Oh, my goodness!" Miss Adeline exclaimed.

"Yes, so...we can't be having her over anymore."

"Well, I can't control where a cat goes and doesn't go, May."

"Sure you can. Keep her inside."

"She lives out of doors. Always has."

"Well, if I see that devil again I'm calling animal control to come out and get it."

"May! For Jesus's sake!"

"For Jesus's sake nothing. Now I have to make dinner 'fore George gets home. Good day."

With that Mama slammed the door in Miss Adeline's face.

That night May broke the happy news to George over supper. He jumped up from the table, taking his wife's hand and dancing her across the linoleum. Mama didn't mention the incident with Miss Adeline or the cat, and neither did Dee.

Two months later, Mama started crying again, and Dee went in search of Sassy.

She found her on Miss Adeline's porch, peering out at the world through a newly installed screen door. Dee slipped through the gate and took a seat on the top step.

Mama's sad again, Dee said.

Oh? Sassy replied.

Do you think another baby died in her tummy?

Perhaps.

Can you please go and see?

It's not a good idea, little one.

I miss talking to you.

And I you.

It scared Mama when I told her what you said.

People fear what they don't understand.

How come no one else but me can talk to you?

Because you're an Orphic.

I don't know what that word means.

It is you, little one. It is what you are.

I'm an Orphic?

Yes.

The front door opened, and Miss Adeline stepped outside.

"Dee, sweetie, your Mama doesn't want you playing with Sassy. You'd better get on home."

"Yes, ma'am," Dee said.

Miss Adeline smiled sadly and shut the door.

I'd better go, Dee said.

Yes. You'd better, Sassy replied.

She waited for the cat to say something else, something comforting perhaps. When it didn't, Dee rose from the porch and went back home.

32

Revier, Ravensbruck Concentration Camp; March 1945

The pain radiating from Dee's broken ribs brought her out of her memory dream. No longer in the *prugelstrafe*, she lay flat on her back in a bed. She raised her head and peered down at her body. She was in her prison uniform, which was damp from hose water. Her vision swam, and she fell back on the thin, straw-filled pillow, getting her bearings.

The sound of someone weeping made her turn her head. A teenager the next bed over gripped her thigh, her skin gray and sweaty, head freshly shaved. Her left calf was wrapped in thick gauze soaked with dark blood. Dee smelled the rotting flesh beneath the bandage from five feet away.

The teenager dug her fingernails into her calf and cried out in Polish.

"Doctor! I need a doctor for God's sake!"

Dee reached across the aisle. "Here," she said. "Take my hand."

The girl grabbed it and burst into tears.

"Squeeze," Dee said, gripping her hand to indicate she

should do the same. "There you go. Good. I don't speak Polish. *Nie Polsku.* I'm sorry."

The girl screamed in agony.

"She needs a doctor!" Dee exclaimed in German.

Bed frames squeaked as the two dozen women in the *revier* sat up to look at the source of the shouting.

"A doctor! Now!"

The Polish teenager wailed. Dee let her hand go and reached up the metal headboard; she grasped the edge and pulled herself up to sitting. White-hot pain washed over her splintered ribs. Dee gritted her teeth and threw her legs over the side of the bed.

Women incapacitated with disease or starvation could only stare as Dee got to her feet, nearly collapsing. She caught herself on the mattress and hobbled to the door.

"We need a doctor in here!" she bellowed into the camp's streets, her smashed ribs flaring.

"The doctor is here," Voss said behind her.

Dr. Voss was dressed in his black suit as before, only now he wore a white coat. A large syringe was perched in his right hand, the sharp tip dripping with some unknown substance.

"Shut the door, please," he said. "You're letting in the cold."

Dee did so.

"Your tolerance for pain is extraordinary, truly," he said. "Three of your ribs are broken, you know."

"She needs help," Dee said, indicating the Polish girl writhing in agony. "You can't just let her suffer like that."

Dr. Voss raised the syringe. "Help is here, fraulein," he said, expressionless. "Now please lie down before you fall down."

Dee staggered back to her mattress and fell into it.

"Now," Voss continued, turning to the young woman, "let us see what the problem is."

Voss set the syringe on a small table between their beds. The Polish teenager appeared terrified of the doctor, shrinking back into her pillow as he stepped toward her.

"Here," said Dee, again extending her hand. She took it.

Voss unwrapped the gauze bandage. When he revealed what was underneath, Dee sucked in her breath.

A ten-inch incision had been cut into her flesh. What appeared to be broken glass jutted out of the wound. Gangrene had clearly set in, the air now thick with its odor.

Voss placed oval spectacles on the end of his nose and peered at the injury. He pressed his finger into a piece of glass, and the girl shrieked.

"What are you doing?" Dee said.

"Examining my patient," Voss replied.

"You're hurting her," Dee said.

Ignoring this, Voss retrieved a syringe from the table.

"She will hurt no more," he said.

The Polish girl let out a blood-curdling scream as Voss brought the needle to her thigh.

"It's okay," Dee said, squeezing her hand, wishing more than anything that she also had learned to speak Polish. Boleslaw Prus's *The Doll* had been on her reading list at the Marietta Library, but she hadn't gotten to it before her deployment.

The teenager shrieked again when Voss inserted the needle just above the wound and depressed the plunger.

"There," he said, withdrawing it, and peered over his glasses at Dee. "No more pain, fraulein. Just as you have asked. Good?"

She was no longer screaming, dazed as she sank back into her pillow.

"Just as you have asked," Voss repeated in English, bowing at the waist. "No more pain."

He placed the syringe in his coat pocket and strode across the room, out through a middle door that led to another part of the *revier*.

"Now she will sleep with Jesus," a woman said in French. Dee turned to an old woman in the next bed over.

"What?" Dee asked in French. "What did you say?"

"I said now she will sleep with Jesus," the woman repeated. "As I will soon. As we all will."

The Polish teenager's grip on Dee's hand went slack and her arm fell, dangling above the floor. Her lips parted, and her last breath rattled in her sunken chest.

Dee turned back to the French woman, who stared at her with light-blue eyes hazy with cataracts.

"You're going to die here, child," she said softly.

33

Red Triangle Barracks, Ravensbruck Concentration Camp; March 1945

Dee folded the deceased Polish girl's hands together, interlocking the fingers. She then brought the sheet over her body and face, giving the hideous wound on her leg one last look. No effort had been made to remove the jagged pieces of glass jammed into the incision.

Just past midnight, a German nurse in a light-brown uniform appeared, casting disinterested glances over the patients in her charge. When she found Dee sitting vigil next to the Polish woman's corpse, she clapped sharply.

"You are not sick anymore. Away you go."

Two Romani girls on work detail led Dee down the camp's streets. The red triangle sewn onto her uniform meant a specific housing assignment, which they approached in the frigid night air. They pushed her toward the door and ran back through the snow, breath steaming around their shaved heads.

Dee opened it to discover a room crowded with women

also wearing red triangles, huddling together for warmth in the low light.

"Dee," a familiar voice said. It was Elsa.

Dee walked down the cramped aisle toward her, three tiered bunks on either side.

"They said you were going to be in here with us," Elsa said, smiling. "Here."

The German gestured to an empty bunk. Dee slid her feet out of her clogs and lay down it.

"Straw," Dee said. "Not feathers."

Elsa lay in the bunk across from her, leaning on an elbow and genuinely excited for the company. "Where did they take you?" she asked Dee.

"Oh, here and there," Dee answered, gently pressing her ribs. "Ended up in what they consider to be a hospital in this place."

"The *revier*," Elsa said, eyes widening. She checked over her shoulder to ensure no one was listening. "Did you see the rabbits?"

Dee considered this for a moment. No, she hadn't seen any rabbits. The only animals she had seen since her arrival were the German shepherds, pulling at their leashes and growling at everyone not in a Nazi uniform.

"No," Dee said. "Why would they keep rabbits in a hospital?"

"Not *really* rabbits, darling," Elsa said. "That's just what they call them. Polish girls. Barely teenagers."

"With glass in their leg," Dee said, suddenly understanding.

Elsa leaned in, her mouth hanging open.

"Is that what you saw?" she whispered.

"They're inflicting the wounds intentionally, aren't they?" Dee asked. "The glass. The cuts."

"That's why they call them rabbits," Elsa said. "That Nazi does all sorts of experiments on them. So I've heard anyway."

"It's true. I saw it myself." Dee tugged at the red triangle on her shirt. "What does this mean?"

"We are enemies of the state." Elsa shrugged. "Political prisoners. That's what that *P* is for."

Dee angled the triangle into the light. A black *P* had in fact been stitched into it. She hadn't noticed it until just then.

"I'm a whore who spreads disease to German soldiers. Those women over there are Soviets. Well, wives and daughters anyway. Red Army."

Dee followed Elsa's finger to a group of Russian women clustered on the other side of the bunkhouse, whispering intently.

"Those Polish girls over there were part of their country's resistance; same with those French girls over there. Austrian communists sleep across from them, Germans the next beds over. They all stick together. Common struggles."

Dee took in the room. The bone-thin women stacked three bunks high murmured, wrapped in dirty blankets and scarves and, in some cases, hay bundled together with string. Hanna, the girl who had given Dee her first bowl of soup, sat with her Polish sisters.

"The gypsies and Jews are one barracks over. The crazies get their own, though the criminals get lumped in with them sometimes too. There's screaming like you wouldn't believe out of that place, especially at night."

Dee eased herself to sitting and pulled her feet up. Her frostbitten toes didn't look much better than they had, but they didn't look much worse either.

The door flew open, and a stout woman with a thick

unibrow and a green triangle on her prison dress marched in, banging a wooden ladle inside an empty metal soup pot.

"Lights out. Lights out. Lights out," she commanded in accented English.

"Who's that?" Dee asked.

"Our *blockova*," Elsa said. "Name's Gustel. She's okay. Better than some, worse than others."

"And what does a *blockova* do?" Dee asked.

"She's in charge," Elsa replied. "Like a babysitter. Lights out, wake up, clean up, you know. They get sausages for dinner."

Gustel walked the rows of bunks, tapping the ladle on the pot, inspecting her charges. When she got to Dee, she stopped. She stared at Dee with eyes that lunged inward toward the bridge of a wide pockmarked nose, and Dee stared back. This went on for a moment until Gustel spoke first.

"You are American?" Gustel asked in English.

"Yes," Dee answered.

"I like Fred *Ah...stare*," she said, and shuffled her feet.

"Sure," Dee said.

"That how you say?"

"Fred Astaire," Dee replied.

"He...*swings*," Gustel continued, and then dropped the ladle in the pot. "Lights out!" she shouted.

Dee and Elsa lay back on their mattresses. Dee shifted until she found a position that made her mending ribs somewhat more comfortable.

The flickering light bulbs went dark, and the whispering died down until it was barely audible.

After a few minutes of silence, a woman started to cry, then another, and then another.

Dee stared into the darkness, listening to the women cry themselves to sleep.

We have to get out of here, she thought.

———

The siren woke them before dawn.

"*Appell! Appell! Appell!*"

The light bulbs switched on, and Gustel stalked up and down the rows, banging her drum.

"Let's go, let's go! *Appell! Appell! Appell!*"

"Her and that fucking soup pot," Elsa said, squaring the blanket under her pillow and smoothing the bedsheet down. "Make your bed," she told Dee. "Quickly."

Ribs aching, Dee rolled out of bed. She slipped on her clogs, pleased to see the swelling in her feet going down.

She remembered her boot camp training and made the bed accordingly. It lacked sheets and a pillowcase, but otherwise everything was right angles and hospital corners by the time Gustel arrived at her bunk for inspection.

"Yes, yes, yes, good," she said in English as she strolled by, stopping short at Elsa's.

"Smooth down your pillow, fat cow!" Gustel commanded in German. Elsa spun around and did as told.

"Don't hold me up again, whore, or I'll smack your fat ass," Gustel continued, waving her ladle. Once the room was reviewed to her standards she again beat the pot.

"*Appell! Appell! Appell!*"

Those who could run ran for the door, the rest limping or being helped by another less-infirm woman. Dee pulled her jacket tight as the morning winter wind rushed into her face, freezing the fluid in her eyes and making the camp appear as if underwater.

"*Appel! Appel! Appel!*"

Dogs barked and snapped as the women formed into their columns, the black-caped blondes back for yet another morning's count. Dee and Elsa lined up shoulder to shoulder, as did thousands of others across the *appellplatz*.

They stood in silence for the next two hours while the guards did their count, prisoners' teeth chattering, limbs shivering. As the third hour approached, Botz emerged, walking the line with a riding crop clutched in her gloved hand.

"That's *Oberaufseherin* Botz," Elsa whispered. "Watch out for her. They call her the Hyena. She's a monster."

"Oh, we've met," Dee said.

Botz stalked her way down the line, scrutinizing the women up and down. When she got to one bent over at the waist, barely standing, she halted.

"Straighten up," Botz snapped.

The prisoner next to the bent woman offered a hand to help. Botz slapped it with her riding crop.

"I said straighten up! *Schnell!*"

The bent woman couldn't do anything but sway from side to side. Botz kicked her in the shin, and she folded in half, hitting the frozen ground head first.

"Up!" Botz commanded, kicking her in the back. "Up, up, up, you useless mouth!" Botz kicked her again.

Dee stepped out of line. "Do it to me," she said.

Botz's face shot up. Her blue eyes widened at the sight of Dee standing apart from the rest.

"What did you say?" Botz asked, stunned.

"I said come over here and do it to me," Dee repeated. "Not her."

"Dee," Elsa whispered. "What in God's name are you doing?"

Botz glared at Dee. She tucked her riding crop under her arm and stalked over, her skin turning as red as her lipstick. When she was within a few feet, she cocked her arm for a backhanded strike across Dee's face and swung.

Dee caught Botz's wrist midair and gripped it tight. Thousands of women lined up on the *appellplatz* collectively inhaled at the sight of it.

Botz's mouth fell open and fear flashed across her face.

"You want to beat on someone, fraulein? Beat on *me*," Dee said. "For all the good it will do you."

Now pale, Botz wrenched her arm free from Dee's grip. Another guard approached, a stocky woman with a severe blond bob. Her German shepherd pulled on its leash, terrorizing the women as they walked down the line.

"*Frau Oberaufseherin?* What seems to be the trouble?"

Botz pointed at Dee, her hand trembling. "That one," she said. "She attacked me."

The blond bob turned from Botz to Dee, a woman half her commanding officer's size. She chose her next words as tactfully as possible.

"*Frau Oberaufseherin,* the morning count is completed," the guard said. "May we commence with work details?"

Botz came back to herself, scanning the *appellplatz,* color returning to her cheeks. Every guard and prisoner was staring at her.

"She attacked me," she said louder, marching back up the line. She tripped, stumbling over her jackboots in the snow, and disappeared among the rows of women.

"Enough nonsense," the blond bob said loud enough for all to hear. "Get to work. *Schnell!*"

34

Camp Streets, Ravensbruck Concentration Camp; March 1945

"I can't believe you did that," Elsa said. She and Dee shuffled out of the *appellplatz* behind hundreds of other blue-striped uniforms. "You're going to get yourself killed, my American friend."

"And so will you, if you stay here," Dee replied. "We all will."

"See that?" Elsa said, indicating the walls. There weren't just fingers in the electrified wire this time but a corpse. The skin was purple with lividity, the striped uniform burned to a crisp. It hung there, stiff in the cold.

"They leave them like that to show what happens if you try and escape," Elsa continued. "Many have tried. Two years ago we had an acrobat. A gypsy. She jumped over the wall like a gazelle, so they say. But they caught her. When she got back, they beat her to death with a chair."

"So what then?" Dee said. "We just sit and wait to die?"

"We sit and wait for the Allies," Elsa said. "They say the Russians are closing in from the east, the Americans from the west. Be here any day now. One way or another, they will come eventually."

Rescue meant the end of the war, which meant Hitler being captured or killed. Dee was running out of time.

She glanced up at the sky, shading her eyes against the harsh winter light.

"There are no birds here," she said. "I haven't heard or seen a single one."

"That's because we ate them," Elsa said. "Those we managed to catch. The ones that got away told their little friends, and they won't come here anymore. Won't even get close."

Dee lowered her gaze to the woman trudging ahead of her, the bones in her spine jutting from the skin.

"I'm not kidding," Elsa said.

"I believe you," Dee replied.

The prisoners were led past a large soup pot, steam rising off the top. Small ceramic cups were produced from uniform pockets, a ladleful of liquid unceremoniously dribbled inside each one by a kitchen worker wearing a green triangle.

"What's that?" Dee asked.

"Breakfast," Elsa said.

"I lost my cup," Dee said.

Elsa handed hers over.

"I couldn't," Dee said.

Elsa put a finger to her lips and produced a second cup from the pocket of her uniform dress. "I'm fat enough that they can't tell what I have in my pockets," she said.

Dee took the cup gratefully and looked back to the bony woman in front of her.

"You wonder how I maintain such a voluptuous physique," Elsa said, reading her mind.

"It had occurred to me," Dee replied.

"Well, you see, on the outside of these walls, I sucked dick in exchange for money," Elsa continued. "In here, I eat pussy for sausage and bread."

She placed her fingers in a *V* around her lips, waggled her tongue through them, and cackled.

They got to the front of the line, and Dee accepted her ration. She drank it while it was still warm, the potato skins and sour cabbage sliding down her throat.

"Sausage is better," Elsa said, peering into the cup.

"I like beans," Dee said. "Ever come across those?"

"I haven't," Elsa said, swallowing with a grimace. "But if I do, you'll be the first to know."

A great stone cylinder lay ahead. It reminded Dee of one of her Mama's rolling pins, only about a thousand times larger. A long metal yoke was attached to either end.

"What's that?" Dee asked.

"Maybe you'll never find out," Elsa said.

Women wearing green triangles gestured toward the road roller and shouted orders in Romany to Dee and Elsa.

Elsa sighed. "Or maybe you will."

A dozen other women picked up an end of one of the ropes or yokes attached to it, so Dee did the same.

The Romani hollered another word Dee didn't understand, and the women pulled, clogs sliding in the snow as they struggled to gain traction. The Romani barked orders, and the women put their backs into it, groaning with effort.

Dee labored with the others, the roller turning in fits and starts along the street.

"Where are we taking this?" Dee asked, ignoring the pain radiating from her ribs and feet.

"That way," Elsa said, winded. "Then back again."

A stout woman in a blue headscarf pulled a rope next to Dee, her face creased with grim determination. Dee recognized her from the group of Soviets in her bunkhouse.

"Good morning," Dee said. The woman appeared surprised to be addressed in Russian.

"Good morning," she answered.

"I'm Damienne. But folks call me Dee. What's your name?"

"Tatiana," the woman said. "But I am called Tati."

"Nice to meet you, Tati."

"And you."

The black-caped blondes strolled about the grounds, German shepherds on their heels. The animals' long pink tongues dangled from their maws as they glared at the women pulling the road roller. Every time Dee made eye contact with one they just turned away, tails wagging, waiting for the order to bite someone.

Can you hear me? Dee asked.

Nothing.

There were still fifty plus yards to go to the end of the road. The rope burned against Dee's palm and shoulder, cutting into the flesh through the thin fabric of her prison uniform. She cast her eyes from the road up to the giant chimney outside the camp walls. The perpetual flames shot up out of its top, dark smoke wafting with the slight breeze.

Gunfire crackled somewhere, and Tati mumbled in Russian.

"What did you say?" Dee asked.

"I said, 'God rest their souls,'" Tati repeated.

"Whose souls?"

"The souls of whoever among us they just shot."

They pulled the stone roller for another half hour, managing only inches a minute. The Romani called out an order, and the women stopped, bending over and grabbing their knees, breathless.

Dee allowed the cold air to dry the sweat running down her face. Now she was almost directly underneath the chimney. She stared up at it, at the unceasing plume of smoke above the orange flames.

The Romani with the green triangle clapped, and the women again picked up their ropes.

Now they rolled it across the *appellplatz*, toward the stone building that housed the camp's offices, the building Dee had been forced to stand in front of all night, barefoot.

Botz was on the top step, a steaming mug of coffee in hand. She sipped it, her unblinking blue-eyed stare never straying from Dee as the women passed.

35

Hauptsturmführer Glockner's Office, Ravensbruck Concentration Camp; March 1945

They dragged the road roller until the sun sat straight overhead, dim and offering no warmth. Elsa appeared ill.

"Are you okay?" Dee asked.

Elsa shook her head; there was a deep red groove across her neck and chest where the rope had lain.

"Just breathe," Dee said. "Nice and slow."

Elsa attempted to catch her breath. Tati approached. "She isn't used to such labor," Tati said. "I grew up on a farm. After my father died, Mother and I pulled the plow."

Tati took Elsa under one arm, Dee the other. They walked her back toward the bunkhouse, Elsa wheezing.

"That was quite a thing you did this morning," Tati said.

"What thing?" Dee asked.

"'What thing?' she says," Tati scoffed. "Grabbing Botz like that. You have guts, *Amerikanskiy*. Guts I like."

"What about you?" Dee asked. "Elsa here tells me you're Red Army. Makes us Allies."

"I fight for Mother Russia, it is true," Tati replied. "Here I have no gun, so *dignity* becomes my weapon. Strength of mind. This they can never take from you. Not unless you give it to them. I am not giving it to them."

They kept on, Elsa's considerable girth made more significant after a half day of pulling a thousand-pound rock back and forth across the camp. The German went in and out of consciousness, stumbling in her clogs.

"Perhaps we take her to the *revier*," Tati offered.

"No," Dee said. "That's no kind of hospital."

They rounded a corner, their bunkhouse now in sight.

"Those gunshots," Dee said. "Who were they killing? Do you know?"

"Jews," Tati replied.

"Why?" Dee asked. "What did they do?"

"They were born Jews," Tati said simply.

They finally arrived, carrying Elsa to her bed and heaving her onto the mattress. She was breathing normally now but unconscious, her eyelids fluttering.

"She won't survive such work," Tati said. "Her heart will give out."

Women sat around the bunkhouse, sipping the midday rations out of cups perched in bony fingers. Tati motioned for Dee to follow her to a quiet corner.

"We've a smuggled radio," Tati whispered. "The Americans aren't far, but my people will be here first. The thing now is to *survive*. Survive until they get here. No more shenanigans like this morning, eh? Do what they say. Resistance is admirable. We resisted when we first got here, like you. And we suffered, like you. But that was then. Now is the time to stay alive."

Dee checked over her shoulder to make sure no one was eavesdropping.

"Tati, I have to get out of here. Soon."

"The only way out is over the wall," Tati said. "You have seen the bodies hanging there, twisting in the wind like chimes, yes? That will be *you* if you try to escape."

"I have to get to Berlin," Dee said. "Before the war is over."

"Berlin? Why?"

"To do what I came here to do," Dee said. "Or this will all have been for nothing. You're Red Army. Don't tell me your people haven't thought about it. Or tried."

Now Tati glanced over her shoulder. "Of course we thought about it. Of course we tried," she whispered. "But I tell you it is impossible. So we smuggle. Coded messages in letters. The Polish rabbits are very talented at this as well."

"Letters?" Dee asked. "What letters?"

"You can write a letter home," Tati said. "They say they will deliver it. Whether they do or not, who can say? But it is something. They censor everything of course. It can only say you are being treated well and are in good health. But we write between the lines."

"How?" Dee asked.

Blushing, Tati leaned in to Dee's ear, whispering in such a way she barely heard the Russian word for "urine."

"Invisible ink," Dee said. This brought a gap-toothed grin to Tati's face.

"Attica!"

Gustel's girth shadowed the doorway into the bunkhouse. "*Hauptsturmführer* wants to see you," she said. "Come at once."

Dee followed the *blockova* across the camp. A line of two hundred women streamed through the gates, covered head to toe in grime, muddy shovels over their shoulders like infantry soldiers returning from battle.

Through the gates, Dee thought. *They work outside the walls.*

Gustel led Dee inside the office building, her body warm for only the second time since her arrival. She was made to stand and wait in the hallway outside the *hauptsturmführer*'s office. After nearly an hour, she was summoned inside.

"Enter."

Glockner was seated, a dead crow on his desk.

"Sit."

Dee sat in the stuffed leather chair. It felt wonderful. She had always taken sitting on cushioned furniture for granted. Never again.

Glockner picked the stiff crow up from the desk by its feet and gazed at it admiringly. "Found it in my backyard," he said. "Poor creature. Magnificent specimen, though."

Dee recalled Elsa's tale of prisoners eating the camp birds out of desperation and wondered what kinds of conversations she might have had with them, given the chance.

Glockner set the crow aside. "And how are you faring, post-interrogation?"

"As you see," Dee said.

"I think you have broken some ribs," Glockner said.

"You would know," Dee replied. "You broke them."

Glockner sat back in his chair, eyes on the ceiling. He stayed like that for a while, as if replaying the events in the *strafeblock* in his mind.

"Yes," he finally said, sitting forward. "Indeed. Most unpleasant, yes? And now you know the difference between an *interrogation* and a *discussion*. Isn't the latter infinitely more preferable? I certainly think so. What do you think?"

Dee said nothing.

"See, this is our problem," Glockner continued. "When I ask a question, I expect an answer. That's how a discussion works."

"All right," Dee said, crossing one leg over the other. "How about you tell me about that chimney?"

Appearing befuddled, Glockner spun around in his chair. "Ah," he said, gesturing to the stone structure across the camp. "What about it?"

"What's burning inside it?"

"Trash."

"Trash."

"Yes."

A silence. Dee stared at the statue of the German shepherd by the globe bar. Its bronze eyes stared back at her, as blank and incommunicative as the real ones lurking about the camp outside.

"Now it's my turn to ask a question, yes?" Glockner said.

Dee said nothing.

"It's the same question I asked when first we met, so perhaps you've had an opportunity to think about it some more. And that question is 'Why are you in Germany, and how did you get here?'"

A knock came at the door.

"Come in," he said, irritated at the interruption.

A young prisoner girl walked in, head bowed, carrying a plate of sausage and bread. Glockner opened his drawer and removed a silver fork and a long, curved knife on a wooden handle.

"*Ja, gut,*" he said as she set the plate down. The girl curt-

sied and all but ran from the room, shutting the door
behind her.

Glockner tucked into his meal, slicing off a hunk of
sausage and cramming it into his mouth. He chewed loudly,
lips smacking.

"*Wurst*?" he asked.

"Sorry?" Dee replied.

"I said," Glockner repeated, sawing off another slice,
"would you like some *wurst*?"

"No," Dee said. "I don't eat meat."

"Neither does *der Führer*," Glockner said, chewing. "Of
course, he's a better man than I."

Glockner stuffed Dee's portion into his maw, working it
down into a swallow. When he finally did, he dabbed his
lips with the cloth napkin the prisoner girl had provided
and set the dish aside.

"It's best when hot," he said. "Now please answer the
question."

Dee uncrossed her legs and let out a sigh. "All right," she
said.

Glockner sat forward, anticipating her response.

"I got into Germany by airplane," Dee said. "I assume
you figured as much, seeing as how I was caught hanging
from my parachute in a tree."

"When you bit off that officer's nose," Glockner said, "it
was all any of us could talk about when we heard. They
thought you were dead when they put you on that train."

"Why would they put me on a train?" Dee asked. "Why
not just leave me there?"

Glockner was chewing on another piece of sausage. He
held up a finger indicating he wished to finish before
answering. "Because," he said, wiping his mouth, "we were
going to cut off your head and present it as a gift to *Reichs-*

führer Himmler. An American woman soldier's shrunken head would have been quite the trophy. But here you are. So...you jumped out of a plane. Understood. Now tell me *why* you are in Germany."

"To find Adolph Hitler and execute him," Dee replied.

Glockner chuckled. "I see. You're an assassin."

Assassin. Dee had never thought of it like that before.

"Yes," she said. "I suppose I am."

"The Americans sent a little girl to kill *der Führer*," Glockner said. "Extraordinary."

"No, they sent me to work a switchboard," Dee said. "I'm here on my own."

Glockner shook his head. "As absolutely absurd as your story sounds, I must say I believe you."

"You should believe me. I'm telling you the truth."

"And now that I know this truth, what is to stop me from taking you outside and putting a bullet in your head?" he asked.

"Nothing," Dee replied.

"Why would I allow a person so determined to end *der Führer's* life continue to breathe air?"

"You shouldn't," Dee said. "It's probably your duty to kill me."

Glockner picked up his fork, slid his last hunk of sausage around his plate, and popped it in his mouth, again chewing as he spoke.

"If I thought for a moment there was the slightest chance you might so much as *touch* our great leader, you'd already be dead," he said. "But of course the notion is absurd. Beyond absurd. No, you are alive because you might be *useful*. There are German prisoners, men whose lives are a thousand times more valuable than yours, with whom we might use you to trade."

Glockner slid his plate across the desk.

"You made me laugh. Have some bread."

Dee took the quarter loaf of fresh baked bread off the china and stuffed it into her dress pocket.

"I look forward to our next *discussion*," he said.

Dee opened the office door. She was about to walk out when she turned back to Glockner.

"You're an intelligent man, in your way," she said. "Intelligent enough to know the war for Germany is already lost. The Russians are coming, I hear."

Glockner's face fell. Dee closed the door behind her.

———

Elsa was still unconscious when Dee returned to the bunkhouse, so she walked the aisles, searching for someone who could benefit from the bread off Glockner's plate. It didn't take long.

Hanna lay curled on her mattress, bony arms folded across her chest, staring at the bottom of the bunk above her head. Dee knelt at her side.

"Hi, Hanna," she said.

The girl brightened.

"Bread," Dee said, bringing it from her pocket. "I have bread."

She brought it out of her pocket, and Hanna sat upright, unable to believe what she was seeing.

Dee tore off a piece. She pressed it into Hanna's palm, and the girl took a bite. She chewed, swallowed, then wept, falling into Dee's arms.

Dee held her tightly, Hanna sobbing into her neck.

"*Shhh, shhh, shhh,*" Dee whispered.

"Her sister was one of the rabbits," Tati said from across

the room, sitting with the other Russians. "She went to the *revier* and never came back."

Dee remembered the teenager with glass in her leg, dying in her bed. Now she saw the resemblance.

The girl shouted in Polish, gripping Dee's neck so tightly she was choking her.

"She says don't leave," Tati said. "Please don't leave me."

"I won't," Dee said, and picked Hanna up, shocked at how little she weighed.

Dee sat back on the mattress, cradling her. The girl's eyes grew heavy then closed.

Dee rocked her gently. She caught Tati's eye, and the women smiled at each other.

"I didn't know you spoke Polish," Dee said.

"Three years in this place, you learn a little," Tati replied.

The sun was setting. Dee leaned back onto the straw mattress, never loosening her grip on Hanna. Soon they both were asleep.

36

The Isle of Kasos, Greece; The Month of Pyanepsion 434 BC

Damien awoke on the island surrounded by curious children, their faces and bodies pocked with rot. The little girl with no face knelt and placed a stubby-fingered hand on his.

"What's your name?" she asked.

"Damien," he whispered.

"Where did you come from?"

Damien tried to swallow. No saliva came forth.

"I only ask because the great ship hasn't yet come," she said.

Damien summoned his courage and reopened his eyes. "What's yours?" he asked.

"Clio," she replied.

"Water, Clio. I beg you."

"You don't have to beg," Clio said, standing.

She gestured to a boy whose ears and nose were black nubs. He ran from the circle.

The children reached down, took Damien by his arms

and legs, and lifted him onto their shoulders. They carried him across the rocks, toward the huts cobbled together from olive trees and driftwood that littered the center of the island.

They brought him inside and laid him on a bed made of palm fronds. The boy missing his ears and nose hurried over with a gourd of water and pressed the mouth to Damien's swollen lips.

Damien drank greedily, burping as his empty stomach took in the warm liquid. The boy pulled it away. Damien twisted his head and vomited, the children cradling his head as the gourd was again put to his mouth. He drank slower this time, his eyes fluttering as he passed out.

He awoke two days later, alone. A basket made of woven seaweed filled with olives had been placed by his bed. Damien greedily shoveled the food into his mouth, picking the pits from between his lips and dropping them into his lap, staining his white smock purple.

A figure shadowed his doorway. Clio walked a few steps inside. "Damien? Are you awake?" she whispered.

"I am," Damien replied, knees drawn to his chest.

"Did you sleep well?"

"Yes," Damien said. "Thank you, Clio."

"Your accent. Where is it from?"

"I'm from Attica."

"Attica? What are you doing here? Are you sick?"

"Sick? No."

"Then why are you here?"

"I...was shipwrecked," Damien said.

Clio's featureless face wrinkled with worry. "You weren't on the *great* ship, were you?"

"Great ship? No. I don't think so."

Clio's shoulders dropped in relief. "Thank the Gods," she said.

"What is the great ship? What is this place?"

"This is Kasos, of course," Clio replied. "I thought everyone knew of us."

"No," Damien said. "I don't anyway. What happened to you? Why are you here?"

"I am here because I am Rotting," she said. "I have been afflicted by the Blackness. The great ship brings us food and wool and wine. So we can live here and not infect the others."

"Wine?" Damien asked.

"Oh, yes. We have all the wine we can drink. Would you like some?"

"Very much," Damien said, trying to appear casual.

Clio laughed. "Come," she said, offering her fingerless hand.

Damien took it, allowing Clio to take him into the sunshine. The island sand glowed in the scorching midday sun, and the girl led him across it, the soles of his feet burning with each step.

Hours later Damien was staggering along the beach, his second krater of wine dangling from his hand. The other children had drunk much more and now scampered along the water's edge. He hadn't eaten a proper meal in some time and it had all gone straight to his head. His fear had vanished, as had his discomfort with the children's appearance.

All was well.

The boy without ears or a nose lingered back from the group so Damien could catch up to him.

"Paris is my name," the boy said. "How do you feel, Damien of Attica?"

"Warm," Damien said, drunk. "Thank you."

"You're very welcome," Paris said, laughing. He ran ahead, and Damien followed. He tripped over his feet and fell into the wet sand.

The children down the shoreline appeared a blur, laughter dimming in Damien's ears. He wobbled after them.

Paris picked up a smooth stone and skipped it across the waves.

"I like it here," Damien said.

"And we like you, Damien of Attica," Paris replied. "Perhaps you'll stay."

"One, two, three...*not it!*" a boy cried, racing down the shoreline. The other children screamed and ran after him. Too shy to join, Damien lagged behind.

"Come on!" Clio called, waving an arm.

Damien ran toward them, surprised at their speed. They played until the sun sank into the sea, building a campfire in the sand and passing a jug of wine. Eventually they fell into drunken sleep, Damien warmed by new friendship and the fire.

He awoke the next morning to a meal of roasted fish, Paris cooking his catch over the glowing embers. They spent another day playing and drinking wine; Damien experienced a peace he had never known before.

Soon his days became his nights and the nights his days.

The weeks passed, then the months, and before Damien had given it much thought, a year.

He would leave Kasos eventually. Until then there was always another game to be played with his new friends, and one more cup of wine.

37

Village Road; March 1945

As she awoke, Dee was convinced she was still on the Isle of Kasos. Damp and heavy, the frigid cold brought her back to reality and settled deep into her bones. She had dreamed about the boy again. Each dream felt more real than the last.

Hanna slept at her side, curled into a ball, her face buried in Dee's blue-and-white-striped dress. It was still dark outside.

"Appell! Appell! Appell!"

The sirens blared, and Gustel burst through the door, banging her ladle against the pot.

"Up, up, up! Up, up, up! Make your beds! Quickly, quickly!"

Hanna awoke with a jolt.

"It's okay," Dee whispered in her ear, knowing she didn't understand the English. "I'm here."

Gustel's sausage breath signaled her presence. The *blockova* stared at them curiously.

"She is sweet on you," Gustel said with a grin, a bit of meat stuck between her gray front teeth. "How nice."

She waited a moment for Dee to say something. When she didn't, she moved on, rousing the bunkhouse's exhausted denizens with her ceaseless drumming.

"Appell! Appell! Appell!"

Dee made her bed and then the next, helping other women too weak to move quickly enough for morning drills. Elsa was up, worse for wear but still alive. She and Dee fell into line, hustling out the door onto the frigid *appellplatz* with the others.

Ravensbruck's population seemed to be increasing by the day, if not the hour. It appeared to Dee's eyes there were a thousand more women standing at attention than the previous morning. These new arrivals learned the daily routine as everyone else had: riding crops slapped across their face, German shepherds snapping at their arms and legs. Screams of terror echoed across the field as the morning count got underway.

The sun rose, and it was still another hour before the count was complete. Then the work lines formed, frozen breath streaming from nostrils as the women lumbered along in multitudes.

Dee stood at attention while a male Nazi guard walked the rows in her section of the *appelplatz*, scrutinizing their physical condition for whatever punishing manual labor lay in store that day. When he came upon any woman not bent over with illness or fever, he pointed to them, and then a wrought iron gate across the field. Those women dutifully half ran, half walked to the gate, where they lined up and waited to receive further orders.

The guard chose several more women, including Dee and Hanna. A half hour later they were in a work detail, shovels over their shoulders like soldiers presenting arms, marching in formation into the woods surrounding Ravensbruck.

The smell of burning paper wafted among the tree branches as they marched, white smoke hovering in the dewy morning air. Hanna tugged on Dee's dress, and she gave the girl a shrug.

A strong gust sent the smoke tumbling away from them, along with the muddy ground's dead winter leaves. The clearer air revealed a meadow up ahead and, to the women's collective astonishment, a lake, crystal blue and beautiful. Nestled in the green valley, it appeared like a mirage or a painting created by one of Europe's masters, hanging in a museum. Several of the prisoners gasped at the sight of it.

A surreal bit of business was playing itself out along the lake's muddy bank. Uniformed Nazis milled about rows of metal filing cabinets, the drawers open, white papers in yellow filing folders fluttering in the breeze coming off the water. It was as if the walls of a large office building simply had vanished, leaving the clerical workers within exposed to the elements.

Empty oil barrels had been placed every twenty feet or so. Flames shot up from each drum, the fires fed by the paperwork being tossed inside by the Nazis. Soldiers licked their index fingers and flipped through stacks of dossiers, communiqués, maps, and clasped manila envelopes marked "*Streng Geheim*" ("Top Secret"). Occasionally a burning piece of paper escaped a barrel, carried by the wind, and traveled to the middle of the lake, alighting onto the still, blue water. Tiny ripples formed as the flames extinguished, the blackened paper sinking into the depths.

"Eyes front!" the guard leading the work detail shouted, and the women immediately turned their heads back toward him.

Twenty minutes later they were on the other side of the lake, cresting a hill and setting eyes on the labor that would occupy them for the rest of the day: a potholed road, leading from the camp and into the adjoining town, a place where German civilians went about their quiet village lives, a million miles away from the concentration camp in their own backyard.

Their orders were simple: shovel gravel from the two-ton pile on the road's shoulder, then drop the gravel into a pothole, then repeat. If a woman stopped to catch her breath, she got a verbal warning. The second time she got a whip across her back. No one stopped a third time.

Dee went about her work, keeping an eye on Hanna. Less was expected of the younger girls, but they still had to keep moving. The Polish child limped along, her shovel barely a third full of the gray pebbles, her skin pink with exertion. The guards on horseback regularly chugged water from canteens on their saddles, one going so far as to swish and spit a mouthful, his issue barely missing an older woman with a sodden rag around her hand, which was spotted with blood. No such hydrating provisions were made for the prisoners in their charge, however.

After three hours, one of the women fell over unconscious, a common sight and one that went ignored for some time. Eventually a guard guided his horse over to her.

"Up!" he hollered, his nasal German echoing through the quiet forest. "Up, you lazy cunt." The woman didn't move.

The guard sighed and called out to his colleague, also on horseback. "Irma."

"What is it, Werner?" Irma replied.

"This one's not getting up."

"Is she dead?" Irma asked, pulling her blond curls into a ponytail.

Werner shrugged. "You," he said, catching Dee's eye. "Yeah, you. See if she's dead."

Dee dropped her shovel and approached the woman lying in the mud, bone thin and waxen. Her eyelids were fluttering.

"She's alive," Dee said in German.

"She's alive!" Werner called to Irma.

"Well," Irma said, "either beat her ass or send her to the *revier*."

Werner sighed again, cracking his neck. "I'm too hungover to beat anyone today."

Irma laughed. "Because you were up drinking schnapps and playing cards with *Hauptsturmführer* Glockner last night. Did you lose all your money again?"

"Are you crazy or something?" Werner said. "Like I could win a hand against the *hauptsturmführer*."

"Then don't play, idiot," Irma retorted. "Come over to my place tonight. Me and some of the girls are cooking *wurst*."

"And will there be drinks with this *wurst*?" Werner asked.

"Naturally. But you have to bring Ben."

"Why? Will Julie be there?"

"Yes, dummy. Why else would I ask you to bring him?"

The collapsed prisoner started to cough. Dee knelt next to her in the mud.

Werner rolled his eyes from Irma across the road down to Dee. "Take her to the *Revier*, bitch."

Dee scooped up the woman underneath her arms and pulled her a few feet. Then she stopped, making a show of being out of breath.

"Need help," she said in German. "She's too heavy."

"She's thin as a stick," Werner spat. "Fucking hell. *Fine*." He searched the workers for an assistant, but Dee beat him to it.

"You," she said, meaning Hanna. "Help me out here."

Hanna dropped her shovel and ran to Dee.

"If it's all right with you, of course," she asked Werner, who sat high in his saddle.

"I don't care. Just get her the fuck out of here," he said. "And hurry. Take too long and you'll get a smack."

Dee indicated to Hanna that she should pick up the woman by the ankles.

They had just made it to the other side of the hill when the unconscious woman lifted her head.

"I'm okay," she said in German. "Put me down, please."

Dee and Hanna did as she asked, the woman taking their hands and pulling herself upright.

"I just wanted a break is all," she continued. "Sorry for the trouble."

"No trouble," Dee said in German. "Now we have a break too."

The woman dusted off her prison dress. "You are the American, no?" Dee nodded. "I'm Brigitte. A whore, like your friend Elsa," she continued. "She was my madam. Say hello for me if you see her." With that the woman patted Hanna on the head, gave a firm handshake to Dee, and walked back through the grass toward the camp. "Beautiful day," Brigitte called over her shoulder.

Dee returned her attention to the Polish girl at her side. Hanna had a hand clamped over her mouth. She jabbed a finger on her other hand toward the trees. Dee shaded her eyes, peering into the forest.

A doe shaded herself beneath a willow tree, her spotted fawn suckling milk. The mother struggled to maintain her balance as the baby pulled her this way and that, feasting greedily.

"Will you look at that?" Dee whispered.

Hanna pulled Dee toward the animals, careful to make as little sound as possible, wincing when their clogs crunched a leaf or snapped a twig.

"Slowly, Hanna," Dee whispered, knowing full well the only non-Polish word the child understood was her name. "Slowly."

The fawn finished her meal and released its mother. The doe stepped cautiously, her ears twisting to the sounds of the Germans burning their papers at the lakeside nearby. Then they were running into the shadowed woods.

Hanna chased after them; Dee followed.

The doe galloped among the trees while her fawn trotted on its stick-like legs, trying to keep up. When the foliage grew thick enough, they slowed, their brown heads high and alert for further threats.

Dee and Hanna spied all this from a distance, crouched behind a fallen tree, which was mossy from recent rain. Hanna whispered at the deer urgently in Polish, her face illuminated with joy.

It was this face and not the deer that captivated Dee's attention. It reminded her of her own childhood and long afternoons with Sassy, walking with the feline along the sidewalks of her Marietta neighborhood. Saying hello to squirrels darting up willow trees and to rabbits scampering among the vegetable patches, a girl alive and free as the birds above.

But there were no birds here, and Dee and Hanna were not free. When the first gunshot rang out, the bullet splintering a thin oak not ten yards from where they crouched, Dee grabbed Hanna and placed a hand over the girl's mouth to stifle a scream.

38

Forest Outside Ravensbruck; March 1945

The deer bolted, gunfire crackling. Bullets sliced the air above their heads, and Dee fell on top of Hanna, shielding the girl with her body. Two disembodied voices, both male, argued in German.

"Did you get it, asshole?"

"I don't know! Fuck off!"

"Keep shooting, moron!"

More gunfire. Hanna trembled, Dee whispering at her to "be quiet. We'll be okay" in languages the girl didn't speak.

Two Nazi soldiers materialized from within the tree grove, smoking luger pistols extended. "I don't see them," one said. "You couldn't hit the broad side of the barn," said the other. "Fucking help me look then" was the reply.

The sound of his Zippo lighter being flipped open echoed here; such was the quiet. There was the sizzle of a cigarette being lit, one of the soldiers strolling toward Dee's and Hanna's position behind the collapsed oak while his companion chased after their prey.

"Are you coming or what?" the voice demanded from a distance.

"Right behind you, fucker," the other voice replied, now mere feet away.

Hanna twisted in Dee's grip, panicking. She stopped twisting when the German soldier sat on the very piece of fallen timber they lay behind, the back of his *feldgrau-*colored uniform looming above them. He raised himself off the log and broke wind, the smell of his flatulence comingling with the odor of his cigarette.

"Any luck?" he called out.

A forest without animals was the strangest silence. Dee heard not just her own heart pounding but also Hanna's, and was amazed the soldier did not.

He stubbed his cigarette out on the wood then hiked up the slope where the deer had made their escape.

"Hey, asshole! Any luck?"

When he laughed, Dee chanced a glance over the log. His companion had returned, the fawn's corpse wrapped around the back of his neck like a mink stole, the front and back hooves gripped in either hand.

"Well, look at you!" he said. "And what will we do with it, hm? Pick our fucking teeth?"

"Meat is meat," the first one shot back. "You remember the last time you ate venison? I don't."

The second punched the other on the shoulder, and they left the way they came. Only after a full minute's quiet did Dee and Hanna release their grip on each other and stand up from the hiding place.

"Dee?" Hanna asked, followed by a string of Polish words. Dee gleaned her meaning from the concern on the child's face.

"No," she said, shaking her head. "They're fine. They got

away." She mimed two deer with the fingers on either hand, running them off into the trees. Hanna beamed back, relieved.

On the way back to their work detail, Hanna picked wild-flowers, the first from the long winter's last snow. She carefully placed them in her dress pocket, blue cornflowers and white Edelweiss.

Back on the village road, they picked up their shovels and resumed hauling gravel for the rest of the afternoon. Every twenty minutes or so, a woman collapsed, was revived by a fellow laborer, and went back to work. The guards sat on their horses, bored, luger pistols dangling from leather holsters.

Dusk illuminated something interesting sticking out of the dirt by the road's shoulder. After Dee checked to make sure no guards were watching, she plucked it from the dirt and dropped it into her pocket in one quick, deft move. She didn't have time to inspect it too closely but had found a ladies comb, most of the teeth missing, fashioned from wood and painted a light blue. Later she would make a present of it to Hanna.

The guards barked orders, and the women lined up, five in a row, many hunched over from exhaustion. Hanna made sure to secure a spot next to Dee, and the Nazi's slaves marched back to the camp, shovels on their shoulders like a finely tuned regiment.

Hanna burst through the bunkhouse door, her cupped hands full of wildflowers. She pushed her way through the crowded aisles, running them to the Polish corner of the barracks, her countrywomen receiving the forest's bounty with delight. Dee slid her swollen feet out of her clogs and found Tati in the Russian section, writing a letter on her straw mattress.

"Ink or urine, comrade?" Dee asked in Russian.

Startled, Tati glanced up from the paper and laughed. "I'll never tell, *Amerikanskiy*."

Rhythmic clapping turned their heads. Hanna danced around the room, the flowers now woven into her matted, dirty hair. The Polish women sang, and Hanna performed a traditional folk dance called the *krakowiak* as best she was able in the tight confines of the bunkhouse. The other women joined in, clapping in rhythm as Hanna spun around, her prison dress billowing off her bone-thin legs. Such was the noise that no one observed Gustel entering, summoned by the unusual sounds coming from the political-prisoner barracks.

The *blockova* positioned herself in a corner, out of sight. Hanna strutted and jumped and twirled, cheered on by the thunderous applause and her sisters singing. Then she took a bow, the women cheering.

The girl then ran to the American and embraced her. A sly smile crept onto Gustel's face as Dee presented the child with what appeared to be a comb. The girl squealed with delight at the gift, begging her sisters to help her remove the flowers so Dee could comb her hair.

The women encircled the duo, Elsa approaching with a bucket of rainwater. Hanna beamed and sat on the floor, leaning backward and lowering her filthy locks into the water. A few minutes later, Dee was running the broken comb through it, and the Polish women replaced the flowers.

A mirror was produced by one of the Russians, a piece of contraband Gustel apparently had missed on her routine inspections. The *blockova* snorted. No matter.

Hanna stared at her reflection with awe. Her hair was straight and neatly parted in the middle, cascading over her shoulders. It was also clean, the chestnut brown revealed from beneath the dirt. The Edelweiss flowers circled her head like a crown, the eyes above her sunken cheeks wide and sparkling. She reached out and took Dee's hand.

"Thank...you," she said, carefully pronouncing the English.

Gustel had seen enough and slipped back out the door. The *blockova* shuffled through the camp's dark streets, toward the administration building. With any luck *Hauptsturmführer* Glockner or, better yet, *Oberaufseherin* Botz were still in their offices. Gustel was sure they would be very interested in what she had just observed. Her mouth watered as she thought of the sausage no doubt given in reward.

39

Munitions Factory; March 1945

Dee stood for morning *appell* as always, along with what were now fifty thousand other women lined shoulder to shoulder for morning roll call. The process took hours, the sight of women collapsing and being kicked or bludgeoned back to standing as routine as the rising sun. This particular morning brought some new faces, however.

A group of German men in suits walked the ranks, studying the women intently. Every now and then, they nodded to one and that prisoner stepped out of line. One of the men, a tall Aryan in an overcoat and tie, passed Dee without a second glance.

"What about her?" Botz asked.

The *oberaufseherin* emerged from the crowd, a black cloak swirling about her uniform and a mischievous smile on her face. Dee caught her stare and held it. Botz blinked first.

"My apologies. Who, fraulein?" the man asked, pursing his thin colorless lips.

"Her," Botz said, pointing at Dee.

The man drew a deep breath and squinted, giving Dee a once-over. "If you insist, *Oberaufseherin* Botz."

"Oh, I do," Botz assured him, grinning.

"Very well," the man said, and motioned for Dee to step out of line.

She and a hundred others were marched out of the gates toward a campus of buildings on a grassy yellow hill in the distance. Women whispered their fears of what might await them behind the walls until Tati spoke up, trudging up the steep incline with a scowl.

"It's a factory," she said in Russian. "Relax."

The women filed inside, sighs of relief filling the air as the building's heat enveloped them.

The ceilings were twenty feet high, halogen lamps illuminating neat rows of workstations that stretched from one end of the facility to the other. Prisoners in striped uniforms labored silently at them, electronic components scattered over the white countertops.

The guards ordered the women to reform their ranks, the ever-present German shepherds herding them like sheep. The man in the overcoat waited until all were assembled before he spoke. A dog barked, and he flinched.

"Good morning, ladies," he said with a curt bow. "My name is *Herr* Keller. I'm the director of operations at this facility." He smiled, a strange gesture given the circumstances. "You will be trained in a very specialized kind of work here. Play close attention and do exactly as you are told, and you will do very well for yourselves."

Dee raised her hand. *Herr* Keller smoothed his blond

hair across his forehead, obviously not expecting any questions.

"Er...yes?" he said, offering a weak smile.

"What kind of work exactly?" Dee said loud enough for everyone in the factory to hear. Women at the benches craned their necks seeking out the female prisoner talking back to a supervisor.

Herr Keller frowned.

"Well, w-we ..." he stammered.

"I'll answer the question, *Herr* Keller," Botz said, her jackboots echoing off the concrete floor. "And do accept my apologies for the interruption. I have tried to teach that one good manners, to no avail."

Dee's eyes slid from Keller to Botz as she approached; the *oberaufseherin* still wore that same curious grin.

"They build munitions here, *fotze*," Botz said. "Things that go...*boom*."

"Then I refuse," Dee said. "Ever heard of the Geneva Convention, *Fraulein*? You can't force us to build weapons that will kill our Allies. We're prisoners of war."

"Yes, yes, yes," Botz said. "I thought you'd say something like that. You are so delightfully predictable."

She slapped her boots together and called out toward the giant bay doors through which the women had marched.

"Bring her in," Botz commanded.

Two male guards entered dragging a limp prisoner between them, the morning light making the tiny figure a silhouette. They dropped the girl into a heap on the floor, and she curled into a ball, hands held protectively over her head.

It was Hanna, her brown eyes wide with fear.

Botz continued her exaggerated goose-stepping, jackboot tips halting inches from Hanna's scalp. She peered down at her, dwarfing the child with her formidable height.

"Beautiful, isn't she?" Botz said. "And so very young. What a waste her life will have been. And all because of you."

Botz produced a pistol from beneath her black cloak and aimed it directly at Hanna's skull. The *oberaufseherin* raised her head, a plucked eyebrow arching over a sky-blue eye, and cocked the trigger.

"Oh, *Blockova* Gustel told me all about you two," she said, smiling. "The little one does depend on you so. Even sleeps in your bed at night, I hear. How touching." Dee sensed the eyes of the factory floor's hundreds of slave workers now on her. "Refuse and she dies," Botz said. "Simple."

Trembling, Hanna raised her head and stared at Dee.

"We'll do a count, shall we?" Botz said. "One…"

The German shepherds tugged impatiently against their restraints.

"Two…"

Herr Keller fidgeted, nervous.

"Three…"

"Don't," Dee said. "Don't do it."

"So you will do what *Herr* Keller asks of you?" Botz asked.

"Yes," Dee said.

"Say, '*Ja*, Frau Oberaufseherin,'" Botz said. "That is how you will address me from now on."

Botz crouched, and pressed the luger's barrel to Hanna's temple. "I can't hear you, *fotze*."

"*Ja*, Frau Oberaufseherin," Dee said.

Botz stood, beaming.

"*Vundebar,*" she said, a gleeful tone in her voice. "And now you may go. Go get your shovel and dig in the dirt."

Dee glanced between Keller and Botz, confused.

Botz eased the hammer back on the pistol and strolled up to Dee.

"I just wanted to see that look on your stupid face," she said, and tapped a gloved finger on Dee's nose. "That one, right here. And to hear you call me 'Frau Oberaufseherin.' It was like Wagner to my ears, hm?" Botz pointed to Hanna on the floor. "Going forward, your insolence will not result in *your* punishment. No. It will result in *hers*. Do you understand?"

Dee nodded. Botz cupped her hand to an ear.

"*Ja*, Frau Oberaufseherin," Dee said.

Botz cackled. "Go. Go dig in the dirt, *fotze.*"

Dee took Hanna's hand and walked the girl back toward the factory bay doors.

Soon they were outside, Botz's laughter ringing in Dee's ears.

40

Kinderzimmer, Ravensbruck Concentration Camp; March 1945

Dee led Hanna back down the hill toward the camp. Shivering with fright, Hanna clutched Dee's hand.

The church at the bottom of the steeple was in view, surrounded by a village. Two-story houses dotted the area just outside the forest, gabardine-clad guards milling about the spacious lawns.

"Look," Dee said, and they stopped to watch for a moment. "That's where the Nazis live," she continued. "Pretty nice houses at that, wouldn't you say?"

Hanna just stared, traumatized from her near-death experience. Dee took her hand.

"Stick with me," Dee said as they trudged down the hill. "You just stick close by me."

When they walked back through the camp gates, they found a pregnant woman on her knees in the mud, screaming. Rivulets of blood and water cascaded down legs bared beneath her prison dress. The women in the marching work gangs looked on in horror, driven along by the crack of guards' whips and the barking dogs.

Dee dropped Hanna's hand and ran to the woman now on her back, face contorted with effort. Dee removed her own tattered uniform jacket and knelt beside her. "Breathe," she said in English, unsure of the woman's nationality. "Breathe."

A crackle of thunder, and the rain fell.

Dee lifted the hem of the woman's dress to reveal a pink head rapidly emerging from the birth canal. The woman cried out, gripping Dee's hand. Hanna observed from a distance, chewing her nails under wide brown eyes.

"Hanna, come here," Dee said. When Hanna didn't move, she waved her over. "Come on now." Hanna reluctantly approached. Dee took her hand and placed it in the woman's. "She needs your help too," Dee said.

Another woman wearing a white coat dropped down in the mud next to them, dripping black hair dangling into a long-boned face etched with premature aging.

"I'm Marie. I work in the *revier*," she said in French. "We must get her inside."

"The baby has other plans," Dee replied.

Marie gasped as she caught the infant's emerging shoulders. The child was born into Dee's jacket seconds later. Marie pinched the umbilical cord with a pair of steel medical clamps from her coat pocket.

"You take the baby. I'll help her," Dee said.

Marie brought the newborn tightly to her chest. Dee helped the new mother to her feet, noticing the yellow triangle on her uniform as she did.

"My name's Dee," she said in Russian, a guess.

"Oksana," the young woman replied, and clutched Dee

as they all made their way across the camp, Hanna following close behind.

They entered a building not far from the *revier*, one so small Dee assumed it was some kind of storage shed. When they entered it was clearly anything but.

The tiny room was furnished with a bunk bed. A dozen babies were arranged across either of the filthy mattresses, crying and mewling and kicking their tiny limbs in the air.

"What is this?" Dee asked in French.

"The Germans call it the *kinderzimmer*," Marie said, placing the newborn in a ceramic bowl on a table by the single window. The baby screamed as she released the clamps and picked up a small pair of scissors off a towel.

Oksana went to her child, weeping with joy and exhaustion. Dee stared at the babies on the mattress for a while before something else caught her eye.

A new mother sat crouched in a corner, holding an infant to her breast, sobbing.

"No milk," she pleaded in French. "No milk."

One of the babies on the bunk bed started crying, and then another, and soon the room was a deafening cacophony, the women shouting over the din. Hanna leaned against a wall, covering her ears.

"Where are their mothers?" Dee said.

"In the *revier*," Marie said, wrapping the *kinderzimmer*'s newest arrival in little more than a rag. "Or working in the factory. They come a few times a day to feed their children. If they can. Like her."

The woman in the corner sobbed along with her baby. "No milk, Marie," she wailed. "No milk."

"Yes, I know, Ines," Marie said, handing Oksana her child.

Ines lowered the baby into her lap, revealing a wilted breast sagging off her skeletal chest.

"May I hold it?" Dee asked, approaching.

"*Him*," Ines whispered. "Bruno."

Dee gently picked Bruno out of Ines's lap and brought him into her arms.

She had never seen a skinny baby in her life. What should have been pink cherubic skin instead hung off his face in wrinkles that were pocked red. He didn't cry; he only stared up at Dee with flat, glassy eyes, like a tiny old man on his deathbed.

Oksana held her daughter closely, incapable of hiding her terror at the stark contrast between the newborns.

"And what will you name her?" Marie asked, placing a hand on Oksana's shoulder. The new mother shrugged, not understanding the French.

"What will you name her?" Dee translated into Russian.

"Lidiya," Oksana said, without hesitation. "After her grandmother."

Marie smiled, deep crow's feet bunching around her exhausted eyes.

"Hanna," Dee said in English, "do you think you can watch these little ones while Marie and I get a breath of fresh air?"

Dee made her arms into a cradle. Hanna nodded.

"Thank you," Marie said as they stepped outside. "I needed a break."

"I can see that," Dee said.

"You are American?" Marie said. "Your French is pretty good."

"I am, and thank you. Are you a doctor?"

"No," Marie said. "A nurse. Voss decided this meant I was qualified to work for him in the *revier*. But after a few weeks I couldn't... I..."

Marie trailed off, her eyes glossing over. "...I couldn't... work there anymore."

"The experiments," Dee said, "on the rabbits."

"In the old days we did abortions," Marie said. "Thousands of them. Then, as the Allies started finding the camps and shutting them down, more and more women came here, many already pregnant. At first the Nazis just tore them out of their mother's arms and killed them. Bashed their little heads against the wall or drowned them in a bucket like rats. But soon there were too many. So they built the *kinderzimmer*. Before the war, you wouldn't let your dog sleep in a place like this. And now it is where we try to raise babies..." Marie trailed off, her eyelids sagging.

"I can help, if you need it," Dee said.

"Voss would have to grant permission," Marie said. "Do you have experience? Children of your own?"

"No and no," Dee said. "Just want to be of help where I can, if I can."

"I will talk to Voss," Marie said. "Come see me in the morning."

"All right. I will," Dee said.

The women shook on it and went back inside the *kinderzimmer*. Ines lay passed out in a heap, Bruno in Hanna's lap. The Polish girl held out a finger, and Bruno reached for it, taking it in his tiny grip.

Oksana sat cross-legged on the floor, Lidiya attached to her breast. "She is feeding," Oksana said, beaming.

Dee hadn't seen a smile so pure since her arrival at the camp.

That night in barracks, Dee lay in her bunk, replaying her morning at the factory over in her mind. It wasn't Botz or her petty games keeping her awake; it was the dogs, drooling and snarling at her with nothing whatsoever behind their eyes.

Never in her life had she encountered anything like it with an animal. Miss Adeline's cat was the first, but even when she was a younger child, the squirrels in the yard and the birds in the trees acknowledged her. She spoke to any animal she chose to, anywhere, and always. Except in this place. Here she was invisible.

"Dee."

She rolled over on her bunk. Tati motioned for her to join the gathering of Soviet women whispering in their nightly meeting.

Dee walked across the bunkhouse. Hanna sat in the middle of their circle.

"Sit, Dee," Tati said. "Please."

Dee took a seat. Hanna's hands were clenched together as if in prayer.

"She has made something very special for you, Dee," Tati said, patting Hanna's knee. The other women in the circle grinned, poking Hanna's legs and teasing her in Russian and Polish.

"For me?" Dee asked. "What is it?"

"Show her," Tati told Hanna. "Go on."

Hanna stretched her arms across her lap and opened her hands like a flower. Inside was a tiny blue bird, carved from the handle of the wooden comb.

"Oh my," Dee said, gently plucking it from Hanna's

palm. As Hanna spoke, Tati translated the Polish into Russian.

"Hanna says...I dreamed you were covered in birds last night, Dee," Tati interpreted. "Birds in your hair. Birds on your shoulders. Birds on your arms and even birds on your feet! Every kind of bird on earth and even birds I'd never seen before. And they were singing, Dee. Singing the most beautiful music in the world. So I made you *this* bird. Perhaps it will sing to you, like in my dream."

Dee held the bird close, her green eyes traveling over the tiny carving. Then her face crumpled into tears. The women wrapped their arms around her. Dee clutched the bird, weeping.

"You don't have to be strong for everybody else all the time, eh?" Tati said, holding Dee tightly. "Everybody needs friends in a place like this."

Dee sobbed as she thought of home, of her mama and daddy.

"*We* are your friends," Tati whispered in her ear. "And we will give you strength to carry on, comrade."

Dee figured she must have cried until she fell asleep. She woke up in the darkness some hours later, Hanna curled on the mattress beside her.

41

Kinderzimmer, Ravensbruck Concentration Camp; March 1945

"Appell! Appell! Appell!"

Dee stroked Hanna's hair as the girl awoke. When she did, Dee held the tiny blue bird in her palm, letting it catch the morning sunlight.

"Thank you for this, Hanna."

"Nie ma za co," Hanna replied.

"And that means 'You're welcome,'" Dee said. "See? I'm learning. Now you go on outside for count. I'll be there soon."

Gustel walked the aisles, rapping the spoon against the metal pot. *"Raus! Raus! Achtung!"*

The *blockova* caught Dee's glare and slowed her march. Hanna slipped off the mattress and ran across the floor to join the Soviet women who were filing out the door to the *appelplatz.*

Gustel stared at Dee, and Dee stared back. Neither woman blinked.

"You got something to say?" Gustel finally asked, hand on her hip.

"Never met a woman who would endanger a child's life for an extra piece of sausage is all," Dee said. "Thought I'd get a good look so I'd remember."

Gustel glowered as Dee followed the others outside, spitting on the floor when the bunkhouse door slammed shut behind her.

After the morning count, Dee made her way to the *kinderzimmer*. She had to push through the crowd of women wearing blank, exhausted expressions, shuffling zombie-like from one place to the next. Marie stood out front, staring at something, her expression catatonic. Dee followed her gaze to the perimeter wall.

Ines's body hung from the electrified fence. The young mother's hands had melted into the razor wire, while her head hung back on its neck, mouth open in a silent scream.

Marie was in a daze when Dee arrived at her side.

"What happened?"

The Frenchwoman regarded her with dark, haunted eyes. "They're dead," she said. "All of them."

The door to the *kinderzimmer* was ajar. Dee pushed it open, dull gray light leaking across the mattresses.

All the babies were quiet and still. Oksana sat slumped on a stool in the corner, paralyzed with shock, Lidiya latched to her breast.

A cold breeze blew through the only window, now shattered. Glass littered the wooden floor.

"Who did this?" Dee asked.

"A German," Marie replied, stepping inside. "Who exactly..." She shrugged.

Dee knelt before the dead babies. Their newly born eyes

were still open, staring lifelessly into a void. Flies alighted on and off their blue skin. It was the most unnatural sight in the world.

"Oh, goodness," a male voice said behind Dee. "How unfortunate."

Dr. Voss ducked under the doorframe and approached the mattresses, expressionless. He lifted a dead baby up in her rag blanket and prodded the cheeks and belly with leather gloved fingers. He wasn't examining her so much as satisfying a morbid curiosity, like a boy poking a dead frog with a stick.

"What happened, Marie?" he asked.

"As you see, *Herr* Doctor," Marie replied, indicating the glass on the floor, "they died in the night. It was too cold."

"Such a mess," Voss said, grabbing a handful of bedsheet on either side of the deceased infants and scooping them up in the sodden linens like fish caught in a net.

"What are you doing?" Dee asked.

"Dee," Marie said, her tone ominous, "let *Herr* Doctor go about his business. It is not our concern."

Voss folded the blanket over and tied it into a large knot.

"I'm taking them back to the *revier*," he said, "since you asked."

"They're dead," Dee said. "They should be given to their mothers to be properly buried."

Voss tightened the knot and peered out the door toward Ines's dangling corpse.

"Mothers like her?" Voss asked. "No. It is too upsetting."

He grunted as he hoisted the bundle in his arms, again ducking his head under the doorway as he stepped back into the thoroughfare.

Dee followed him, and Marie reached out, grabbing her arm. "No," Marie said. "Please."

"What is he doing with those babies?" Dee replied, turning back to her.

"Why does it matter? They are dead."

"And when their mothers come back, what will you tell them? That they just disappeared? A mama needs to see her child go into the ground. She needs to be the one who puts it there."

Oksana let out a small whine from the corner. The new mother held baby Lidiya out to them, tears streaming down her face. "No milk," she said in Russian. "No milk."

Dee tailed Voss through the camp streets. When the doctor got to the *revier,* he knocked on the door with the tip of a highly polished black boot, arms full of infant corpses. A German nurse in a brown uniform opened it for him and curtseyed her respect.

Dee caught the door just before it closed. She peeked through the crack, allowing Voss and the nurse to go through another door before slipping off her clogs and stepping inside. Bedridden women tracked Dee with their red eyes as she tiptoed barefoot across the ward and crouched to the second door's keyhole. Voss was on the other side, his *Totenkopf* cap disappearing as he descended a staircase.

Dee followed him, gingerly closing the door behind her. The stench of decomposing flesh became more and more unbearable with each step down the stairs. Dee pulled her dress collar over her nose as Voss's boots echoed ahead.

At the bottom there was a tunnel, light bulbs strung on either side of the stone corridor. Voss disappeared into the shadows at the tunnel's end, footsteps fading. Rats scurried along the floor.

What is this place? Dee asked them. The rodents said nothing in reply, only marked her warily with their beady black eyes.

Dee hurried down the underground passageway before arriving at a thick metal door. The source of the stench was just on the other side. It was slightly ajar, and she pushed it open.

The corpses of hundreds of emaciated women lay stacked on long metal tables, naked and contorted with rigor mortis. Some of their eyes were open, some closed, and some dangled out of their sockets. All were in various states of putrescence.

Dee walked among the dead. They were like discarded dolls, dropped in the cold mud by a child who no longer had a use for them.

A latch clicked shut, and Dee spun on her heel. A low, orange light flickered beneath a door across the mortuary. She heard Voss grunt behind it.

She twisted the knob. Cold, dank air filled her nostrils as she eased it open and peered into the room. Dozens of large glass jars crammed onto metal shelves surrounded a pair of autopsy tables. A specimen floated in each one, suspended in dark amber fluid.

Dee crept toward them, careful not to make a sound. Now she saw the jars contained fetuses in every stage of development, a Nazi doctor's collection of the unborn.

Voss emerged from behind a shelf, setting the *kinderzimmer's* blanket across one of the the autopsy tables and arranging the dead babies in a neat row.

"Close the door, please," he said without turning around. "You're letting in the stink."

"What are you going to do with them?" Dee asked.

"Shut the door, and I will tell you," he said.

Dee reached behind her, and did as Voss asked.

"I have wanted to examine you since your arrival, you know," Voss said, picking one of the lifeless babies off the table and palming the crown of her crooked head. He twisted it until the spine straightened, a sickening crack echoing off the brick walls.

"I have an idea," he continued, setting the infant down and turning from his workbench. His thin lips were parted slightly, and he licked a bit of spittle off them. "Why don't you take a seat, and I can satisfy my curiosity?"

"You're not cutting me," Dee said. "Or poisoning me or doing anything like that."

"Of course I'm not, for pity's sake," Voss said, sounding genuinely offended. "I said I want to *examine* you."

"You're not touching me," Dee said. "Ever."

Sighing, Voss leaned back against the table's edge. "Some of our first experiments in this camp involved sterilization. We used young gypsy girls who had just begun their menstruation..."

Voss trailed off. He scrutinized the formaldehyde jars a moment before continuing.

"Those experiments didn't go well. All of them died. We simply didn't have the right technique. Their uteruses became inflamed, and the girls expired, one after the other. Terrible deaths. So much screaming."

He went to a bookshelf and slid a fetus jar two inches to the left, making it equidistant to the jars on either side of it. He stepped back to admire his handiwork.

"I have a theory that it was their gypsy blood that caused these experiments to fail," he went on. "Had I not been so preoccupied with typhus and dysentery outbreaks those many months, I might have continued this work on the so-called rabbits…Polish girls, like that little one you seem so fond of. *Hanna*, I believe is her name."

Dee clenched a fist.

"I can request that *Oberaufseherin* Botz bring Hanna to me, I suppose," Voss said. "To further my experimentation."

Dee drew in a sharp breath.

"Unless I'm otherwise engaged, of course," he offered.

Voss's deep-set brown eyes slid over to the other autopsy table. "Have a seat," he said. "Please."

Dee imagined Hanna in this room, going under Voss's knife surrounded by aborted fetuses and decaying bodies. The girl would never be the same, if she even survived such an ordeal.

Dee clutched the tiny blue bird in her dress pocket and slowly walked toward the table. Voss reached out to her, and she took the Nazi doctor's hand.

42

Mortuary, Ravensbruck Concentration Camp; March 1945

Dee was about to sit on the autopsy table when something pricked the back of her right arm, just above the elbow.

"What was that?" Dee said. "What did you inject me with?"

"A sedative," Voss said, yanking out the syringe. "One I take myself sometimes. It's nothing to worry about. Quite the opposite. Now relax."

Dee's knees went warm, and she thought she might fall over. Voss gripped her hand and helped her onto the table, laying her onto the cold metal surface.

"There, there," he said, his voice low and monotone. "There, there. Let yourself enjoy the potion's effects."

The silver skull and crossbones on Voss's *Totenkopf* cap shimmered, as did the rest of the room. Her limbs were heavy, too heavy to move. She sank into the table.

"Which of your parents has eyes like these?" Voss asked, pulling Dee's eyelids wide between his thumb and forefingers. "*Mutter*? *Vater*?"

"N-neither," Dee slurred. The ceiling kept rising. She wondered how high it might go.

"Fascinating," Voss said. "Never in my life have I seen such a color green in a human eye."

Dee's prison dress slid up her body. Voss yanked it over her head, and her arms flopped back on the table, paralyzed. Next came his hands, no longer gloved. They slithered up her thighs, then her stomach, and finally rested on her rib cage, just below her breasts.

"Your bones haven't yet completely healed," Voss whispered. "Nor have your feet. Such suffering you endure. It's theoretically possible that you possess a unique pain tolerance previously unknown to Aryan science, but I don't think this is the case." Voss walked to his workbench. "I think instead the miraculous properties can be found in your blood."

The ceiling stopped rising. Tiny white dots flooded Dee's vision. Another needle jabbed her in the crook of her elbow.

"D- don't..." she said, the word dribbling from her lips.

"*Shhh,*" Voss whispered. "*Shhhh.*"

He pulled out the syringe and held it up to the light. It was full of blood.

Her blood.

"My work, however disagreeable you may find it, is all in aid of saving German soldiers' lives," Voss said, returning to his bench. "I imagine the Americans are undergoing similar experiments for their own countrymen's benefit."

"Don't count on it," Dee said, her words barely audible.

"No?" Voss said, setting the syringe inside a beaker. "My understanding is the United States has detained thousands of Japanese immigrants in California. And what of the Blacks? You presume it isn't possible that they aren't being used under similar circumstances as this? When the war is over, we shall find out I'm right."

"When the war's over, you'll hang," Dee mumbled. The floating white dots had quadrupled in size.

"Let us have quiet now," Voss said, and Dee received another injection in her thigh.

The light grows so bright Dee has to close her eyes. When she opens them, the light is still there, but now she can see it's the sun, high overhead in a cloudless blue sky. She's seated on a horse, endless desert fanning out in every direction. Purple mountains ring the horizon, the song of the locusts buzzing in the sagebrush. Her skin feels hot and dry, gloriously so.

"That's more like it," she says, and gently tugs on her horse's reins.

43

Costilla, New Mexico Territory; August 1854

Dee rides through the high-desert town of Costilla, New Mexico. She wears a hat pulled low, two six-shooter pistols hanging off a gun belt made from a dark red sash, liberated from a soldier's corpse in Mexico.

Here she is the Outlaw, once again.

An old cattle rancher with a tangled white beard and peeling, sunburned skin ambles up to her, a wad of worn dollar bills in his hand. She takes them from him and counts. Satisfied, she spits, and jams the bills into the back pocket of threadbare pants that threaten to slide off her bony hips.

The town's only road dead-ends on a two-story rooming house, a large bonfire crackling before it. Dee dismounts and saunters toward it, taking in the enormous blue sky that sits on the town like a dome.

A man with a bloated, pockmarked face rocks in a wooden chair, smirking. He wears a black kerchief around his right arm, as do the other five men emerging from the structure.

Dee plants her boot heels in the dirt outside the gang's headquarters, hands dangling just above her pistols. She takes the black-banded men in with a slow, steady gaze.

"Name's Attica," Dee announces. "You all the Bannon Gang?"

The man on the porch gets to his feet and holds up a hand to the others. He gives Dee a once-over then approaches her until they're mere feet apart.

"We are," he says. "I'm Bannon."

"Nice to make your acquaintance," she says, tipping her wide-brimmed hat. "Heard quite a bit about you."

"State your business," Bannon says.

"My business is with the people of Costilla," Dee continues. "They've paid me a sum of money to see to it that you leave their town and that you do so at once."

The gang members chortle. Dee looks over her shoulder back down the road. The faces of frightened Costilla citizens peek out from behind broken windows.

"Did they now?" Bannon says with a sneer. "That was a mistake."

"They will no longer tolerate being extorted by you or your men," Dee says. "You need to leave, Mr. Bannon. All of you. Now."

"Say again?" Bannon asks.

"Say what again, Mr. Bannon?"

"That word. Ex-something."

"Extorted."

"Yeah. What the hell does that mean?"

"It means that for the past year you have required these good people pay your gang a significant amount of their meager incomes for protection," Dee explains. "The irony being that the only threat they currently face is the very gang to which they pay."

"That's what 'extorted' means?"

"Yes."

"Ed? Write that down," Bannon tells one of his minions. "That's a good word. *Extorted.* I like that." He turns back to Dee, his chin waddle creasing as his thick lips stretch into a smile. "What'd you say your name was again? *Attica?*"

"Yes," Dee says.

"Well, how about this, Attica? We're gonna give you fifty paces back down that road behind ya before we start shooting. That way it won't be so easy. Make it a contest, like. Boys get bored, you see. Gotta offer up some entertainment now and again."

"I take it you aren't leaving then," Dee says.

"Even give you a ten count," Bannon replies. "One...two."

Dee yanks a Bowie knife out of her belt. She throws it up into the air, catches the handle with her left hand, then slashes Bannon's throat open so fast her victim doesn't realize what has happened.

Before the gang can react, her index finger is deep inside the incision, and when it finds what it's searching for pulls it out of Bannon's body. It's the man's tongue, now dangling out of the gash in his throat.

Her right hand has simultaneously withdrawn a pistol, so when one of the gang takes aim, she's already squeezing the trigger, the bullet finding the shooter in the space between his right eye and the bridge of his nose. He collapses to the dirt as Bannon falls over dead. The rest of the gang drops their weapons and raises their hands high.

"Gentleman, behold what I have dubbed the 'Attica necktie,'" Dee says, gesturing to Bannon's gruesome injury, "a result of my recent discovery that the human tongue is, on average, ten centimeters long and originates in the back of the throat. Please understand the perfect execution of this technique, as I have so ably demonstrated here, is the result of much practice on violators such as all of you. Should you not vacate the town of Costilla this instant, I will be more than happy to continue to perfect my craft on each and every one of you in turn."

The remaining gang members look to their deceased boss, the front of his tan cotton shirt soaked in gore, then back to Dee.

"That means you should run," she says. "Right now."

They do so, scrambling for the open desert, abandoning their horses hitched to posts in front of the rooming house.

The rancher with the white beard is now at Dee's side, his hat tilted back, taking in Bannon's bloodied corpse. "I'd heard rumors," he says. "Looks like they was all true."

"Are you satisfied with the work, sir?" Dee asks.

"I am."

"Do me a favor, then, if you would," she says. The rancher gawks at the man on the ground now wearing his tongue like a garment. "Make sure everyone knows it was me. I have a reputation to uphold."

She grips the brim of her hat and bows slightly, then heads for her horse, which is tied to a post on the other end of town. The townsfolk watch her walk back down the thoroughfare, eyes wide in brown dusty faces.

A sparrow alights on her shoulder. Dee extends her index finger, and the bird hops to it.

This is who you are, the bird says, cocking its tiny head up to her. *This is what you do.*

Then why will no one in Ravensbruck talk to me? Dee asks.

Because they can't hear your song, the bird says.

I don't know what I'm doing wrong, Dee says. *Tell me.*

You must sing.

I thought I was.

You aren't singing. You are mute.

I don't understand.

You are asleep.

Help me. Please.

You must wake, Orphic, the bird says. *Time is running out.*

The bird flies away, up into the noonday sun. Then the sun is a light bulb, hanging over Dee's bed in the *revier.*

"Ah," *Oberaufseherin* Botz said, standing over Dee. "She's awake. *Vundebar.*"

Heinrich Himmler joined Botz, peering down at Dee over his round wire spectacles. Then there was Voss, shaking his head.

"Unbelievable," Voss said. "Simply unbelievable."

"Why is her head twisted like that, Doctor?" Himmler asked.

"Excellent question, *Herr Reichsführer,*" Voss replied. "A few days ago I injected her with tetanus, which when left untreated causes grotesque contortions such as this. Without proper antibiotics, she should have died, *Reichsführer*. Should have but did not."

"Extraordinary," Himmler said.

"There's something in her blood that causes this astonishing tolerance to pain," Voss said. "I drew a considerable amount of it for analysis."

"Excellent work, *Herr* Doctor," Himmler said.

"You are most gracious, my esteemed *reichsführer*. But there is still more to do. I am next embarking on another round of my gunshot experiments. The first trials didn't go well, as you know. All the subjects died. But this one might prove to be the exception."

"Where do you shoot them?" Botz asked, her eyes brightening.

"In the leg," Voss replied. "Just above the knee."

"May I?" Botz asked.

"If you wish, *Frau Oberaufseherin,*" Voss said. "Unless *Herr Reichsführer* has any objection."

"Not at all, *Fraulein,*" Himmler assured her.

Botz withdrew her luger from beneath her black cloak.

"Please step back, *Herr Reichsführer,*" Voss said. "And cover your ears."

"Ah," Himmler said, doing so. "Good idea."

Dee moved her eyes to Botz, the only part of her body she *could* move. The *Oberaufseherin* grinned as she pulled back the hammer and aimed it at Dee's left leg.

Then she pulled the trigger.

44

Cargo Truck, Ten Miles Outside Ravensbruck; March 1945

Clementine clung to the inside of the cargo truck as it bounced along the shelled road, packed with prisoners. A terrified woman lying in the fetal position at her feet grasped her leg.

"Where are we going, do you think?" she asked her.

Clementine glanced out at the countryside. "I don't know."

"Ravensbruck," an emaciated old woman wrapped in a filthy blanket said from the opposite bench. "It's a camp for women. Only women."

"Do they have cigarettes there?" Clementine said with a smirk.

"If they do, they're not for us," the old woman said.

"Pity."

They were the last lucky few put on a truck at Bergen-Belsen, the rest forced to march the three hundred kilometers across Germany to their next place of internment. Mere days away from an Allied liberation, the Nazis weren't about to leave a single prisoner behind who might testify to the atrocities committed in the concentration camp. Clementine had barely survived, tens of thousands dying of disease in her first month as a Nazi prisoner.

After another few hours, the truck entered a wooded area, thick with trees, then lumbered to a stop.

Any hopes Clementine held that Ravensbruck might be an improvement over Bergen-Belsen vanished as she was pushed and shoved through its gates. A sea of hollow-eyed women milled about, staring at the latest batch of arrivals as if they were mirages. Female guards with light-blond perms cracked whips and screeched orders, while snarling German shepherds pulled on their masters' leashes, now such a common sight the prisoners barely flinched at them. Clementine stuffed her hands into her blue-and-white striped uniform pockets and followed the others to the intake building.

As in Bergen-Belsen, her head, underarms, and pubic area were shaved, and a fresh red triangle was sewn to her uniform. She liked the patch, considering it a badge of honor to officially be labeled the Reich's enemy. She was ordered to a barracks, a painted red *P* above the door indicating she would now be housed with the rest of the political prisoners.

Inside there was little room to maneuver. A sour-faced *blockova* clapped meaty palms and assigned them soiled straw mattresses on the floor. She introduced herself as Gustel, informed the newly arrived she didn't tolerate any shit and to pay attention to what the others did and how they did it, as they knew the rules.

Clementine wondered what the *blockova* was doing to

stay so fat in a death camp. When the Allies eventually reached Ravensbruck, she thought she might find out, perhaps with Gustel at the end of a knife.

Clementine made her bed on the floor and bunched a tattered blanket under her head. She stared up at the ceiling, trying not to think too much about Chesterfield cigarettes and good coffee.

Night fell and Gustel left the bunkhouse, presumably to stuff food in her face with the Nazis. No sooner had the door closed than the women arranged themselves into groups and whispered to each other urgently.

Clementine understood none of it, most speaking Polish or Russian, with some German popping up here and there. She had just closed her eyes when a woman spoke a familiar name. She sat upright, searching the room for the source.

An older woman was addressing a gathering of Soviets in Russian, gesturing emphatically. She thrust a finger toward the window and slammed a fist into her palm, repeating it.

Dee.

Clementine drew closer to them, listening intently. The Red Army women caught her eavesdropping and hushed up.

Tati jumped to her feet, squaring herself with the tall French woman, puffing her chest. She rattled off a few words in Russian and made a gesture at Clementine to *go away*.

"*Patienter,*" Clementine said, folding her hands in prayer. "*S'il vous plait. Avez-vous...*Dee?"

Tati and the others all shrugged at the French.

"Dee," Clementine repeated. "*Americaine*?"

Tati's eyes went wide. "*Amerikanskiy?*" she said.

"*Oui, oui, oui,*" Clementine said, clutching Tati by the shoulders. "Dee! *Americaine!*"

"*Da,*" Tati said. "*Da, Amerikanets po imeni,* Dee!"

"*Ou*?" Clementine said, and when Tati shook her head, she started waving her hands. "*Ou, ou, ou?*"

"*Da, da,*" Tati said, and searched for a word Clementine might understand. "Hostel."

Clementine shook her head, confused.

"Hospital," one of the Soviets corrected.

"*Infermerie*?" Clementine said. Another Russian nodded to Tati that this was correct.

"*Da, da, da. Bolnitsa. Infer...merie.*"

"We go," Clementine said in English. She pointed to herself, to Tati, and to the door.

"*Da,*" Tati said. "We go."

45

Revier, Ravensbruck Concentration Camp; March 1945

Raw human sewage now flowed in rivers throughout the camp, trickling through muddy rivulets made by the recent spring thaw. Clementine and Tati trekked through this filth toward the *revier*, excrement splattering over their shins as they did.

Whatever order there had once been at Ravensbruck was rapidly deteriorating. The barracks were now so over-populated that giant canvas tents completely lacking plumbing or sanitation housed newly arrived prisoners. A kind of anarchy was flourishing along with the sheer numbers, and Tati along with other Soviets capitalized on it, enjoying a booming business smuggling potatoes, one of which she now clutched in her uniform pocket at the ready to bribe her way inside the *revier*.

"*Tam, tam,*" she said to Clementine, indicating a building with a red cross painted on it.

"*Oui, je vois,*" Clementine replied.

They arrived at the front door, and Tati pounded on it with her fist. It cracked slightly, and a taciturn Romani *blockova* poked her face out, a long black braid dangling over her shoulders.

"*So keres?*" the *blockova* asked.

"Dee," Tati said. "*Amerikanskiy.*"

The Romani raised an eyebrow as if to say, "*What have you brought?*"

Tati produced the potato, and the *blockova* palmed it, stuffing it down into her enormous cleavage. She then jerked her head: *Come in.*

Clementine made a step to follow Tati and the *blockova* shook her head.

"*Bi-lacho,*" she said, wagging her finger in Clementine's face.

Tati smacked her hand, and the women squabbled at each other in their respective languages, neither understanding a word the other was saying. The *blockova* snatched the potato out from between her breasts and attempted to close the door in their faces.

Clementine stepped in front of Tati, grabbed the Romani by the cheeks, and planted a kiss on her mouth.

The potato dropped out of the *blockova*'s hand, her body going limp. Clementine kissed her deeply, passionately, and the woman fell back against the door in a swoon.

Tati retrieved her potato from the mud. Clementine slowly pulled her head back, the Romani's lower lip stretching out in the Frenchwoman's gentle bite. She released it and the *blockova* gasped.

"*Puis-je entrer?*" Clementine cooed, stroking the woman's cheek. The *blockova* understood not a word but moved aside and allowed both women to pass.

"*Merci, mon amie,*" Clementine said, and she and Tati stepped inside the *revier*.

The smell of death choked their senses as they entered.

Clementine pinched her nose and followed Tati down a corridor of the soon-to-be dead.

They found her on a bed covered in swarming black flies. Clementine cried out her name.

Dee's eyes were half open, the green irises dull and floating in yellow pools. Her breathing was shallow and labored.

"Dee," Clementine said, placing a hand on hers. "Dee, it's me. Clementine. Look at me, my friend. Please look at me."

Dee's eyes rolled up to her, flashing with recognition. "No, no. They'll kill you," she mumbled. "Get out of here."

"They haven't killed me," Clementine said. "Not yet, anyway."

"What are you doing here?" Dee said.

"I was captured," Clementine replied. "Same as you."

Tati inspected the thick bandage around Dee's left leg, waving the flies away and cursing in Russian. The gauze was soaked with blood, and she smelled the gangrene setting in.

"The babies are in the jars downstairs," Dee rambled, delirious with fever. "Don't tell their mothers."

Clementine gripped her hand. "What happened, my friend? What happened to you?"

Dee coughed, her body convulsing. Tati ran to the head of the bed and gripped her shoulders. "Help me get her up," she said.

Dee hacked and wheezed as she was pulled up to sitting. After a while the coughing subsided, and Clementine sat on the mattress, cradling Dee in her arms.

"Oh, my friend," Clementine said, her voice choked with tears. "What have they done to you?"

Dee sank into Clementine's warm embrace, thinking that if she died like this, maybe that would be okay.

46

Isle of Kasos, Greece, The Month of Elaphebolion; 433 BC

The great ship dropped anchor, no one save Damien witnessing its arrival. He emptied his krater of wine down his throat and tossed it onto the ground, staring with intoxicated curiosity at a red crab darting toward it, intending the cup as a new means of shelter. Whether it was the stink or the lack of space, Damien couldn't say, but the crab abandoned it, untouched.

Wooden tender boats ferried the ship's wares toward the silent beach. Grecian sailors relieved themselves in the waves, feet digging into soil for the first time in weeks. They rolled barrels out of the surf and onto the land, righted them, and popped the lids with crude tools.

The giant wooden boat's gangplank crashed open. Damien shaded his eyes from the sun and observed what happened next.

Children trickled out of the vessel's lower holds, herded forward down the gangplank by a sailor cracking a bullwhip, his nose and mouth covered with a bandana. They squealed when they hit the frigid water, squinting up at the cloudless sky as they dog paddled for land.

Damien continued toward them. As he got closer, he observed they had one thing in common: they all suffered from deformity, disease, or both. Little boys and girls much like Clio and Paris trudged up onto the shore, skin blackened with leprosy. Others clung to each other's tunics, the blind leading the blind. The rest was a smattering of birth defects and congenital ailments, huddling in fear as they took in the remote, featureless island they would now call home.

Damien waved at the group as they passed, trying to appear friendly. Those who could see or comprehend what was happening cast wary glances his way then looked back to the rocky path before them. Confident they could find their way around the island without his help, as he had, he made his way toward the black ship, an enormous carving of the god Poseidon serving as the vessel's figurehead.

The sailors reemerged naked and dove into the surf, shrieking with relief as weeks of sweat and grime washed off their fetid skin. Damien was content to pass some of his afternoon drunk observing the unusual spectacle.

A swarthy man with an enormous belly arrived in the final tender boat, dressed in loose-fitting linens that flapped about his girth in the wind. A dirty sash tied around his head covered his left eye, and a gourd sloshing with liquid dangled from a rope around his waist. He swigged off it and let out a loud belch.

"Stay back, boy," he growled. "You stay the fuck back."

Damien raised his hands. "I'm not like the others," he told him. "I don't have the Blackness or any other ailments, sir."

The ship's captain regarded him curiously, wiping off

some of the liquor that had dribbled down his many whiskered chins. "What's your name, boy?"

"Damien, sir. Damien of Attica."

"Attica? That's Athenian."

"Yes, sir."

"How in the world did you end up in this fucking place?"

"My father and I were fishermen," Damien lied. "Our boat sank, and he drowned."

The captain took a swig off the goat bladder. He spat on the hot rocks and held out his hand for Damien to shake. "I am Basham," he said, "of Lindos."

"Pleased to meet you, Basham of Lindos," Damien replied, shaking the big man's hand. He eyeballed the bladder, curious what was inside it.

"Your father gave you a taste for the drink, didn't he, boy?" Basham said with a grin. "Just like mine. Long days out at sea, Damien of Attica. A little of this can pass the time, eh?"

Basham tugged a smaller flask off his belt and held it out to Damien, who took it eagerly.

"Slowly now, boy," Basham instructed. "That's strong stuff."

Damien took a slug, reveling in the burn that trickled down his throat before holding the flask back out to the captain.

"There's more where that came from," Basham said, taking it. "Along with other distractions you might find enticing, if we let you on board. What say you, boy? Those little balls of yours dropped yet? You ever fucked?"

Damien shook his head.

"Slave girl on board. Clean. Well, clean enough. She'll suck you off, anyways."

"Who are all these children?" Damien asked. "And why have you brought them here?"

"Who? The idiots?" Basham replied.

"Is that what you call them?"

"It's not what I call them, boy. It's what they're called."

"Some are merely blind," Damien said. "Some are sick. Some have difficulty speaking or walking. They're all different."

Basham chuckled. "No distinction between idiots that I'm aware of."

Damien squinted at the sun radiating off the water, the cries of the gulls and sailors intermingling with the sound of the pounding surf.

"Come," Basham said, jerking his head. "Meet the men."

A few of the sailors had gone on a hunting expedition and slaughtered a goat, one of the many animals who lived on the craggy rock edifices that jutted over the sea. Damien took part in none of it, instead quickly devouring a basket of dates that had thus far gone untouched next to the fire.

He took in the blanket of stars overhead as he ate, the odor of the sailors and the crackling animal fat comingling in a nauseating combination. Basham turned from the men's idle chatter, handing out what was left of the goat's roasted femur in a clenched fist.

"Eat, boy."

Damien shook his head and popped another date in his mouth.

"What, you don't favor meats?" Basham asked, incredulous.

Damien again shook his head. Basham lowered the goat flesh.

"Strange boy," he said.

The sailors found beds in the soft sand. Basham sat idly before the fire, crunching on the end of the goat leg, lost in thought. After a while he caught Damien staring and dropped the bone into the fire, kicking up sparks.

"Something on your mind?" the captain asked.

Damien rose from the sand, brushing off his tunic. He walked toward the captain and sat across from him, the fire crackling between them.

"I need your help," Damien said.

"I imagine so," Basham said, pulling the flask off his belt. He guzzled clumsily from its funneled end, then handed it across the fire. Damien drank from it deeply, delighting in its intoxicating effects.

"I want to get off this island," Damien said, passing it back.

"No shit you do," Bashan replied. "Only question is what's in it for me?"

"I knew that's what you'd say."

"You have an answer, then, boy?"

"Yes."

"Speak on it."

Damien drew himself up straight before the flames.

"There's Athenian silver on this island."

Basham blinked as if he couldn't believe what Damien had just told him.

"You heard me," Damien said.

Basham slurped down the flask until it was empty and tossed it aside. "Say it again."

"Athenian silver," Damien repeated. "I found some. Here. On this island."

Athenian silver was the most highly prized currency throughout Greece. It was the silver standard, the metal from which all commerce and lending were based on. The silver was parceled out in small coins; an image of an owl stamped into the bullion identified its purity. To discover its source was to mint money.

"Where?" Basham asked, the man's pupils dilating across the fire.

"Promise me passage home and I will tell you."

"Tell me or I'll wring that skinny neck of yours."

"Wring my neck and you won't know where the silver is."

"I'll find it."

"You sure about that?"

Basham's intoxicated thoughts turned over. When they reached their inevitable conclusion, he sniffed. "Your passage is assured," he said.

"In the sea," Damien replied. "Just beyond the shore."

Basham followed Damien's finger to the black waves.

"Silver under the sea?" Basham asked. "Never heard of that."

"That doesn't mean it isn't so," Damien said. "I didn't dare go near the others—the 'idiots,' as you call them. If I did, I'd risk infection. I've done nothing but explore this island on my own. For a year. One day I saw something on the ocean floor. Something shining in the sun. I dove as deep as I could go. Didn't go far the first day. Didn't go far the day after either. But in time I could dive very deep. Very deep indeed. Like a fish. I dug into the soil and I found it. It means nothing, here. Less than nothing. But back in Athens..." Damien allowed his voice to trail off as he stared out onto the water. "Back in Athens, I'd have made my fortune."

Basham cracked his knuckles.

"What say you?" Damien asked.

Basham grinned, revealing a mouthful of rotting gums. "I say you've earned a roll below decks, boy."

The great ship's bowels stunk of fish guts and human sweat. Damien held his nose against it as he descended into the vessel's humid, dark belly. He had to take a breath eventually; the smell of the crisping whale fat in Basham's torch made his eyes water.

At the end of the narrow passageway sat a tiny figure, barely visible, legs drawn up protectively against her chest.

"Call her whatever you like," Basham slurred. "But do your business quickly, eh?"

The captain pulled himself back up the stairwell, the wood threatening to splinter under his weight.

When he was sure he was gone, Damien sat on the floor, crossing his legs. The slave girl stared at him with wide darkly circled brown eyes, her matted ginger hair filthy.

As the hours passed, she understood Damien intended to only sit and fell into a deep sleep.

Damien sat this way, cross-legged, until the break of dawn. He had spent the long night singing to the denizens of the sea and praying to the Gods to heed his call for aid.

In the morning Basham announced to his minions that Athenian silver was for the taking, just beneath the waves offshore.

The men stripped themselves naked and charged into

the water, whooping and hollering at the prospect of securing their futures with handfuls of the precious metal.

They dove again and again into the surf, coming up empty with each turn and diving back under, ever hopeful. Damien observed all this from the beach, chewing on a leftover date.

Later that morning, Captain Basham waddled down the gangplank. He widened his arms at Damien as if it say, "*Where is it?*"

"There," Damien called out to him, pointing out a spot of ocean the sailors hadn't yet explored. "It's over there."

Basham followed Damien's finger, hitched his linens over his belly, and ran out into the surf.

The captain belly flopped into the water, the splash drawing the other sailors' attention. When they realized what their boss was doing, they dove in after him, arms and legs carving through the water.

Damien sighed with relief at the first shark fin's appearance, which was soon joined by several others.

Then came the screaming. Bones cracked, bodies bitten cleanly in half. The water foamed red, guts and viscera bubbling to the surface.

Damien sprinted across the sand and dove into the surf, swimming through the bloody waves to the school of feeding sharks.

He arrived at the great white that had carried him to Kasos, the creature who had saved his life.

Damien asked, in so many words, if they were even.

The giant fish offered something like a smile, its razor-sharp teeth stained with the blood of its prey.

The ocean is forever, and you are a child of the Gods, it said.

Damien accepted this and swam back for land.

Once there, he pulled himself onto the sand, catching

his breath, the blood of dozens of sailors rinsing off his skin in crimson ribbons.

Damien gazed out at the waves. After a while, Captain Basham's severed head floated past, bobbing like a fat cork.

As the sun set, Damien searched for Clio and Paris. He found them in the village, huddled around a bonfire with the new arrivals. They passed a gourd of wine, the freshmen crying out for their mothers and fathers and home.

Clio explained that they could never go home and that the wine took away their sadness, if they drank enough of it. Damien dipped his hand inside an open barrel and slurped up a drink of his own. Then he addressed the group.

"Have your fill and then get a good night's rest. In the morning we sail for Athens."

Paris hopped to his feet and approached Damien, his noseless face twisted in confusion. "Athens?" he asked. "What do you mean?"

"I mean we're going there," Damien replied. "First thing in the morning."

"And how are we getting there exactly?"

"On the great ship."

"The great ship?" Paris asked. "That's impossible. Those men won't let us within a hundred paces of them."

"Those men are dead," Damien said.

Paris took a step back.

"What happened to them?" Clio asked.

"I killed them," Damien replied.

"Why?" Paris asked.

"Because they needed killing," Damien said simply.

"And now you're going back to Athens?"

Damien went back to the barrel, cupping his hands and bringing up as much wine as they could hold. He slurped greedily, wiped his palms down his blood-stained tunic, and belched.

"*We're* going back to Athens," he said. "All of us."

47

Red Triangle Barracks, Ravensbruck Concentration Camp;
April 1945

"The Russians are coming. *Dee.* The Russians are coming."

Dee opened her eyes. Clementine was at her bedside, sitting on the straw mattress. "She's awake!" she exclaimed in English. Tati, Elsa, and Hanna ran across the room, joining the Frenchwoman at Dee's bedside.

"The Nazis are rounding everybody up," Clementine continued. "The *blockovas* say they're going to make us walk to some place called Mecklenburg. That's a hundred kilometers away. It's a death march, my friend. Do you hear me? We won't survive it."

Dee now sensed the throbbing pain above her left knee. "Where am I?" she croaked.

"Your bed," Clementine said. "You've been in a coma for over a week."

Panic shot through Dee's body, reawakening the rest of her injuries. "A *week*?" she said.

"Yes, my dear, sweet Dee," Clementine said. "And so now you must do *the thing*."

"Thing? What...*thing?*" Dee replied, her words coming thick and slow.

"The thing you did in the woods with the owls," Clementine said. "Now. Today."

Dee's next breath left her body with a shaky rasp. "I can't," she said.

"Why the hell not?" Clementine demanded.

"I'm dying," Dee said.

"*No*," Clementine snapped. "No. I won't let you. Where is that woman, eh? The lieutenant and her birds. The crazy American who looked me in the eyes and told me she was going to Berlin to kill Hitler. The woman I *believed*. Show her to me. I demand to see her."

Dee exhaled, lungs gurgling. "I don't think I can."

Hanna spoke urgently to her in Polish. Tati translated.

"You must not die," Tati said for Hanna. "I love you as I loved my own sisters. Do not leave me. Please."

Elsa gently lifted Dee's head, rested it on her lap, and stroked Dee's forehead.

"There are those green eyes of yours," the German said. "I missed the sight of them."

Dee sighed, surrounded by the warmth of her friends. "I'm tired," she said in English.

The women looked among one another, not understanding.

"My mama and daddy," Dee continued. "If you make it back home, tell them I was here. Tell them what you saw."

Dee closed her eyes and went still.

"Dee," Clementine said, her voice choked with fear. "Dee. Wake up."

Hanna started to cry when Dee didn't respond. Tati knelt and whispered urgently into her ear.

"Dee. What I told you is truer now than ever! You must hang on to life just a little longer," the Russian implored her. "Our comrades are coming."

Tears rolled down Elsa's ruddy face, sprinkling onto Dee's forehead. She gently wiped them away.

"She is leaving us," Elsa said. "She is going to be with God."

Overcome with grief, Hanna wailed. Clementine punched the bunk's wooden frame, bloodying her knuckles. "Not her," she said, pacing. "*Not her.*"

The bunkhouse doors opened, and Gustel entered, tailed by another *blockova*, carrying a stretcher between them. Clementine clenched her bloodied fist and made a move to strike.

"No," Tati said, catching the Frenchwoman's elbow. "Our time will come. But it isn't now."

Gustel dropped the stretcher on the floor by Dee's bed, smirking at Clementine all the while. The two *blockovas* grabbed Dee's unconscious body by the arms and legs and dragged her onto the litter.

"Where are you taking her?" Elsa demanded.

"Where do you think, cow?" Gustel replied.

The women stared helplessly as Dee's body was lugged out of the bunkhouse and into the camp's sewage-flooded streets.

Clementine, Elsa, and Tati crowded the doorway. Dee's limp arm dragged along the mud as she was carried toward the crematorium's ever-churning smokestacks.

"Remember your owls, Dee!" Clementine cried after her.

48

House, Ravensbruck Concentration Camp Outskirts; April 1945

Dee woke up in a warm bed under a thick wool blanket. The walls were painted eggshell white, the window curtains light pink with lace trim. The scent of pine oil wafted up from the hardwood floor.

I'm dead, Dee thought. *I died.*

"Well, well, well," a gravelly female voice said in English. "Look who's finally awake."

Dee rolled her head over on the feather pillow. A thin, gray-haired woman sat in a rocking chair, her soft brown eyes peering out from beneath heavy eyelids. She wore a black dress with a high collar, and she fidgeted with a beaded necklace draped around bony fingers.

"Hello, young lady," the woman said.

Dee figured she might muster the strength to sit up on her pillow. When she did, the old woman grinned broadly.

"Some life left in you yet," she said. "Well, done, kid."

"Who...*are* you?" Dee asked.

"I'm Gemma," the woman replied. "LaGuardia. And who the heck are you, if I may ask?"

"Dee. Attica."

"*Dee.* That short for something?"

"Damienne."

"Well that's an unusual name," Gemma said. "And may I say it's a real pleasure chatting. Haven't had anybody to talk to in who knows *how* long. Just been staring at you lying there, like a bump on a log."

Dee gripped the bedspread and pulled it off her legs. The gunshot wound above her knee was now a faded scar.

"Easy now, honey," Gemma said. "Don't rush it, kiddo."

Dee couldn't remember the last time she had seen a lamp on a nightstand, or a rug, or a vase. All those things were in the room, and more.

"Where am I?" Dee asked.

"Say what?" Gemma asked, leaning forward and cupping her ear.

"I said where am I?" Dee repeated, amazed she could bend her knees and plant her feet on the floor below the bed.

Gemma appeared genuinely perplexed by the question. Before she had a chance to answer, the room's mahogany pocket doors slid open, revealing an oval table set for dinner.

A young Nazi in uniform gestured to the white China bowls atop the table, an anxious cook in white linens peering out at the women from the kitchen.

"Eat, frauleins," the guard said in German. "Eat."

———

Dee poked at a bowl of baked beans with a spoon, reassuring herself it wasn't a drug-induced hallucination. Gemma slurped down a bowl of chicken soup, lips smacking. The Nazi guard returned with a carafe of red wine and two glasses. He poured one for Gemma, who took it and drank half in one gulp. He poured the second and placed it in front of Dee, who pushed it away.

"What, you don't partake?" Gemma asked.

"No," Dee replied. "I don't." Gemma shrugged and took it for herself, pouring Dee's share into her own glass, filling it to the brim.

Dee brought a spoonful of the beans to her nostrils, savoring their scent.

"Eat it while it's hot," Gemma said.

Dee did, a soft moan escaping her lips as the warm beans coated her tongue.

"Taste good?" Gemma asked. Dee could only nod. "They make decent enough food...for a bunch of Nazi pricks."

Dee ran her fingers over the finely woven linen tablecloth. It was soft, very much like the one on her mama's table.

"So where are you from in the world?" Gemma asked. "America, specifically. That accent of yours says definitely somewhere due South."

"Marietta," Dee said, sinking the silver spoon back into the gooey beans, "Georgia."

"I know where Marietta is," Gemma replied, draining her bowl, some of which dribbled over her dress. She set it on the table and sat back in her chair with a contented sigh.

"They're fattening us up, you know," she said, wiping her front with a linen napkin.

Dee swallowed another spoonful, tears springing in her eyes at the familiar tastes.

"For what?" she asked, in a daze.

"So we look good for the newspapers," Gemma replied.

"Newspapers?"

"Sure, kiddo," Gemma said. "Don't you know?"

The pocket doors slid open. There were two Nazis now.

"Bedtime," said the taller one. *"Schnell."*

Dee was allowed to brush her teeth for the first time in months. Blood dribbled off her swollen gums and down her forearm, splashing into the porcelain sink.

She settled into a warm bath, dirt fizzling off her skin and foaming into brown bubbles. A tapping at the bathroom door, and it creaked opened. Dee drew up her legs, expecting Botz or Voss or Glockner, instruments of torture at the ready.

It was Gemma, or at least her face, eyes squeezed shut in deference to Dee's privacy.

"Here's some soap," Gemma said, angling a wrinkled arm around the doorframe. A fragrant ball plopped into the bath, and Dee snatched it off the dirty surface, clutching it to her face and breathing in its delicious scent.

"Thank you, Gemma," Dee said. "Much obliged."

Gemma smiled, eyes still closed. "You're welcome, doll," she said, and shut the door.

That night, Dee lay under cool sheets, the thunder of mortar shells in the distance lulling her into a deep, peaceful, dreamless sleep.

Breakfast the next day was buckwheat pancakes. Dee almost choked herself stuffing forkful after forkful into her mouth.

"Easy, honey," Gemma said, spooning up the yolk out of a soft-boiled egg sitting in a cup. "Take it slow."

Dee fell back in her chair, clutching her swollen stomach. Gemma daintily sipped yolk as if it were hot soup, dabbing her lips after each bite.

"What about you?" Dee asked. "Where are you from?"

"Like you couldn't guess," Gemma replied with a cackle.

"Somewhere...*east*," Dee said.

"Got it in one," Gemma said with a wink.

Dee approached the kitchen window and slid the pink curtains open. Ravensbruck sat in the valley below, ringed by its barbed wire fence, tiny bodies swarming underneath a hazy blue sky. She leaned her forehead against the glass.

"Why am I here?" she asked Gemma. "Why aren't I dead?"

"Dunno," Gemma replied, joining her at the window. "Why aren't I?"

Dee contemplated the old woman with the funny accent, the kind hard-boiled detectives and cabbies and newspapermen spoke with in the movies at the Strand Theater in downtown Marietta.

"Who are you?" Dee asked. "Really."

"Me?" Gemma asked with a shrug. "I'm nobody."

The two women peered out at the camp.

"*My brother*, on the other hand," Gemma continued, "my brother is the friggin' mayor of New York City."

49

Road, Ravensbruck Concentration Camp; April 1945

Dee and Gemma bounded along in the backseat of a Daimler-Benz G4, back toward Ravensbruck. The driver was the same Nazi guard who had ordered them to eat dinner, the passenger the one who had sent them to bed. Mortar shells exploded every few minutes in the nearby vicinity. The men's shoulders jumped at the sound of each one.

Gemma leaned over and whispered into Dee's ear, eggs and coffee on her breath.

"They're close."

Dee shook her head, not understanding.

The Russians, Gemma mouthed. A pothole sent the pair scrambling to hold on to something.

"*Scheisse,*" one of the Germans muttered, wrestling with the wheel.

Thousands of women streamed out of the camp's front gates in a column as the black car approached. The Nazi in the passenger seat directed the driver to go around the back. Dee turned in her seat, searching the crowd for any sign of her friends.

They rounded the corner, the vehicle shuddering. The driver downshifted and again cursed in German.

"Gas," he spat. "We're out of fucking gas."

The Benz crept to a stop and the Germans threw their doors open, red faced.

"Follow us," they commanded the women. "*Schnell.*"

Dee and Gemma got out of the car and followed their captors back inside the walls of Ravensbruck.

Women now moved freely about the grounds, clad in clothing salvaged from the dead or those soon to be. Soup pots and broken plates littered the *appelplatz*, while Nazi guards hurried across the field, arms heavy with luggage.

"What's happening?" Dee said.

"The Russians, like I said," Gemma said. "Be here any day now."

The crackle of artillery thunder sent everyone to the ground.

"I said any day?" Gemma said. "Try any *minute.*"

Their captors ordered them back on their feet, pushing the women toward the stone building that housed the camp's offices.

The lobby proved as disordered as the camp at large. Loose typing paper lay scattered across abandoned desks, while shattered inkwells stained the floor. The painting of Hitler now hung askew as panicked clerks shoved their way past the foursome on their way out the exit. The air was thick with the smell of sweat and smoke.

"Upstairs," one of the guards commanded them, his voice cracking. "Go."

Glockner's office door was ajar as they approached. A frightened woman in a brown skirt backed into the hallway, dragging the *hauptsturmführer*'s globe bar down the hall, the wheels squeaking against the linoleum.

"Is *Herr Hauptsturmführer* in, *fraulein*?" one of the guards asked. The woman didn't answer, only hurried toward the end of the corridor. A bottle of schnapps tumbled off as she entered the stairwell, the glass exploding.

They entered Glockner's office. He appeared nervous, pacing in front of his window. The walls and floor were bare, save his desk, the art and specimens pilfered from the homes and galleries of Europe nowhere to be found. Another bottle of schnapps sat on the desktop, half empty, a glass of the pungent liqueur in his hand.

"Give her the uniform," he said, shooting his drink.

Dee couldn't believe her eyes. Draped over a chair back was her army uniform, clean and pressed and, underneath it, her boots. She hadn't seen either since her first day in the camp.

"I don't understand," Dee said to Glockner. "What is this? Where am I going?"

"Where do you think?" Glockner replied.

"Home, baby," Gemma said, resting a hand on Dee's shoulder. "We're going home."

"Home? How?" Dee asked.

"Prisoner exchange," Glockner said, pouring himself another shot with a trembling hand. "American for German. German for American."

The office windows rattled as another mortar shell exploded outside the camp. Brown liquid dribbled over the *hauptsturmführer's* fingers as he fumbled the next round to his lips.

"Get dressed, honey," Gemma said. "We have to go. Now."

A female guard in a black cape entered, a German shepherd trailing behind her on a chain leash.

The woman snapped a smart Nazi salute, the dog at her side panting with thirst.

"Heil Hitler, *Herr Hauptsturmführer! Hundeführerin* Fassnacht reporting as instructed. I am here to assist with the prisoners' transport!"

"Fine, fine," Glockner said, pouring another drink. "Be quick about it."

Fassnacht robotically faced Dee and Gemma, her sunken blue eyes ringed with fatigue. "Prepare yourselves to follow me at once," she barked. "*Schnell.*"

"That can't be," Dee said. "Home? Me? Why?"

"Because the American press got wind of your capture," Glockner slurred. "Coded messages in letters home from the fucking Russians. Or the Poles. Doesn't matter." He slurped down another shot. "And now you are of value to the Reich...as I predicted you would be."

Dee shook her head. "No," she said. "I..."

"Dee, baby, listen," Gemma said, gently taking Dee's hands in hers. "You got a mother and father back home waiting for you, right?"

Dee nodded.

"You're gonna see them, hon. Gonna see them real soon. Think how happy that'll make 'em. See their pretty daughter again. Yeah? Now get dressed, baby. Go on. Hurry."

Dee regarded her uniform, which was draped over the chair.

"*Home,* Dee," Gemma said. "Let's go *home.*"

Dee thought of her mama and daddy and Southern-style beans minus the ham. She recalled cool spring evenings on the porch and cozy winter days inside with a fire. And she fondly remembered washing the dishes with her mama after dinner, hips swaying to the radio broadcast of Duke Ellington or Ella Fitzgerald or Bing Crosby.

Dee felt hope for the first time since her arrival at Ravensbruck.

The leashed German shepherd let out a sharp, high-pitched whine, as if in pain. It lowered itself to the ground, ears flattened back against its head. Everyone in the room looked at the animal.

The dog crawled backward on its belly, its wide eyes meeting Dee's.

Forgive me, it told her. *I didn't see you there.*

Dee's heart leapt in her chest.

What did you say? she asked it.

I said I did not see you until just this moment, the dog repeated. *Please believe me.*

You can hear me? Dee asked.

Yes, the German shepherd said. *I beg your forgiveness.*

Dark-yellow urine pooled beneath the canine's sandy fur. Then there was the sound of tapping against glass, and everyone turned to the windows.

Birds of every kind lined the sills: sparrows and gulls and pigeons and doves. They drummed their beaks against the windowpanes.

Glockner stumbled backward into his chair.

"Holy Toledo," Gemma said, squinting at the birds. "Will ya look at that?"

Sing, the birds told Dee. *Sing, Orphic.*

Sing.

Sing.

Sing.

Sing.   .

Sing.

And all at once, Dee understood.

From the moment she had awoken on the train to Ravensbruck, she had felt only one thing. This feeling had clouded her every thought and ruled her every action. It had robbed her of her sense of self: who she was, where she had come from, and most important, why she was here.

It was fear.

Fear.

And now here, thousands of miles away from everything she'd ever known, she was being offered the chance to return to all that was familiar and comfortable and safe. To *go home*. And in that one, brief moment, the moment she knew she was *going home*, she felt like herself again.

She felt like Dee.

And in the absence of that fear, a Nazi guard dog heard her.

And the little birds that had abandoned the camp heard her.

Sing, they implored her, thrusting their beaks against the window.

Sing. Sing. Sing. Sing. Sing.

Dee eyed the German shepherd cowering in its own filth.

Look at me, she said.

The animal mustered its courage and pulled itself up on quivering legs.

You will do as I ask, Dee said.

Yes, the dog replied.

You and the others.

Yes. I swear it.

Then all will be forgiven, Dee said.

You are most wise and merciful, Orphic, it replied. *I thank you.*

The German shepherd raised its head and glared up at the uniformed blond woman holding its chain leash. A low growl emanated from deep within its throat.

Hundeführerin Fassnacht took a protective step backward. Dee addressed Glockner in her full voice.

"I'm not going home," she told him.

"What?" Glockner asked. "Why?"

"Yeah," Gemma chimed in. "Why?"

"Because, *Hauptsturmführer* ..." Dee said. "Because, Gemma..."

Dee closed her eyes and slowly lowered herself onto her knees, resting an open palm on the floor.

"Because home is not where Adolph Hitler is."

Sing, the birds on the windowsill begged her.

Dee remembered Bo McInnes; the Klansman spitting on the mailbox her daddy had painstakingly hand-lettered ATTICA onto with pride.

Sing.

She remembered the girl on the train, and the fly alighting on her dead, still eye.

Sing.

The old Frenchwoman shoveling snow, shot in the neck.

Sing.

The Polish "rabbit" on Voss's table, her mutilated leg filled with glass.

Sing.

And the dead babies on the cots, their mothers' bodies unable to make milk to feed them.

Sing.

Dee took in all this pain, all this suffering, and detonated it like a bomb deep inside her heart.

The camp's German Shepherds threw their heads back, howling to the sky. The birds shot up off the windowsill, joining the thousands of others that now flocked above the concentration camp, a dark cloud blotting out the sun.

Clementine stood jammed in the crowded bunkhouse with others awaiting their fate. Joyful tears streamed down her cheeks. Tati and Elsa and Hanna huddled around her.

"*There* she is!" Clementine shouted above the howling dogs and screeching birds. "*There's* my friend! *Vive la* France! *Vive* America! *Vive* Dee!"

Sing, Orphic, the birds cried, flocking.

Sing!

Dee opened her big, black, shining eyes.

And sang.

PART III

DEE-DAY

50

Ravensbruck Concentration Camp; April 1945

The camp's German shepherds, hundreds of them, acted as one.

Dogs across the *appelplatz* turned on their Nazi masters. Screams echoed along the campus as canine teeth sank into arms and legs.

The thunder of a mortar shell shook the ground, the Russian army that had fired it now mere yards away.

Dee rose from the floor, her black eyes wide.

Hundeführerin Fassnacht flattened against Glockner's office wall, her dog snarling. Glockner spun around in his chair, drunk and bewildered.

Dee jerked the semiautomatic luger out of Fassnacht's holster, placed it to the Nazi guard's forehead, and blew her brains out. Fassnacht's knees buckled, Glockner's wall now coated with gore.

Gemma LaGuardia stared at the surreal chaos unfolding outside the window. Camp guards fled in every direction, their German shepherds pursuing like wolves chasing prey, chain leashes dragging along the ground behind them.

"Holy moly," Gemma said, covering her mouth.

The German shepherd bowed its head to Dee.

Watch Glockner, Dee ordered it. *I'm not finished with him yet.*

Yes, the dog said. *I will do all that you ask.*

Dee turned around to Gemma, dark eyes swirling. The mayor of New York's sister took this in without comment. At this point, she had seen it all.

"Stay here," Dee told the old woman, and handed her the luger. "I'll be right back."

Gemma took the weapon and aimed it at Glockner. "Don't you move a fuckin' muscle, guy," she told him.

Dee descended the stairs; the administration building's lobby was bedlam. Office personnel desperately tried for the exits, beset upon by dogs and birds, the latter of which poured through the open doors on the back of the spring winds, pecking at the Nazi office workers' eyes and faces.

In the maelstrom, one guard had dropped his pistol and crawled along the ground toward it. Dee picked up the weapon, slid a round into the chamber, and executed him with a bullet to the back of the head. The sound of the gunshot elicited screams from Ravensbruck's secretarial pool, and Dee used the panic to her advantage, firing bullets into them with lethal precision. The remaining dozen or so office personnel wearing Nazi uniforms soon collapsed, dead.

One of those dead uniforms had an MP40 machine gun strapped to their back. Dee liberated it and checked its ammo.

Now she had two guns.

She was about to exit the administration building's front doors then stopped herself.

She needed to change into her US Army uniform first.

Back upstairs, Glockner was slumped in his chair, fingers in his ears against what was now unceasing mortar shelling, guarded by Gemma and the snarling dog.

"War's over maybe, looks like," Gemma said, gesturing out the window.

"Not quite," Dee said, straightening the jacket of her lieutenant's uniform over her skeletal shoulders. "Almost."

"Be careful, hon," Gemma said.

"You do the same," Dee replied. "And Glockner? You *stay*," she told the camp *kommandant*. The German shepherd growled to reinforce its new master's command.

Dee stepped over Fassnacht's corpse on her way back downstairs.

Clementine, Tati, and Elsa exited the bunkhouse into a brand-new world. Uniformed Nazis ran every which way, dogs and birds relentlessly pursuing them.

"Dee," Clementine whispered in a reverential tone, taking in the scene. "My God."

Hanna emerged from the bunkhouse, ran up to the Frenchwoman, and gripped her tightly around a thigh.

"*La, la, mon petite,*" Clementine said, covering the girl's eyes with her hand. "*Shh, shh, shh.*"

The Polish girl removed Clementine's hand and took in the camp with wide, determined eyes.

"Dee," Hanna said in English. "Where's Dee?"

The clopping of horse hooves on the black tar road answered the question as soon as she asked it. Dee sat high in the saddle of a German Warmblood liberated from the camp's stables, the silver horse shaking its mane. It reared up, hooves waving in the air.

Dee had collected every weapon she could get her hands on, leather straps crisscrossing over her chest. Automatic weapons, most still warm, dangled off her torso.

Thin white smoke trailed up from the ground outside the camp's stone walls, mortar fire exploding in thirty-second intervals. Dee pulled guns off around her neck and tossed them down to Elsa, Tati, and Clementine.

"Dr. Voss," Dee said. "Find him."

"Where are you going?" Clementine asked.

"Botz," Dee replied. "She's getting away."

"Then go get her," Clementine said, cocking back her machine gun. "We'll handle the doctor."

"Don't kill him," Dee instructed. "Just hold him till I get back."

Clementine saluted sharply. Dee wrapped her arms around the thoroughbred's muscular neck and whispered in its ear. The horse again reared back and broke into a sprint.

Frau Oberaufseherin Ursula Botz saw the dogs turning on their Nazi masters and ran for her life.

Before the war, she had been a common village girl in the countryside outside Berlin. After it started, she was made a concentration camp guard and soon thereafter a God, dealing out pain and death as she saw fit.

Now she was just that girl again. Running.

Botz sprinted past the camp wall and into the surrounding forest. Russian soldiers dotted a hill in the distance, and she pivoted, heading toward the lake. If she could make it there, she would dive in and swim across.

Clop, clop, clop, clop, clop.

Panting, she broke out of the treeline and into the open field.

Clop, clop, clop, clop, clop.

The lake was just ahead. She didn't dare turn around to the incessant galloping encroaching from behind, closer and closer.

Clopclopclopclopclop.

"*Mutter!*" Botz gasped, her legs pumping as hard as she could will them to. "*Vatter!*"

CLOPCLOPCLOPCLOPCLOPCLOPCLOPCLOP.

"*Nein!*"

Dee grabbed Botz's blond hair bun and dragged her beside the horse.

"*Nein!*" Botz screamed again.

"*Ja, fraulein,*" Dee corrected her. "*Ja.*"

Dee turned back for Ravensbruck, the *Oberaufseherin* wailing all the way.

51

Ravensbruck Concentration Camp; April 1945

Clementine fired her MP40 into the backs of fleeing Nazis until white smoke curled hot off the barrel. The Frenchwoman's nostrils flared as she exhaled, relishing the sound of their death agonies.

The first bullet out of Tati's machine gun stove piped, and she struggled to clear the jam.

"*Da, da, papasha,*" Tati cooed, as if the weapon were a person. Clementine smiled. She had picked up a little Russian in the Bergen-Belsen camp.

"*Papasha*" meant "Daddy."

The machine gun's action cleared, and Tati threw her head back, letting out a guttural war cry and charging into the fray.

Elsa sidled up to Clementine, out of breath, a freshly fired pistol in each hand. Tati's short legs were a blur as she ran after the Nazi guards trying to make it to the other side of the camp's wall alive. Elsa and Clementine joined in the chase.

When these women had awoken earlier that morning,

they were prisoners of the Reich. Now they were an Allied gun squad, locked and loaded.

The trio charged ahead, firing into fleeing Germans, screeching like banshees.

Hanna huddled against the empty bunkhouse wall, hands pressed over her ears and her eyes squeezed shut. Soft fur brushed against her arm, and she opened them, breath catching in her throat.

A dozen German shepherds surrounded her, tongues wagging. Hanna screamed. The dogs crouched to their haunches, whining anxiously.

Hanna sobbed. The dogs' presence terrified her and with good reason. Nothing she had seen in the previous months gave her any reason to believe they were anything but mindless killing machines.

The shepherds backed away, ashamed at having scared the young girl. Hanna stopped crying, confused by their sudden retreat.

Then a hummingbird flew into the room. The bird's iridescent feathers shimmered in the dim sunlight, its tiny body darting around her head. Hanna wiped her tears away. The hummingbird hovered inches from her nose, thrumming wings tickling her face. Hanna giggled. The bird alighted over each of the dog's heads, floating a few seconds before moving to the next one. Then it rocketed back toward her face, and Hanna squealed with delight. Tiny feet thrust from its feathers, seeking a perch. Hanna lifted a finger, and the bird landed on it.

"Oh!" Hanna said, delighted.

The bird's head cocked left and right, right and left,

wings fluttering as it balanced on Hanna's finger. Hanna's shoulders dropped, an ethereal calm washing down her body. She hadn't perceived this sensation for as long as she could remember.

The hummingbird winked. Hanna gasped.

The bird winked again and flew off her finger, to the open doorway.

Mortar shells shook the ground like an earthquake, an event that normally would have sent Hanna under a bunk bed. She ignored it, walking toward the bird, smiling.

The dogs followed her, slow and gentle, like docile pets.

The hummingbird's aquamarine feathers flashed, a beacon guiding the young Polish girl through the end of the Second World War.

A portion of the camp's Eastern wall lay flattened by mortar fire. The bird led Hanna and the dogs through spaces in the fallen electrified fence, dead grass catching flame under the twisted wire.

Now they were outside the camp's perimeter. They walked for a while, Hanna looking to the sky above as if seeing it for the first time. The dogs panted happily, running their backs under the girl's fingers, hoping for a scratch. She obliged them, rubbing between their ears and laughing when they licked her palms in thanks.

They soon crested a hill. Hanna couldn't believe what awaited them below.

Oberaufseherin Botz hung suspended from the branch of a great oak tree, wrapped in dog-leash chains. Dozens of German shepherds sat obediently in a ring around the tree.

Dee stood before it all, strapped with machine guns.

Hanna followed the bird down the hill. The dogs all sank onto their bellies as she approached.

Dee turned around to Hanna, her black eyes shining. "Hello, Hanna."

Hanna's gaze went from Dee's dark eyes to *Frau Oberaufseherin*, dangling like a worm on a hook. Botz was screaming words in German, none of which Hanna understood.

The Nazi writhed in her chains, the leashes she had made her dogs wear around their necks now knotted together and wrapped around her limbs.

Dee turned from Hanna back to Botz, speaking in German. Hanna didn't know the exact translation but gleaned her meaning anyway.

The *Oberaufseherin* was about to die a terrible death.

The *revier*'s surviving patients listened to the sounds of the camp's liberation with half-lidded, yellow eyes. When the hospital doors flew open, Clementine charging inside with a machine gun and leading a trio of similarly armed women, they were hard pressed to believe what they were seeing.

"*Voss!*" Clementine shouted, lifting her MP40, moving the weapon wherever her blue eyes went. "*Voss!*"

A Romani succumbing to dysentery pointed to the floor.

"Basement!" Clementine hollered in French, and Tati and Elsa followed, gun barrels sweeping the air as they stomped through the *revier* toward the stairs.

The women descended the steps and went into the tunnel, the concrete floor carpeted in oily, writhing rats. Mortar fire had driven every rodent in the camp underground.

"Oh, fuck me," Elsa said.

Tati soldiered ahead, kicking a path through the slithering animals with her clogs. Squeals echoed in the cramped tunnel, the rats scrambling over one another's backs in an effort to escape being crushed.

Elsa and Clementine followed Tati down the corridor. At the end of the tunnel was a thick metal door, slightly ajar. The smell of rotting corpses wafted from the other side, an odor the women unwittingly had become accustomed to.

They didn't acknowledge the stacks of decaying bodies piled on tables across the underground mortuary. An orange light flickered under the door on the other side of the room.

"*Ja,*" Elsa whispered.

"*Da,*" Tati affirmed.

"*Oui,*" Clementine answered, and took a deep breath, her guts turning over at the putrid air filling her lungs.

Tati took the lead; hitting the door shoulder first and slamming it open on rusted hinges. Voss stood in front of the autopsy table; one arm wrapped around Marie's throat, the other holding a luger to her temple.

"Back!" he yelled in German. "You stay the fuck back!"

Clementine had a shot: bullet through his jugular, exiting out the spinal column. It would drop him instantly, but she remembered Dee's orders and lowered her weapon.

"All in good time, Doctor," she said in French, finger still on the trigger.

"Where are you from, *camarade*?" Marie asked Clementine, whose expression brightened at the French.

"*Cannes,*" Clementine replied. "By the sea. You?"

"*Lourmarin,*" Marie replied. "By the hills."

"We'll be home soon, *camarade*," Clementine said. "I promise."

Voss spat a volley of invectives in German, tightening his grip around Marie's neck.

"The American," Marie said, unperturbed by her captor. "*Dee*. She's coming, isn't she?"

Clementine, Elsa, and Tati exchanged looks, smiling at the sound of their friend's name.

"Oh, yes," Clementine said, replacing her gun sights on Voss. "Dee's coming all right."

Oberaufseherin Botz twirled in her chains, red faced, eyes watering with fear and rage.

"Let me down!" she screamed. "I'll have you shot for this!"

The oak tree's branch crackled under her weight, and Botz dropped another inch down toward the pack of German shepherds sitting in a circle beneath her, licking their chops.

Hanna reached up and took Dee by the hand. The hummingbird zipped from Botz to Dee, Dee to Botz.

Dee extended her palm, and the bird rested in it, its green-feathered tail twitching. She brought the bird close to her face and kissed its tiny head. The hummingbird shot straight up into the sky, chirping all the way.

Hanna shaded her eyes, the bird becoming a little black speck against the pale-blue sky. Then the German Shepherds rose as one, tongues tucking back inside their drooling maws.

"*Oberaufseherin* Botz," Dee said in German. "Do you have any last words?"

Botz craned her neck, twisting in a circle mere feet above

the dogs. The shepherds stared up at their former master, impassive.

"Let me free," she whined. "Please."

Dee shook her head.

"*Please*," Botz implored her. "I was just following orders. Yes? You know this. You are a soldier, like me. Women such as us, we have no choice in these matters. We are powerless. *Powerless*. Yes? This world of men. They do what they want. When they want. And nobody stops them. All we can do is survive. I'm just a stupid peasant girl for men to do what they want with. I had no choice. *No choice.* You see? Dee? Dee. *Dee.*"

"Are you finished, *Oberaufseherin?*" Dee asked her.

Botz burst into tears, crying hysterically. "I'm sorry I called you a cunt!" she screamed. "Okay? I'm sorry! *I'm sorry! I'm sorry! I'm sorry!*"

Dee waited until she ran out of breath. "Done?"

"*Nein!*" Botz implored her captor. "*Nein, nein, nein!*"

Dee tapped Hanna on the shoulder. When the girl glanced up to her, she made a motion as if to say, "*Close your eyes.*"

Hanna did as asked.

Dee raised her right palm and dropped it to her side.

Botz howled as the dogs devoured her legs, shredding the calves off her femurs.

They ripped the fingers from the palms, chewed the biceps off her arms. The tree branch splintered under their relentless tugging, sending the *oberaufseherin* into the dirt.

The canines descended on her. When the largest German shepherd tore Botz's face off her skull like a Halloween mask, Dee scooped Hanna into her arms and headed back up the hill.

52

Mortuary, Ravensbruck Concentration Camp; April 1945

There came the sound of a thousand tiny claws skittering on stone and then squealing, louder and louder.

"Rats," Clementine gasped.

The black bodies flooded the mortuary's operating room, flesh-colored tails twitching. Elsa shot her pistols at the floor, as did Voss, inadvertently unhanding Marie in the process.

"Cease fire! Cease fire!" Clementine shouted, waving her hand. Tati's and Elsa's trigger fingers went slack.

The rats weren't coming anywhere near them, instead flowing around their clogs like a parted sea. Marie stepped toward the armed trio, and where her feet landed, the rats vacated, allowing her free passage to the other side of the room.

Voss wasn't so lucky. The rats climbed him like a tree, sending the Nazi doctor to the floor.

As soon as the luger had dropped from his hand, they released him and scrambled back out of the room. Tati picked up his weapon and trained it on Voss, now covered from head to toe in bloody rat bites.

He hadn't made a sound and now regarded his wounds clinically, as if they were on one of the Polish rabbits, not his own flesh.

"You look unwell, Doctor," Dee said in German, stepping through the doorway, Hanna at her side. Rats swirled around her feet, disappearing down the corridor. "Do you require treatment?"

Voss tilted his head at her, a scientist presented with a curious new specimen. Dee smiled.

"Marie, please prepare a sedative for the doctor," she said in French. "And we shall see to his injuries."

Marie slipped out of the room.

No one said a word for a long while, bits of concrete raining on their heads as Russian artillery exploded above. Hanna gripped Dee's hand tightly.

"Can we shoot him?" Clementine asked, breaking the silence.

"The doctor requires our care," Dee replied. "He's now a prisoner of war. He'll stand before a court of law, then be hanged for his crimes. That's the American way. And the French way, for that matter. But first we must see to his well-being."

Clementine's jaw flexed, her eyes narrowed at the bleeding Nazi.

"*Merde,*" she cursed, pacing. "Fine."

Marie returned, a syringe held in a shaky hand.

Dee took it from her. "Have a seat, Doctor," she said. "Please."

Voss sniffed and opened his mouth to speak. Before he uttered a word, Elsa was across the room, placing her weapon's muzzle against his temple, addressing him in his native German.

"She said *sit,* asshole," Elsa said.

Voss did as told, blood from the rat bites drooling down his face. When he had seated himself on the autopsy table, as requested, Dee approached, syringe held aloft, the needle slowly traveling toward his neck.

"Don't worry, Doctor," she assured him. "You won't feel a thing."

Voss went under, the terrible smells and sounds of the *revier* fading away.

He dreamt of his boyhood in Bavaria, a time spent skiing and thinking about art and music, and how he might spend his life as the son of a successful farm-machinery factory owner. He had abandoned his destiny as a businessman for philosophy and then medicine, starting his practice a few years before *Der Führer* had waged war against the world. Voss had never wanted for anything in life and assumed that after the war's conclusion he would resume his position of privilege among the elite of German society.

Once he was anointed an officer of the Reich, the world became his for the taking. When the war's tide turned, he plotted his next move, perhaps some arrangement with the Allies that secured his bank account and kept him out of jail.

Instead he now found himself waking from a drug-induced slumber on his own autopsy table, naked but for a filthy sheet procured from the *revier* one floor above.

Five female faces hovered over him as he recovered his faculties.

"He's waking up," said the Russian.

"He sure is," said the German.

"*Bonjour*, motherfucker," the French one chimed in.

The Polish girl, a child the doctor recognized as a relation of one of the rabbits, peered down at him curiously, held in Dee's arms. He stared up at his curved reflection in the American's pitch-black eyes.

Dee set Hanna down and pointed to a jar on a table across the room. "Hanna, please."

Hanna retrieved it obediently and handed it to Dee.

"The procedure is complete, Dr. Voss," Dee said. "Let's sit you up."

Tati held out a hand for Voss to take, but he waved it away. He got onto his elbows, brow creasing at the strange sensation presenting itself below his navel.

Something was *missing*. What, he couldn't be sure of just yet.

"Something wrong, Doctor?" Tati asked in Russian.

Voss pulled his head forward and peered down at the white sheet draped over his naked body. It traveled over his torso like a blanket of snow on a ski slope in his native Bavaria. Smooth. Flat. Uninterrupted.

Flat.

"Doctor?" Clementine asked in French. "You feeling okay?"

Voss gripped the edge of the sheet and ripped it away. Black, knotted stitches stood up from his crotch where the genitals had been.

"Looking for these?" Dee asked him in German, holding the jar up to his face.

Voss's eyes flicked up from the stitches to the contents inside the glass. His limp, severed penis floated in formaldehyde, blue testicles tumbling around either side of the freshly dissected scrotal sac, now a deflated balloon.

Voss screamed. And screamed. And screamed.

"There, there, Doctor," Dee said, her tone soothing. "It's merely an *experiment*, much like the ones you enjoyed performing. Ours is: 'How long can a Nazi survive without his manhood?' We'll find out, I guess. Marie here will take notes."

Voss's bulging eyes went from his former reproductive organs to his former prison nurse, clipboard in hand.

"You seem distressed, Doctor," Marie said, producing another syringe. "Allow me to help."

Voss's shrieks faded in his ears with the needle prick in his neck, along with the women's voices.

"Make sure he lives," Dee said. "Long enough to hand him to the Allies, in any case."

"Oh, he'll live," Marie replied. "Trust me."

"Where to next, Lieutenant?" Clementine asked.

"Glockner," Dee said, tossing the jar to the floor, where it shattered.

Voss managed to turn his head in time to see a pair of rats scamper through the puddle of formaldehyde, fighting over the meal they would soon make of his sex organs.

"Fall out," Dee said, and the women followed her out the door.

Voss pulled his fading vision from the feasting rats to his former nurse, a wide grin spread across her face.

It was the first time he had ever seen her smile.

53

Ravensbruck Concentration Camp; April 1945

Not long after Voss awoke from surgery, the Russian army arrived at Ravensbruck.

Human life no longer had meaning for these soldiers. They had witnessed their villages burned, their families slaughtered, their country upended by a German madman hell bent on world domination. Their tanks had rolled across the eastern front, pressing their own dead into the ground like withered flowers into potting soil, men and boys trained to believe they were born to stop a Nazi bullet, and nothing more.

And now here, thousands of miles away, they found themselves inside what would soon be known the world over as a "concentration camp." Here they found the only things capable of giving them anything even remotely approaching joy: Nazi soldiers and defenseless women.

The Russian soldiers fell on both without mercy.

Gustel, the once-privileged *blockova*, ran for the gates, hoping to escape the roving rape squads. She had nearly made it when she was tackled into the dirt, a Red Army private's rotted breath washing over her face.

"Don't fight, darling," the boy soldier said, panting. "I'll be gentle."

Gustel cried out as the prison uniform was stripped off her body. Protectively she wrapped her arms over her naked breasts, her thighs pulled apart by the men atop her.

"Me first," an officer hollered, unzipping his pants.

"Yes, sir," the private said. As he made room for the superior officer, a German shepherd tackled him to the ground.

Dozens of others joined it, jaws finding purchase around Russian throats. Machine-gun fire crackled before abruptly stopping, the rape gang subdued.

Dee stepped over the men pinned to the ground by dogs and offered a hand to the former *blockova*. Gustel took it and was pulled to standing.

"I'm sorry, Dee," Gustel blubbered. "Please don't hurt me. Please."

A Russian colonel cursed, wrenching his forearm free of a German shepherd's grip and shooting the animal in its flank. The other dogs howled.

Dee raised her right hand then dropped it sharply at her side.

A thousand birds of prey descended on the camp like lightning, shredding the marauding Russian soldiers with their talons, a tornado of hawks and owls and eagles. The sky went dark under the cloud of raptors spiraling back up toward the sun. Hanna emerged from among the Russians, picking up Gustel's ripped uniform dress and handing it to her.

Gustel quickly dressed, taking in the new world order. "I really am sorry," she said.

"Then help us," Dee said, looking to the smoking chimney on the other side of the camp's wall.

The Russian soldiers picked themselves up from the ground, going for their weapons. Dee pulled off a machine gun hanging from a strap around her neck. She raised it into the air, and the birds above formed a circle, like the eye of a hurricane. Dee fired the weapon into the sky through its center.

Bullets fell back into the grass like metal rain. Then there was perfect silence, one that hadn't existed within the camp's walls in more than four years.

"My name is Lieutenant Damienne Attica," she bellowed, her voice echoing across the *appelplatz*. "And Ravensbruck is now liberated. Anyone who doesn't offer safe passage to its former prisoners dies at my hand."

The Russians took this in, passive expressions belying their terror. They stood like this for what seemed an eternity to all present, a moment none would recount to their children or grandchildren after the war. They figured no one would believe them even if they did.

A Soviet boy soldier picked up his battered rifle. The shepherds snarled.

He held it out in front of his body and walked forward, the weapon cradled in shaking palms. When he got a few feet from Dee and her squad, he went down to one knee.

He rested it at their feet, afraid to look the American in her black eyes.

"No, *comrade*," she said. "You will need that when we get to Berlin."

The boy's eyes shot up and met hers.

"What is your name?" Dee asked him.

"Adrik, Lieutenant," he replied.

"Do you want to kill Nazis, Adrik?" she asked him in his native tongue.

"*Da*, Lieutenant."

"Then follow me," she said. "Or will you not take orders from a woman?"

"I will do as you command, Lieutenant," Adrik said, saluting.

"Then today you are a man," Dee said, and glanced back to the cold chimney in the distance.

Glockner clung to the office's windowsill, his drunk, bleary eyes following the flock of birds and pack of German shepherds, now turning as one and heading straight toward the administration building.

Straight toward *him*.

Gemma LaGuardia pulled back the hammer on the luger and took a step toward him. "Try to jump and I'll shoot you before you hit the ground," she growled.

Clementine kicked the door in. Tati and Elsa brought up the rear, weapons in hand. Hanna peeked inside from the hallway.

"You all with Dee?" Gemma asked.

"Dee," Elsa replied. "*Ja*. You?"

"Yep," Gemma said, lowering the pistol. "Let's get this show on the road then."

Tati and Elsa took Glockner under the armpits and dragged the *hauptsturmführer* into the hallway and down the stairs, Gemma, Clementine, and Hanna close behind.

Dee stared up at the cold, still smokestack. She dropped her gaze to the hundreds of naked female corpses, piled high in the grass.

"What's in there?" she asked Gustel, indicating a small brick structure at the smokestack's base.

"I show you," Gustel said in English.

They went inside a tiny building, really a small room roughly three hundred square feet, walls covered in lime-green tile. Shower nozzles dangled from the ceiling. A single hole offered sunlight. It was situated between the nozzles; a round iron cover flopped open on a hinge.

Directly below it was a black canister, the size of a large coffee can. Dee picked it up and turned it over until the white stencils painted onto the black exterior were readable: *"Zyklon-B."*

She dropped the can and walked into an even smaller room adjoining the larger. Nude women slumped against the walls, dead. Their eyes were wide open, expressions frozen in horror at their final realization on earth: that the smoke pumped through the shower nozzles was not to rid their hair of lice but to stop their breathing. Dee took in every woman's dead stare before walking back outside, Gustel following.

Furnaces stood in a row, the kind that ships and trains carried to fuel their engines. The doors hung ajar, the skulls and ribs and femurs within reduced to ash. Beneath them lay cordwood, still smoldering.

Dee found fresh kindling and stacked it underneath one of the ovens. Gustel pitched in, and soon the iron oven was red-hot, the door glowing.

Glockner's bewildered babbling raised her spirits. Clementine, Hanna, and Gemma emerged from the treeline, Elsa and Tati dropping the *hauptsturmführer* onto a pile of the previous winter's dry pine needles. He rolled onto his back, grimacing.

Birds landed in the trees above, branches sagging underneath their weight. They peered down at him, little faces twisting this way and that, their black eyes on the man who mere days before had been saluted as the camp's *kommandant*.

"Greetings, *Hauptsturmführer*," Dee said. "The extraordinary circumstances of this meeting are not lost on me."

She grabbed his wrists and dragged him toward the glowing open oven. Clementine picked up his ankles.

"*Un*," Dee said.

"*Deux*," Clementine said.

"*Trois*," Dee finished.

They tossed him inside. Like all men who considered themselves above the law, he didn't believe his punishment was real until moments after it was imposed.

Dee shut the furnace door and jammed the handle down until it locked. Half a bottle of schnapps wasn't enough to dull Glockner's senses against being roasted alive. He was fully conscious as his ribs and buttocks and thighs were cooked in their own fatty juices. He screamed and thrashed against the oven walls until his body died, tongue dumb but the brain awake as his extremities were immolated.

Gemma broke the subsequent silence. "Goddamn," she said. "That was awesome."

The women laughed beneath the chimney, Glockner's ashes drifting onto their hair like black snow.

54

Outside Ravensbruck; April 1945

A hundred horses were congregated in the forest surrounding Ravensbruck, all hoping the Orphic would choose them as her steed. Russian soldiers drifted among them, shell-shocked eyes moving between the horses standing at attention and the hawks swirling in the clouds above.

Dee and her squad stepped through Ravensbruck's gates. Adrik followed them like a puppy, stopping short at the sight of the crowded forest. "My God," he said, rifle slipping. Red faced, he picked it up from the ground.

Dee approached a chestnut-colored Morgan. The horse bowed its head, honored at having been chosen. She mounted it with ease, as did Clementine hers, a gray Appaloosa with a flowing black tail.

Tati chose a Holsteiner white as snow, tall and proud. Elsa meanwhile had picked the shortest among the herd, a Shetland pony struggling to hold its ground as the rotund German attempted to climb onto its back.

"The poor thing," Clementine said.

"What'd she say?" Tati asked.

Dee translated, pulling young Hanna up onto the Morgan. The Polish girl clutched her waist.

Arms and legs flailing like an overturned crab trying to right itself, Elsa situated herself onto the pony's back. "*Scheisse*," she cursed.

Adrik stepped in to help, arranging Elsa into a position that might sustain her over a hundred-kilometer journey.

Gemma didn't choose a horse, instead approaching Dee's with an outstretched hand. Dee took it, and the two women shook.

"This is where I get off, doll," she said. "I'm gonna hang tight and wait for our boys to get my butt back to New York —if my no-good brother bothered to send anybody for me, that is."

"Thank you, Miss LaGuardia," Dee said. "You take care of yourself now."

"I'll look after her," Gustel said. The former *blockova* approached and took Gemma's hand. "She will be safe," Gustel continued in halting English. "I swear this."

"Thank you, Gustel," Dee said.

"I am...*ashamed*...of me," Gustel said, her eyes watering.

"I know," Dee said, picking up the horse's reigns. "I know you are."

Dee clucked her tongue, and the horses galloped toward Berlin.

———

It felt like freedom.

Clementine breathed in the countryside air, crisp and sweet in her nose. Tati tried to stifle her tears but was unable, her cheeks wet and cool. Elsa giggled despite herself, the pony struggling to keep up with the bigger horses charging ahead.

Hanna buried her cheek into Dee's back, hugging the American's waist. She could count her savior's ribs if she had wanted to, much as she could her own, such was their malnourishment.

The Morgan kept a steady pace, slaloming among the trees with the rest of the herd. German shepherds ran underfoot, tongues wagging. The thousand-strong bird flock fluttered above their heads, wings beating steady as rain.

They rode through the night and into the next morning. When Hanna's grip loosened, Dee whispered to the Morgan without voice.

Slow.

The horse would have run until it died had the Orphic asked it to. It obeyed her command, going from a gallop to a trot. Everyone behind them did the same.

Clementine sidled up next to Dee, her tired eyes affixed on the sun rising over Nazi Germany.

"Beautiful," she said in French, her voice husky with fatigue.

The crackle of gunfire peppered the air ahead.

"We're close," Tati said, pulling up on her Holsteiner. "Berlin is half a day's ride away. We should press on."

Dee directed her attention to the army at their backs.

Hundreds of dogs sat obediently in the grass, a bird flock ten times their numbers in the sky and trees above their heads. Soviet soldiers brought up the rear, most marching, the rest riding atop BT-2 tanks, eyes red with exhaustion.

"We rest here," Dee said.

55

The Great Ship, Greece; The Month of Elaphebolion 433 BC

A boy named Jace was a fisherman's son, so he was charged with hoisting the sail. Those children with the physical ability to do so assisted in the effort, Damien among them. A white sail emblazoned with the image of a bull's horned head flapped to life. The sea breeze made it bulge, mast creaking.

Jace called for the others to help him pull the rigging and move the sails. The ship lurched forward; Jace and his misfit crew tied down the ropes, carried by the wind out to sea.

The children cheered, the Isle of Kasos fading into the distance.

Damien stood at the bow, his eyes closed, the salty breeze rushing through his hair. He craved a drink. As if reading his mind, Paris appeared at his side, cup in hand.

"There's whole barrels of this stuff," he said, handing it over.

Damien grinned and sniffed the liquid, pleased it was the same potion that he had shared with Basham around the fire the night before. "Thank you," he said, and drank half of the cup in one swallow. Paris did the same.

"My hands shake in the morning sometimes," Paris said. "But drinking more makes them stop."

"Mine too," Damien replied.

The boys finished their drinks. Paris sighed into his empty cup. "There's a girl below decks. I tried to talk to her, but she hissed at me."

"Leave her be," Damien said.

"As you wish. Do you want another drink?"

"Well," Damien said, pretending at indecision. "I'm not sure. Do...you?"

Paris shrugged. "I'd have some if you did."

"Suppose I will," Damien replied.

"Okay."

Damien went back to his view as Paris retreated for the barrel of liquor. One little girl took a single swallow, bent over the port-side bow, and vomited into the ocean.

Paris returned soon after, and Damien took the drink he offered before heading down the stairs to the decks below.

The slave girl lay on her side. Damien sat in the lotus position several feet away.

"What's your name?" he asked.

The girl sat up, brushing tangled, dirty hair off her forehead. She stared at Damien blankly, her pale-brown eyes flat and expressionless.

"Please tell me," Damien said.

Her answer came in a rasp. "Oya."

"It's good to meet you, Oya," he replied. "I'm Damien, of Attica. You are now under my protection. No harm will come to you. Any person who attempts to mistreat you will die at my hand. I swear this to you in the name of the great Orpheus, may he be blessed. Where are you from?"

"Cyprus," Oya answered, her voice barely audible.

"This ship is headed in the opposite direction, toward Athens."

Oya crossed her legs like Damien's and smoothed the hair out of her face. Damien knew why the pirates had taken her. She was beautiful and would have fetched a high price in the next port of call.

"My family was killed by the Assyrians this past winter," she said, her voice coming forth a bit stronger. "I have no home to go back to."

"My family is also dead," Damien said. "I am an orphan, like you. Or was. The Orphic Temple is now my home. Would you like to come with me?"

Oya's eyes widened, and she slid backward into the shadows. "I...I don't know," she said.

"That's okay. And you don't have to come," Damien assured her. "You don't have to do anything you don't want to, as a matter of fact. Ever again."

Lost in thought, Oya stared at the floor a while. "What is...*Orphic*?" she finally asked.

"Orphics are people who study the ways of Orpheus, may he be blessed," Damien said. "Orpheus was a man who spoke to the animals and birds and trees and even the rocks. He sang his song, and they sang their songs to him."

"Is that...true? Or a story?" Oya asked.

"It's all true. I promise."

"And they...*Orphics*...kill people?"

"Oh, no," Damien said, shaking his head. "Not at all. Just me."

"You kill people?"

"Yes."

"Why?"

"Because some people need to be killed."

Oya's forehead wrinkled. "I don't want to kill anybody."

"Most people don't," Damien said. "That's for the best, I suppose. They won't teach you how to kill at the temple, Oya. That's something I study special, just me and my master."

"I see," Oya said.

"That's how I came to this island. Master Scylax said that he knew what scared me most and rowed me out to sea. He pushed me overboard, and I nearly drowned. I didn't, though, obviously."

"How did you...not die?" Oya asked.

"I called upon the birds and the sharks for help, and they came to my rescue," Damien said. "It was all a test, you see. Master Scylax knew my greatest fear was drowning. Although I suppose I was never really that afraid of the water or drowning until then, when I thought it might actually happen. But Master Scylax must have known deep down that's what scared me most. Now I'm not afraid of drowning at all. It was a pretty simple test, really. I think he'll be most pleased that I passed it."

"I see," Oya said.

They sat in silence for a while, Oya unnerved by Damien's gaze. There was something in his eyes that she found unsettling. They were eyes that belonged more to a wolf or a reptile than the boy who sat before her.

"I'm very tired, Damien," she said after a while. "I think I'll sleep."

Damien jumped to his feet and bowed at the waist. "As I said, you're under my protection. No one will enter this room without my permission, and no one will receive that permission even if they asked. Sleep as if behind a locked door and only you have the key."

Damien bowed again and walked back to the upper deck.

Oya stared at the space where he had sat until her eyes grew so heavy she could no longer keep them open.

The dolphins leapt in and out of the ship's wake as the sun sank below the horizon. Damien, Paris, and Clio stood on either side of the carved figurehead of Poseidon, the orange light of the setting sun bathing their faces.

Damien peered down at the dolphins, ocean mist clouding his vision. The sea creatures told him the great ship was heading ever so slightly northeast and to please allow them to correct its course. Damien thanked them. The sail was adjusted, and the children cheered, navigating off the dolphins charging ahead, backs glittering in the light of the moon.

Damien stumbled down the steps that led below decks, missing one and falling head over heels down the remainder. He landed in such a way that the wind was briefly knocked out of him. He rolled onto his back, paralyzed.

The other children laughed at him, drunk. Damien made an obscene gesture at them, and they returned it in kind, whooping and hollering and telling any other child in earshot what the strange boy had just done to himself.

Damien ignored them, opting to crawl the rest of the way. He arrived in the cargo hold, Oya sound asleep, right where he had left her. He flopped onto his stomach and blacked out.

The next morning Damien pulled himself up the steps from beneath the ship, head throbbing. There was only one cure for his current state, of course, and he immediately ventured to the barrel and dipped his dried goat bladder inside, mouth salivating.

He couldn't wait for it to fill completely, putting it to his lips with a shaky hand and sucking it down. He belched and pulled it away, waiting to see if he threw up, as he sometimes did. When he didn't, he resumed his chugging, topping off a bloodstream still coursing with alcohol from the night before.

"Land! Land ahoy!" Jace cried, and the children rushed starboard.

Damien corked his flask and pushed his way through the throng. In the new morning sun, a strip of white sand glowed in the distance. He recognized it as the shoreline just south of Athens.

"There!" Damien exclaimed. "That's home!"

They reached the shore early that afternoon, Athenian sailors waving their arms and guiding the ship into port. They were expecting Basham and his merry band of pirates, so when Paris and Damien released the gangplank, nearly a hundred of what these men called "idiots" behind them, their mouths dropped open.

Damien walked down the gangplank, the children bunched up behind him like ducklings.

"By the Gods, that's an ugly bunch," one said, and the others laughed.

"That one there's eyes go every which way but straight forward!"

"Look at that girl's face. Should've been drowned at birth, that one."

"They all shoulda."

"That's a face you can't unsee. That one, there, looks like something my dog coughed up."

"Best burn this ship to the water, what we should do, lads."

Damien raised a hand. "I am Damien of Attica," he announced. "And these children will be conducted to the Orphic Temple under my safeguard."

One of the dockworkers spat and stepped forward. "Who you say you were, boy?"

"Damien. Of Attica."

"That supposed to mean something?"

A sly smile spread across Damien's face, and he took another few steps down to the dock.

"May I assume you know the story of the murder of Nicomedes of Athens? Murdered at the hands of a boy younger than I?"

"Yeah. So?" the dockworker said.

"I am the boy who murdered him. It was I who cleaved his chest open and exposed his still-beating heart. It was I who was banished from the city walls and made Orphic. I stand before you now and tell you any man who impedes our passage will meet a similar fate. Is that clear?"

The men eyeballed one another, worry now cast over their faces.

"That's what I thought," Damien said.

He led the gaggle of children down the plank and through the dockyards, toward Athens. Oya emerged last, running to catch up.

56

Field, Outside Berlin; April 1945

Dee jolted awake in the tall cold grass, unsure where she was in the world. The Morgan stared down at her, tall ears twisting on its head like radar dishes, listening to mortar shells detonating miles away.

A sparrow landed on the horse's head and peered down at Dee. It chirped in greeting. *Hitler,* it said.

Dee sat up. It appeared to be the same brown sparrow that had tapped on her window in her girlhood home in Marietta.

It *was* the same sparrow, in fact.

Dee stood, adjusting her uniform.

Hitler, the sparrow repeated.

You have come very far, Dee said.

So have you, the sparrow replied. It flapped its wings and coasted to a Russian KV-8 flamethrower tank fifty yards away. It landed on the gun mantlet, twittering.

Hitler.

Dee stepped over sleeping soldiers, eyes fixed on the

chemical tank. She smelled gasoline, the charred barrel beckoning her hypnotically.

The turret cover opened, and Adrik emerged, his thick brown hair matted down around his large ears. "Good morning," he said in Russian.

"'Morning," Dee replied.

Dee rested a hand on the tank's exterior, running her palm along it as if it were her daddy's freshly waxed coupe, not a rolling piece of artillery.

"You were assigned to this tank, Private?" Dee asked him.

"*Da*, Lieutenant."

"And all your comrades are dead," Dee continued.

"*Da*, Lieutenant," Adrik said.

"The Germans execute flame tankers on sight," she continued, fingers traveling reverentially over the exterior. "But you survived."

"Yes, ma'am," Adrik replied.

"Have you named it?"

"No."

"Why not?"

Adrik shrugged.

"Let's fix that then." Dee picked up a stone from the grass and scratched out a name into the hull: BENNY.

Adrik offered a hand. Dee took it and climbed into the hatch; her wide green eyes peered through the periscope. She gripped the handles, twisting them and taking in her surroundings. Dogs and birds and soldiers lay in the field, slack with hunger and exhaustion. The sparrow landed on the periscope and bent forward, rapping on the glass with its beak.

Hitler. Hitler. Hitler. Hitler. Hitler.

Clementine's and Tati's arms were intertwined, Hanna

between them, deep asleep. Elsa was nearby, curled in the fetal position, feeling safe for the first time since the war's outbreak.

Dee smiled and started the tank's engine.

57

Führerbunker; Berlin, Germany; April 1945

Traudl ran a rag over the same vase for the tenth time while *Der Führer* gargled in the nearby bathroom, readying himself for his wedding.

Adolph Hitler emerged, freshly dressed in a pressed gabardine suit. His head bobbed uncontrollably atop his shoulders, his tiny hands flapping like moths. He made a beeline for the pharmacy on the other side of the room, specifically the big white pills in glass bottles topped with cotton. He crunched a handful with a grimace then fretfully smoothed down the square black mustache over his lip with trembling fingers.

He made what Traudl had privately dubbed his "nervous sounds." Little hums and grunts, as if acknowledging a person speaking to him no one else could see.

Hitler dry swallowed what his secretary knew to be the last oxycodone found anywhere in the Reich chancellery. She highly doubted her boss grasped that and didn't dare dream of telling him.

"Are we ready?" Hitler inquired of his secretary, his nasal voice shaking.

"I will check, *Mein Führer,*" Traudl replied, dropping the cleaning rag and straightening her pencil skirt.

She hurried across the concrete bunker's floor and pushed the Map Room's double doors open. Eva Braun, Hitler's bride-to-be, sat limply in a chair. She stared at nothing, her auburn hair pinned back from her haggard face.

"Are you ready?" Traudl asked.

"I suppose so," Eva said robotically. "Yes."

Blondi sat back on her haunches, whining with hunger. The German shepherd hadn't been fed in days, nor had anyone else hiding in the bunker beneath the burning streets of Berlin. A Nazi soldier-priest glared down at her from the altar in front of the bookcase, the dog unaware the man was planning to make her his supper after the ceremony.

The sitting room doors parted, and Eva slipped in, unsteady on her feet.

"Ah," the priest said. "Welcome on this most happiest of days, *Fraulein* Braun."

A mortar shell shook the earth, bits of ceiling falling onto Eva's hair. She took her place at the makeshift altar.

The doors parted, and Traudl entered, Hitler on her heels. His pale-blue eyes bugged from their sockets. He didn't seem to see Eva or anyone else for that matter, allowing himself to be positioned across from his mistress like a piece of furniture.

The soldier-priest cleared his throat. "We gather in the presence of God today to bring this man and woman together in..."

"Just get on with it!" Eva shouted.

Traudl let out a yelp. Hitler perceived none of it.

"*J-ja, fraulein,*" the soldier-priest stammered. "Do you take this man to be your husband?"

Eva shrugged and spun her finger in a circle, as if to say, "*Hurry up.*"

"And you, *Mein Fuhrer,*" the soldier-priest continued. "Do you take this woman to be your wife?"

Hitler stared into a void, vast and unknowable.

Traudl rested a hand on his shoulder. "This man is speaking to you, sir," she said. "Listen, Adolph. Yes?"

No one besides Eva addressed him by his first name. The sound of it caught his attention. "Hm?" he grunted.

"You are being asked to take Fraulein Eva's hand in marriage," Traudl said. Another shell shook the ceiling. She knew she would soon be dead, knew they all would be. The thought of it brought nothing but comfort.

Hitler blinked, seeing the exhausted blond woman across from him for the first time that day.

"Well," he said, "*ja.*"

"I now pronounce you man and wife," the soldier-priest said, and stalked out of the sitting room, leaving the door open behind him.

Eva closed her eyes and wept.

Traudl didn't know where to look. Eva sobbed, Hitler affixing the wailing woman with a vacant stare.

"My will," he said to neither of them.

"I'm sorry, sir?" Traudl asked. Eva sank to the floor, overcome. She lay on her side, sobbing.

"My will!" Hitler squawked, jabbing a finger to the open door.

"Yes, of course," Traudl said.

The secretary helped Hitler into his desk chair, leather and overstuffed. His head bobbled, his dress shoes tapping against the floor.

"I, Adolph Hitler," he bellowed, and Traudl fumbled for a pen and paper on the oak desk, "do hereby bequeath..."

Traudl scratched down the opening stanza of *Der Führer's* last will and testament. She crossed the *t* in *bequeath* and held the pen above the paper, a drop of black ink hanging from the tip like blood off a syringe.

Traudl's eyes caught Hitler's. Adolph was staring at something above her head. She turned around.

A sparrow sat atop the grandfather clock. Its head bobbed back and forth, much like the German chancellor staring at it from across the room.

"How on earth did you get in here?" Traudl asked, standing from her chair. She set the pen down and wagged the paper at it. "Go on! Shoo!"

The sparrow chirped and fluttered off the clock, banking right and sailing out of the library on two brown wings.

"Shoo! Shoo!" Traudl continued, stepping over Eva's prostrate body. The bird landed on top of the open door that led upstairs to the chancellery, one of the last government buildings in Berlin untouched by fire or shelling.

A purple-faced colonel sat by the door, having recently ingested a cyanide capsule. "Why is this unlocked?" she asked him, and the sparrow flew up the stairwell.

It bobbed slightly as Traudl closed the door behind it, the wind current shifting just enough to alter its trajectory.

Fortunately the upper door that led into the bunker was still slightly ajar. The guard on the other side was crouched low, picking cigarette butts off the ground left by previous shifts. Out of matches, he lit one butt off another, sucking down nicotine from the inch-long rolls of tobacco.

He took no more notice of the sparrow than he had when it had flown in. The bird flapped its wings, ascending to the sky.

Below it sat the shell of a city populated by the shells of human beings. What had once been one of Europe's great metropolises was now a smoking heap of ash and decay. Piles of bodies lined the shoulders of roads packed with suitcase-toting refugees, mostly women and girls fleeing the Russians who were steamrolling their way toward the Reich chancellery.

The sparrow affixed its gaze to the heavens, asking the gods for strength to sustain the journey back to its Orphic master.

The clouds are mountains I must climb, the bird reminded itself, then opened its beak and sang a song of joy.

Adrik drove Benny forward over hill and dale, mindful of the KV-8's depleting gas. The nearly imperceptible click of tiny feet heralded the arrival of Dee's guide. She peered through the scope, smiling at the sight of the exhausted sparrow. It winked, sensing her presence.

Hello, she said.

Hitler, the sparrow replied.

Well done, Dee said.

The sparrow chittered gleefully at the compliment, then spoke of its adventures in the city ahead, outlining coordinates and road hazards Dee and her advancing army would do well to be mindful of when they invaded.

Adrik polished a pistol on his uniform pant leg, the

weapon glinting in the sun streaming through the tank's open hatch. From time to time, the sunlight faded as if going behind a cloud; really the flock of raptors flying above the KV-8 were as obedient as the now-thousand-strong pack of dogs galloping behind it in the grass.

A normal boy might have found the sight too extraordinary to contemplate, but Adrik was no normal boy. He had seen a farmhouse in his Russian village filled with men, women, and children torched to the ground, the occupants burned alive. The Nazi officer who had ordered the village's torching had watched it all from the front seat of his Volkswagen, laughing hysterically. Nothing on earth would ever truly shock him again, not once in the remaining eighty-three years of his life.

"We're close," Dee said in Russian. "*Hitler* is close."

Adrik holstered his weapon. "How do you know that?" he asked.

Dee turned from the tank's scope, green eyes twinkling. "A little bird told me," she said.

58

Outside the Führerbunker; Berlin, Germany; April 1945

Nazi Germany's last remaining warriors were boys and old men, patrolling the streets with low-caliber rifles, bayonets fashioned out of wood tied to the barrels with twine. Death at the hands of the Allies was inevitable, but nonetheless they stood their ground as *Der Führer* had commanded.

The Russians were minutes away. A KV-8 tank rumbled around the corner, the last remaining conscripts stoically awaiting their deaths.

Instead a thousand dogs filled the streets, tongues wagging.

The men blinked at the sight, bewildered. The German shepherds, only a tenth of whom were from Ravensbruck, took the lead, bounding toward the Reich chancellery. The rest, canine conscripts who had answered a village neighbor's howl, brought up the rear, barking. They took no notice of the men and their pathetic armaments. The Germans didn't discharge their weapons at the dogs or at the women on horses directly behind them.

Clementine, Tati, and Elsa charged through Berlin on horseback. Hanna now rode with Clementine, gripping the Frenchwoman tightly.

Then there was the K-V8, tracks grinding over what remained of the cobblestone. Above it was what appeared to be a thunderhead, threatening rain. A boy ten years of age corrected their general assumption.

"It's not a cloud. It's birds," he said. "So many birds."

German soldiers descended the Reich chancellery's steps, aiming broken weapons.

"*Mein Gott,*" one of them said, taking in the scene.

The dog pack charged up the stairs, enveloping the tattered remains of the Wehrmacht like locusts consuming wheat stalks. The K-V8 tank was directly behind, angling its massive body toward the steps. The belch of air escaping the gun turret belied the fireball to come.

The dogs scattered, leaving Hitler's last line of defense exposed. Dee pulled the tank's trigger, a strip of fire-soaked fuel ejaculating from its nozzle and slapping down onto them. The citizen soldiers in the streets below watched slack jawed as their countrymen's skin melted off their bones.

Inside the tank, Dee's eyes were black. The sparrow guided her toward the door that opened on the staircase that led down to the *Führerbunker*.

This way, the bird said.

Thank you, Dee replied, twisting the tank's wheel. *You've been so helpful.*

The young guard at the *Führerbunker*'s door spotted the flame tank and ran, leaving a smoking cigarette butt in his wake. There was a crackle of gunfire as a few remaining Nazi soldiers took their own lives, preferring a quick bullet to whatever the Russians were offering. Dee waited until everyone had sorted themselves out then pushed open the tank's roof hatch.

"Ah," she said, breathing in the smoky air. "Berlin."

59

Führerbunker, Berlin, Germany; April 1945

Hitler had bequeathed property that he would soon no longer own to people who would soon no longer be alive. Faithful to the last, Traudl scribbled down his last living will and testament, which no one would ever read.

"*Ja.*" Hitler sighed in his leather chair, finished with his dictation. "*Gut.*"

A scream turned his attention to the bunker door one room over.

Traudl shot up from her seat, backing into a wooden bookshelf lined with dozens of copies of *Mein Kampf*. Three of the first editions tumbled off the shelves, pages fanning open.

"Oh, my," she said.

No one moved as the footsteps grew closer. Then there was a gunshot.

Then another. And another.

The office door crashed open, Clementine's blue eyes moving in sync with the machine gun in her grip.

"Hands up," she said in German. "Up."

Hitler and Traudl raised their hands.

Tati pushed her way inside. The Russian now had a loaded gun pointed at Adolph Hitler. She was living the dream of millions around the world.

Huffing and puffing, Elsa entered behind them both. "Dee wants him out there," she said, throwing a thumb over her shoulder.

Clementine and Tati clapped hands on Hitler's wrists. Then they yanked him out of his chair, over his desk, and dragged him into the hallway.

Traudl followed them into the Map Room. Some fifty years later, Hitler's secretary at last would write of what happened next, read it over, then burn the pages in her kitchen sink.

Dee leaned against the Map Room's fireplace, favoring her good leg, something clenched in her right hand. A warm fire crackled in the hearth behind her knees, sparks drifting in the stifling air like fireflies. Next to her feet was a can of gasoline, half full, the last one to be found in the KV-8 tank.

She had spent a rare moment of quiet thinking of her mama, of her daddy, of Marietta. The sparrow landed on her shoulder.

Seems like a long time ago, Dee said.

Yes, the sparrow replied. *It does.*

The Map Room's doors slapped open. Clementine and Tati backed into it, dragging Hitler over the carpet and dropping him facedown, inches from Dee's boot tips.

"Look at her, you piece of shit," Clementine said, kicking him.

Tati hacked up a mouthful of saliva and spat on *Der Führer*.

Dee raised a hand, and the women backed off. She hunkered down, grabbed Hitler's shoulder, and rolled him onto his back. Adolph made his little nervous sounds, blue eyes rolling around in their sockets for a while before finally settling on Dee, whose black eyes sparkled like diamonds.

Dee unclenched her right hand. The left grabbed the thinning hair atop Hitler's head and yanked his attention toward what lay in her palm.

It was Hanna's little blue bird. Hitler swallowed hard, blinking at it.

"Always wondered what I'd do, you and me ever found ourselves in the same room together," Dee said. "Now that we are, doesn't quite seem real. *You* don't seem real." Dee twisted Hitler's face in such a way that it looked upon her own. "But here you are."

Hanna was on the other side of the room, hiding behind Adrik. "Dee?" she whispered, fear in her voice.

Dee turned from Hitler to the little girl. "Come here, honey," she said, her black eyes returning to green. "It's okay." Hanna ran from behind Adrik and into Dee's arms. Dee scooped her up. "Don't be afraid," Dee said. "Okay?"

Hanna buried her face into Dee's shoulder. Clementine entered the room, lighting a cigarette taken from the shirt pocket of a dead German soldier outside the Map Room doors.

"Let me take her," Clementine said.

Dee handed the little girl to Clementine. The French-woman rushed Hanna from the room as her friend's eyes returned to black.

Dee picked up the gasoline can, unscrewed the cap, and splashed the contents over Hitler's squirming face and body.

"I came all this way to light you up, Adolph," Dee said in German, her voice low. "All the way from Marietta, Georgia. But I want you to hear something first."

Hitler whimpered. Dee wiped the gasoline out of his eyes with her thumbs and forced them open, pulling the lids wide and taut.

"That little girl's name is Hanna," Dee said. "And she's gonna grow up. Find love. Perhaps raise a child. Maybe two. Maybe more. All of them Jews, like their mother. And they'll grow up. Have her grandchildren. *Jews*, each and every one."

Hitler found his full voice—a voice that had inspired an entire country to pursue a fever dream—one last time. "Traudl!" he cried out. "Eva!"

Dee rested her bad knee into his sunken chest, stopping him from speaking.

"They'll go on, *Herr* Hitler," Dee said. "All of these women will. As for you? Your thousand-year Reich is over before it even started. *Kaput.*"

"Traudl!" Hitler screamed again. "Eva!"

Clementine reentered with Elsa, dragging deeply off her cigarette, the cherry glowing blood red. Dee extended two fingers, and Clementine handed it to her.

On April thirtieth, 1945, Lieutenant Damienne "Dee" Attica lit Adolph Hitler on fire. She did it just like she had the doll she had made of him four thousand miles away in Georgia, *Der Führer's* face cut out in black and white from *Life* magazine. She touched Clementine's cigarette to his foot; Dee always started with the foot and always the *right* foot. She didn't know why. It's just how she liked to play her game.

Hitler went up like a torch. Dee's knees went weak, and

she sat on the floor, the flames dancing in the reflection of her black-marbled gaze, the sensation of pure bliss pumping through her veins. Intoxicated with ecstasy, she sighed.

Eva Braun appeared in the doorway, observing her newly wedded husband's body jerk and writhe on the floor. Then it stopped moving. Eva breathed a sigh of relief.

"Thank you," she said.

Eva helped Dee to her feet. They gazed at Hitler's charred, smoking body, his mustache white with ash.

Blondi the German shepherd trotted into the room, taking in her former master's remains. Then she bowed her head to Dee.

I see you, the dog said to her.

Dee scratched Blondi between her ears.

"Thank you," Traudl said from the Map Room doorway, echoing Eva's sentiments.

Dee smiled, her black eyes going back to a brilliant green. "You're welcome," she said.

The women took each other's hands, ringing Adolph Hitler's corpse. The bunker was quiet for a good long while, save the hammering of mortar shells overhead.

"It is finished," Dee said, breaking the silence.

Dee emerged from beneath the Reich chancellery. The dog pack was in full attack mode, chasing away what remained of Hitler's defenses in the city center. Clementine, Tati, and Elsa followed close behind, *Der Führer's* seared flesh still pungent in their nostrils.

The birds cleaned up after the German shepherds, feasting on the dead and dying Nazi soldiers in the streets.

Adrik brought up the rear carrying Hanna, the little girl's face resting on his shoulder.

"She's asleep," Adrik said.

"Good," said Tati. "That child has seen enough horror to last two lifetimes...more."

Dee regarded her comrades. Her green eyes seemed duller now, her face drawn and tired.

"You need sleep, too," Clementine told her.

Adrik jerked his head toward the flame tank.

"I can drive," he said.

"Where?" Tati asked. "Where do we go now?"

Hanna stirred, and Tati took her from the boy soldier. "*Shh, shh, shh,*" she cooed. "Stay in your dreams, little one."

"Home," Dee said, raptors circling overhead. "You'll go home. We all will."

"I don't have a home to go back to," Adrik said.

"Nor I," Tati agreed.

Their horses galloped around the corner of a crumbled government building, manes glittering in the pre-dusk light.

"Then you'll make a new one," Dee said, raising a hand to the sky.

The dogs and birds packed up around the Allies like disciples gathering to hear Mass. The streets fell silent, German refugees staring at the scene in muted awe.

Dee beheld the thousands of assembled creatures. They barked and chirped as the Orphic's gaze met theirs.

"They will guide you back to safety," Dee told the women. "And to food and shelter. Follow them. Trust them with your lives."

Dee turned from the animals to Clementine, Tati, Elsa, Adrik, and Hanna.

"As I have trusted you with mine."

"Where are you going?" Clementine asked, alarmed.

"Like I said," Dee replied. "Home."

The Morgan trotted up the steps, and Dee climbed on its back.

"Don't leave us, not yet," Tati said, but she knew that Dee knew all she really wanted was a long, sad goodbye. No such scene would play out here on the Reich chancellery steps, however.

Dee dared a last look at her compatriots, a flash of tears in her emerald gaze.

Then she patted the Morgan's neck, and it bolted, vaulting over bodies and overturned lampposts and piles of disintegrated brick.

Her friends watched her ride into the setting sun until she was gone.

Dee rode until she could no longer keep her eyes open. She settled for a meadow miles west of Berlin, falling off the horse and into soft grass, which was still warm from a humid spring day.

The horse folded its legs and got down next to her. Dee rested a hand on its flank, allowing the rise and fall of its breathing to send her into the deepest sleep she had slept in months, and the dreams that came with it.

Cape Sounion, Attica Peninsula; The Month of Elpahebolion 433 BC

The children reached the Orphic Temple at nightfall. Torchlight glowed from within, flickering in the arched windows carved out of stone.

"Wait here," Damien commanded them. "First I will announce you. Then we'll all go inside and have something to eat." The boys and girls murmured with excitement.

Scylax had written him off for dead, of that Damien was sure. Now this so-called master would see that his pupil had not only survived but also returned wiser, stronger, and more powerful than he could possibly fathom. Perhaps in time Damien might be recognized for what he truly was: a young master in his own right.

He pushed his way through the heavy oak doors and breathed in the familiar scents of the Temple's halls. They were dark and smelled of smoke. A familiar voice whispered his name.

"Damien of Attica," Scylax said. "You have returned, just as I knew you would."

Damien's eyes adjusted to the dim light. He made out Scylax and the enormous stone wheel behind him ringed by torches. Orphic monks also surrounded the altar, their heads bowed beneath hooded robes dyed red with their own blood.

Someone was going to die on that wheel tonight.

"Come in, Damien," Scylax said. "But do leave your new friends outside."

This was wrong. Nothing at all like the triumphant return he had fantasized about, drunk on wine.

"No, thank you, Master," Damien said, his voice cracking.

"Oh, but Damien," Scylax said, lowering the hood off his bald, gray head, "I wasn't asking."

The monks didn't look up as Damien walked down the center aisle, finding his seat on a stone bench, the exact same spot where he had witnessed the Orphic named Markos spill his blood years earlier. It was in the time before he remembered how he had come to the temple in the first place, before he remembered the murder of his father, and the slow, agonizing decline of his beloved mother. Ignatia had brought him here, squeezing his hands to comfort him as she tried to coax the memories buried deep within his psyche.

Ignatia. Damien longed to see her, to hug her, to bury his face in her hair and feel the sense of safety she alone brought him. He missed her desperately.

I can watch this and be okay, he thought. *I can do and see things that frighten me. Fear is an illusion. It is a monster in my head. If I ignore it, it goes away. If I ignore it, it goes away. If I ignore it, it goes away.*

Scylax took a seat on the bench opposite Damien, who stared straight ahead, determined not to turn toward the master. Scylax just stared, a grin stretched across his ashen face.

The room sat silent for a long time. Then a monk in the front row rose. He was small and very thin, his red robe pooling around his feet as he shuffled to the front of the room. When he spoke his voice was surprisingly high and feminine.

"I am blessed by the Gods," the monk said.

"And also are we," Damien repeated, along with the rest of the room.

"I am made of flesh and a mortal sinner," the monk continued.

"And also are we."

"I am a seeker of communion with the Gods."

"And also are we."

"I ask that my initiator come forth," the monk said. To Damien's astonishment, Scylax rose from his seat and walked down the aisle.

Scylax circled the monk once, stopped, then curled thin fingers over his shoulders. He then withdrew the hood from the monk's head, which was shaved to the scalp.

"Raise your eyes," Scylax commanded, and the monk did so.

It was Ignatia.

Damien leapt from his seat, but half a dozen monks intercepted him as he rushed the altar. They held him fast, struggling to subdue his slapping, clawing hands.

Scylax's grin broadened as he withdrew a long, thin blade from within one of the sleeves of his robe and rested its sharpened edge at the base of Ignatia's throat.

Damien screamed.

"Silence!" Scylax bellowed, and one of the monks

holding Damien clamped a hand over his mouth. The boy writhed in his powerful grasp, immobilized.

"And now, Damien of Attica, I present the conclusion of your lesson," Scylax said. "You will now face that which you fear most, as promised." Scylax leaned over Ignatia's shoulder, his yellow eyes wide. "What did you imagine I presumed your greatest fear to be?" he continued. "Water? Drowning? Sharks? Little blind children? *Boats*?" Scylax chuckled. "No, Damien. You don't fear those things. You only fear *one thing* and one thing alone. Do you know what it is yet? Would you like to guess? Or shall I tell you?"

Damien bucked and twisted in the monks' collective grip, swallowing his screams.

"Very well," Scylax said, and withdrew the knife from Ignatia's throat. He marched back up the aisle to Damien, stopping inches short of the boy and crouching so they were face-to-face. His next words came in a whisper. *"Your greatest fear is that those you love will die and leave you all alone."*

Tears sprang into Damien's eyes and rolled down his cheeks.

"Yes," Scylax said, straightening himself. "That's what I thought."

He returned to Ignatia, his voice filling the Great Round Room to the rafters.

"A soul reunites with its body ten times, chained to the wheel of incarnation," he intoned. "Sister Ignatia seeks freedom from her grievous cycle. Tonight we will send her on her quest."

Scylax reached into the pocket of his black robe and brought out a thin necklace. He let it dangle, the torchlight catching the locket crafted from gold. It was made in the shape of a butterfly.

Scylax draped it over Ignatia's head and fastened it around her neck.

The monks not holding Damien rose as one, Ignatia falling into their arms as they surrounded her. They carried her to the wheel and laid her on it, where they secured her wrists and ankles with rope.

"A river runs through Hades. The departed bathe in it, rinsing away all recollection of their existence on Earth," Scylax said. "Though your tongue is withered, do not dare drink from it. Seek instead the Pool of Memory. Seated atop a great stone is a sentinel. A demon. What will you tell her?"

Ignatia took a deep breath before speaking. "I will tell her I am but mortal flesh, a child of the gods," she recited. "Take pity on me, and allow me to drink from the sacred water."

Scylax placed his blade on Ignatia's jugular. "We pray the infernal monarch hears your plea. Your thirst quenched, may you reincarnate and continue on the Grievous Cycle."

Damien knew what came next and all at once found the strength that had betrayed him. He slammed his head backward into the monk holding him, breaking his nose, and in the ensuing chaos managed to twist free of the others, landing blows and sending them stumbling backward over the stone benches in front of the wheel. The other monks piled on top of Damien, who fought them with everything he had.

"*Damien!*" Ignatia shouted, a dozen monks dragging him up the aisle, an anguished cry from the pit of his soul filling the room. "I will *always* be with you!" Ignatia cried. "Do you hear me, Damien? *I will always be with you!*"

Scylax didn't let her say another word, pulling her head down to the wheel and drawing the blade deeply across her throat.

Damien burst forth from beneath the pile as Ignatia's lifeblood gushed from the slash. He crawled over the monks toward Scylax; his face snarled with otherworldly rage, his green eyes now black.

"Let him come!" Scylax commanded. He strode down from the altar's steps toward Damien, hundreds of scorpions pouring from beneath his robe.

"The ocean is forever, and you are a child of the Gods," Scylax said, stalking up the aisle, arachnids crawling every which way from under him. "That's what they say to you, isn't it? The birds? Yes?"

Damien stumbled back as the scorpions scrambled toward him, barbed tails high.

"But there are many Gods," Scylax continued. "Whose child are you then? I think you know, Damien of Attica. I think we *both* know."

Damien ran for the doors as the scorpions reached him, crawling up his legs. He screamed as they stung him, their tails like needles.

"Run, boy! Run, before I catch you," Scylax said, laughing, sending Damien into the hallway, fleeing for his life.

He burst through the oak doors and staggered outside, the children of Kasos gasping at the sight of him, now nearly covered from head to toe in scorpions. The man who followed behind Damien sent the children running into the shadows, terrified of the tall man with the yellow eyes.

"Do you not hear the scorpion's voices? Do they not also sing to you, child?" Scylax bellowed. "You are the young prodigy, yes? The great Damien of Attica who sentences others to death as he sees fit? Or are you not who you thought you were?"

Damien fell to the ground, the scorpions' venom coursing through his veins.

"The scorpion would sooner sting itself to death than lose a battle against its foe!" Scylax roared. "And I tell you now that you *are* a child of the Gods. Grandson of the Titans Cronus and Rhea. Nephew of Demeter, Hestia, and Hera. Of Zeus and Poseidon. *Son of Hades, rise to your feet!*"

Damien, his veins pulsing with scorpion venom, did as Scylax commanded. In an outstretched hand, the master held out the bloody dagger that had sliced open Ignatia's throat.

"Take it," Scylax said. "Use it. Send me to hell."

Damien panted, catching his breath, glancing between the blade and Scylax.

"Master Ignatia prayed for this," Scylax continued, his voice softening. "She took a vow of silence. Studied the scriptures. Prayed to the Gods. Devoted herself to the Orphic teachings."

The master stepped toward Damien, the knife balanced in his palm.

"I am not afraid of death, Damien, for it is but a step in a journey that has no end. Use this knife and my journey continues. Nothing more. My soul is prepared for Hades. Is yours?"

Now the knife was within Damien's reach. He stared at it, his eyes dark.

"Your mind is chaos. The gift bestowed upon you is being wasted," Scylax said. "Only discipline can reveal its potential. Daily practice. Study. Pledge yourself to that work, and I promise to hone your talent as sharp as the edge of this blade."

Damien's eyes faded back to green.

"You want to hunt evil?" Scylax continued. "Bring bad men to their knees? Kill me and you still will. For a while, anyway. But eventually your limited skills will betray you.

You'll be murdered too. Again and again and again. Forever running across the sands of Hades to the next life and the next. It will take thousands of years to learn what I can teach you in two. Bow to me, Damien of Attica. Call me your master once again. And when we are through, you will be so much more than a common killer. You will be an *Orphic* assassin."

Damien snatched the blade from Scylax's hand and plunged it into the master's throat. When he pulled it out, blood spurted from the gash, coating his face. The monks emerged from within the chamber, silently watching as Scylax fell to his knees, eyes cast to the heavens. At last he closed them and fell over into the grass.

The monks parted as Damien walked back into the Great Round Room, his eyes as black as the night sky above.

Damien stood by Ignatia's body for a while, until every fiber of his being understood that what lay before him was an empty vessel, a husk, and that the person Damien had loved more than anyone in the world was gone forever. He dropped the dagger and removed the pendant from around her neck, the one shaped like a butterfly. He made a vow to always keep it so he'd never forget.

Oya entered. She walked up to Damien and wrapped her arms around him, squeezing him tightly. She held him like this for a long while, Damien's face running with tears and Scylax's blood.

61

US Army Outpost; Antwerp, Belgium; May 1945

The *Stars and Stripes* front page was plastered on every telephone pole of the US Army outpost in Antwerp, newsprint soaked by recent rain and fluttering in the cool breeze. The headline read: *HITLER DEAD.*

Soldiers milled about behind the barbed wire, eating thick ham sandwiches and drinking hot coffee, happier than they'd ever been in their young lives. An MP in a silver helmet spotted someone on horseback approaching and kicked his feet off the sandbag perimeter, standing for a better look.

"What's that now?" a fellow sergeant said, shading his eyes.

"Looks like a lady," the MP said, and picked a pair of binoculars dangling off a hook. He pulled focus on what was now clearly a woman on a horse, riding toward them. She wore a uniform, US Army issued.

"Huh," the MP said.

The MP held out a stiff palm, and Dee slowed the horse

to a stop. She got down to the ground and straightened her uniform shirt.

The MP and his fellow sergeant didn't quite know what to make of the situation. For her part, Dee kept her hands slightly raised, careful to keep her pace deliberate but not aggressive. When she was within earshot she addressed them both.

"My name is Damienne Attica," she said. "Lieutenant, 3341st Battalion. I abandoned my post. You need to arrest me."

A few phone calls confirmed her story. Damienne Attica was indeed a commissioned officer in the United States Army and had indeed gone AWOL from her posting in Paris. She was held under suspicion of desertion in the outpost's brig.

Three weeks later, the intelligence officer arrived, a Colonel Lambrecht. He had been fully briefed on the matter concerning the lieutenant, copious notes stuffed in the attaché on his lap as his vehicle was waved inside. Salutes and handshakes were exchanged as he made his way to the cellblock, arriving to find a friendly woman with a kind smile and striking green eyes.

She first thanked him and her captors for honoring her request of a daily ration of beans before cheerfully submitting to questioning. Dee and Lambrecht spoke for hours that day, and most of the next. Lambrecht left Antwerp with three more notepads filled with names and places.

In ascertaining the veracity of her account, he found that Captain Etheridge was real, and yes, he had a French girlfriend named Clementine. Iggy (short for "Ignatius") was real too, a young mechanic-sergeant from Illinois who by his telling had been kidnapped by German agents that he had managed to escape, falling in with the Free French Army. His story was more than a little suspect, but that could be dealt with later.

Lambrecht interviewed them all, the consistency in their recollections and the total lack of discrepancy between accounts propelling him further and further toward an inevitable conclusion. When everything was compiled, he requested an appointment with a man whose very existence was so secretive within army intelligence he was referred to on paper and in speech only by a code name: G-2.

62

National Mall, Washington, DC; August 1945

Sitting on a bench in a black jacket and black fedora, G-2 squinted his battleship-gray eyes across the National Mall. A father on lunch break tossed a baseball with his son, the mother leaning against the family Studebaker parked on the curb. The Washington monument towered above them, gleaming white in the midday sun.

Lambrecht was told G-2 would have a black umbrella with a red handle in case of rain. He sat next to that man on the bench, rubbing his palms together.

"Don't do that," G-2 said without looking at him. "Makes you look nervous."

Lambrecht rested his palms flat on his slacks; eyeglasses sliding down the bridge of his thin nose in the summer heat.

"Thank you for not bringing notes," G-2 said. "A lot of people bring notes."

"Sir, do I then just..."

"Yes. Just."

Lambrecht drew a breath. "Sir, I'm not sure what you already know."

"Pretend I don't know anything."

"Yes, sir." Lambrecht composed himself and started at the beginning. His story took nearly half an hour, with pauses only for passersby who veered too close to the bench, along with the irritating lullabies of an ice cream truck. When he was finished, G-2 removed a handkerchief and wiped his mouth as if he had just sat back from a big meal.

"Do you think she really did it?" he asked.

Lambrecht replied without hesitation. "Yes, sir. I really do."

"Say it, then."

Lambrecht crossed his leg, his knee popping audibly. "Sir, I believe Lieutenant Damienne Attica assassinated Adolph Hitler."

G-2 sighed. "A WAC switchboard operator."

"Yes sir."

After...escaping...and *laying siege to*...a concentration camp we knew next to nothing about just north of Berlin."

"Yes, sir."

G-2 made eye contact with his subordinate for the first time that afternoon. "No, Colonel. She didn't."

"Sir?"

"She *didn't*."

There was nothing in G-2's tone that indicated he didn't believe the tale he had just listened to. He was merely stating the government's position on the matter, dispassionately.

"Yes, sir," Lambrecht finally said.

G-2 touched Lambrecht's knee—*pat, pat*—and stood, taking his red-handled umbrella with him and disappearing into the thick Washington humidity like a mirage.

Men whose job it was to concoct such things designed the narrative that became American history now and forever: Adolph Hitler and Eva Braun had committed suicide in the *Führerbunker*, their bodies burned beyond identification in a ditch. That Eva was now in Switzerland with a new identity meant little, that a woman from Marietta, Georgia, had really burned Adolph Hitler alive, even less. The war was over.

And good had triumphed over evil.

63

Attica Residence, Marietta, Georgia; August 1945

Mama and Daddy had kept her room just as she'd left it.

Dee sat on her childhood bed, the familiar smells of home overwhelming her. The cold bunk at Ravensbruck was much more than a world away from here; it was another universe, another dimension even. She sank into the mattress, running her fingers over the comforter. She felt *bigger* now, somehow, a giant in a dollhouse.

Dee got down to the floor and peered under the bed, expecting to find nothing but mopped hardwood. To her amazement, her Nazi dolls were still there, as if patiently awaiting her return, Hitler and Goring and Himmler right where she had left them. She scooped them up, laid them on their backs across the blankets, and blew the dust off their black-and-white faces. They appeared to her now the toys of a silly girl, one with a dark secret she couldn't share with anyone. Now Dee had shared that secret and more, with friends she predicted she'd never see again.

The United States Army had unceremoniously released her from the Antwerp lockup and put her on a troop transport plane back to London. From there it was one more transatlantic voyage to New York, a train to Atlanta via Chicago, and then that final bus ride to Marietta. She was never again asked to recount her experiences overseas, only handed a brown envelope on her way out of the brig. It contained her boarding papers for the *Queen Mary*, her train ticket for Chicago, and a bus token once she arrived in Atlanta. All of that, and her honorable discharge papers from the United States Army. Dee Attica was a civilian again.

When she stepped off the bus, her mama had kicked off her shoes and run in stocking feet to embrace her daughter. Her daddy was right behind her, both weeping and thanking Jesus for returning their daughter home. Dee had been listed missing in action and presumed dead. Until word of her capture had made the *Atlanta Journal-Constitution*, her parents couldn't be sure she was still alive.

Whether it was the Russians or the Poles, some brave soul in the camp had written Dee's name and city of birth between the lines of a letter home, most likely in their own urine. That censored letter extolling the magnanimous virtues of her German captors was sent to America, the recipient then running the back of the paper over a candle or a match. That same someone had then alerted the Atlanta press, perhaps via letter, maybe even telegram.

Dee owed a debt of gratitude to whomever that person was and likely would never discover their identity.

The *Marietta Daily Journal* wrote a blurb about her return in the section behind the Sunday coupon circular. *Local WAC Returns Home from Europe,* the headline had read, as if World War Two were a sightseeing tour. It made no mention of her time in a concentration camp, of course, or of the not-insignificant accomplishment of assassinating

Adolph Hitler. The *Journal* followed up with a similar story, a single-column that did note she had been a POW "in a camp for female prisoners."

No one who hadn't witnessed Ravensbruck for themselves could understand what that meant, of course, not that they would believe it if Dee told them. May had clipped and framed the articles handsomely before setting them on the fireplace mantel.

In those first weeks home, her mama had made her Hoppin' John and beans Southern style without the ham and anything else she wanted. At night they did the dishes side by side, swaying their hips to the radio, as if the war had never happened.

But it had happened, and sometimes at night Dee woke up with the taste of blood in her mouth, realizing in her half-conscious state that she was biting her tongue, bracing for another blow in the *prugelstrafe*. Then she remembered Botz being eaten by her dogs or Voss and his vivisected manhood or Glockner's burning ashes, and managed to fall back to sleep.

There were no more Nazis to kill, at least not in her sleepy Southern town, and it made her sad. More than anything she had learned it was the *anticipation* of things that made life exciting, and that achieving one's goals was never as satisfying as one expected they might be. The journey was the good part. And now her journey was over.

"Dee! Mail!"

Dee opened her eyes, giving up on her nap. She was sleeping more and more these days, a development her mother had decided was her daughter "catching up on her rest."

She descended the stairs, green eyes half lidded, her hair pulled taut under a headscarf.

"Mail?" she asked. "For me?"

Two envelopes sat on the kitchen table. Dee read the return addresses and ran up the stairs with them, shouting with surprise and delight. George got out of his chair at the sound, giving his wife a quizzical look.

"What's got into her?" he asked.

May shrugged. "Guess she got word from someone special."

Woods; Marietta, Georgia; August 1945

Dee slipped out her window and climbed the trellis to the ground just as she had those nights when she snuck off to burn her Nazi dolls. She ran into the woods, clutching the letters in her dress pocket.

She read the first letter walking among the trees, leaves rustling on their branches overhead. The French lettering was fine and delicate, much unlike the warrior she remembered who had written it.

Dearest Dee,

Mike says in America you have "phone books" with everyone's home address. Someone at your fort in Georgia "looked you up" (Mike's English phrase) and here I am, writing to you, here in our new home in Amiens. It will be a short letter I'm afraid, as I am quite pregnant and cannot sustain a sitting position for any length of time. Blah, blah, I will not bore you with my petty complaints.

I think of you often. I miss your pretty green eyes and the way you made me think that maybe anything in the world could be accomplished. Was any of it real? I sometimes think I dreamed of the places we went and things we saw (none of which I will give name to here—the past is the past, and it should stay there, my American friend.)

I just wanted you to know if our baby is a girl, I will name her Damienne. And if a boy, Damien. And I hope one day you will visit us or perhaps we will visit America (Mike's parents live in "Sacrament-Oh"—sorry I don't know how to spell American towns). And I trust you are well and wonder where you are all the time. All the time.

Are you with your owls, mon amie?

Love, always love,

Clementine

Dee refolded the letter and tucked it back in her dress pocket. She opened the second letter, stepping out of the forest and onto the county road. This one was written in large, blocky print:

Ma'am,

Hope this note finds you and yours well. Just wanted to say that I told the truth about you to the army and what you set out to accomplish. Spent some time in lockup for it, but no matter, was happy to do it. You take good care now and maybe one day drop me a line too. Be well, ma'am and same to your folks and God bless you.

Sincerely

Iggy

p.s. I still have those dreams I told you about sometimes.

·   ·   ·

Dee reread it one more time. The sound of a pick-up truck's brakes squealing turned her around.

———

It had followed Dee a ways, creeping along as she meandered down the shoulder reading Iggy's letter. Inside the truck's cab were three men, sitting shoulder to shoulder. The one in the middle was short, with a red beard and Dee guessed a potbelly, just like his brother Bo.

The driver asked the two men at his side a question Dee heard through the windshield.

"That her?"

The trio slid out, Red Beard lagging a moment, searching for something in the glove compartment, the hinges squeaking as it fell open.

The driver was tall, with a greasy brown beard. He spat before speaking.

"Ya'll that girl been in 'em papers, ain'tcha?" he asked, and spat again.

"War hero," the other man said, muscles made large by factory work.

Dee folded Iggy's letter and placed it in her dress pocket, finding Hanna's blue bird between her fingers. She squeezed it.

"Yes," she answered. "I suppose I am." Birds, mostly sparrows, landed in the trees that lined the county road.

"I know who you are," Red Beard said, slamming the truck door closed. "I know *just* who the fuck you are." Something was gripped in his hand. Something pink.

He waddled toward her, his girth much more prodigious than his deceased brother's. When he got within ten feet of Dee, she took a step back, and he grinned. Then he opened his hand and tossed the pink things on the ground at her feet. They were turned inside out, the red stitching inside the lining readable even from a distance.

Oh, Mama, Dee thought. *You figured maybe I would lose them, didn't you?*

Dee had burned Bocephus McInnes in the hay barn, removing her mittens so as to avoid getting gasoline on them. She had accidentally left them behind, but what would have been an innocuous clue was now a smoking gun: her mother had carefully stitched her name inside each one.

When she glanced up from them, the trio had encircled her. The muscular one was holding a long chain, brown with rust.

The birds went silent. Then Red Beard cried, "Git her!"

The largest man tackled Dee around the waist, landing on top of her and cracking her forehead against the gravel. She blacked out for a while; when she came to, the chain was wrapped around her knees, secured with a padlock. The other end was being threaded through the truck's trailer hitch.

The birds were screaming, flocking above their heads. The truck engine roared to life.

"See anybody?"

"No! Get in, goddamn it!"

Red Beard laughed, spittle flopping off his lips.

"*Yee-haw!*" he cried, panting with anticipation. "What ya gots to say now, huh? You killed my little brother. God knows you did. You'sa 'bout to get what's coming to you, yes, you are. What's ya gots to say now, huh? What? Say somethin'!"

Dee smiled, blood from her head wound running into her bright-green eyes.

"I'll be right back," she said.

The men jumped into the truck and hit the gas. Dee slid along the ground behind it, her body twisting over the gravel road. When the vehicle hit fifty miles an hour, she bounced once, twice, and then she was falling, straight into hell.

65

Hades, Asphodel Fields

Dee fell.

The chain around her legs disintegrated, as did her clothes and hair.

The ocean is forever.

Her ancient throat wound reopened, the cut bestowed upon her in the Orphic Temple on the morning of her death centuries earlier.

And you are a child of the Gods.

She twisted and turned as she plummeted, like a leaf in a storm.

Dee opened her eyes to the sound of growling echoing off ash-white canyon walls. When she tried to scream, she found no voice to do so.

The hell beast Cerberus took a step forward on giant paws, fangs bared in each of its three dog heads, jowls dripping with blood. Dee defiantly thrust her hand forward.

Cerberus threw its head back, howling. It was a terrible sound, one that threatened to crack her skull like an egg.

Prostrate thyself, Orphic! Cerberus commanded. *You have no power here.*

Dee ran.

She ran as she had around the track at Fort Oglethorpe, counting the days into weeks, weeks into months, and eventually months into years.

When she hit a hundred, she stopped counting.

———

Dee had long since lost her sanity when the rock appeared.

A shimmering of light and it was there, tall and white and the color of bone. Upon it was the demon, clawed hands raised high, the rivers of veins running beneath her diaphanous skin pulsating with light.

"Oh, my Chindi! You are a *beauty*!" the demon cried. "A gorgeous, wonderful, *beauty*!"

Dee collapsed to her knees, what little life remained in her draining out of her legs and into the scorched white ground.

"I had no idea if you'd make it or not. *No. Idea*," the demon said.

Dee opened her mouth to reply but had no more ability to speak than she had possessed a hundred years earlier, with Cerberus.

"I'm going to miss you, you know that?" the demon said. "Even more than the cowboy. Now he was something else. But *you* ..."

The demon trailed off, reaching down and gently brushing a black talon across Dee's cheek.

"You...I *liked*," the demon said, sadness in her voice. "I really, really...*liked*."

A pond sprang up from the wasteland like a flower. Dee swallowed, her tongue thick and dry.

"Well," the demon continued, "this next life should prove interesting for you. At least, I *hope* it will. Now get on with it."

Damienne reached behind her neck and removed the golden chain. She opened the cylinder and let the parchment slip out, silently mouthing the words written across it.

"I can't read your mind, Chindi, much as I'd like to," the demon said. "Read it out loud."

"I am but mortal flesh, a child of the gods," Dee recited, barely audible. "Take pity on me, and allow me to drink from the sacred water."

"Yes, yes, yes," the demon said with a wave. "Now. *Drink.*"

Dee dipped a shaking hand into the pool.

"*Before you do*," the demon thundered, freezing Dee's hand in place, "do try to have some *fun* with this one, hm? It's a goody."

Dee plunged her face beneath the water and drank.

66

El Toro Discotheque; Albuquerque, New Mexico; July 1978

Gloria Gaynor's "I Will Survive" concludes, and the record scratches. DJ Ibarra flips the vinyl off the turntable and replaces it with another.

A twelve-year-old boy drops his sombrero in the center of the club's illuminated floor and bows to the crowd, a large bell-bottomed assembly packed to the rafters, drunk on tequila.

Kool and the Gang's "Jungle Boogie" blasts through the speakers, and he dances.

He sweeps his right leg behind him and then his left.

Right, left. Right, left.

He raises his arms in a pinwheel, turns in a circle, and locks his joints.

And then he unlocks them.

No one here has ever seen a boy dance like this before.

He walks backward, sliding the soles of his feet along the ground, as if floating on air.

He spins, does the splits, and snaps back to standing,

rolling his shoulders into his arms, and his arms into his fingers in one continuous motion, like a wave.

His thumbs pop up, like little pistols. He "fires" them and winks.

The crowd laughs and bursts into applause. But this part of the display isn't what they came for. That part comes next.

The boy dances the "Disco Finger." Parrots and parakeets flutter down from the discotheque's rafters, aligning themselves in a neat little row in front of the boy, chirping and squawking in rhythm with the funk thundering from the DJ's turntables.

The boy keeps dancing. And the birds, miraculously, dance with him.

He raises his arms, and the birds raise their wings. He spins in a circle, and the birds spin in a circle. The boy does a back flip, and the birds do a back flip.

His audience can't believe what they are seeing.

The *tias* and *abuleitas* in the club's kitchen making tamales for the drunks cross themselves, muttering prayers to God. What the boy is doing is not natural. It isn't of this earth.

The boy does one last spin and stops. His handsome brown face breaks into a smile, green eyes shining.

"Jungle Boogie" concludes, and DJ Ibarra swaps the record, the Bee Gee's "Night Fever" exploding through the red-velour-covered speakers.

"Let's hear it for our *boy-eeeeeee!*" DJ Ibarra hollers into the booth's microphone, and the disco's crowd chants his name.

"*Demián!*"

"I can't *hear yooooou!*" the DJ shouts.

"*Demián!*"

"I still can't *hear yooooou!*" the DJ repeats.

"*Demián!*"

"One more *tiiiiiime!*" the DJ commands.

"*Demián!*"

EPILOGUE

Los Angeles, California; Present Day

Damien came back to the present with a gasp. He sat up, his skin prickling in the air conditioning, shirt plastered with sweat.

"Here," Angela said, and he took the glass of water she offered.

He drank it dry and set it on the end table next to his chair, rubbing his stiff neck.

"You're quite the singer, Damien, I must say," she said.

Damien dropped his hand. "I sang?"

"Yep," Angela replied, smiling.

"What'd I sing?"

Angela shrugged. "Doesn't matter. For now."

She stretched her arms over her head, dropped her spiral notepad thick with scribbling on her chair, and tapped off the recording function on her phone.

"Sit tight."

She walked out, leaving the door open behind her. When the bathroom door on the other side of the suite opened and closed, Damien glanced at the notepad covered in Angela's handwriting:

NAZI DOLLS AND MOTHER REACTION (ANXIETY) RECURRENCE SEEMS A SIGNIFICANT BREAK WITH FAMILY VALUES (CHRISTIAN? SOUTHERN BAPTIST? HE/SHE WON'T GO THERE RIGHT NOW)—"IGGY"/"IGNATIA"...FOLLOW UP ON THIS—BOOT CAMP RECURRENCE —QUICK PARIS RECALL AND THEN WE'RE AT THE RAVENSBRUCK CAMP AGAIN—3:06 P.M. HE'S TREMBLING; I ALMOST WANT TO END THE SESSION—NOT SURE WHAT TO DO—<u>RESEARCH RAVENSBRUCK.</u>

Dizzy, Damien pulled out his phone and checked the time. He had been under hypnosis for six and a half hours.

He turned the page.

I THINK HE'S SINGING THAT BEE GEES SONG???—HA-HA

Max had put on a suit and tie for his interview with the FBI, an absurd sartorial affectation in the Los Angeles Department of Fish and Wildlife Offices, where short-sleeved button downs with jeans or khakis were the norm. He pretended to check his e-mail, eyes flicking to the clock. When Agent Aja Arkadia walked through the door, obviously a federal agent, he sucked in his gut and stood from his chair.

Aja asked for him by name. Jackie, the office secretary,

pointed to Max, who waved, regretting the awkward gesture as soon as he offered it.

Agent Arkadia approached him, hand extended. It was her eyes that struck him first, enormous and beautiful and green, and then her hair, black and swirling about her shoulders as she walked.

He shook her hand, his palm sweaty.

"Mr. Berke," she said. "Thank you for meeting with me."

"Pleasure. Of course," Max replied. He turned back to his cubicle, as if there might be a place for her to sit.

"Hoping I might take you to lunch," Agent Arkadia said.

"Lunch," Max said. "Great."

―――――

They chose a burger stand at a triangular intersection, his suggestion for lack of a better one. He ordered a Number One with seasoned fries and a large root beer. Agent Arkadia ordered onion rings and nothing else.

They set their plastic orange trays on a patio table, and Agent Arkadia popped an onion ring into her mouth. She chewed, jaw flexing under flawless olive skin, her green eyes boring into his.

"Why did you call the FBI, Max?" she asked.

Max swallowed a mouthful of burger then sipped off his root beer before answering. "Well, um, you know," he said. "I saw the picture. And you know...was like, *wow*. Okay. That's the guy."

"What guy?" Aja asked.

"The guy from the picture."

"What picture?"

"From the FBI site."

Aja picked up her phone and turned it around to him.

The forensic sketch of a dark-haired white man with green eyes stared at him through the screen.

"This one?"

Max wiped sauce off his chin with a napkin and nodded.

"That's the guy I met."

"At his house, you said."

"Yup."

"Why did you go to his house?" Agent Arkadia asked.

"Well," Max said, dabbing fries into his pile of ketchup, "we were tracking a mountain lion."

"A mountain lion."

"Yes. Yes, ma'am."

"Go on."

"C-33," Max said. "That's her alpha-numeric designation. We tranked her—*tranquilized* her—and took a reading of the microprocessor in her collar."

"Uh-huh," Agent Arkadia said, and pointed to Max's root beer. He shrugged his permission, and she picked it up and sipped deeply off the straw.

"So yeah, we were tracking her," Max continued. "She kept going to the same place over and over."

"Is that unusual?" Agent Arkadia asked, setting the drink down. Max eyed the lipstick-stained straw as nonchalantly as he was able.

"Well, yeah, kinda. Yeah," Max replied. "Mountain lions are very cautious. They're wild animals, they don't...*yes*. It was extremely unusual."

"What was his name?" Aja asked. "The guy."

"Damien," Max said. "Like I told Agent Summers."

Aja shook her head and took a bite out of another onion ring.

"Don't know Agent Summers," she said. "You're talking to me now."

"Okay. Yes."

"Just talk to me."

"Yes."

"Good."

Max regained his bearings. "The animal, the mountain lion, was returning to his house again and again."

"Returning how?" Aja asked.

"To the front porch. Or thereabouts."

"I see."

"Yeah. Pretty incredible."

"Why incredible?"

"Just the behavior."

"*Unusual*," Aja offered.

"Yes. Oh, yes. Definitely," Max assured her.

"And this is the man you met," Aja said, again picking up the phone and showing him the FBI forensic sketch on the screen.

"Yeah. That's the guy," Max said. "Or, not *the* guy—it's a drawing, obviously, but yeah, you know." Max picked up his soda and sucked out a mouthful. Aja smiled.

"Got an address?" she asked.

Someone's coming.

Damien's eyes fluttered open, and he sat up on his couch. The mountain lion stood squared off in the entryway, ears flat against her head, glowering at the Spanish colonial's front door with giant cat eyes.

What? Damien asked it.

Someone's coming, she repeated.

Who?

Leave. Now.

Who is it?

Leave. Now.

Damien didn't ask a third time. He slipped his socked feet into the shoes in front of his couch and hurried to the planter beneath a picture-frame window overlooking the Hollywood Hills. He retrieved a 9mm pistol, slid it into his waistband, and exited via a bedroom window.

There was the sound of an engine revving, tires peeling out against the driveway. The mountain lion let out a held breath, whiskers fluttering.

Two minutes later there was a knock at the door. C-33 took a step forward on the talavera tile, sniffing the air. Another knock. The cat took a step back as the doorknob jiggled, a lock pick disengaging the cylinder within.

The door creaked open and Aja stood in the entryway, framed by the hazy Los Angeles sunshine, gun drawn. She stared at the mountain lion, and the mountain lion stared back at her.

Am I going to have a problem with you? Aja asked the animal.

The mountain lion bowed her head. Aja holstered her weapon and stepped inside.

She pulled her phone out of a pocket in her jacket and tapped the voice memo app.

"Empty, sparsely furnished," she said, narrating into the phone. "Open floor plan, kitchen to the right. Covered pot on stove. Removing cover. Beans, cold. Clean floors. Very clean. Clean everything. Minimal furniture. Couch. Expensive. Art books, picture books. Coffee-table stuff. Expensive. Bookshelves. All the novels you're supposed to read. Spines cracked. Walking into bedroom. Window open. Suspect left recently. Very recently. Bathroom adjacent. Toothbrush, toothpaste, soap in shower. All clean. *Too* clean."

Aja lowered the phone. The mountain lion's claws clicking along the hardwood turned her gaze. When the FBI Agent's green eyes met the cougar's yellow ones, the cat again lowered her head.

"He doesn't really live here," Aja said into her phone. "Nothing here is his. Rental. Vacation. Whatever. Find out who owns house. Stepping through window."

Aja planted her boots into a succulent garden beneath the sill, crushing the plants under her dress-boot heel.

"Footsteps. Fresh. Leading away from the house to the driveway."

Aja walked the house's perimeter, the phone beneath her chin.

"There was a gardener here but not anytime recently. Peeling paint. Coming back around to driveway. Footprints in tire tracks. He's gone."

Aja carefully stepped around the evidence, again arriving in the house's entryway. The mountain lion sat back on her haunches, cleaning her whiskers with a giant paw.

Where did he go? Aja asked.

The cat lowered her paw from her face and again bowed her head.

I don't stand on ceremony, Aja said. *I just want to know where he went.*

C-33 lifted her eyes to Aja's. *Cannot say*, he cougar said.

Can't say or won't say? Aja replied.

Both.

Your loyalty is misguided, Aja said, *however admirable it may be.*

Perhaps, C-33 said. *Perhaps not.*

Aja rolled her eyes. Experience had taught her there was no use arguing with a cat.

Damien drove up the 101 Freeway, his eyes occasionally moving from the desert landscape to the convertible's gas gauge, which was nearing empty. No matter. He was almost there.

The Desert Bloom Trailer Park lay just inside Los Angeles County, by design. Known among the locals as "Pedophile Park," the trailers within the gray concrete walls exclusively housed men convicted of sex crimes, most incapable of securing housing or work in neighborhoods that wanted nothing to do with them. Here in the middle of nowhere they lived in relative peace, traveling hours in every direction to menial-labor jobs or whatever living they managed to procure under their present circumstances.

Damien parked in the driveway in front of the remote-controlled gate. A rent-a-cop emerged from his shack and approached Damien as he exited the convertible.

"Help you, sir?"

Damien stepped out of the car, squinting at his phone.

"I think I'm kinda lost," he said. "Can't get a signal out here. Is this really where I am?" He turned the phone's screen to the approaching guard, the chubby man's sunburned nose crinkling as he tried to get a better look.

"Lemme see," he said.

When he was within striking distance, Damien grabbed him by the collar, spun him around, and placed his neck in a sleeper hold. He struggled, but Damien's grip was ironclad, the rent-a-cop's skin going crimson, lips sputtering as he passed out.

Damien gently sat him against his shack, a rattling air conditioning unit jammed in the window leaking rusty-colored water down the metal wall. Damien took the guard's keycard and swiped himself inside the mobile home park.

"*Olly olly oxen free!*" he shouted, racking a round into his pistol's chamber.

Dusty horizontal blinds rattled within the trailers, fingers making gaps as their occupants peered out into the bright, white sunshine.

"*Come out, come out, wherever you are!*" Damien roared, and when the first door opened, Damien recognized him immediately.

It was Ben Claaseen, a forty-seven-year-old man who had raped a sixteen-year-old girl named Jackie in downtown Los Angeles a decade earlier. Ben had struck as Jackie had withdrawn cash from an ATM, funds she had saved to buy her mother a necklace for her fiftieth birthday. He had dragged her into an adjacent alley, subduing her with a brick to the temple. The teenager had nearly died of the head injury.

Ben had been released on parole a few months ago. Damien had followed the convict's progress through the criminal justice system on a variety of sex offender websites. He knew all about this man. Knew all about these *men*.

"Hey, Ben," Damien said.

"Who the fuck are you?" Ben asked.

Damien raised the barrel of the 9mm and smiled.

"Damien," he said, green eyes swirling into blackness. "Damien Attica."

The sound of the first shot sent a nearby flock of sagebrush sparrows up into the sky. They pirouetted above the trailer park on the warm desert winds, swirling among one another in the breeze. Another shot rang out and then another and then another.

The sparrows sang.

ACKNOWLEDGMENTS

As always the Paramount Movie Club: Heather, my wife, who doesn't let bad pages leave our apartment. And my pal Mike, who really, really reads what I give him.

Angela, my editor, for making me a better writer.

And Renee, for steering me in the right direction at a critical moment in the story's development.

ABOUT THE AUTHOR

Sam Luna is the author of *Powder Burns: An Orphic Assassin Novel*. He lives in a very small apartment in Los Angeles with his patient wife, spending his free time hiking in Griffith Park and drinking too much iced tea. Much unlike the Orphic Assassin, he has fainted twice at the sight of blood.

He invites you to visit his website samlunabooks.com where you can sign up for email updates.

ALSO BY SAM LUNA

Powder Burns: An Orphic Assassin Novel

Made in the USA
Middletown, DE
13 February 2022

60959711R00255